ROSIE'S MIRACLE

ROSIE'S MIRACLE

A Novel

Arthur Kornhaber

SUNSTONE
PRESS

SANTA FE

This is a work of fiction based on historical events. Any resemblance to persons, living or dead, or any group, location, organization or institution, is purely coincidental.

Sunstone books may be purchased for educational, business, or sales promotional use. For information please write: Special Markets Department, Sunstone Press, P.O. Box 2321, Santa Fe, New Mexico 87504-2321.

Book and Cover design ® Vicki Ahl
Body typeface ® Californian FB
Printed on acid free paper

Library of Congress Cataloging-in-Publication Data

Kornhaber, Arthur.
  Rosie's miracle : a novel / by Arthur Kornhaber.
    p. cm.
  ISBN 978-0-86534-806-6 (softcover : alk. paper)
  1. Life change events--Fiction. 2. Miracles--Fiction. I. Title.
  PS3611.O7436R67 2011
  813'.6--dc22

                              2011010536

Published in
Santa Fe

WWW.SUNSTONEPRESS.COM
SUNSTONE PRESS / POST OFFICE BOX 2321 / SANTA FE, NM 87504-2321 /USA
(505) 988-4418 / ORDERS ONLY (800) 243-5644 / FAX (505) 988-1025

With Love

Our Most Recent Miracles
Granddaughter Ceili
Great-Granddaughter Ellie

In Memory

Paul Kornhaber

Only a miracle makes the impossible ... possible.

Contents

Acknowledgements

Although this is not my first book, *Rosie's Miracle* is my first novel. I will be eternally grateful for all that I learned, and all of the kind and generous help I received along the way.

I would like to thank my dear wife, Carol, for her cheerleading and editorial assistance. Not only for the book, but also for our life together.

I would also like to thank the lovely people from the towns and the pueblos that I met in my stay in New Mexico during the 1990s. My personal experience with them, their culture and their history, inspired me to write this book. I also want to thank those scholars, writers and researchers, many from the University of New Mexico, whose works have taught me so much about Crypto-Jewish issues.

I could not have completed this work without the support and assistance of the friends and colleagues who "got it," when I first explained the idea of the book to them. My special thanks to those who helped me personally and professionally: June Behar, Michael Denneny, Mary Goldberg, Arthur Morey, Joan Peters, David Punch, Judy Rothman, Holly White, and others who know who they are.

And, of course, thanks to the folks at Sunstone Press who made this process a satisfying and fruitful experience.

1

Rosie's Run

August 5, 2000

The university summer term was over and 23 year-old Rosie Flores felt herself dreading going home. There was no longer any way the young graduate student could put off telling her beloved friends and family her news. She had decided to marry Jon after she finished graduate school the following year. However, in spite of her happiness, she faced a major obstacle. Her family would never accept her marrying Jon. Every time she thought of returning home to announce her decision, Rosie felt sick to her stomach.

This was her last day on campus. A fitful sleep had left her groggy. All that remained for her to do today was to turn in her undergraduate student's grades, pack up her books and clothes, and drive home to Santa Rosita. When she sat up on the edge of her bed, her usual stream of worries flooded her mind. She sighed to herself, maybe a run along the riverbed would wash them away. Rosie sleepily pulled on her jogging suit, and slowly shuffled out of her dorm into a sea of sunlight so bright that it jolted her awake. The light was especially intense because the rain and winds of the previous night had scoured the desert air as clean as crystal. Rosie shivered for a moment in the cool air, took a deep breath, stretched her arms upward, and yawned out loud. Normally, she went through her warm up mindlessly, but not today.

She tried to distract herself by fixing her gaze on a broad shaft of sunlight slowly flashing its way across the university parking lot. She counted the sunbursts bouncing from one car windshield to another. One, two, three. Three was a good number, a sign perhaps? Help from anywhere would be welcome.

Warm up over, Rosie stretched up to her full five-foot-five and shook her head vigorously to shake out whatever cobwebs remained from last evening. Too much tequila, she chided herself, but don't beat yourself up about it! End of classes, right? She took in a slow, deep breath, wriggled her shoulders slightly to help settle her full breasts into the running bra, stretched both arms back and then launched herself into a slow jog. "Head not too bad, no aches and pain, knee feels better," she mumbled out loud, and switched to autopilot. Her body knew what it had to do: start slowly, find the groove, and try to keep a steady 10K pace, six point two miles an hour.

Her worries quickly re-appeared, minor topics first. How did I make out on the graduate political science exam . . . missed the second question... if only I had studied more . . . should have stuck with my first answer. Prof. Waterston, she never liked me, says I am too lenient with my students. One more year and she's outta my life. Ay! Gotta service the car or I'll never make it home. My parents are always on my case about the car. Jon too. Well, I did let the registration run out, got two parking tickets. Maybe they have a point.

"Quit it!" she scolded her consciousness and shook her head as if she could fling away her fears. Especially her biggest one, lurking in the wings of her mind, patiently waiting to make its appearance.

When Rosie reached the main road, she picked up her pace and began to tighten the bright red headband her brother Ike had made for her. Too loose, and it could fall down over her eyes at the wrong time. Satisfied that it would stay in position, she reached back and gathered up fistfuls of her long jet-black hair, twisted them into a tight ponytail and snapped the end with a band. Now she could feel the bracing sting of cool air on her neck.

By now, she had reached the stand of pinon trees that marked the entrance to an ancient trail running along the bank of the Rio Grande River. Only known to a few, this path snakes it's way north-south along the river and through scrubby masses of chamisa, sage, and aged cacti Indians know it as 'the way of the ancestors.' They claim there are portals along the road where the boundaries of time and space dissolves allowing spirits of the departed, now dwelling in other dimensions of the universe, to enter and take shape here.

Legend has it that people with the 'gift of open awareness' may travel the road unharmed, but only if they are first taught how to understand and manage the spirits and energies. This gift runs in families. Rosie, like her grandmother, Abuelita, and her Auntie Paz, had the gift. Rosie's mother, Sarah, didn't have the gift, but knew all about it. Everyone knew that without understanding, the gift could be frightening. That's why when Rosie was seven, and began to complain about being frightened by things she couldn't understand, Sarah had to ask her mother to come to Rosie's aid.

"Do not be afraid," Abuelita hugged Rosie lovingly, "when you see or hear things you cannot understand. That's because you have the special gift, like Paz and me. Accept what you experience, observe it, and know you are strongly loved and protected. Especially by our Rosita. She will not let you be harmed. Enjoy what is beautiful, but always tell us if you ever get scared."

By the time Rosie was ten, she communicated often with the spirit of Rosita, embodied within the ornate wooden statue of mysterious origin nestled in a nicho at the back of the Santa Rosita church. Otherwise, because of her feisty temperament and rebellious nature, she could be skeptical about giving other spirits and mysteries their due respect. Abuelita worried about this and discussed her concerns with Raymond, Rosie's childhood friend. He agreed. "You are right that Rosie needs to be more respectful and not anger the spirits. I am worried what will happen when she is at the university and I am not around to watch over her."

Raymond, who was raised on the pueblo and graduated from the University of New Mexico six years earlier, promised Abuelita he would talk to her. He knew Rosie liked to run in isolated places, and since the best place for that in Albuquerque was the riverbed trail, he took Rosie aside at her send-off party and tried to warn her about the exceptional powers inhabiting the trail.

"Don't run on the riverbed alone," he cautioned her. From her skeptical expression, he immediately knew she would ignore his advice. "First time, go there with someone who knows the place well. Alone, it might be dangerous. If you like I can come down some weekend and show you the ropes."

Her defiant words were predictable to him: "Never mind, you don't have to come. Don't you think I can take care of myself?"

Raymond grinned. "Not all of the time. Well, I promised Abuelita I would say what I said. You know my phone number."

Rosie awakened early on her first morning at the university and made straight for the riverbed. I'll show Raymond, she thought. The first five minutes on the trail were uneventful, so her initial anxiety lessened. Ha! She laughed out loud, and began rehearsing how she would tell Raymond how wrong he had been. I'm not a kid anymore and don't treat me like that, she was thinking. Suddenly, she felt queasy. Her mind filled with frightening thoughts and images: she saw burning buildings, women and children running, old people being slaughtered by men on horses. She heard their screaming. Her skin began to tingle and her stomach turned over—body signs that the spirits were moving. Although she knew she was still moving ahead, the landscape seemed to stand still.

"Ay!" she cried, giving voice to a wrenching feeling of sorrow rising within her. So intense, she feared her chest would burst. Through her tears, she saw blurred shapes of people, some grotesque and strangely dressed, whirling around her. She remembered how Abuelita had instructed her to question spirits that frightened her. Summoning her courage, she shouted at them, "Who, what, are you?" But these spirits didn't answer. By now, she was too paralyzed by fear to continue running so she dropped to her knees. She squeezed her eyes shut, and visualized Rosita gazing down at her from her nicho. "Rosita, help me," Rosie screamed, "Rosita, I'm scared." No response. "Please, do something."

She slowly opened her eyes and spied a bearded male presence materializing at her side. She saw him reach out and lightly touch her shoulder, but felt no pressure. When she turned to face this apparition, it vanished in a flash. Remarkably, it took her fears with it. She had no memory of what followed except waking in her own bed several hours later.

When she came back to her senses, she phoned Raymond to tell him what happened. He just laughed.

"What did I tell you?"

Rosie was not about to lose face and countered that it hadn't really been so bad. Raymond scolded her: "Next time you listen. The place is loaded with spirits: my ancients for one. And many of your people as well. Lots of them who came here hundreds of years ago and started to kill us, so we had to kill them. Unfortunately, some only get ornery when they are disturbed; others are just plain bad all the time. They will get you for no reason. You stirred them up! I bet you didn't pay respect before you barged in there, did you?" He laughed again, "But I bet someone saved you, right?"

"Well there was a man . . ."

"Probably one of your ancestors . . . ."

Rosie remembered the apparition. "He had a very long beard."

Raymond paused for a moment, some things can be spoken about, and others not. "We don't need to say anything more." He continued in a gentler, more reverent, tone. "Actually it is not a bad place, if you follow the rules."

"Rules?" Rosie shook her head and rolled her eyes disdainfully.

"Yeah," Raymond nodded, "Rules, everybody knows how much you like to follow rules." He laughed. "Alright, you don't like rules. How about principles? For example, never, ever get caught there in the dark. The bad spirits like the dark. And before you set foot on the trail, you must ask permission to enter. Once you are in, you need to ask for protection. You will feel it if you have it. If things do not feel good to you, get out of there. When you leave, be sure to give thanks. You can always try again. Above all, do not ever shout or call anyone by name. You need to watch your mouth. Even if you stub your toe or twist an ankle; no cursing allowed!"

"Right," Rosie snorted. "Having fun, I hope."

Raymond smiled, "You just got a good lesson in respect, didn't you? You needed that."

Rosie grumbled, and dismissed him, "Okay, Professor." Never one to hold a grudge, she found she couldn't be irritated with Ray for more than a moment. He didn't react to her moods the way her that some of her hot-tempered friends and relatives did. Raymond's way was to react calmly. Who could fight with someone who doesn't fight back? This left Rosie to look at herself and face up to her impulsive behavior. She was appreciative that Ray gave her the emotional space to vent to her heart's content. As she told her boyfriend Jon, "Ray would make a great psychiatrist. When I freak out he doesn't react, just lets me stew in my own juices."

Abuelita had informed her that her 'gift' would not be easy to live with.

"Do not discuss your gift with those who do not have it, or understand it," she warned. "If you talk about it to anyone else they will think you are loco."

Rosie however, true to form, needed to learn for herself. To begin with, she asked herself, "If I can feel and understand such things, why can't everybody else? In our town of Santa Rosita, isn't everybody the same? Don't we say that no one is exceptional? Isn't anyone who thinks they are better than anyone else just a loser?"

To test this idea, she had asked a group of her schoolmates if they ever heard Rosita speak to them when they were at church. They just laughed at her. A teacher found out what she was asking and warned her, "Rosie, such things are not talked about, and you are a bad girl for asking questions."

Not one to surrender easily, Rosie tried again during her high school senior year. She had only to mention the subject and her boyfriend of the moment labeled her "Miss Woo-Woo."

Lesson learned, she went underground on the subject of spirits until her first year at university. Surely, she thought, my roommate, Donna, will understand, she is a psychology major, after all. She is a sophisticated girl from Las Cruces, isn't she?

The time seemed right one evening when Rosie and Donna were alone in their dorm room and Donna was about to open her third bottle of beer.

Rosie asked her, "Donna, what do you think about Jung's ideas about the collective unconscious that we discussed in psychology class?"

"Hey, girl," Donna laughed, "I'm kicking back tonight. Save that talk for the classroom."

Rosie went on, unfazed, "Jung says, I think, that human awareness contains all that has ever come before."

"Sounds good to me." Donna was dismissing her.

Rosie said, "Donna, sometimes I feel I can plug into this layer of awareness and to see and feel things not readily apparent to other people." The more determined she sounded; the more Donna's eyes grew uncomfortably wide.

"Well, good for you," Donna said. "Shall we call for pizza?"

"Yeah!" Rosie laughed and popped the cap off a beer. "Enough of that."

Donna slapped Rosie's back. "Hey, girl. You had me worried for a while."

@

The sun was just cresting above the mountains when Rosie exited the stand of pinon trees and arrived at the overlook above the riverbed. She asked permission to enter, announced her thanks aloud, and crossed herself. As soon as she made her way down the hillside and reached the trail, her same obsessive daydream began to play in her mind like a second-rate movie: She is back home in Santa Rosita for summer vacation. She has informed her family that she will make an important announcement at their Friday night family dinner. Cut to Friday night Grandmother's house. Everyone in her family is seated around Abuelita's table. Rosie stands up, gets everyone's attention, and ceremoniously makes the announcement.

Chaos! Her mother, Sarah, whips her hands up to her forehead and falls back in a faint. Her father, Jaime, turns beet red and grabs his chest. How could she? Poppa's jaw drops. In turn, he goes white as a sheet, then blue with cyanosis, then red with rage, feeling double-crossed by his darling granddaughter. Her brother, Jake, already so edgy that he gets upset about being upset, jumps up from his chair and curses her out for causing trouble. "Goddam, Rosie," he screams, "Why can't you do things like everybody else?"

Jake's wife, Carmela, becomes steely-eyed, a sign she is cautiously analyzing the situation. Think before acting, count to ten first, Carmela taught Rosie, but it seems to have done no good. Now Carmela leans back in her chair and eyes Rosie carefully. Abuelita's eyes grow wide with worry. Do troubles never end? Of course not. She bites hard on her lower lip, even though she has a premonition about what Rosie is going to say, because of her gift. At that moment, however, she is more concerned about everyone else's reaction.

Auntie Paz looks...well, Rosie cannot exactly picture how Auntie Paz will react. She'll know all right, but not as much as Abuelita, because she isn't that old. And there is dear brother Ike. He leaps to his feet, boiling over with anger, happy to have a new topic to blow off about, to make himself look good. Now she has handed him a doozy. He points at Rosie and begins to unload.

"Ay!" Rosie yelled, bursting the bubble of her fantasy. The image of Ike on the attack was too real. Her cry scaled the steep rock walls of the canyon, and bounced back twice as loud. She clamped her hand hard over her mouth hoping she didn't wake the spirits. Ike is going to use this to get one up on me, she worried.

Ike's rivalry with Rosie over the years has always been a source of distress for the family, especially her parents.

"Sure, Ike fights with Rosie a lot," complains their father, Jaime, who tries to see the bright side of things. "All kids fight." Her mother Sarah, who is more realistic, adds, "Ike calls Rosie the 'Brain'" and thinks we spoil her.

Jaime and Sarah have been defensive about Ike for a long time. As Jake explained to the sentencing judge after Ike got a DUI citation, "My boy has had a hard time. Look at what happened to him when Rosie went to school. Ike is two years older but he was left back, so he was only one grade ahead of Rosie when she went to first grade. They said he couldn't pay attention enough to learn. So they left him back a year. Rosie was too smart so they wanted her to skip a grade. But that couldn't happen, so she had to stay where she was."

Sarah jumped in. "You know how we do things in Santa Rosita, Judge. How everybody's family members are expected to remain in their place. How no one is allowed to even try to outdo anybody else, especially girls with older brothers. You know that girls shouldn't marry until their older sisters marry. I couldn't marry Jaime when I wanted to because my sister, Paz, wasn't married. We had to wait two years until Paz formally announced she had no intention to marry."

"If Rosie got promoted over Ike, it would shame him," Jaime said.

"But look at him now," Sarah smiled. "He left school on his sixteenth birthday but he seems to be doing better since Poppa started watching over him. Now, from a weaver to a designer, and even now a supervisor, with one employee?"

"You don't have to be book smart, to be smart," Jaime summed it up.

"I see here he is involved in La Tierra, is that true?" the judge asked. "This 'New Mexico for New Mexicans' group sure stirs up a lot of trouble."

"All the guys in the family were members at one time or another," Jaime straightened up to his full height to answer. "Me, his brother, and Poppa, his grandfather, all members sometime. Jake and I still have tattoos, see." Jaime rolled up his sleeve. "For the last few years, we don't have much to do with them. Too much drugs, and the old guys are all in politics in Santa Fe. The guys in it today are a different breed; they don't grow out of it like us older guys, not a good influence on Ike."

"Judge, we are all waiting for Ike to grow up," Sarah pleaded, "My family thinks he'll turn out okay, so can't you give him a break?"

☙

Rosie searched for a daydream, memory, anything, to replace Ike in her thoughts. Something pleasant. How about the first time she met Jon, she told herself. She remembered the time two years earlier, when she left her guitar class at the university feeling hot, sweaty and nauseated. Her chest hurt, too. She was too dizzy to walk any further, and flopped down on a bench. Rita, a classmate, was passing by and saw how sick Rosie looked.

"You need some help, girl," she said. But when Rosie said she was okay, Rita decided to take charge and felt Rosie's forehead. "You are on fire," she shouted. "Let's go, girl."

She grabbed Rosie's arm and headed for the Student Health Center. It was past five and regular office hours were over. Only one on-call doctor and a couple of night nurses were there, but that didn't stop Rita from yelling 'emergency' and pounding on the door. When a nurse told her outpatient hours were over, Rita screamed, "This girl is dying!"

Fortunately, a doctor just leaving the clinic was curious enough about the ruckus to look at Rosie. When he saw how sick she was, they brought

Rosie inside. He examined her, ordered a throat culture, blood tests and a chest x-ray, and had the nurse put her to bed. He returned in an hour, announced she had pneumonia and started her on antibiotics.

The next morning after the doctor pronounced her progress as satisfactory, he spied Rosie's guitar leaning against the wall. He examined it and casually mentioned, in his best bedside manner, that he had once played classical guitar but gave it up because his fingernails kept breaking. Rosie thought it was a nice thing to share; at least he was not a stiff. In fact, he seemed very nice, if a little too serious. Not bad looking either, with a pleasant enough face, square jaw, kind eyes. Maybe thirty years old. The best thing was, he was respectful and didn't talk down to her, even though she was the patient and a student, and he was the doctor.

She remembered falling asleep, seeing his silhouette in the doorway and wondering how tall he was. So when the nurse told her, next day, that she was recovering enough to be discharged, Rosie asked if she could see the doctor to thank him for being so nice.

"Dr. Jon Spielman," the nurse replied in such a way that Rosie thought she answered that question often, "is off duty for the next three days, so another doctor will see to your after-care."

Rosie was surprised that she felt so disappointed.

For days after her discharge, she could not get the doctor out of her mind. She criticized herself mercilessly for wanting to see him again. What are you doing, girl, she chided herself. He's not your kind, and besides, why should he care? She finally gave in to her impulse. But how to do it? Would it be too pushy to return to the health center to thank him? What if she waited a week, or two, then thanked him? That was not being pushy. Okay, one week.

A week later, Rosie stopped by the health center. The nurse informed her that Dr. Spielman had just left to get his passport. He was off to South America at the end of the term, and after he came back, he was taking a job up north.

"Up north where?" Rosie asked, "Up north as in Canada?"

The nurse laughed. Make a nurse laugh and she will tell you anything. "Up north," she rolled her eyes, "with you nortenos, in the boonies. We'll see how long he lasts." She chuckled loudly.

As the days passed, and try as hard as she could, Rosie still could not banish the doctor from her daydreams. She questioned herself: Why am I thinking so much about him? What was so special about him? She had never felt quite this way before. In Santa Rosita, she had never really had a chance to get close to any boy because her family would never let anyone 'mess' with her on pain of death, or worse. Her high school boyfriends were nothing serious.

The two boyfriends from the university, especially 'Luis the Unfaithful,' were people from her own background, but she never daydreamed about them. They were fun while they lasted, but too young, too macho, and too interested in collecting female scalps. She was not going to be a handmaid to some brainless guy. She was even savvy enough to end the affair with her married, control freak, pothead music teacher after three months, keeping the sex as a trophy memory.

She even mentally asked Rosita what it meant if she couldn't get the doctor out of her mind. Could it be love?

The answer came one evening when Rosie was alone in a corner of the library, dozing over her books. It was a gentle sweet voice that she heard in her head. It said, "You have met the man you will marry." Rosie jumped up with a start. "Who said that, Rosita, you?" she entreated the voice. No other answer came, but she knew she did not need one.

@

A thick cloud of smoke, wafting up from a rundown adobe in the canyon below interrupted Rosie's reverie. She started to cough and choke and covered her nose and mouth quickly. She picked up her pace to outrun the smoke. Keep thinking nice thoughts, she urged herself. Make it to the big blue gate, and turn around. Stay in the moment, control your feelings, don't forget to put gas in the car, keep a lookout for tea plants, good sage, and Indian paintbrush. Abuelita wants me to bring some home. She ran up a steep hill and caught sight of the blue cattle gate about a mile up the road—the halfway mark. Once at the gate, she tapped it with the middle finger of her right hand, circled it twice, and started back. Twice around was good luck, but, of course, it had to be done just right. Run to the left only.

As she completed the turn, her mind drifted once more to memories of her first few meetings with Jon. She was standing at the registrar's office choosing classes for the fall term. The doctor passed by. He spotted her and waved.

"Miss Flores, you are looking much better," he grinned. At first, she did not recognize him without the white coat. She thought, is this the same person I've been mooning over? He was dressed 'regular,' denim shirt, leather vest, bolo tie, fancy belt, jeans, and boots. Not those too fancy boots, like the homeboys wear. That was good. He appeared a bit thinner than she thought, but his shoulders passed muster. Rosie liked men with square shoulders; all the men in her family were built that way.

Rosie made a conscious effort to rein in her enthusiasm. "Cool it, girl. Be polite, say hello and leave. Don't make trouble, he ain't for you," she cautioned herself. Nevertheless, her first impulse prevailed as usual. She would deal with her conscience later. "Oh. Doctor Spielman. I am fine, thanks for fixing me up. How are you?" She sounded stupid to herself.

"Good, thanks for asking," he answered. "Patients don't often ask the doctor how he is."

Rosie noticed that he seemed more subdued than he had been at the hospital. Was he shy, depressed? She sensed no danger. Go for it, she told herself.

"How was South America?" she bubbled.

"Really depressing," he sighed. "Corrupt, the people are exploited, health care is awful, and the governments don't give a damn. A few rich families run the whole show. Pathetic." He stopped. "Sorry to be a downer, but I get worked up about it."

"I went by the hospital to thank you for what you did for me; the nurses told me that you are leaving again." Am I going too far? She wondered. He is a doctor. I'm a country hick. Why am I talking him up anyway?

"Yes. Got a job up north, way up north," he said. "I learned that I don't have to go a thousand miles away to work with underserved people. There's a need right in my own backyard. That's what Margaret Mead said."

"The anthropologist?"

"That's her."

"Where up north?" she asked, calmly and politely.

"Santa Rosita, the clinic there," he said with enthusiasm.

Rosie shrieked, "That's my home town. I don't believe it!"

"Really?" he moved closer. "The Santa Rosita way up north?"

"Born and raised," she spoke quickly. "And I've been volunteering at that clinic ever since I was in high school. Last summer when you were away, and next summer too. I'm doing my work-study program there...in business administration and..."

"That's something." He paused. "It's a shame we'll miss each other. I start there after you go back to school."

"How did you come to get a job up there? We usually hire just our own people" she smiled self-consciously, "you know what I mean." Am I being too pushy, she wondered?

Jon paused. Did he really want to answer such a personal question? Why not, he thought, such a pretty girl, so full of life. "My specialty is rural medicine, and Mr. Alonzo, he seems to run things up there needed a doctor... the old one died."

"Yeah, old Doc Garcia." She felt her heart pounding, her eyes widened. "Mr. Alonzo, that's my Poppa, my grandfather. Everyone calls him Patron."

"Yes. Patron. He's your grandfather? He did one hell of a job selling me to the people up there."

Suddenly she felt protective towards this poor gringo. Did he know what he was getting into? "That's Poppa. Do you know much about Santa Rosita, Doctor Spielman?"

"Call me Jon."

"Then you can call me Rosie. That's one thing we do in Santa Rosita, call people by their first name or a nickname. Do you know anyone else up there besides people at the clinic?"

"I have one friend there. Raymond and his family. He came back to the pueblo from Boston."

"My God! That Ray! I grew up with him."

Jon laughed. "Small world, isn't it? We met here when he was a graduate student in physics and I was in med school. Ray answered a notice I posted on the bulletin board asking if anyone from the North Country wanted to share expenses driving home on weekends. I brought him up to Santa Fe and he hitchhiked home from there. We even spent weekends together at each other's homes. He introduced me to his folks at the pueblo."

"I know them well," Rosie chimed in.

Jon continued, "After he went off to M.I.T. in Boston, I visited him a few times, and now we'll be able to get together more when I go up there."

Rosie said, "We are all so happy he's back. We used to travel together, with the teachers representing our school in the state competitions. Raymond was the top high school math student, and I was the best speller in elementary school."

"So, you are a champion speller?" Jon laughed.

"Used to be!" Rosie rolled her eyes. "How well do you know Raymond? He is very laid back, you know, like a lot of the Indians."

Jon said, "I don't know what I don't know. Like what?"

She took a deep breath. "Do you know that he uses his math and computer skills to enhance his designs? That his art carries on the tradition of pueblo artisans known for their beautiful earth-colored plates and pots decorated with turquoise and obsidian. Do you know that our Santa Rosita is as well-known for this art as San Ildefonso is for black pottery, and Acoma pueblo is for the checkered patterns in its black and white pots?"

"Not really." Jon admitted.

"And that Raymond's work was just featured in a national magazine?"

Jon was impressed. "He never told me."

"Told you he was modest. See here, I saved a copy." Rosie opened the book she was carrying and took out a clipping. "I just saved it for him."

She read out loud: "The mythical and haunting themes of Mr. Martinez's plates and pots come to life with the application of precious stones arranged in a precise, mathematically harmonious mosaic. If art can be compared to music, he is truly the Bach of ceramics."

Jon shook his head and chuckled. "The Bach of ceramics! He is never going to live that one down." Jon recalled, "He told me he was taught, as the oldest male child in the family, that he had to carry on the art traditions and use them to help the family. He also told me one of his earliest memories; his grandmother took him far away and showed him how to find the family's sources of clay, plants for dyes, and stones like turquoise and obsidian."

Rosie interrupted. "Did he tell you what a rough time he had at home when he turned out to be the school's math genius? Especially after the principal entered him in competitions and he won? Did he tell you how his parents gave him grief for spending too much time in the 'outside' world? They were scared they might lose him!"

Jon asked, "Not a word. What was that about?"

"Well," Rosie smiled, she was just getting warmed up on Ray: "After he got a perfect score on his SAT math exam, the press came around, and the state Secretary of Education got all excited. Can you imagine that reporters invaded our town? The Albuquerque newspaper called him the 'Pueblo Boy' who 'aced' the SAT. Ray and his family were invited to the State Capitol and the Governor gave him a plaque and a thousand-dollar check. The Governor had to make a personal plea to his parents for them to let Raymond come here on a full scholarship. My Poppa and Ray's father and grandfather couldn't refuse such a request from the Governor, especially since he was a war veteran. Warriors honor each other. That's our way, you know."

"I do now," Jon had to sigh. "Ray did tell me that after two years at the university his professors told him he had learned all the math they could teach him, and got him into M.I.T. Full tuition paid."

Yes," Rosie remembered, "He went east. That was hard on his family. But grandfather already knew, in his own way, that Raymond wouldn't be there very long. You probably know the rest."

"I was visiting him in Boston the night he got the call from his mother to come home because his father was sick. I couldn't believe how he took the news in stride. Next day I asked him how he felt about leaving, and I remember every word: 'I'm fine about leaving, but my department head is disappointed. Makes him look good to have an Indian around. But I told him neither M.I.T. nor his department really mattered in the grand scheme of things. He looked at me funny. I don't think he got what I said because he is so immersed in his work and his status. I said that my spirit is at peace at home with my family, that physics is only discovering what is there anyway, and when you think about it, what is the point?'"

"Ray can go on a rant," Rosie laughed.

"And he wasn't finished," Jon said. "When I went on about talent being the number one commodity at M.I.T., he set me straight on his values. He felt that being there was interesting but talent was no reason for a son to avoid his duty. It meant everything to him that he could please his father, especially at the end. He was willing to go home, marry Chenoa and make his parents happy at the prospect of a grandchild."

Rosie thought back, that was Ray alright. Then Jon went on: "Ray said he could put on an Indian act, but that wasn't him. Remember in Plato how people might think shadows were reality? That's kind of how it was for him at M.I.T. People were ignoring their spirits, running around, knocking themselves out, acting self-important, and looking for some guru to make sense of their lives. Ray was even sensitive to the women, who might or might not complain. It hurt him that there were so many unhappy women there, smart, pretty, good-hearted, but lost souls. He was at peace with going home where he belonged. And he asked me where I belonged."

Rosie looked pensive; "I remember how happy his family was when he came back and got married."

Jon looked at her quizzically. "I was at the wedding. I didn't see you."

"Bummer, I went to Haiti with some friends that summer to build houses, help some kids...you know." She saw Jon smile at her.

"That's a nice thing to do," he smiled warmly.

Rosie felt herself beginning to blush when the talk turned to her. "What else do you know about our town? The life, the people, the church . . .?"

"I've been to the pueblo, and the clinic, but I don't really know much else."

"Did you meet any other people besides my grandfather?" she asked.

"In the town, not really, just a few the people at the clinic when I interviewed there."

"Dr. Jon, I don't know if Ray told you about, really..."

Jon finished her sentence for her: "...what the town is really like?"

Rosie realized they were talking as though they had known each other for a long time. She had to warn him about what he was getting into.

"You know, Santa Rosita isn't like here, or Santa Fe. People in Santa Rosita have strong attitudes and many hate outsiders. It doesn't matter whether they're Anglos or other tribes; outsiders don't settle in Santa Rosita because there isn't any room for them, even when there is. Know what I mean? I'm amazed Poppa asked you to come work at the clinic. Because you're you, I mean." Rosie's face reddened.

Jon understood; Rosie was wondering what had forced her grandfather to bring an outsider in to take such an important job. "Temporary is okay," she sighed. "That's a separate category."

"I don't consider myself an outsider. I was born in Santa Fe, I went to school here, and I speak the language. I've worked with patients all over the state, Taos, Las Cruces, the pueblos."

"Sure, but those people aren't from my isolated Mestizo Catholic town in the north with plenty of attitude and loco ideas thrown in. You are in for a surprise," Rosie laughed. She shook her head and clicked her tongue. "Santa Fe is cosmopolitan, gentrified Albuquerque-lite. The pueblos near there even have casinos." Rosie thought for a moment. "Religion, for example. Are you Catholic?" she asked.

Jon laughed and shook his head. "Hardly. I was born Jewish. Patron already asked me about that and I told him I'm not religious."

Rosie told herself, this guy is going to be eaten alive. A Gringo, Jewish, an outsider, a real strike three." She pursed her lips and looked him straight in the eyes. "Jon, you are heading for big trouble."

Jon only smiled. "I'll find out for myself I guess," and Rosie knew she had not scared him away. Was it flirting a little when she hinted he might need a local guide in Santa Rosita? She held back her goodbye, as if something told her this meeting wasn't over.

Jon looked her square in the eye. "Miss Flores. Rosie. There is a guitar concert Saturday night, flamenco; the Garcia singers and dancers are coming from Santa Fe. Would you like to go with me?"

Rosie was caught off guard. She was still speculating about what would happen to him in Santa Rosita. Her answer, "Sure," popped out before her rational mind had time to stifle it. The she blinked her eyes and teased, "After the performance, I'll tell you what the tourists don't know about Santa Rosita."

By the time the Saturday night concert was over, Jon and Rosie were holding hands. "Want some coffee and we can talk some more?" Jon asked. At the café, she gave a little challenge: "Ready to learn more about what you are getting into?"

"Shoot," he ordered, and reached for her hand.

Rosie looked deep into his eyes, then quickly away, but left her hand in his. "Well," she said earnestly, "If you read the tourist brochure, it says that Santa Rosita is an important historical, cultural and religious venue dating back to the 1700's when our founder, Fr. Miguel, built his church here." Jon was impressed. Rosie continued, "Santa Rosita County includes two separate entities, the town and the pueblo."

"That I know, "Jon laughed.

"There's a tribal council run by Raymond's grandfather, Elmer Ceoptewa, or grandfather, as you know him. No one knows how old he is, but he has to be very old! Did you know he was a soldier in World War II and won two silver stars for bravery in action?"

Jon shook his head, "I didn't know that."

"He started the Pueblo Veterans Association after the war, and he runs all the patriotic celebrations." Rosie said enthusiastically, then paused. "He lost his wife, Millie, several years ago."

Jon's face grew sad. "Ray told me."

Jon is a kind person, Rosie thought, and continued, stifling the urge to make direct eye contact.

"My grandfather, as you know, Ruben Alonzo, is the town's Alcalde, the mayor. Everyone calls him Patron because he manages the town's business. He's eighty and still gets a kick out of dressing up occasionally like a Spanish colonial big shot. People say his eyes are so piercing that he can see through anything, so it's a waste of time to try games with him."

"I saw that for myself," Jon agreed with a smile.

"Poppa knows everything going on in town, especially when it comes to politics. He is the church leader, social worker, enforcer, psychotherapist, power broker, and troubleshooter. Let's see, anything else, oh yes, wheeler-dealer and philanthropist at the same time. He is our most important link to the state government, so he keeps control over funds that come in by grants, gifts, and even donations from the 'Wannabe Santa Rositans.' That's what La Tierra calls the 'liberal gringos' who want to come up and save us."

"Is that me?" Jon asked.

"Could be," Rosie admitted with a laugh. "Anyway, Poppa isn't so narrow-minded. He knows how to ask for advice when he needs it. Especially from Fr. Raul and the church executive board, and grandfather, and Ray, now that he is back home, and the tribal council."

"That's good to know."

Rosie noted how Jon was a good listener and was warming to the subject: "He can play rough when it comes to business, but he is a sweetie to the people he loves, especially Abuelita. They have been married for sixty years. She doesn't tell her age, but she says she is much younger than Poppa. Did you notice that she has one brown eye and one black? That's the mark of a healer. My Auntie Paz also has different colored eyes and the gift as well. Me too, see?"

Jon looked into her eyes. "So you do, and so beautiful, too. I met your grandmother, Abuelita, and I'm interested in what she does."

"You do the same things in different ways. In our town, she is a curandera, a folk healer. Cures people with prayers, herbs, and plants. Do you know she can read the thoughts of her loved ones? No kidding! Sometimes we have to stop her from finishing our sentences. Her ancestors were settlers who earned a living in the lodging and trading business. Our family started the Santa Rosita Inn and the Familia Gallegos 'Restaurant y Cantina'"

Jon smiled. "That's where Ray and I hang out. Great margaritas."

"Our family's flagship enterprise, as Poppa calls it—he likes to read business magazines—is the Santa Rosita Arts and Crafts Center. This is his way to link the interests of the townspeople with the native people. Everything is there—the family rug business, the arts and crafts store, and the Inn- Cantina complex. Poppa expanded the business that had been just weaving rugs for generations to include other craft media. Now we have one of the most successful arts and fabric businesses in New Mexico. We even sell international. You must have seen our rugs."

Jon said only, "I'm sure..."

"Well," Rosie took a deep breath, "our rugs are famous for their striking colors, from our own secret recipes, and intricate designs. They also contain very old patterns and sacred letters passed down in the family over many generations. When people ask about them, Ike never explains their meaning. He tells them that we just weave them and that we don't have to know what they mean. If they were good enough for our ancestors, they are good enough for us."

She paused. "Ike has an attitude, but Poppa, he's a diplomat. Our family was especially proud of the way he helped satisfy some resentful Indian artists who felt the Center was disrespecting them and treating them as employees. He listened politely to their complaints, agreed with them, and offered them equal partnership in the business. With Elmer and Raymond's help, he worked out the financing to build a two-story adobe, complete with an outdoor oven, right next to the Arts and Crafts complex. You have seen it, haven't you?"

Jon nodded. "Yes, looks like it's been there for ages. It's so...authentic... beautiful."

"Now the tourists can wander among the artists as they work, ask questions and buy beautiful handmade things. Win-win. That's Poppa. I'm going to work with him in the business when I finish graduate school."

Jon laughed, "You are a lucky girl."

"Thanks. Am I talking too much?" She excitedly patted his hand. "I am, aren't I? Now you, tell me how was it being raised in Santa Fe." She leaned forward and squeezed his other hand.

"Different, believe me, very different," he smiled. "Hey, time to go. They are closing up the place."

As Rosie neared the end of her run, her pleasant feelings were quickly dissipated by a string of concerns. What's Poppa going to do when I tell him about Jon and me? Will he want to disown me or help us? After all, he did hire Jon. She visualized her grandfather seated at the dinner table. All-powerful Poppa, the Alcalde of Santa Rosita. The Patron. He will be happy I'm coming home, but after that? Maybe I just shouldn't go home. Maybe we should stay here, or move to another state. After all, even before I met Jon, didn't I question myself if I should go back home?

Several years earlier, the more Rosie became involved in university life, the smaller and more provincial Santa Rosita seemed. Even the mystical world she shared with her grandmother and Auntie Paz began receding into a narrow corner of her consciousness. That sacred space was now being invaded by thoughts of earthly temptations: business, money, pleasure, travel, material goods. By her third year at university, she had become so troubled by these thoughts she needed advice from her school counselor.

"My head and my heart are going at each other," she told him. "My head," she groaned, "tells me to go out into the world where there is more action, excitement, opportunity, and possibilities. My heart says the opposite. It says that I love my family and I made a promise to return. So what's more important? I would like to go out and see the world, but how can I not go home when that is what my Poppa, and everybody else, is waiting for me to do?"

The counselor reassured her. "Enjoy where you are today. You have plenty of time to figure it out."

"Well," Rosie sighed, "maybe there is another option. Find a guy from Santa Rosita who likes to travel. The problem is, guys from Santa Rosita don't travel. They either live there full time, or leave forever. Gotta look somewhere else."

Rosie started smiling with satisfaction at the thought that she did, after all, find a guy from somewhere else. She almost laughed aloud when she recalled her friend Donna's enthusiastic reaction the first time she told her about Jon. "Wow. Way to go chickie, have a ball," Donna crooned in her singsong voice. Like many native New Mexicans, Donna spoke with a musical intonation—gradually raising the pitch of each word until the last word in the sentence. Rosie playfully exaggerated this tonality when joking with her friends. "Yeah, he asked meeee. I didn't expect that and I got so flus-tered. You know him being who he is, a doc-torrr, and me being meeee, and me thinking that this isn't right, because we are so diff-er-ent, and in almost every possible waaa-yy. But hey, we are in Albuquerque, the big city, where anything goes.

As soon as he asked me out, all the entire practical stuff, the outsider thing, or how my family would freak out if they knew I was going out with him, all that flew out of my mind. I was on my own. There was no family around. I wanted to get to know him better.'

"And I guess you did, girl."

"Yeah, but it hasn't been easy. Gotta lie low back home. Some Friday nights we have drinks together with Ray at the Cantina but that is it. No touching, no sleeping together. We tried to get together one night and we almost got nabbed by some drunken punks. So it can only happen here, for now."

Donna admonished her, waving her finger back and forth. "It's okay to have a good time, you know what I mean, but a strike three guy isn't for you. I fooled around with some gringos, sure, but that was foolin' around. I am going to marry my own kind when I go home. That is what we do. That's what you gotta do, too."

Rosie felt hesitant. Was she telling Donna too much? Could she keep a secret? Better be cautious. "Yeah, I know he is not for my family, but I'm having a ball."

Donna warned. "Trouble, Chiquita, you are heading for a lot of trouble. Girls like us, from where we come from, we don't marry any gringos. By the way, Spielman, what's that?"

"Jewish, but he isn't religious."

Donna exploded. "Ay, Rosie, you are even more loco than I thought. He doesn't even believe in Jesus Christ!"

Soon after this conversation, Rosie began to notice that some of her Hispanic friends at the university were, as she told Jon, "looking at me funny." Did Donna talk too much? No doubt that the word had gotten out, because some 'home boys' sent Luis, a former boyfriend, to work on her.

"Rosie, you are just shoving it to your parents and your family. Who do you think you are, shaming your people?" Fortunately, such appeals left Rosie unmoved. She knew that no one would dare to squeal on her to the people at home. The code had it that whatever happens in Albuquerque, stays there. Everyone had too much on one another.

"Jerk!" Rosie cried out loud, thinking about Luis. A moment after she slowed her pace to a walk, she saw a black line of stinkbugs crossing the path ahead of her. Sensing her approach, they stopped as one, bowed their heads into the ground and lifted their rears in defense, lock and load, ready for anything. "Pretty cocky, huh?" She shouted and bounded over them. "So what are you telling me? That I am sticking my head in the ground, exposing my backside to misery, huh?"

Sum it up, girl, she told herself. Column A and column B. A. It would be nice to go home, except B, they won't accept Jon. That's the cannonball in the pit of my stomach. There is a column C. Jon and I can always move somewhere else. She pictured herself saying goodbye to her brokenhearted parents and grandparents. So old, so vulnerable and she loved them so much. How could she leave her grandparents? So no column C. I do not want to move somewhere else. I can make this happen, she thought resolutely. So I have to quit acting like a stinkbug and do what I gotta do.

She thanked the spirits after she left the riverbed and walked into a black cloud of doubt; there was no chance. She wasn't leaving. That left column A or column B. But how?

Back in her room, she closed her eyes and watched a daydream play out on the back of her eyelids. She was in church attending Sunday mass. Fr. Raul stood at the altar, his back to the people. Rosita looked down upon the assemblage from her nicho to the left of the altar. Rosie froze the scene around her. She walked down the aisle, up to the altar, and around Fr. Raul, until she was at Rosita's feet. She looked up and stared deeply into her beautiful eyes. When the familiar turquoise light appeared, she began her plea.

Dear Rosita, I know I am always bothering you for help. But this time I really need you. Just like when I was six years old, remember, when Abuelita was so sick, and I came here and kneeled down before you, and asked you to make Abuelita better. And you smiled down on me. And Abuelita got better. Remember that? Well, now I'm stuck, terribly stuck. There is no way I know how to make my family accept me and Jon getting married. No way. You have to help me again. Please.

Amen.

2

Santa Rosita

At the same time Rosie was preparing to go home for the summer, Patron and Elmer were mulling over their shared problems.

"Even though tourist income is up fifty percent since we opened the Arts and Crafts Center," Patron was complaining to Elmer, "we still aren't making enough money to support everybody at the pueblo."

Elmer was shaking his head, "Our younger ones are talking about building a casino like the other tribes. Very bad. That would be the end of us."

"I agree," Patron said. "Ike told me that Alcalde knows La Tierra doesn't want a casino either."

"Us old guys gotta come up with something," Elmer frowned. "Or we are gonna be in big trouble."

Elmer decided to discuss the casino idea with Raymond when they took their regular soak in the hot spring. They headed out before dawn, so Elmer could converse with the night spirits before they entered the water, always a good idea. They reached the river, then walked toward the area where the reed-covered spring was hidden. They stripped and made their way cautiously over the slick stones to an acrid smelling, steamy, bubbling pool. Elmer pinched his nose and frowned. "Extra sulfur today." Raymond grinned and reached out to help Elmer into the spring but Elmer shooed him away.

"I ain't that old yet," he whispered, and grinned again. Raymond felt happy that his grandfather was in a good mood. Elmer settled himself down on the soft, sandy bottom and mused, "Extra hot this morning. No more talking for a while."

They rested in silence, watching the first light of the morning silver-plate the reed stalks. When the gleam disappeared, Elmer began to speak softly, "The night spirits have gone. Now I can say to you what is on my mind. I am troubled that a casino would be the end of us. We would become like those other tribes. Gobbled up!" He pointed off to the south, toward the string of casinos along the freeway running north-south through the center of the state.

Raymond playfully flicked a handful of water in Elmer's direction. "Gobbled up?"

Elmer nodded. "Our young will catch their money-minds and get their spirits rubbed out. Like we caught their diseases. More business in the mind, the less room for spirit." He spoke slowly and deliberately. "When I see a beautiful prairie next to a river, my heart soars. I want to enjoy it and leave it alone. Those others don't understand; they see a beautiful prairie next to a river, they see a housing development. If we become casino operators ... well... our kids will grow up thinking about card games and slot machines, about schemes to separate people from their money. They could give in to jealousy and rivalry, and drink, and drugs, even more than they do now, and more lung cancer from the smoke, get STDs and AIDS...and more money to get fat."

His voice trailed off until he was silent.

Raymond slipped down into the pool until his mouth was just above the waterline. The water was getting intolerably hot for him, but it didn't seem to bother grandfather. Elmer starting talking again. "Can't avoid this problem. Gotta do something about it. We need some counsel. I will go to the top of the mesa and ask the Great Spirit."

Raymond was feeling proud that grandfather said 'we' need counsel. He asked softly. "For what?"

Elmer answered. "For a way forward." Elmer wiped his brow. "Extra hot today. I'm getting cooked." Raymond began to get up when Elmer motioned to him to stay. "Grandson, tell me, college boy or not, you don't really believe that only human beings run this show, do you?"

"Who are you asking, the Indian me or the university me?"

"My grandson, the Indian you."

"Well, people seem to run the show, but I guess the Great Spirit runs the people."

"That's good enough. Your education didn't ruin you completely."

Elmer laughed, got up, and patted Raymond's shoulder. "I have rubber legs now, so you need to help me out."

Raymond boosted him onto the edge of the pool. He was light as a pinon tree branch. Elmer eyed their steaming chests and chuckled. "Now we really look like redskins."

Patron was grumbling to Esther that he was having trouble coming up with ideas to help with the pueblo's financial problems.

Esther was listening, uncritically and quietly, an encouraging smile illuminating her face. She was well known in the town and pueblo to be Patron's secret weapon.

"Don't worry Ruben, you always come up with something, otherwise you wouldn't be where you are today. Think about what you did for Jake with the job at the recycling center, and Lisa. And that doctor, too. I remember back when you told your cousin, Armando, the boss at the State Waste Management Department, that Jake should run our recycling center. Remember, Armando said Jake didn't have credentials, and doubted that Jake knew enough about environmental issues. And you leaned back in the chair, didn't say a word, slowly took your old charm out of your pocket and began to fiddle with it. You looked Armando straight in the eye and nailed him. 'Who helped your son get off when he shot the drug dealer?' Remember how Armando almost choked on his cigar?"

Patron laughed, "He said, 'Okay. So your cousin, Chico, the attorney, got him off. But Jake needs to do a good job. I am accountable to the feds.'"

Esther went on, happy that her Ruben was laughing. "And what about getting that five-year grant for the director's job at the senior center for Lisa? Even though she only has a home economics degree from community college and the job required a full college degree and five years' experience in geriatrics. Remember when you invited the grant committee here, told them Lisa is one of us, and they should throw out the application of that geriatric specialist who wanted to move here? And you said it was more important that Lisa knew about actually caring for old people, like her grandmother who was so sick all those years."

"True," Patron nodded. "True. And I said that the job would keep her at home with her family, where she belongs. They liked that."

Esther nodded with a sweet smile. "And what about the Doc? You had to go outside to fill that job after Doc Garcia passed away, or the grant money might have gone out the window. And what did you do?"

Patron sat up straighter and winked at her. "Never lose free money, that's my motto. I remember when I told Jake I needed to have a doctor on board, and quick, or we'd lose the funding for the clinic. The only one who wanted to come here was a doctor from the university. That was one hard sell, especially to the clinic staff and La Tierra."

Esther nodded and smiled, "Susannah gave me a play-by-play on what happened with the Doc at the clinic, when they tried him out. It was very funny. He was a good Doc, smart, kind, and professional, Susannah said, but he didn't flirt with anybody. The nurses decided to test him to see if he might be gay. You remember Maria, the lab tech who dated Ike?"

Patron nodded. "Sure." Who could forget the build on her, he was thinking, Lucky Ike.

"Well," Esther continued. "They gave him the test."

"The test?" Patron asked.

"You don't know about the test?" Esther laughed.

"I don't know everything." Less said the better, he thought.

"Well," Esther continued. She was thinking, Ruben says he doesn't know, my foot. "Anyway, the next morning Maria walks into work wearing her lowest-cut peasant blouse. She gave him the 'test' in the morning and made her official report at lunch. He passed! She said she bent over in front of the Doc a couple of times. He saw what he had to see, and she said his eyes almost popped out. Susannah said that Doc took a serious peek and another when he thought she wasn't looking. Susannah said that the Doc ain't gay, that he just doesn't want to play where he works."

"Good story," Patron laughed. "That Susannah..." He thought for a moment, "Good thing too. Imagine if the Doc were gay, he wouldn't last a minute in town. Can you imagine? A gringo, Jewish, and gay! That's mountain lion bait for La Tierra." Patron shook his head. "They almost screwed up my deal to get the Doc."

"I remember," Esther sighed. "That was a close call."

"I had everybody on my side; grandfather and the tribal council, the church board. I had started my speech when Ike and his La Tierra friends showed up. I was saying we needed a permanent doctor for the town. I reminded them that people really like our temporary Doc, and I wanted to ask him to stay on. I asked if anybody had a problem with him. No one made a sound, but then Jorge from La Tierra opened his mouth.

"'Yeah, the Doc ain't too bad. But he ain't one of us, he's an outsider, and a gringo, and you know he is a Jew.' Jorge looked around for approval, and his pals, even our Ike, were snickering. Then one of the guys yelled 'Jews. They steal your money!' And Ike joined him, 'No Jews in this town! Never had any. Don't need any.' And old Teresa shouted, 'Ike, don't interrupt your grandfather, it's not respectful.' I was getting annoyed, but I went on speaking. I said that Doc speaks perfect Spanish and some dialects, too. I was almost shouting them down. I said that he's not like the other outsiders, and he's a good friend of Raymond's... from the university. Raymond vouches for him. I yelled out that Rosie knows him from the university, too. He's the good doctor who saved her life when she had pneumonia! But I wasn't convincing them, so I thought I might have to compare him to something worse. So I said that even though Doc may be an outsider, he is not that much of an outsider! The crowd liked that one. Remember when someone shouted out: 'At least he isn't from the East.'

"Everybody laughed. I got the crowd on my side again. Right, I told them, he comes from a family in Santa Fe that goes back to the early 1800's. Nothing compared to how far we go back, of course.

"Then Jorge yelled, 'but he is a Jew...' I raised both hands in the air and I said that I don't think he follows any religion. Then, I think it was Vincente who yelled out, 'What kind of a man is that?'"

Esther interrupted, "I remember, then some drunk shouted, 'Keep the Jews in Albuquerque with the rest of the crooks.'"

"Yes," Patron laughed, "then a woman yelled out 'I heard he was gay.' It was good that Susannah immediately shouted out that he passed the test."

Patron and Esther were both having a good time. Patron went on. "Everyone loved that one. When I felt the crowd softening up, I decided to let them have it. Remember, I said, that if we don't keep the Doc we could lose $175,000 in grant money. Then I pointed to Susannah and Sylvia in the back and said if we didn't get the money, they would be back on unemployment."

"Everyone Ooohed and Aaahed at that one," Esther laughed. "Remember macho Miguel, with his shirt open and gold chain hanging down that hairy chest, who thinks he's God's gift to women, yelled, 'Well, now that's different. If the gringo stays, the money stays...'"

Patron was laughing so hard he had to stop and catch his breath. "And I said, Correcto, Miguel, and said at least Miguel gets it! And he looked around grinning and proud of himself. That's when I knew it was time to quit and maybe fight another day."

"And then you did it, like I said," Esther patted his shoulder, "at the hospital fundraiser you called the Doc up to the front, put your right hand on his forehead, and said, 'Thank you.' They were wondering why you were blessing the Doc, an outsider. You just held your head up, cleared your throat until everybody shut up, and announced that the clinic had gotten a new $100,000 grant for rural health care, and it was the Doc's connections that did it. Then you pointed to the two clinic girls you told to stand in the front, and said that now Celia and Estella have jobs, and Sylvia and Susannah can keep theirs, too. My dear husband, everybody loved that. I was so proud of you."

Patron had stopped laughing; his mood changed to serious. "Sarah, I am worried about Ike. He acted strange at that meeting."

"He was drinking too much with his buddy, Sal. Celia told me that after Ike heard what you said he told Sal, 'Look at those pendejos cheering. They're sell-outs; give 'em a buck and they kiss the gringo's ass.'"

"'Yeah, sell-outs!'" Sal yelled, too, and high-fived Ike.

"'La Tierra,' Ike shouted.' It ain't over.'"

Patron recalled Ike's disturbing behavior: "When I finished talking he staggered over to me, kissed me on both cheeks and offered me a swig of his beer. I didn't want any of that. I patted his cheek and tried to let him know that I understand how he feels, but I owe the Doc a lot."

"He should understand that," Esther said.

"Yes, he didn't expect that kind of an answer. He knows that honoring a debt is a big part of our code. So I got personal and told him it's not just about grants for the clinic, the Doc is good. He found out why those sores on my leg weren't healing, and now I'm getting better with the medicine he gave me. I thought Ike would accept that."

"Instead he lost it," Esther threw up her hands. "Remember he started in, 'If you let gringos in, this place will be another Albuquerque, overrun with outsiders. Not just gringos, blacks, Asians, wetbacks sneaking in. We could lose our identity, our culture, and our way of life. This is our land, remember? We need to protect ourselves. You told me that when I was a kid. Remember?'"

"Yes, poor nieto. He thinks I'm letting him down. In a sense he's right. In the old days, I used to think the same way he does. But now I've changed. I told Ike the old ways don't work anymore. Read the newspaper, I told him, watch TV, look at reality. Maybe it's my old age, I told him, but I'm beginning to think it's not about gringos, blacks, reds, browns, yellows, anymore But about good people and bad people. Not how they look or what they believe in. It all boils down to good or bad. No?"

Esther interrupted, "Yes. You're right. Live and learn. Like it or not."

"I told him that I want to keep our town just for us. But the reality is that if we're going to survive, we need to do business with outsiders. They buy our artwork and crafts, don't they? So maybe we need to give some of them a chance—one by one, of course."

"'But that means change, Ike said. 'You always said you are against change, Poppa. Keep the old ways, you said.' The poor kid was turning colors, he was so confused. I put my arm around him, told him, 'You are a good boy, Ike. But things now are not like they were. There have to be new-old ways. You understand?' And I hugged him and told him, 'You got the fire, mi nieto. You got the fire.'"

Esther patted Patron's hand. "That was the right thing. Ike's emotional, like his mother and me."

Tell me about it, Patron thought. "Ike told me, with tears in his eyes, that he thought he knew what I wanted from him, but now, he doesn't get it. I told him that nothing stays the same. I said he needs to grow up more and his parents agree with me. But for now, I told him, not too much to drink, lay off the drugs, and watch out for the clap."

Esther felt the need to comfort him. "Ruben, remember when you were his age and joined La Tierra, how you were all mad because so many of us thought we were getting the best of the outsiders when we sold desert land to them. Then when property values went up, we got furious because they made big profits. Remember your angry speeches about these being our lands. Our historic home, settled by our Spanish Catholic ancestors!"

"Yes," Patron mumbled.

"Well, Ike is only being like you, and Jake, and his father. You all felt the same."

"Yes," Patron responded with a downcast expression.

"Now, Ruben, Ike may have some emotional problems, but he is also a dreamer and artist like you. He does beautiful work at the shop, and did you see the fine logo he designed for La Tierra, the one on his headband?"

"True," Patron sat up a little straighter. "The flaming red Spanish sword in the shape of a cross that stabs through the map of New Mexico. That would make a beautiful rug, too."

Esther's eyes began to shine. "That beautiful dye he mixed, calls it 'Sangre de Cristo Red.'"

They locked eyes. Esther reached out to stroke Patron's face. Her touch was silky, and light as a feather. "Don't worry, dear. You will save the day. Just wait and see."

Patron took both her hands in his and drew her close. "From your mouth to God's ears. Thank God Rosie will help when she comes home for the summer."

Esther smiled softly. "Of course dear. Rosie will help, but right now, she has other things on her mind. Serious things." She said these words in a way that mystified Patron. Was more trouble on the way?

@

Esther keeps a running scorecard on the state of each of her beloved family members. Recently, at the annual meeting of curanderas and folk healers in Santa Fe, she had her turn to update the senior members on the state of her family.

"My oldest daughter, Paz, is fifty-seven; she is still not married, which is a long story. Paz runs our hotel and restaurant business. We bicker a lot but always make up. Sarah, my second daughter, is fifty-seven, married to Jaime Flores, age fifty-nine. Sarah never fights with anyone, and needs to stand up for herself more. Jaime is a quiet and respectful person who does not make trouble. Not much fun at a party, but he is a hard worker, and he worships Sarah and my husband. They have three children; oldest son is Jake, who is 37. He's been a good man since he left the gang, came back from the service and grew up. He is married to Carmela, same age, who... is a good person...but well—how should I put it? She cares most about herself! Jake and Carmela have Lisa, my granddaughter who is an adorable young lady. She does great work as our Senior Center director, a job that my husband got for her. Our grandson, Ike, works in our rug business. He needs to grow up. Right now, he keeps me awake with worry because he has some crazy ideas and raises hell. I pray a lot for him. Then there is my beautiful granddaughter, Rosie. We are so proud of her because she is going to graduate school at the University of New Mexico (pause for applause). Rosie is coming home to pick out a nice guy and get married, make me some great-grandchildren before too long. She's the one to continue our healing tradition and modernize the family businesses."

One of the women asked about Carmela. Was this the same Carmela who traveled to Albuquerque on business? Esther launched into more about her daughter-in-law:

"Carmela prides herself on being more cosmopolitan than us because her father, who came from our town, was a military officer. He met his future wife, Esperanza, when he was on duty in Spain. Carmela's mother, although the poor thing died too early, put ideas in that young girl's head that she came from noble ancestry. Esperanza always made a fuss about her skin being lighter than ours. 'It's not that darker skin color is bad,' she would say, 'it's just that white is the best color for skin. So Carmela should never go out in the sun unless she covers up completely.'"

Esther continued: "Carmela's mother had the old attitude that the early Spanish settlers had, thinking they were better than the mestizos, born of mixed parentage. But our people have skin in a spectrum of beautiful colors from copper to brown. We have had centuries of intermarriage, so our body types and facial shapes can be different even among blood relatives. For example, Rosie has bronze skin and very high cheekbones. Jake has a flatter nose and broad cheekbones, and his complexion is darker than Ike's or Rosie's. Lisa, his daughter, inherited her mother's pale skin, also Jake's nose and high cheekbones. Paz has the longest and narrowest nose in the family! We wonder where that came from."

Esther took a deep breath. "Unfortunately, some of her mother's ideas impressed Carmela; we saw that when she and Jake fell in love. My daughter Sarah and Jaime were very sympathetic to Carmela. She was an only child left without a mother, but they felt she was putting on airs, like carrying a parasol so the direct sunlight never touched her face. Jake explained to us that Carmela's attitude wasn't her fault, since her parents had made such a big fuss over her light skin. They told that made her special. But I think she looks anemic, and I tell her to take her iron pills! "

Esther smiled. "The more we got to know her, we found she has a good heart. She does projects at the church and helps the needy. A few mean-spirited people call her 'Miss Wannabe Gringo' but Carmela puts that down to their being jealous. We have come to love her and my husband is quite proud of her contributions to the family business. She is perfect in the rug store, with an elegant bearing and manners that charm the customers. But after a few margaritas, without salt because it makes her retain water, she reminds us of her ancestors among the Spanish royalty."

⊚

Esther retired from the family business several years ago and often suggests to Patron that he do the same. The subject came up again one evening as they relaxed on the patio and a spectacular sunset painted the sky. He had just finished reading an article "Knowing When to Retire," and filled out the questionnaire next to it. His score made it plain: it was time for him to pass on control of the business while he was still healthy and clear-headed.

He waved the magazine in her direction. "Dear, this says I should get out while the getting is good. So, since I know I will not live forever, I am coming to a decision."

"Good," Esther murmured. She had heard this before.

"I have decided to turn the business over to the children. This time for real." She only smiled and nodded. Patron continued. "But I feel that it is easier said than done."

Esther laughed out loud. "The first thing you will need to learn is how to bite your tongue. That's because you already know things the younger ones are going to have to find out for themselves."

"True," Patron grimaced. How smart she is. "Our kids think they know it all, I guess everybody thinks they know it all. I did until I passed seventy. Then..."

"We realize we don't know so much. Yes, Ruben, that's the way God planned it."

Patron admired the way Esther could deal so calmly with things he agonized about, as if she had already experienced everything.

"So do I have to stand by and watch the children make mistakes? Does everything I know go down the drain?"

"No, sometimes it skips the children, but that's what grandchildren are for. They get it. Like Rosie." Esther reached over and patted his arm.

"What if I end up just feeling useless?"

Esther laughed again. "That will be the day." She flashed Patron a flirty side-glance. "You have other work to do. Remember, helping grandfather. Besides, amor, you will always be useful to me."

"You mean shopping, going on trips. Right?" Patron nudged her.

"That's only part of it," Esther teased.

Once he had made up his mind, Patron went into action. Strike while the iron is hot, he told himself, and immediately called a family meeting.

"He finally did it," Esther confided to her closest friend. "Ruben has given the daily responsibility for running all the businesses to our son-in-law, Jaime. He's quiet, but responsible. Jaime always felt he 'married up' with our Sarah, so he has been working to prove himself to Patron ever since. He will coordinate the work of three divisions. Our grandson, Ike, will be in charge of rug design and production; our daughter-in-law, Carmela, will still be in charge of sales and marketing, and our daughter, Paz will continue to manage the Inn and Restaurant y Cantina. Ruben is thinking about where to place Rosie in the business after she finishes school."

Patron had a meeting with Jaime to talk about Rosie. "Even though Rosie is beautiful, she has the best head in the family for numbers. So she will be our chief financial officer." He remembered how he had glowed with pride when Rosie told him about her dreams for the family business.

"Poppa," she had said, "I'll work out a business plan for adding on a mail order catalog and something brand new, a website, and I'll use the computer to manage all our inventory, financials, payroll, everything!"

Music to Patron's ears. Like everybody else in the family, he eagerly awaited her return from the university. So did her Auntie Paz and Carmela, leaders of the town posse to find Rosie a suitable husband. This quest naturally flowed from Paz's spiritual connection to Rosie, which began when she was born—when she first noticed that Rosie's eyes were of different colors, and put the first bow in Rosie's sparse hair, and clipped on her little earrings. That is what godmothers do. And when Rosie was old enough to take an interest, Carmela became her fashion consultant. All through Rosie's high school days, Carmela was ready and willing to help her pick out the perfect outfit and do her makeup before a big date. Carmela knew all about such things.

But lately, Paz got the sense that Rosie was troubled. She shared her concern with Esther, who felt the same way, but wasn't ready to speculate why. "Let's wait until Rosie gets back," Esther advised. "I think it's something we need to talk about face-to-face." Of course, Esther, who was far more experienced than Paz in matters of the heart, knew more than she was saying.

3

Back Home

Rosie arrived home late on a Sunday afternoon. After greeting her joyful parents, she wearily announced that she was 'wasted' and only wanted to get into pajamas, flop on her bed and stay there until she was 'all slept out.' After she called her grandparents and Paz, she managed to leave a phone message for Jon, who was attending a medical conference in Albuquerque.

By Tuesday, Rosie felt rested enough to start the summer job Patron had created for her using a summer rural service grant. It brought her a modest salary, as well as school credits in health care business administration. Patron was proud of her work, and she had made a big improvement in the clinic's record-keeping and financial management. After lunch with her indulgent mother, Rosie strolled over to the clinic just as the staff was ending their lunch break.

"Our college girl is back!" Susannah shouted. "Come over here and give me a hug." After many embraces Rosie headed to her office, the former 'curandera' room, where as a teenager she had helped her grandmother tend to the sick. She arranged things to her liking and then, with the encouragement of the staff, decided to call it a short day. She would go home and use the rest of the time to think and plan.

One step at a time, she cautioned herself. Time to check with Ray to see if any word about her and Jon had gotten out. She grabbed the phone and dialed Ray's number. No answer. She left a message. "Hi Ray, Hi Chenoa. It's me. Chenoa, can I borrow Ray sometime? Need to talk to him at the Cantina. Thursday night will work. Thanks. Jon should be back from Albuquerque by then and he will join us. Love you, Chenoa girl." She took a deep breath and hung up. Step one done!

Rosie worked at the clinic the next couple of days and visited all her relatives except Auntie Paz, who was away. After work on Thursday, she took a nap, ate a bite, and headed out to meet Raymond. It had started to rain, so she grabbed an umbrella and strolled down the hill through the drizzle to the Cantina. She paused in the doorway for a moment to take in the familiar surroundings. There was Raymond parked on a barstool, his large body silhouetted against a colorful array of whiskey bottles arranged on glass shelves and reflected in the bar mirror. He was staring at a flashing neon sign over the bar: 'Juan, PhD in Mixology.' She crept up behind Ray and placed her hands over his eyes. "Guess who?"

Ray received her greeting in the Indian way—sitting upright, with no physical response except for a bright sparkle in his eyes when he turned around to face her. "Rosie, of course! What makes you think you can sneak up on an Indian?"

"Hi, Ray, long time no see." Rosie looked around for her aunt. "Auntie Paz not back yet?" Ray shook his head. "Nope. Did you hear? It's a hard rain coming tonight. By the way, Jon is back, but he had an emergency. He'll come over after he finishes."

"That's OK; you and I haven't talked alone for a long time. Ray, I'm so uptight." Rosie sat beside him and let loose a torrent of words, all about her fear of telling her family about Jon and her. Then she interrupted herself, "Hey, I need a drink. Where is Juan?"

Ray pointed to the man on the far side of the room cleaning a table. "Hector's here tonight." The man, hearing his name mentioned, and without turning around, raised his hand to acknowledge Rosie. "Juan's off."

Rosie waved at Hector who didn't see her, then turned back to Ray and screwed up her face: "His margaritas are awful." She whispered, "Beergaritas .. . the worst!"

Raymond shook his head. "Juan won't give anybody his recipes."

"Oh, hell! I'll drink anything tonight. Hey, Hector," Rosie called. When he looked their way, Raymond wiggled his index finger. That meant a margarita; middle finger meant beergarita. Rosie turned around again to ask him why the place was so empty, and he said people knew a big storm was coming.

"Music?" Rosie twirled her index finger in the air.

Hector sounded grouchy. "No music and no time for margaritas. Tequila only, Chiquita, then I clean up and go home." He walked over and poured Rosie a shot of tequila.

She downed it quickly, swung around on the barstool, and looked hard into Raymond's soft black eyes. They smiled at each other.

"Lots happening," he smiled sympathetically.

Her soulful response vanished from her face when a clatter of hailstones hit the roof so hard it made her jerk her head around. "My God!" she shouted.

"Here it comes!" Hector bellowed back. "Gonna be bad out there, guys. I'm closing up."

Rosie calmed down. "Oh! Not yet," she smiled her best. "Hector, please?" She begged, flashing her broadest smile.

Hector rolled his eyes upward; he knew her game, tried to frown, but he couldn't resist Rosie's charm. He poured her another drink.

"Okay, only for you, Rosie. But you gotta tell my wife why I stayed if I get killed on the way home."

Rosie smiled and motioned to Raymond to move to a back booth with her. "I'm dropping the bomb tomorrow."

Raymond clucked his tongue. "Rosie, why torment yourself? Stay in Albuquerque. It isn't that far away. They can't get at you, and you can sneak a visit once in a while."

"Don't say that," Rosie moaned. "I need you to tell me everything is going to be all right."

"I can tell you what you want to hear, or I can tell you the truth." He raised his voice a bit. "Do you really think nobody here knows about you and Jon?"

"Of course!" She sat up straight. "So does Jon."

"Folie a deux as we say in French." Raymond shook his head and spoke deliberately, "He was worried that maybe Juan suspected something because he sees you together sometimes. He is also concerned about your family's reaction . . . if they will go loco when they find out. I told him that I wished I could reassure him, but, just like I'm saying to you, something out of the box is your only hope. Something unforeseen, unexpected, out of our hands. What grandfather is looking for by going up to the mesa to ask for guidance about the casino." Raymond stopped short and looked up at the shaking roof. "He's up there right now."

Rosie became alarmed. "In this weather? He's an old man. Maybe we should go . . ."

Raymond shrugged her off. "He wouldn't like that. Besides, he can take care of himself."

"I wish I'd known he was going to the mesa. I would have asked him to put in a word for me with the big guy." Rosie pouted.

"You don't have to. He knows something's up with you."

She wasn't surprised. "Yeah, he would," Rosie sighed. "Well, back to what you asked, I don't think anyone in town knows anything. Believe me, if the girls at the clinic knew about us, they would have laid into me. That's gossip central."

Raymond teased her, "Maybe they're waiting for the right time to out you so they can do the most damage." He turned serious. "What I am really worried about is if the La Tierra guys find out, Jon could be in danger, run out of town, that's the least!"

"Hey!" Rosie interrupted. "I'm telling you no one knows. Just you, maybe Abuelita and grandfather, Auntie Paz, they may sense something, but they don't know the whole story."

"Your parents?"

"Nope," Rosie answered smugly. "Especially not my parents."

"Well, if that's true, you are making Santa Rosita history."

"Bite your tongue, Ray!"

"You know what people will say when they find out? 'Hey, college girl, ain't anyone here good enough for you? Patron's granddaughter going to marry an outsider?' You know about losing face."

Rosie drummed fingers on the table. "Okay, I got your point; now you are supposed to cheer me up."

A five-second-long roll of thunder shook the room. Hector threw his arms up, a motion to get them to go. Raymond ignored him. "Let's stall until Jon comes. Change the subject. How about our new buzz-phrase, cultural sensitivity? It's in all the grant applications."

"Ray, what the hell are you talking about?"

"Didn't Jon tell you what he learned about cultural sensitivity last week?"

"Ray, are you losing it? I'm worried about my whole life here, and you are going on about, what are you going on about?"

Raymond saw that he had piqued her curiosity. He waved to Hector, "Okay. A couple more minutes. Jon's on the way. We'll wait for him in the lobby." He turned to Rosie. "This is worth hearing. C'mon, it's a good story to pass the time until Jon shows up."

He took Rosie by the arm and escorted her up the stairs and into the lobby.

"Last Friday Jon told me that he learned the downside of having close family ties. I asked him if he meant that family members could drive each other nuts. He said no. It was about family he had seen in the clinic, but he wouldn't tell me their name because of confidentiality. He said it was a local family that's been feuding with another family for centuries.

"Oh, that has to be Lopez and Abales, I said, they can get loco. I hear the Lopez kid got popped. Pete, right? Jon wouldn't say and I told him he didn't have to, and that he wouldn't be sued for telling on his patients because there are no secrets in Santa Rosita.

"'Well,' he said, 'since you know it all, I saw Pete in the clinic. He's 17, the grandson of ....' Yeah, Vincente Lopez, I interrupted. Not a bad person. A little too straight and uptight, but that comes from living out in the desert. We have many guys like him at the pueblo.

"Jon said they brought Pete in because one of the Abales shot him in the leg. I told him the Abales never shoot to kill, and the Lopez people don't either.

"Well, Rosie," Raymond chuckled, "Jon talked so fast he started tripping over his words. He said that Pete came to the clinic in a two-truck procession, with his parents, grandparents, sister, and brother. After the kid was fixed up, Vincente bragged that Pete was a warrior defending the family name. The grandfather was grinning about Pete having popped two of them in the caps; he was sure they wouldn't come near this clinic because of all the Lopez family waiting outside. Apparently, the Abale guy had to be taken to

Taos to be patched up. Then old Vincente showed his left ear to Jon, at least what remained of it. Said an Abale tough guy shot it off thirty years earlier. I hinted to Jon that ears may have been the target in the past, but now its kneecaps.

"Then Jon started talking again, waving his arms in the air. 'I couldn't believe what Mr. Lopez was saying. This is the 21st century, for God's sake! When he told me that Pete is like him, a warrior, he patted the kid's head. The whole family was smiling and nodding . . . When I asked Pete about his life, he told me he had left school. He bragged that wasting the Abales was going to be his career. After that, his family all smiled and his father high-fived him. Raymond, nobody even cared about him dropping out of school. And when I asked what started the feud with the Abales. Would you believe it, nobody remembered! Mr. Lopez said his family had always hated them. Some fellow long ago knocked up one of their girls.'"

Raymond was respectful of Jon's efforts to understand the culture. He told Rosie, "Jon knows the kid dropped out, has no prospects and headed for trouble. But he sees this kid feeling good about himself because his family respects him. That's great, but wouldn't it be better if his family were giving him encouragement to stay school, become a man who could earn a good living, things like that?

"I let Jon know he was only at the beginning of learning our ways, but he definitely was becoming culturally sensitive to Santa Rosita life. Family togetherness usually means staying here and ignoring the rest of the world. Jon disagreed; he said that does not necessarily have to be bad. Most of the little kids he sees are fine. It's the teenagers who feel stifled and act up. Yeah, I told him, but most of them calm down when they get older, and then mostly take after their parents. My people do this too: they want the kids to stay, but they can't give them much when they do, except love and respect. As great as it is to have this as home base, it only goes so far. When our young people leave, they feel disoriented and get depressed. I felt that way when I went away to M.I.T. But it wasn't that bad for me, because I grew up some at school in Albuquerque. I told Jon what we really need is a way to have both family and the big world out there all in one package."

Rosie just closed her eyes and sighed.

Raymond asked, "Did I get your mind off your worries?"

Rosie grinned back. "For a minute." She gestured up at the roof, where the rain sounded like a tribal drum beat. "So is that saying something?

Raymond grinned. "Why not?"

The phone rang and Hector answered. "Rosie, it's for you," he called.

Rosie picked up the phone. "Oh, Jon, you okay? Yes, I miss you, too. Okay, Okay. Just get some sleep. You'll need it. No. I understand. See you tomorrow. Yes, I'll tell him. Love you too."

She called to Ray. "Jon has to stay with his patient tonight. Ambulance can't make it up here. The rain is coming north and flooded the road to Albuquerque. It's gonna be a bad one"

"Then we'd better go. Goodnight, Hector," Raymond waved.

Hector returned the gesture. "Drive careful."

Raymond put his arm gently around Rosie's shoulder. "So . . . when are you outing yourself?" he asked.

"Tomorrow night," Rosie said. "'I'm praying for a miracle."

"Why not?" Raymond laughed. "Want to get together afterward?"

"Sure," Rosie agreed.

"Then I'll see you both here tomorrow night. I'll bring the bandages."

Rosie kissed Raymond on the cheek. "Till tomorrow then and here's one for Chenoa, too." She kissed him on the other cheek.

.   Raymond smiled. "I'll give her all the dirt when she gets back from work."

4

The Same God

Although Raymond had been skeptical that Rosie's romance would stay secret, she was correct in assuming that no one in town knew she and Jon were an item. Not that the possibility wasn't considered when Rosie worked at the clinic during spring break, but no one came up with any hard evidence. Jon had been working there for six months before Rosie arrived, and was already accepted as much as he could be. The staff was pleased that he didn't act high and mighty or think he was better than anyone else because he was a doctor. They saw his dedication and gentle way with children, agreeing among themselves that even the shyest kids took to him. A few were wary about Jon being Jewish, but only a couple of people took to watchful waiting for the stereotype behavior they thought he might show: pushy attitude, being cheap and so on.

Susannah and the other nursing staff knew Jon had treated Rosie at the university, so she made it her self-appointed mission to check out whether Rosie and Jon had something going on. She started by teasing Rosie in the cafeteria, "Oh, Chiquita, I noticed the Doc, he's checking you out," and enjoyed it when the other women there all laughed. But Rosie didn't take the bait, just changed the subject. Susannah was quieted for the time being. However, the notion that the Doc might have taken to Rosie was too titillating to ignore. Priscilla, the head nurse, noticed Rosie seemed to be more than eager to come to work. That was unusual behavior in Santa Rosita. In fact, Priscilla noted that some mornings Rosie even arrived before anyone else. "Hmmm," she thought, "the only person there is Doc, who sleeps at the clinic; and the other night Rosie stayed late to do the books; at least that's what she said."

Priscilla fancied that more than a casual glance passed between Rosie and Jon, so she mentioned it to Susannah: "Rosie comes in early sometimes and stays late. Nobody is here except the Doc. Most chiquitas Rosie's age and pretty like her would be out drinking with their friends and coming in late hung-over. Could something be going on with them?"

Susannah thought for a moment. "I dunno. She brushed me off when I teased her. She wouldn't act like that if she had a guilty conscience. Maybe she really needs to do extra work for school."

"Yeah," Priscilla agreed, "Rosie wouldn't mess with an outsider. She's too smart to do that. She is one of us through and through and, besides, her family would kill her. Anyway I got more important things on my mind than Rosie's love life, like my borracho husband and my three daughters in heat." End of inquiry.

Rosie and Jon were able to keep secretive in Santa Rosita because they acted formally there. They were careful to carry on the romance out of town, quite easy to do while she attended the university. Rosie's family didn't question her much about what she did on weekends. When they did, she found it easy to make up excuses for remaining at the university on semester breaks, or going on field trips. Jon kept no secrets from his father, who took to Rosie right away, accepted her, and never even mentioned their cultural and religious differences. The elder Spielman was sensitive enough to understand his only son's choice, and was not about to alienate him. He knew Jon would have to come to terms with Rosie about religion anyway.

Jon had discussed this religious question with Rosie one morning when he picked her up after church. She only had to tell him how good it felt her to go to church for him to respond with a kind smile, "That's all that matters."

When Rosie asked him about his faith, he told her that he believed in a higher power but, unlike her, he didn't have the need to belong to any organized religion.

Rosie pushed for details. "I don't know anything about Jews. Did you ever go to Sunday school?"

Jon shook his head. "Not really. My parents and grandparents taught me about Judaism. As simple as it may sound, they taught me that learning is being close to God, and so is helping people who need it. And we don't need an intermediary between God and man. That's about it. Live and let live. I was never taught to hate other religions or think Judaism was the only way. And later I studied the Kabbalah on my own for a while."

"What's that?" Rosie asked.

"Jewish mysticism. It must be similar to ideas that grandfather and Raymond believe—very spiritual, intangible. I think these ideas helped me become a doctor." Jon was feeling self-conscious about revealing his deep feelings. This made Rosie more eager to mine him for more information

Jon said, "Don't laugh. It started when I was a little boy. My mother was very sick and my father called a doctor. When the doctor left, everybody felt so much better..."

"And..."

"And." Jon hesitated again, searching for the right words. "I was so impressed by the doctor's ability to make everybody feel better. When I went to bed, I talked with God and said I wanted to take care of people. And he said that if I take care of people, he will take care of me."

Rosie leaned over, snuggled up to him, and stroked his face. He heard God speak to him, she thought. She crooned, "That is so sweet ..." Then she asked in a little girl voice, "Are you sure that me being Catholic and wanting to stay that way, and bring up our kids that way, doesn't bother you? You know you could become Catholic too. Then we would have less of a problem living in Santa Rosita."

Jon laughed. "And what if you became Jewish?"

Rosie jolted herself out of his arms. "I could never become Jewish. It would kill my family, and we never could live in Santa Rosita. Besides, I love my church."

"So I guess we have a problem," Jon teased. "I'm not going to become Catholic and you are not going to become Jewish."

"This could be serious." Tears welled up in Rosie's eyes, and she sniffled. "Jon, I don't like to talk about this."

Jon was surprised by Rosie's response and backed off. He smiled. "Rosie, let's enjoy where we are right now, and not where we are not." But she was not ready to end the conversation. "I don't understand. If religion doesn't mean anything to you, why can't you become Catholic? For me."

Jon reflected for a moment. "Because I don't believe in any religion, nor why people have a need to divide themselves into groups that worship the same God differently. It's lame-brained to me."

"So I'm lame-brained?" Rosie cried.

"Well, no. You do what you feel is right."

"We should be together on this." Rosie started to move away but Jon put his arms around her shoulders. "Look, we don't have to think the same way about everything. Whether we bring our children up in both faiths, or one, or none, is all the same to me. God is God. What does he, or she, care? I'll respect your beliefs, you respect mine, and we'll do fine."

"And the kids?"

"We'll expose them to everything. They'll be fine."

"This is trouble, trouble," Rosie's tears started up again.

They sat quietly until Jon interrupted the silence. "I don't have a problem accepting that your church is very important to you, like my Dad's synagogue is important to him. Can't that be enough?"

Rosie thought for a moment. "Won't your father feel bad if our kids are not brought up Jewish? My family will go loco if they are not Catholic."

"I can't speak for him but I'm sure he would want our kids to know our family heritage, history..."

Rosie responded urgently, and earnestly, "It's not only the religion; it's the life, the community ... my church is another home, a connection, for me ... Padre ... Rosita."

Jon pulled her close. "You are my home."

Rosie's mind started to race. Ay! It wasn't only how much family trouble she would make for herself if she married Jon, but how much of herself would she have to give up? And how could she ever raise her children in Santa Rosita if they weren't involved in the church like everybody else? Maybe this was not such a good idea.

Jon sensed her dismay and pulled her close. She nestled in his arms. He whispered, "God is God, right? So what's the problem? "

"That's one way of looking at it." Rosie sighed. "But that's not the way it is."

On Friday nights, Rosie's beloved grandmother, Esther, devotes most of her day to preparing the evening meal. After breakfast, she lays her antique white linen tablecloth over the dining room table and carefully sets each place with her well-worn blue and white Talavera dishes. Next, she sets one heavy, azure-colored wine glass and one water glass on the far side of the plates, wine glass on the right. Then she carefully folds each white linen napkin into a fan shape and inserts it into each water glass. This done, she fills the silver candlesticks, wall sconces and candelabras with fresh candles before she places the appropriate pieces of cutlery; ornately decorated knives, forks, and spoons at each setting. Her Friday night menu is relatively consistent: pan trenzada—traditional braided bread is a staple. Sopapillas with honey are a special treat. The first course is chicken soup and posole, followed by assorted tapas, a variety of small corn, chicken and beef tamales served with rice, beans, and salad. The main course is Esther's mouth-watering piece de resistance—'Polla Alonzo,' Patron's favorite—chicken roasted in spicy salsa. There is also wine and beer. After dinner, Esther serves up her renowned flan for dessert. During coffee, some members of the family relax and catch up on their news, while others play cards, dominos, or other games. To assure the family's togetherness, Esther pulls the plug on the TV.

Early Friday morning, Rosie was awakened by a phone call. It was Susannah from the clinic. Rosie did not have to come in to work that day because all services were closing down, except for emergencies, because of the heavy rain. Good news. That left the day for her to plan how she would 'out' herself to her family that evening.

Rehearse what you need to do and say, she told herself as she lay back on her pillows and closed her eyes. After dessert, I will stand up, and tap my glass with a knife to get everybody's attention. Then, with strength and authority — I will not ask them, I will tell them. I will say, 'I have an announcement; quiet, please.' Then I will say, 'Jon and I are in love and want to get engaged this summer, and get married after I finish graduate school next year.' She interrupted herself with a question. Would it be better to alert everybody before we eat that I have an important announcement to make after dinner? You know, tell 'em what I am going to tell 'em? Rosie sat up suddenly. Shit! Maybe this plan is no good. Telling all of them at once may not be the best way to do it. Maybe I'd better go slower, drop a hint to someone first, someone who will not freak out. Test the waters. Yeah, one step at a time is better. Get some people on my side. Esther and Auntie Paz probably sense something's up. Yes. I will start with Auntie Paz today. She is always on my side.

Rehearsal over. Rosie congratulated herself. Talking with Auntie Paz was a good idea. Mom respects Paz, and when Mom finds out . . . Yes. That is the best plan. Soon after she got out of bed, exercised and showered, she called Paz who was, as usual, overjoyed to hear her voice.

"Absolutely, dear, come to the Cantina this afternoon. One o'clock. Don't forget a raincoat and an umbrella, boots too. The weather report said this is one of those hundred-year rains. A once in a lifetime El Nino or something. "

@

By noon on Friday, it was raining so hard that people began to worry. The TV began alerting people to stay inside because the rain was dislodging walls of mud and causing large boulders to tumble down the mountainsides. Rosie had more important things on her mind and decided to brave the rain. She bundled herself in her yellow slicker, opened her umbrella, and began to splash her way down her blacktop driveway toward the restaurant and Cantina. It took only a few minutes for her to reach the plaza, where she took time to play hopscotch between the deep puddles of water. Paz was standing outside holding a large golf umbrella and stretching hard to pass a tarpaulin up to a worker on the roof.

"Hi, Rosie," she called enthusiastically. "Ay! This roof wasn't made for rain like this. Be right with you, dear." When Paz turned back to the worker, Rosie became transfixed by the progress of a large raindrop sliding down Paz's nose. She watched it dip beneath her nostrils, track down her upper lip and disappear into her mouth. She laughed to herself, and felt her love for Paz, zany Paz.

"Need help?" Rosie shouted.

Paz responded by grabbing her by the hand and pulling her under the portal and through the front door of the restaurant. "Inside, quick. Hungry, honey?"

"Not right now thanks." Paz was always pushing food.

Paz turned away and shook her head from side to side, spraying droplets out of her hair. "Learned that from my dog," she laughed. "I am bone-chilled; how about some tea?" Rosie nodded yes.

"Now I need to get these boots off," Paz sighed. "You're pretty soaked too." As Paz took off her coat and boots, Rosie noticed that, rain or not, Paz was well dressed as usual.

"You look pretty sexy under that raincoat."

"Too soggy to feel sexy," Paz wiggled her hips.

Rosie laughed, "Looks like you lost some weight. Huh!"

"Yeah, but I don't want to lose too much. Don't forget, round goes with sensuous, goes with . . . hot!"

Rosie laughed, rolled her eyes and complimented Paz on her colorful red, yellow and blue dress. As usual, Paz wore three silver and turquoise bracelets around each wrist, and a silver belt containing many gemstones. A silver and turquoise chain hung loose around her neck, holding an oversized silver crucifix that rested semi-horizontally on the broad shelf of her bosom. The cross shimmered with her every movement, reflecting light that illuminated her dark brown hair and almond shaped eyes, one brown and one black. Rosie picked up Paz's hand and stared down at her fingernails.

"Wow, that's a wild purple. Auntie Paz, your nails are awesome."

"Thanks," Paz beamed. "My manicurist thinks this purple is a little outrageous, but what the hell."

Paz walked over to the boiling teakettle. "I got peppermint and chamomile."

"Peppermint."

"So, Rosie, what's so important that you're jumping out of your skin?"

"How do you know I am jumping out of my skin?"

"I know, you know that I know. But I don't know why."

"Okay, I have news, great news."

"News," Paz echoed. "I love news. Great news is even better. How exciting."

One deep breath and the cork was out of the bottle. "Paz . . . Jon and I are in love and we want to get married." Rosie fell back into a chair. "There! I did it."

Paz smacked herself on the forehead with the palm of her hand. "Whoa! Love! Married! John who? Someone in Albuquerque?" Then she stopped cold. "My God! Not . . . not ...him . . . the Doctor, here?"

Rosie nodded, "Yes."

"Oooh. I knew something was up with you. I knew it! But Doctor Jon, that's a big surprise."

"So?" Rosie raised her eyebrows at her aunt. Paz fell silent, preoccupied with her failed detective skills. "Hmmm," she reflected. "You've been hangin' at the Cantina with him and Raymond." She looked squarely at Rosie and laughed. "I knew that you came back from college a woman, I mean a complete woman. That was in your eyes."

Paz reached over and gently stroked Rosie's cheek, and Rosie felt the heat. When Paz looked deep into your eyes, she could see your soul.

"So you knew."

"Your mother and I talked about it. You know, college girl and all that. We decided it was your business; after all, aren't you are a modern woman?" Paz nudged her. "So who else have you told about your Jon?"

"No one except Raymond."

"Did you think that maybe I knew?"

"Felt it, yes. Knew it, possible."

Paz liked that. "What about your parents?"

Rosie swallowed hard. "Not yet," she answered. "I had to make sure I was sure of Jon and that I wanted to come back home to live. You know, if I told even one person, everybody would know. Then I would have to deal with a madhouse, which I am trying to avoid."

Paz agreed. "Abuelita feels something is going on. Poppa's reaction is going to be predictable; the old line, we marry our own, Hispanic heritage, pure blood, stay with the faith. Tradition."

"But he is mellowing out in his old age, isn't he? And Jon being his doctor . . ."

"Mellowing, Jon being his doctor! Honey, this is Poppa we are dealing with." Paz sighed.

"Thanks for the we." Rosie smiled weakly.

Paz was reflecting, "What goes around comes around . . . so the old man is going to have another turn." Did Rosie spot a sly grin crossing her face?

Rosie got it. "You mean what happened to you?"

"All over again." Paz laughed loudly. "You know the whole story?"

Rosie shook her head, no. "Just the G-rated kid version."

"Wanna hear the adult version?" Paz asked.

"Sure." Assured that Paz was on her side, Rosie was happy to change the subject. Paz leaned forward and gently cradled Rosie's hands in hers. The cross on her necklace slipped off her bosom and began to slowly swing back and forth over the table. "Look, Rosie," she chuckled. "When my cross swings from left to right, whatever it is, is not good. When it swings in a circle, its right."

The cross began to rotate in wider and wider circles as she spoke. "See, a good sign. Now here I go." Their eyes locked. "When I was twenty, I fell in love with Bill, an artist from the East who came here to paint. He was good-looking, tall, fair-skinned, blond-haired, hot, too, for a gringo. And I was ready: twenty, gorgeous and a flirt. But no one ever got into my pants because they were scared of Poppa. So, through no choice of my own, I was still a virgin. I was working in the restaurant when he walked in. So help me, God, I almost peed my pants. I thought heaven sent him to me, and by special delivery. Not only was he gorgeous, he seemed so nice too, polite, laid back, mature, not a macho boy on the make like the others. We got to talking, and he asked me if I would show him around the town, and help him to visit the secret places that all of us who grew up here know about, so he could paint the flowers and the scenery there. I said of course, so we started to spend a lot of time together and one thing led to another. I was so in love with him.

"Bill didn't know enough about our rules to be afraid of Poppa. He asked me if he could meet my family. So I put it to Poppa, and of course, he had a fit. Even Momma took Poppa's side. In those days, she agreed with him more than she does now. They told me that they didn't want neighbors to talk, to say that a guy from Santa Rosita wasn't good enough for me, and you know the old song about outsiders, the family would lose respect, especially Poppa being Patron."

"That's exactly what I'm afraid of," Rosie lamented.

Paz leaned back, releasing Rosie's hands. The cross around her neck nestled back on her chest. It seemed to like it there. "So Bill and I snuck around together. You know, the whole thing, out through the window every night until Poppa snagged me. He followed me to Bill's place and caught us making out, well, more than that. He opened the bedroom door and walked right into Bill's naked backside sticking up in the air ... and me underneath. Poppa slammed the door and screamed for me to dress and come outside, and for Bill not to come after me, or else. Poppa said he had a gun in his truck. When he got me home, Poppa cried and said I disgraced the family, and if I continued to see Bill he would disown me, and he would have Bill taken care of. Momma and Sarah calmed him down or I think he would have hit me. Two days later, Bill told me that some people put a sign on his house saying the gringo got 48 hours to leave or see his cojones swinging from a tree. I wanted us to run away together, but we were flat broke. So Bill took off. I received a letter after that saying that he loved me, but there was no way for us to be together. He could not afford to get married, he had to travel and paint, and that anyway my relatives were crazy. If he stayed in Santa Rosita he would be killed, and even if he asked me to join him where he was, they would probably come after us and kill us both."

"Ooooh, Auntie Paz," Rosie cried sympathetically, and reached for a napkin to wipe away her tears.

Paz patted her hand. "Chiquita, take another napkin, I'm not finished. I found out I was pregnant and started bleeding all the time and finally had to go to the hospital in Santa Fe. Momma tried to cover for me. She told Poppa I was having female trouble, endometriosis. I knew Poppa suspected different, but he preferred to ignore it. Endometriosis was okay. He could tell everybody I was having female trouble and going to take care of it. No one ever said to his face that I had anything but endometriosis. I lost the baby and got depressed, even thought about doing myself in. After I came home, I started going over to the church every night to talk with Rosita. Well, one night, she rolled her eyes up and looked right at me. I almost fainted. Then I heard her voice in my mind. She talked slowly and softly, you know how she does."

"What did she say?" Rosie asked.

"She told me I had to live. She said she would always be my friend and that God does not want people to kill themselves. Then she looked way up, like she was seeing God."

"Wow."

"That's her, Rosita."

"Sure."

Paz laughed and gently elbowed Rosie. "Do I sound nutty?"

"Makes two of us. Rosita smiled at me once when I was a little girl. I saw her eyes move, too."

Paz smiled softly. "We are not supposed to talk about this."

"That will never happen. Is your story finished?"

"Almost," Paz caught her breath. "Poppa behaved differently toward me after Bill. To tell the truth, I still resent him for the way he acted toward me after that, and especially in church. Before Bill, we used to sit together in church on Sunday mornings. Everyone knew our family arrangement. I sat on Poppa's left side, with your mother, Sarah, next to me. Momma sat on his right side and Jake next to her. After my affair with Bill, Poppa made me sit next to Momma, away from his side, and moved Sarah and Jake next to him. Can you imagine how I felt? Especially because I was already paranoid about who knew about me, and who was staring at the back of my head. Poppa felt I had shamed him, being Patron and all. It made me feel terrible to see him moping around with such a sad look on his face. Like he was going to cry. I felt my life was over. Of course, the men stopped coming around, and some lousy rats, the La Tierra turds, made remarks to me about my illness having two arms and legs. I guess I should have moved away to Santa Fe or Albuquerque, but I stayed. Rosie, I am a homie. I need my family. So I stayed."

Paz blew her nose loudly. "End of story, adult version."

Rosie gathered up the used napkins. "Anyone since?"

"In Santa Rosita! No way. After things simmered down, and people had someone else's misery to gossip about, I threw myself into the business. All the guys I knew here were losers, except for Marin, remember him?"

"Yeah, a nice guy."

"He went off and got killed in the war. The other muchachos used to tell me that I was conceited and thought I was too good for anyone here. So I decided, since the pickings were so slim, that if I had to marry my 'own' like Poppa said, I was not going to marry."

"What about, you know?" Rosie asked.

"Sex? Sure. Well, I go on a cruise occasionally. And I have a fellow in Albuquerque I see once in a while. But he is married. Not happily so he says, like they all do. Anyway he's not available for much more than a . . ."

"Auntie Paz!" Rosie squealed.

"Don't worry, dear. I get what I want when I need it. There is something about being single that makes life simple. I have a lot to be grateful for, and I try not to miss what I don't have. But you know the old joke, enough about me. What about you?"

Rosie sighed. "What about me?"

Paz spoke reassuringly. "We can always hope that since times have changed, you might have a much better chance with Poppa. He isn't as feisty as he used to be, although he is too stubborn to admit it. Maybe he learned something from what he did to me."

"That would be nice."

"You can count on your parents freaking out when you tell them. Your Dad for sure will bust a gut. You have always been able to twist him around your little finger, but now you will need to do a lot more than twisting. Your Mom is a total softie. She is sure to have a panic attack, but she won't make waves, she'll follow your father's lead. They will look to Abuelita and Poppa for their reactions first. Jake, I dunno. You know how he is with makin' waves. He won't like the idea at all. Mostly it's Ike and his friends we need to worry about. You know how he is when he gets hyper."

"I can handle Ike," Rosie said. "Jon can take care of himself, too. He feels he has a right to live where he want to. It's his state and his country too."

"Makes sense," Paz sighed deeply. "But it still won't do him much good up here."

Rosie took her hand and kissed it gently. "So you're not mad at me that I didn't tell you before?"

Paz nudged her affectionately. "Silly. Tell you what. I will go have a chat with our Rosita and say some prayers for you. Also, it would be a good idea for you to talk with Fr. Raul, but go early in the morning."

"For sure," Rosie laughed.

"Okay," Paz inhaled deeply, now all business. "As soon as I get home, I will ask Guadalupe and the rest of my homies for help. I will see you tonight at Abuelita's. Be sure to let her know beforehand that you want to say something to the family tonight."

"I'll do exactly as you say." Rosie kissed her goodbye and walked out into a driving rain that beat down so hard on her face it hurt her eyes. She sought shelter under the portales attached to the houses lining the plaza, and weaved her way homeward. When she reached her front door, she began to rehearse her announcement to hear how it sounded. "Dear family . . ." But that was as far as she could go. Fear made her question herself. "Should I wait for another time?"

Rosie went into her room and phoned Jon. She was choking back tears. "I'm afraid I might chicken out but I won't. Do or die, tonight is the night. I am dropping the bomb after dinner. We have Paz on our side and I'm so scared."

Jon tried to lighten her mood. "Hey, the worst thing they can do is to run us out of town. Or if we want to stay here, we can always buy an Army tank to live in."

"Not funny," she sniffled.

"I know. Sorry. I wish I could be there when you tell them," he said softly.

"That's better," she almost laughed.

"Bon courage as they say in French. I'll wait for you at the Cantina. Ray promised to keep me company until you come. Whatever happens, my love, we will work it out, I promise. And . . ."

"And what?"

"I'll keep the car door open and the motor running just in case."

5

Gathering the Saints

Patron and Esther live in a hacienda passed down through his family for the past two hundred years. The 500-acre property occupies the broad expanse of an incline that overlooks the town. Within the eight-foot-high, red adobe walls are five white adobe homes. The largest is a centrally placed horseshoe-shaped main house. It is bordered by four other adobe homes, each on a 20-acre parcel at the corners of the estate. The main house is set on a rise at the center of the property overlooking a large courtyard with an ornate fountain at its center. Rosie's family home occupies the northeast corner of the property, adjacent to the stables, barns, and servants' quarters.

At six o'clock Friday evening, Rosie informed her parents that, raining or not, she preferred to walk over to her grandparents' house rather than driving with them. She paused for a moment in anticipation of her father's loving, teasing response. He did not disappoint her.

"Walk over! In that rain! You will get swept away." He stopped himself. After all, his daughter was not a child anymore, although he is sorry she ever grew up. "Well," he added facetiously, "since you are a college girl, you should know what is good for you. Us uneducated folks think you should drive over, but what do we know, we just use common sense. You are going to do what you are going to do anyway, my headstrong daughter."

Jaime noted that Rosie didn't answer back, which was unusual. "So, why the grim face? Can't be something wrong. School's over. You got a month to rest. So let's see that smile."

"Later, Dad. Bye."

"Oh, oh. Mysteries, huh! Rosie, I got enough troubles. Don't need mysteries. Well, just be careful. If you see lightning out there, run like hell."

No sooner did Rosie step outside when a blast of wind blew her umbrella inside out. That made her wonder if walking was such a good idea. Moments later, her parents drove by.

"Quick, get in," Sarah cried.

"Go ahead. I'm okay." She waved them on and watched their car slowly disappear around a corner. Rosie was finally in view of her grandparents' house when a thunderclap exploded behind her. In full panic, she dropped her umbrella, sprinted up the driveway as fast as she could, flew through the courtyard past the parked cars, vaulted over the side of the lighted fountain, raced up the few steps to the house and threw herself against the massive wooden front door that her parents had left partially open for her. With a sigh, she stumbled into the quiet of the warm, front vestibule.

Safe at last! A pile of wet boots littered the floor. Several wet umbrellas filled the ceramic blue and yellow umbrella stand. Raingear was scattered over the old wooden benches lining the walls.

"Everyone is here, already!" Rosie mumbled. She stood up tall; aware she was correcting her posture, took a deep breath, and cautiously slipped under the archway trimmed with blue and white Talavera tile, into the gallery leading to the spacious living room. She spotted Paz at the far end of the gallery, standing on the bottom step of the great stairway leading to the second floor. "Shhh," Paz whispered and pointed upwards. "Come upstairs first. They are in the dining room."

Rosie tiptoed up the red-carpeted stairs, sliding her hand over the highly polished banister, counting the steps just as she did as a child: "Twenty-one, twenty-two . . ." She grinned to herself, remembering how many times she gleefully slid down that banister straight into her father's outstretched arms, her mother's words echoing, "Jaime, you are going to kill her."

Paz opened the door cautiously. "Shhh. It creaks," she whispered conspiratorially. Rosie walked inside and stifled a sneeze. Paz laughed.

"I staged the room this afternoon. Look, over there." Paz pointed to a wide shelf over her bed, where she had positioned a variety of wooden statues of her saints, as well as several stone Indian fetishes. "I've assembled my homies," she said, raising her eyebrows. One figure stood above the others, a foot-high blue and gold statue of Nuestra Senora de Guadalupe. Paz had placed flowers at her feet, as well as the feet of a smaller statue of St. Francis, finely carved from blue-black ironwood. "I asked Saint Francis for help," she said, "and Saint Jude, the saint of lost causes. He is good at times like this."

"Thanks a lot, Auntie Paz," Rosie held back a giggle.

"And I gave everybody of my little stone friends here, bear, turtle and eagle, some corn meal, with ground turquoise. They will give you strength and patience and far sight." Paz took Rosie's hands in hers. "You have always had such beautiful little hands...Oh! Another thing. I spoke with Rosita for a long time today. She kept looking up at the sky and told me to tell you to wait."

"Wait?"

"Yes. Wait. I guess she is looking into things. Isn't that exciting?"

"I hope so. I haven't talked to her yet." Rosie turned to inspect the rest of the room; she had not been in Paz's room for a long time. She spotted a ten-inch high, delicately carved statue of an old, wizened man holding a staff on the end table next to Paz's bed.

"I never saw him before." Rosie pointed to the figure.

"Oh, that's Mosie. I found him in Abuelita's old family chest. Y'know, the one with all the moldy old stuff that nobody knows what to do with. I don't exactly know his story or where he came from, but I remember that my grandmother, your great-grandmother, told me he is almost as old as Rosita. Mosie is a good listener. Take him home if you like."

"Not right now, Auntie," Rosie smiled and pointed to another figure leaning against the wall. "Why is Saint Anthony over there upside down?"

"Oh, him," Paz scowled. "I am fed up with him. I stood him on his head to punish him. For two weeks I've been asking him to help me find my lost earrings, my best ones. What has he done? Nothing. Nada. So I am letting him know how it feels to be upset."

"How long are you going to keep him upside down?" Rosie laughed.

"I can't tell you now. I don't want him to hear." She nudged Rosie toward the door and lowered her voice. "Until next week," she whispered. "By then if he doesn't come through I'll probably feel sorry for him. But I don't want him to know."

Rosie shook her head, rolled her eyes upward, and hugged her. "What can I say? Now we'd better go downstairs."

Paz smiled. "Hey! You know I do not talk like this to just anyone. Only to you, and Abuelita and Poppa. By the way, you are still using the dream-catcher I gave you to take to school, right?"

"Sure."

"Good, be sure to shake it out every morning, especially now. Dream-catchers can only hold so much before they need to be emptied. You go ahead. I'll be down in a minute."

"Okay, Auntie Paz." Rosie chuckled. "Shake out my dream-catcher, right! Auntie Paz, I gotta tell ya' . . . you . . . you . . ."

Paz kissed her. "Yeah, I am a nut. But you love me, right?"

Rosie stepped out of Paz's doorway onto the balcony, and into the din of the rain pounding on the latilla roof above the living room. Feeling apprehensive, she ambled over to the railing, and glanced down. Her parents were entering the dining room but she felt no hurry to join them. Better to spend a moment savoring the memory of the lovely moments she spent on this balcony in her childhood. To wonder for a while . . .

How would it go tonight? What was she putting on the line? Would she have to give this all up? How could her family ever accept what she wanted? She leaned over the railing and soaked up the beauty of the living room below. A word she learned in French class came to mind. 'Sortileges,'—memories, a beautiful word. She rolled it around in her mind for a moment. This balcony was a sortilege.

Rosie began to squint her eyes open and shut, just as she did when she was a little girl. Squinting could transform the world. By squinting, she could change those colorful rugs scattered over the Saltillo floor below into a beautiful mosaic. By squinting, she could make the brilliant colors pouring out from the beehive fireplace in the far corner of the room into a glorious abstract painting. "Sortileges," she reflected, can have smells. She inhaled once, then very deeply again, absorbing the delicious aroma of pinon wood floating up from the fireplace. How many times in the past had she climbed these stairs and stood on this balcony just so she could bathe in this smoke? Often it made her woozy. Holy smoke. Smoke dreams. Her mind was bouncing around. Recuerdos, another beautiful word, memories. All of a sudden, the image of Raymond's grandfather appeared in her mind. He was sitting next to the fire in the cave on the mesa. She hoped he was not lonely or cold, so she sent him warmth. Why did grandfather just come to me? She asked herself. Am I on my mesa too?

Rosie started down the stairs, very slowly, hand on the banister. A wash of gratitude came over her. How lucky I am to have been born into this family, and to have such a beautiful house—my grandparents' house. Please God that my own daughter can stand here one day. By the time she reached the bottom of the stairs, her sense of well-being vanished. I know I am going to make them crazy. She sighed. But you gotta do what you gotta do.

Rosie had reached the bottom of the stairs and was summoning her courage to enter the living room, when Esther walked into her. Esther's head was covered by a shawl, so she couldn't see.

"Ay!" Esther cried out.

"Abuelita," Rosie hugged her.

"Is that my Rosie? Did I hurt you?"

"No, Abuelita," Rosie chuckled. "What's goin' on?"

"My shawl is stuck on an earring. Give me some help."

Rosie untangled the shawl and spotted the culprit. It was one of a pair of beautiful red hoop earrings that she, her mother, Paz and Carmela had made Abuelita buy on a shopping trip to Santa Fe last year. Esther was dressed up tonight. Her bright red dress was a perfect background for her large Zuni silver necklace, set with obsidian and turquoise stones. In Patron's words, "Abuelita always gets decked out when something is up."

Rosie noticed that, for the first time, the necklace seemed a little outsized for Abuelita. She banished a frightening thought that Abuelita was growing old and hugged her extra hard. "Abuelita. Lookin' gorgeous tonight, Carmela will be pleased."

Esther fingered her necklace. "For you after I go." Then she blushed self-consciously, jangled her jewelry and shifted her eyes in the sultry way she did when she knew she looked good.

Rosie mimicked her eye movements. "Oh. Oh. Have you finished with, you know what, in there, your Friday night special?" Rosie pointed to the butler's pantry.

"Of course," Esther answered coyly.

"Candles as usual?"

Esther was about to answer when a lightning flash drained all color from the room and turned it into a black and white movie set. Two seconds later, the companion thunderclap rattled the windows. Esther put her arms around Rosie, and kissed her cheek. "So, I light candles. My grandmother did it, so I do it. Why? You always ask me, and I always say I do not know. Or maybe I do, but I don't know how to explain it. Sometimes, words don't work. Lighting candles on Friday nights brings back sweet memories, from a place within me where there are no words. Good feelings I felt when I was a little girl holding on to my grandmother's skirt when she lit the candles. Or those special sounds, expressions or cries to God, that I learned from her, and she learned from her mother. Maybe someday, you . . ."

Rosie made an effort to be respectful. "But Abuelita, Mama doesn't do it, and she didn't want me to do it with you when I was little."

Esther nodded in a gentle, understanding way. "Your Mama was never interested, but Paz was, is. That's okay, only one in every generation has to do it. Enough of that. Oh! Before I forget, if you go out near the river, I could use more plants for medicine. I need more yellow flower, yucca, Indian paintbrush, sage, and St. John's Wort. Allergy season is coming."

"Sure, let's go together when the rain stops."

"It's a date. Now we eat." Esther kissed Rosie hard on her cheek. "You are my precious baby, Rosie, mi linda. I love you so much it hurts, here." Abuelita pointed to her heart, "it hurts good."

Rosie returned her kiss, adding a strong embrace. "Abuelita." Rosie's voice trembled.

"You don't have to say anything. I know," Esther nodded.

"What, how, do you know?"

Esther interrupted her by putting a finger to her lips. "Comes with the candles."

She winked and smiled what Patron calls her 'Mona Lisa' smile. Another thunderclap shook the room; the lights flickered on and off. "We better eat before the house caves in." Esther turned toward the kitchen. "You go in now."

Rosie walked through the living room and entered the large rectangular dining room. The lights had gone off, so the room was lit with only candlelight from an array of silver candelabras, one on each end of the table, and three more along the long sideboard. Five black metal wall sconces lit up the walls and ceiling. Rosie's appearance was heralded by another series of thunderclaps that shook the windows. "Holy shit," shouted Jake. "It's the end of the world."

"Jake, please dear," Carmela scolded, "Language! It's Friday night."

Everyone was seated at their assigned place, according to Esther's rules. Patron sat upright in his elaborately carved wooden chair, posted at the head of the table. Esther was at the opposite end, from which she runs the dinner show. Rosie's place is to Patron's right, in front of the sideboard where the dishes are kept — convenient for the youngest female to serve and clear the table. Paz is on Patron's left. Behind her is a precious family heirloom— an expansive antique tapestry that often serves as a source of family entertainment, especially for the children. Figuratively, the tapestry depicts the hustle and bustle of a typical village market scene. But there is more. When seen by candlelight, and through the squinted eyes of people with the gift, which most children have for a while, the figures in the tapestry appear to come to life. From time to time family members sitting across from the tapestry interrupt their dinner conversation to point out such activity.

When Ike, who sits between Rosie and his parents, was young, he often gained praise for describing the figures' movements. "Even," as his father noted, "when they don't." Carmela and Jake, who sit next to Paz with their backs to the tapestry, most often don't bother to look behind them.

Rosie saw that Patron was staring transfixed at the ceiling, and knew why. "Leaks, Poppa?" she asked mischievously. It was a family joke that Patron hated leaks. Without shifting his eyes he answered, "I'm checking." She noticed that the candlelight playing over Patron's face seemed to erase his wrinkles. Poppa was born to sit where he sits. How lucky I am to have someone like him to love and protect me, she thought. How lucky. How could I ever hurt him?

"You are a good lookin' dude, Poppa," Rosie winked.

"So I hear you got news for us, Rosie." Patron beckoned her over, and stuck out his cheek for a kiss. Rosie kissed him tentatively. She was wondering, is he going to want me to kiss him when he hears what I have to say?

"Ah," he grinned, "What kind of a kiss is that? Is something is the matter?"

She cleared her throat. "Maybe yes, maybe no. That's to see. Gotta eat first," she said. "Then I'll . . ."

Jake interrupted, "Hey, Poppa. Look out there. The TV said a hundred-year-rain, a lot of traffic is stuck. The dirt roads are all muddy. Even the blacktop roads are cracking. Potholes all over the place. Good thing I got a four-wheel drive or we couldn't have made it. Better eat quick and run."

"Eating quick is not good for you," Esther admonished with a wave of her finger.

"I've seen a bunch of hundred-year rains," Patron shrugged. "I'm still here." He picked up a bottle of wine. "Who wants?" he stopped for a moment and added proudly. "Except Jake, of course."

"Well, we don't live too far to swim so let's enjoy," Jaime suggested and everybody laughed. That pleased Sarah because Jaime doesn't often make jokes. Jamie happily grabbed the wine bottle and filled his glass to the top.

No sooner had Rosie slipped into her seat, than Paz flashed her a series of sly winks of the eye and under the table nudges. Patron noticed how Rosie winced now and then. If Paz is involved, he thought, something is up. He sat himself up just a little straighter.

Esther hurried into the room with her head high and her hands full. "This is for Jake," she said proudly, and handed Jake a mug of non-alcoholic beer, "in the glass you sent me from the Army." Patron winked at her and smiled. Carmela, who is always appreciative of noble gestures, smiled and said, "Abuelita, you look beautiful in that outfit we bought you even though you didn't want it."

Esther acknowledged her comment regally and signaled that she was ready to sit down. Jake popped out of his seat and rushed to pull her chair out for her. She acknowledged the gesture with a graceful, almost imperial nod, and sat down. Patron smiled at her with admiration. Truly, his Esther was a lady, a lady through and through.

"Jake, dear, you may cut the bread," she announced.

"Cut even slices this time, Jake, even slices," whispered Carmela. She immediately regretted that perhaps she spoke out of turn. Not respectful to say this to my husband in front of his family, she thought, especially at his parents' house on Friday night.

Sarah rose to her son's defense. "Jake cuts them pretty even!"

"Whoops," Jake chipped off a piece of bread on purpose and popped it in his mouth. "Mmm."

Carmela shook her head in disapproval: "Manners, Jake. Friday night. That's not funny."

"Okay," Jake pretended to sulk, and glanced around to see if anyone was smiling. Enough teasing, he thought, his Carmela was such an easy mark. Grinning, he sliced the bread slowly and evenly, mimicking a surgeon. "Look at this, perfecto. Just like my Abuelita taught me."

"Ay! He will never grow up," Sarah lamented and rolled her eyes in mock exasperation.

"And we don't want him to," added Rosie, purposely buttering him up. Jake winked approvingly at her.

Esther chuckled. "Pass the soup."

Ike gulped down his soup, sat back, and cleared his throat noisily. Time to be heard from.

"So what's the big news, college girl?" he oozed sarcasm, at the same time softly brushing his long, jet-black, hair away from his eyes. This gesture, an imitation of the bandito's movements in the Pancho Villa movie, took Ike a long time to perfect.

Ike's 'groupie girls,' as he calls them, especially love this move. Voted the best-looking guy in high school, Ike knows he looks good. Not as tall as he would like to be, but to compensate he has a clear bronze complexion, piercing black eyes, high cheekbones, and an aquiline nose, all above a well-formed jaw. Tonight he was dressed in his standard Friday night attire — his #1 cowboy shirt, jeans, silver belt and motorcycle boots.

Ike rose from his chair to speak, taking a moment to tuck his hair in his shirt collar, and straighten his La Tierra headband. He was savoring a thought. This might be the night to get her, and in front of the family, too.

"So, Rosie," he began, looking around the table. "We hear you are keeping secrets."

"Secrets; look who's talking," Rosie parried.

Ike ignored her remark. "You movin' to Los Angeles? You pregnant? You gettin' married to a gringo, maybe?" Ike snickered, languidly running his open hand through his hair.

Esther glowered at Ike and laid a finger over her lips to shush him.

Rosie stuck her tongue out at him. "Grow up, Ike. I'll finish my soup before I start with what I have to say." She knew that when Ike messed with his hair, trouble was coming.

"She's right. Let's finish dinner first," said Paz reassuringly.

"So we won't choke when we hear her big news," Ike grinned mockingly. He was determined to give her a hard time.

A sudden thunderclap, shook the rafters like a remonstration from above, and interrupted Ike. Patron quickly glanced up at the ceiling. No leaks . . . yet.

Esther crossed herself and motioned for Sarah and Paz to accompany her to the kitchen. When they returned with the serving dishes, the family set to eating. However, it soon became impossible to ignore the rain, the noise, the shaking rafters and the flickering lights.

"Geez, sounds like artillery out there," Jake, laughed nervously. There was apprehension in his voice; after all, he had seen the real thing. Carmela knew what he was feeling. She reached under the table, patted his knee, and leaned over and whispered in his ear. "You will protect me amor, no?" Jake turned to her and smiled. "Do that again. A little more to the right." She slapped his knee and looked around, a bit pleased, to see if anyone was paying attention.

Esther capitulated to the storm. "I'm getting worried so I guess everybody had better go soon," she said sorrowfully. This was the shortest Friday night dinner in the history of the Alonzo family. Rosie, Paz and Sarah got up to clear the table and Esther went into the kitchen and brought out the flan.

"Yum," said Ike, licking his lips and staring hungrily as Esther placed the delectable golden flan on the table.

"You slice it, my dear," Abuelita nodded to Rosie. "We are so happy you are home from school."

"A big piece for me," said Ike, spreading his arms apart and pointing to his plate with his middle fingers curled and his little finger and thumb outstretched, a La Tierra sign.

"If you are nice, macho boy," Rosie said and playfully flipped him a tiny sliver of flan.

"Ayyy," Ike yelled. "Mom, Dad . . ."

Rosie followed quickly with a generous slice, silencing his complaint. Ike dipped his spoon into the flan and stuffed it into his mouth. "Mmmm."

"As good as mine?" Rosie asked.

"Good as yours!" Ike howled and looked around. "Hah, you don't make flan, you make glop. College girls can't cook!"

Jaime cleared his throat loudly. His kids were at it again. "Enough, you two. Now let's hear what's on Rosie's mind before we go."

"Yes, everybody quiet," Sarah added with some authority.

"Yes," Carmela added. "Shhh."

Patron leaned back in his chair, reached into his vest pocket and without thinking took out his lucky charm as an involuntary precaution. His eyes began to smart. An early warning sign that something was up. Esther had taught him to always pay attention to what his body was telling him.

"Not to worry. I'm happy and I'm healthy. Everything's fine," Rosie smiled at Patron. Esther nodded, "Good."

Patron chuckled nervously. "Don't tell us you got a job in New York?" He teased, hoping that his worst fear, that the university would corrupt his granddaughter, wasn't coming true. After all, he did take a chance sending her there.

"No, Poppa, I'm not going anywhere." Rosie replied with poised assurance. She knew what Patron wanted to hear, so she delivered.

Patron sighed with relief and flashed her the thumbs-up sign. "Then we have no problem." He began to slip his lucky charm back into its place. False alarm.

"Then, what? What is it, Rosie?" Carmela pressed her.

Rosie stalled by taking a big bite of her flan.

"Soooo. We are sitting here getting older, Sis," Ike whined.

"I don't talk with my mouth full, like you." Rosie mumbled. The lights in the kitchen flickered again, and then the electricity went off.

"Ay!" Sarah shouted.

"She's here!" Paz whispered, but loud enough for all to hear.

"Who?" asked Jake.

"Take it easy, no one's here," Patron snapped, hoping that Paz would not go on. "Don't worry about the electricity. There are extra candles in the kitchen if we need them, and plenty of wood for the fire. Dark or light, we can listen to Rosie."

The loudest thunderclap yet launched Jake up from his chair. "Poppa, if we don't leave now, we won't make it home."

Carmela looked at Esther and Sarah. Her eyes said, "Remember Jake's PTSD, from the war."

"The house won't fall down, dear," Esther reassured Jake with a warm smile. Sarah got the message. She reached over and gently squeezed Jake's hand. He squeezed back. Jaime patted Sara's thigh in approval. Carmela winked at them.

Abuelita raised a hand. "Let's hear what Rosie has to say before everybody leaves."

"Yeah," Ike chimed in, "Spill it, Rosie."

"C'mon Rosie," Jake urged. "Make it quick."

Paz nudged Jake gently and scowled at him. "Be nice, Jake. Can't you see she is uptight?"

Jake answered, "All I see, Auntie Paz, is that it's pouring out there, and I want Carmela and me to get home in one piece. Can't we save this pow-wow for another night? What is so important that it can't wait? "

Patron raised his right hand to interrupt them. He felt his eyes starting to burn and his left eye beginning to twitch. Esther saw it and went on the alert.

"Rosie, say what you got to say." He turned to Paz. "Paz, do you know what she is going to say?"

Paz waited until all eyes were on her. "Not exactly, Poppa. But we women do know things that . . . well, how do I put it . . . things that men have to find out." She winked at Patron, and slowly swung her chair around until she met Esther's eyes. Esther half-smiled and nodded back. Carmela and Sarah nodded solemnly. After all, one for the girls is one for the girls.

"Yeah, like how to bust a guy's chops," Ike yelled, and Jake laughed. Jaime started tapping his fingers loudly on the table.

"Ike," Esther wagged her finger. "That's not nice. Apologize to Paz."

Esther asked herself, I wonder why Rosie didn't talk with Sarah or me before tonight. Patron was thinking that when women band together, it usually means trouble. He had better pay attention.

Jaime cleared his throat noisily. After all, Rosie was his daughter. "Rosie, spill it, we are all ears, and then we have to go home."

Ike twisted around to meet Rosie head on. "Okay, I'll be nice. Are you getting engaged or something else? Rosie? Hah?" Ike pointed to his stomach.

"Enough, Ike, show respect." Jake swept an arm across the table to make his point and knocked over Carmela's half-full wine glass. "Damn."

"Oh, Jake," Carmela groaned and jumped out of her chair.

"Don't worry, dear, I've got something to get out the stain," Esther reassured them. The lights in the kitchen flickered on and off again, giving enough light for Carmela to get some paper towels and begin wiping up the excess wine. "Hey, it's like a disco in here, anyone wanna dance?" Ike kidded.

"Sure, me!" Carmela laughed.

Jake passed the wine bottle to Ike. "Here, you might need this if we are going to be here all night."

Ike took the bottle and filled his glass. Then, aware that Jake was watching, he conspicuously downed the contents of his glass in two swallows and refilled it. "Maybe Rosie turned lesbo at school. Or she's going into a convent."

"Cool it, Ephraim," Rosie warned. "Or I'll tighten your headband."

"Don't call me Ephraim!" Ike chucked his napkin at Rosie.

Jaime groaned, "Don't you two ever stop?"

Sarah needed to say something. After all, these were her kids acting up in front of her parents. "Rosie, stop, Ike doesn't like that name. Have respect."

Esther scolded Ike with a wave of her finger. Ephraim was her great-grandfather's name and she loved and respected him very much.

Ike was looking at Rosie and didn't see Abuelita's glare. "Yeah, have respect Rosie." Ike parroted his mother. Approval and support at last! He leaned back in his chair, grinning with a smug expression.

"Yeah, respect," Jake repeated. "Remember, everyone is someone."

As soon as he uttered these words, Carmela saw an opportunity to collect some points for what she felt was her sorely underestimated husband. She leaned forward. "Yes, everyone is someone. Jake made that up. Isn't that a good phrase? I told Jake, he should be a writer. Jake, tell them what you said to that dentist last week. Listen, this is a story worth hearing."

These were welcome words for Rosie. She was already having second thoughts about making her announcement. "Sure, big brother, tell us what happened," Rosie smiled her best smile. No doubt about it, she thought, she was getting more and more chicken every second.

Paz watched her niece's ambivalence and sent her a telepathic message that she should forge ahead. She was not alone; Rosita was on the move. The lights always flicker when Rosita is on the move. Other energies are working. She caught Rosie's eye, pointed outside at the rain and mouthed the word, "Rosita."

@

"Well," Jake sat up in his chair, "We better get home but . . ." He scanned the room, and all eyes were upon him. Too good an opportunity to miss. "I'll make it fast. You know the dentist from Albuquerque, Al Perkins, or Plotkins, who comes here every week, tall, thin guy, might be a Jew."

"Perkins, Al Perkins." Patron corrected him.

Jake nodded respectfully to Patron, who had obtained the funding support to pay the dentist's salary.

"Sure," everybody chimed in. Rosie swallowed hard. Jew, is it? She thought, where was this going? Carmela was beaming; her Jake now had everybody's attention. She began to inspect each of her fingernails. Yes, could use a manicure. Maybe go with the black nail polish.

"Well," Jake looked around the table, "Perkins, or whatever his name is, showed up at my recycling center to dump some wine bottles, boxes and stuff. I saw him coming and I said, 'Hi Al, how are you today?' You know I try to be friendly with the public."

"Of course," Sarah said and looked over to Patron for approval. He smiled. Jake continued, "Well, first he looked at me funny. Then he told me I should call him 'Doctor.' Can you imagine? I got pissed off, but I did not lose my temper."

Jake slowly turned and met everybody's eyes. Everyone smiled back in approval. Jake's explosive temper was a problem in the past. "I told him that I don't call people 'Doctor' or anything else. In Santa Rosita, I told him, we call everybody by their first name, except our priest. There are no special people here. 'In Santa Rosita,' I told him, 'everyone is someone. So if you think you are better than anyone else, and I can't call you Al, dump your crap somewhere else.' That's what I said."

"Way to tell that gringo, Bro." Ike high-fived him across the table. "Who the hell does he think he is?" Ike threw Patron a high-five in the air, too. Patron was sitting too far away to slap palms so he managed a smile. Jaime showed thumbs up. Sarah proudly glanced around as if to say, "See how well Jake is turning out after all we've been through with him."

"Good one," Patron grinned. "Everyone is someone. I will use that line. Says a lot, nieto, says a lot. Everyone is someone. Yes. Perkins is not a Jew. He told me he is one of those Episco . . . pali, something."

Jake answered that it didn't matter. He was an asshole anyway.

This gave Rosie the opportunity to get Ike. "I understand what you mean about respect, and everyone being someone. But how can I respect Ike running around with those loser La Tierra jerks who never take a bath. All they do is talk trash, bother strangers and hang out in that scummy Diego's bar with all the other druggies."

Ike banged his fist on the table. "La Tierrans are not losers; we are brothers, artisans, guardians of our land, our heritage and culture. Diego's is our headquarters. All the men at this table know Diego's." Jaime and Jake glanced surreptitiously at each other, hoping Ike would shut up.

Rosie shouted back. "Guardians of what? Trouble, drugs, and wild parties. Face it, we stole the land from the Indians, Ephraim, This is not our land, they were here way before us. Lots of things happened here before us."

"Ike doesn't do drugs," Sarah came to his rescue.

"Mom, really!" Rosie shot back, "Alcohol is no drug, and pot?" A new series of thunderclaps drowned out the rest of the conversation. When the noise abated, Ike was putting on his jacket. "I don't need to listen to this," he growled.

"Hold it." Jaime slammed a glass on the table. "Ike, sit down. Show respect. This is your grandparents' house."

"Ahhh!" Ike groaned, fell hard back into his chair and clamped both arms over his chest.

Esther winced, and then commanded, but softly. "Ike, dear, easy on the chair."

Rosie suddenly realized that she might be pushing things too far and decided to make a peace offering. She reached for Ike's arm and grabbed it tight when he tried to pull it away. "Ike, I only bust your chops because I think you are better than those La Tierra losers."

He succeeded to brush her hand away, not too hard, and scowled. "Man, Rosie, that university has fuc . . . screwed you up bad. Are still one of us, or . . .?"

"Enough! Both of you!" Sarah whined, then shouted. "Ow!" She brought her hand up to her right cheek and tapped it several times. "TMJ," she said, "TMJ. I get it when I am tense."

Jake asked what TMJ was and Carmela coolly replied that it was tempero-mandibular-joint pain, and she didn't have it. Esther looked sympathetically at Sarah, and said that she would give her some salve to rub on it. With a grunt, Esther rose from her chair.

"Quiet, please," she said softly but firmly. Dead silence. "Ay, damned arthritis," she complained. Esther raised herself up to her full height, and held that position. She looked like a stern schoolteacher waiting patiently for her class to calm down, but her family knew different. In fact, Esther had left her body. In silence, everybody waited for her to return. Time had stopped for Esther. When she returned, she nodded her head, and stared directly at Ike. "Dear, you are helping Rosie out, even though you don't know it. You always look out for her." Although bewildered by Esther's remark, Ike felt a good feeling come over him. Approval from the older generation. That was in the code. Take care of your younger siblings. He decided to go with it.

"Yeah, Abuelita, I am glad you see that, and you understand how Rosie doesn't appreciate me."

Patron leaned his chair back as far as it would go without tipping over. How my Esther can turn things around for the good, he reflected with pride. But what else was going on? What did Esther and Paz know that he didn't?

Esther read his thoughts, and winked. She was taking charge. "Say what you have to say, Rosie." Her smile covered Rosie like a warm coat.

Taking courage, Rosie stood up slowly, almost mimicking her grandmother's movements, and slowly swiveled her gaze around the table, halting briefly to lock into everybody's eyes, one by one. Even Ike. Games over. "Tell them, not ask them," Rosie took heart. "Okay. No interruptions, okay? Here goes. I found my man. Okay, we are going to get married next year, after I finish school."

Dead silence. Even the noise of the pounding rain seemed to disappear. Sarah cleared her throat loudly and proceeded to massage her cheek with the TMJ. Patron started tapping his right foot against the bottom of his chair. Jaime froze and felt that his brain was beginning to rotate inside his skull. Esther leaned closer to Rosie, magnifying her presence. Paz whipped her hand up to her mouth to cover her smile. Jake slid his chair back from the table and muttered, "More trouble." Carmela pulled her chair so close into the table, she hurt her stomach.

Ike jumped up and out came a torrent of words. "You . . . married! He must be one crazy dude to want to marry you!"

"Silencio!" Jaime interrupted, shouting much louder than he wanted to. "Rosie," he said sternly, for him, "maybe we should talk about this at home." His plea fell on deaf ears. No sense going on, he knew it was too late for him to save face, so he settled back in his chair and began to rub his chest slowly, making wide circles. Although he was staring right at Rosie, he was straining out of the corner of his eye to read Patron's reaction. "Of course," he tried to speak casually but croaked weakly, "We knew you were seeing guys at school. Which one is this?"

"Well, someone I did not tell anyone about. I have been seeing him for the last year, Daddy." Rosie emphasized the 'Daddy' and flashed him the smile that usually worked wonders. However, for the first time in her life she saw that it did not register. Not good.

"For a year?" her mother gasped.

"Right," Rosie answered.

How could they all have missed it? Doesn't everybody know all about everybody else in Santa Rosita?

"Someone from here?" Sarah squeaked and swallowed hard.

Rosie shook her head, "kind of, but not when I met him."

"Hmmm. Not when I met him." Patron began to rub his chin, as if he was stroking an imaginary beard. "You met him at the university, right? So he's an outsider, right?"

Rosie answered, "Not exactly." Patron's face softened. He blinked three times very rapidly. "Not an outsider, but not one of us." Then he interrupted himself, "Rosie, you are sure you are not going to move away. Right?"

Move away! A bargaining chip at last. "No, Poppa, I don't want to move away."

"That's all I want to hear," sighed Patron. "All I want to hear." The others echoed his sigh of relief.

Ike broke the spell. "Rosie, quit milking it!" He wanted to be the first to crack Rosie's secret. Rosie knew what he was up to and tossed him her most dismissive look. "He is someone you all know, and I might say most of you like him, too." Then turning up her nose to Ike, "At least normal people seem to like him." Then she smiled her most dazzling smile, turned up the sparkle in her eyes, and blinked her long black eyelashes several times.

Patron was scrutinizing Paz's reactions out of the corner of his eye. What was she up to? His musings were interrupted by a crash of lightening, and the ensuing thunder that rattled every piece of glassware in the house. When the noise subsided, Patron glanced up at the latilla ceiling at the far corner of the room, focusing on the point where the roof joined the adobe wall. Was that a water trail dripping down the wall? His mind turned back to Rosie. I need to wait and see, he told himself. Keep my mouth shut. Rosie said she does not want to leave. He leaned to the left so he could see around the candelabras and make eye contact with Esther. Her eyes were waiting for him. She smiled reassuringly, feeling the turmoil of his thoughts. Ay, Ruben, she told his mind, this is going to hurt.

Jaime was mumbling to himself. Damn. Rosie should have discussed this at home. This is between us, a parent-daughter discussion. Rosie is supposed to tell us first, and then we tell everybody else. That is the right way. This is not the right way. This does not look good. They will think I can't rule my own family. Damn!

Sarah knew what he was thinking and reached down to squeeze his hand under the table. "I knew it," she whispered, "I just knew something was going on with Rosie." He did not squeeze back.

Ike tried again. "Soooo, not exactly an outsider? And not exactly one of us, either? If it's a guy, I mean." He cradled his chin in his hand and brushed his hair with the other.

Sarah forced a smile. "Rosie dear, I had an idea that you were interested in someone," she said, haltingly. This time Jaime squeezed her arm reassuringly. What she said was good for us, he thought. Parental unity.

Patron needed to make certain. "Rosie, you are sure, very sure, that you are not moving away?"

"Poppa, how could I live without you?"

Patron smiled back weakly. Rosie was doing well. Charm oozing from her pores. He sighed with relief. "So get it over with. Say what you want to say. It can't be that bad."

Rosie shook her head and smiled. "That depends on . . ."

Ike interrupted. "Is it Raymond?" He laughed. "He's married, but you hang with him at the Cantina. Or some guy at the clinic? What about that Jew doctor? Who else is there? Juan, he's married, too."

"Be serious, Ike." Jaime brushed him off with a wave of his hand.

Patron was thinking, probably someone from the university. But what about the Doctor? No, she can't see him that much. He is here during the week when Rosie is away in school. Anyway, he's not one of us, and Rosie knows better.

Ike sensed Patron's puzzlement and pressed the point. "Well, Rosie and the Doc were in Albuquerque together for a long time. And they hang at the Cantina with Ray when Rosie is home." Now Ike had everybody's attention. He rested a hand in his hair and stroked his head gently.

"If it's him, Rosie, there ain't any way. You are my little sister. I have a say in this family, and I have a responsibility towards you. You need to listen to me."

"Hah!" Rosie blurted out. "Then act like a big brother."

"Quit it," Jaime shouted to both of them. "Let her be," he growled at Ike under his breath. "It's my place to be mad at her." Sarah patted his leg and said. "Shhh. Blood pressure . . ."

Carmela smiled at Rosie. "Go ahead, dear," she urged. "Tell us who he is." Then she nudged Jake, shifting back and forth in his seat, to get ready. He mumbled that he and Carmela needed to leave soon, but no one paid any attention. A bolt of lightning hit the ground near the fountain, silhouetting Patron against the window.

"An omen," Paz whispered. Rosie ignored the lightening flash.

"The man I love is someone I met at the university, and you know him." Rosie blurted out the rest: "Poppa knows him. Abuelita knows him. We all know him in one way or another."

Patron felt his foot going at it again. Tap, tap, tap and picking up speed. Who is she talking about? Am I losing my touch? How can I not know what my granddaughter is up to? He blinked hard three times to relieve the tension. Blinking helped, but he thought it looked weird, so he camouflaged his nervous tic by rubbing his eyes and clearing his throat.

Carmela leaned toward Rosie in anticipation, and, always multi-tasking, lifted her left hand slightly to admire her spectacular turquoise ring out of the corner of her eye. She addressed Rosie in her most charming sales-executive-way: "Who is it, sweetie?" Her tone made Rosie wonder if Carmela was with her or against her.

Patron became distracted by a distinct water stain spreading across the ceiling. Same spot as ten years ago, he complained to himself; all that money for the new tile roof gone to waste. Then he heard Rosie.

"The person is . . . Jon Spielman, Dr. Jon Spielman," she declared. "We love each other and we want get married next year and live here, and Jon wants to stay at the clinic, and I will work in the family business."

All heads spun in Patron's direction. How was he going to respond? He sat expressionless, no sound, except for his stomach which emitted a loud gurgle.

Ike broke the silence. "A gringo, an outsider, a Jew," he yelled. "Son of a bitch. I figured it out, didn't I? With my sister!" Ike searched the group for support.

However, all he saw was a variety of wide-open eyes and mouths, a collage of bewildered expressions. All except Paz, who sat grinning like a Cheshire cat. Ike continued his rant. "You," he pointed at Rosie. "One of our people isn't good enough for you! I told them not to send you to the university. You should have stayed at home like me!"

"Jeez, Ike, enough with your one-of-us stuff," Jaime wheezed haltingly, and then spoke more forcefully as his breath returned. "And get it straight, you didn't go to the university because you dropped out of school, remember? You ran around raising hell with your friends and racing cars!" He glanced over at Patron and felt ashamed. His kids were fighting in front of the man he respected so much, the same man who invited him into the family, who gave him an important job, who treats him like his own son. What would Patron think of him now? He had to keep control: "Tone it down, son," he cautioned Ike.

Ike shouted. "You always stick up for her, Dad. Do you hear what she said?" Ike shook his fist at Rosie. "Look how she sprung this on us."

Jaime waited a moment, aware that all eyes were on him and Ike. "Well, you are right about her springing it on us. Rosie, you did spring this on us. But cool it, Ike, cool it." Jaime spoke slowly. That usually helped when Ike was losing it. "We are all just trying to deal with what Rosie said, without going off the deep end. You get so mad you don't leave room for anyone else to react."

"You are pissed, right, Dad?" Ike asked in a tentative voice.

"Pissed, maybe, more blown away. But that's not going to help right now. This is a private matter. Rosie, we need to talk."

Sarah put her head in her hands and moaned. "Ay!"

Jake complained. "Shit is more like it."

Carmela flashed him a disapproving look.

"Enough, everybody" Esther banged her hand on the table and called, "Ruben!"

Patron was considering whether he should blame himself; after all, he was the one who brought the Doc up here in the first place. No, he recalled, Rosie met Jon at the university. But he was the one who pushed Rosie to go to the university, enough of that. How could he have known? He was off the hook.

Patron sat up straight, cleared his throat to say something, but nothing came out. Memories of Paz's love affair flickered through his mind. Not again, he thought, not again. This time he would have to move carefully. Rosie looked pleadingly at Patron, but all she saw was hurt, and he suddenly looked very old to her.

Paz fixed her eyes on Patron so intently; he could no longer avoid her stare. He turned to face her. She nodded her head very slightly several times, and slowly raised her eyebrows as a silent communication, "What goes around comes around." Patron got her message.

Esther shook her head slowly from side to side and pursed her lips tightly together to remonstrate with Paz. Poppa had enough trouble.

Jaime's throat closed tightly around his words. Knowing what his daughter was up to was one thing, but knowing who with, was another. It was his duty as her father to take the lead. "Juan mentioned that you and Doc and Raymond had drinks together. And we knew Doc treated you when you were sick at school."

Good for Juan. Rosie smiled inside, didn't spill the beans.

Sarah grinned sheepishly. "A mother knows when her daughter . . . but with Doc? Well, Rosie, you know this just can't be." She caught Jaime's eye and felt they were united. It was important that they be on the same side. She knew that family unity was part of the code, important to him too.

"Mom's right," Jake scowled. "We understand about these things, Sis, but marriage, no way. You pick a nice local guy and make things simple. We have never had an outsider in the family, and we don't need one now. Besides, no one from outside ever moved here and lasted! We are all the same here; we have been this way forever. That's what makes us special, and we like it this way. The Doc may be OK, but he is not like us. So how can it work out?"

"Sorry, Jake," Rosie sniffled, tears running down her cheeks. "I've thought about every word you said hundreds of times. I don't want to hurt you, but we are in love. Doesn't that matter?"

Jake pushed his chair back hard, shot to his feet, and bolted toward the door. "Right now, Rosie, I am trying not to get pissed off, or going over and punching that Doc, Jon, whatever you call him. We let him work up here and he breaks our rules. He should know better."

Carmela got up and gently navigated him back to the table.

Esther signaled to him with her eyes, "Be careful with the chair."

More thunder and everybody stopped talking. As the long moment ticked away, Patron examined the walls and the roof for more leaks. Esther's thoughts flashed back to the time she was sixteen and fell madly in love with 'the white guy from Santa Fe' who delivered beer to her family's restaurant. When her father found them talking in the storeroom, he grabbed the guy, dragged him to his truck, and told him to leave town and never come back. Or else. Esther cried for three days. He never came back. It always boiled her that it was so unfair; men could get away with whatever they wanted, even bragging about their women, especially the gringo women they worked for, but as for women? Maybe now it was Rosie's turn to test the waters.

Carmela was computing the cost-benefit ratio of having a Jewish doctor in the family. Of course, it could be embarrassing if Rosie married an outsider, she told herself. On the other hand, a doctor in the family, a Jewish outsider, sure, but a doctor. Could this be good for the family's standing? After all, he was white, new blood for the family, lighten up the kids, head of the clinic, and I have never heard anyone badmouth him. He's not one of us, and he's a Jew . . . well, that's not so great . . . but a doctor in the family is fine. Think of the money we would save."

Carmela decided to defer judgment until she heard more. In the meantime, she edged into her purse for her compact and lipstick, and proceeded to adjust her make-up.

Sarah was holding her head in her hands and moving her jaw from side to side as if she were chewing her cud. Can we talk Rosie out of this? What if she doesn't change her mind? Can she marry a Jew in a church? What about the children? Will they let them in the church if their father is Jewish? Can they be baptized? Dios! I could have grandchildren with a different religion. People could be prejudiced against my grandchildren. Ay! This cannot happen. Jake and Jaime look like they are going to bust a blood vessel Ay! Ike, and his friends, Sal, and Romeo, what are they going to do? This Doc doesn't know what he is getting into.

Ike cursed Jon in his mind. That sneaky son of a bitch! He broke the silence. "Poppa, you ain't going to let this happen, are you? Dad, we know what to do. Right? What you did with outsiders when you were my age. And you, Jake, my bro? Let's take this bastard out!"

Jake sighed. "That would be okay years ago, before I had a family, before there were so many lawyers to find something to sue over. Remember when I punched Sergio in the face and it cost us a bundle? Ike, I can't think about this right now. I just want to go home."

Patron was about to raise his right hand to restore order when a powerful blast of wind shook the house to its timbers and blew out two candles. He jumped up from his seat and peered through the window. The fountain was dark. "I've changed my mind. This is the worst storm I've ever seen," he murmured to himself. Was this thing with the Doc a lark for Rosie, or the real thing? He had to find out. If it was the real thing, he had to play his cards right. He looked up at the ceiling again, it was dripping water in two places. "Boys, help me. Get a pail, rags!" he called.

"In the kitchen closet," Esther yelled, and followed them. Jaime returned quickly with two pails and set them under the leak. Rosie helped mop the floor.

"This will do for now," Patron said. "I got two more pails out there when these get full." He motioned for everybody to sit down. The best thing to do now, he thought, was to do nothing. "Look. This news is too sudden and the weather is terrible. You must all go home quick, otherwise you will be stuck here for the night. We can talk about this later."

Rosie interrupted, "But I want . . ."

Patron put up a quieting hand. "Not now. You need to talk with your parents first. That's what you should have done in the first place." Rosie sulked. Ike grinned, at last Poppa nailed her. Jaime frowned. "Poppa's right."

Rosie bowed her head and stared down at the floor like a chastised puppy. Paz and Esther both wanted to get up and comfort her, but thought better of it.

"Right," Ike added. "And I got to talk to El Gringo."

"No, you won't," Rosie came back to life.

"Just try and stop me," Ike barked back. Patron motioned for Ike to calm down.

Rosie cried. "I was afraid it would be like this. Ike, I want you all to be okay with what I want to do. I want to come back home and work in the business. Please, Ike, help me. Lay off Jon. Please. Dad, Poppa?"

Esther moved next to Rosie, and put up her hand. "Enough for now. No one is going to do anything. Right now, everybody goes home."

Jake walked over to Rosie, gently took hold of her shoulders, looked deep into her eyes, and, restraining his temper, said, "I could really get mad about this, but I don't want to. Ten years ago, brother or not, I would have helped lock you up for your own good until you got over him." Jaime and Ike nodded in agreement. "I know times have changed, but this is not good. I don't know why you are looking for trouble. The outsider thing is one strike; the religion part is another. We never had a Jew in the family. You know this town, the people around here; they don't want outsiders, Jews or anyone else. Jews hate Christians; some are cheap and greedy, and will screw a guy for a buck. I want to play with your children and I don't want half-Jewish nieces and nephews. They won't fit in here, so get over this. It hurts, but in time you'll forget about him. I am telling you, people get over these things."

Then Jake remembered the Vietnamese girl he had fallen in love with during his service overseas. A piece of his past Carmela did not know about. Jake went out with her for six months, and she told him she loved him. They even had a scare about a baby. Once back home, he never wrote to her because he knew they were too different to have a future together. He still thought about her. If he was able to cut her off, Rosie could do the same.

Rosie replied. "I tried not to love him, but I couldn't do it."

"Then there is going to be trouble," Jake said angrily.

Ike added, "Better believe it."

Esther nodded to Patron, who got the message. "Time to go," he commanded.

Jake turned around. "Right, Poppa, we are out of here. Remember what I said, Rosie."

Jaime waved goodbye to Jake and Carmela, then beckoned to Sarah and Rosie. "Sarah, bring your coffee into the living room. We need to talk with Rosie." Rosie was on her way to the door when she heard Jaime's order.

"Dad, can't it wait until later?"

Jaime motioned for her to come closer. "Haven't we been good parents? Why didn't you tell us first? I feel ashamed, disrespected. You made us look bad." Jaime rubbed his stomach while he spoke.

Ike interrupted, "Give it to her, Dad. No way is this going to happen if I have anything to do with it."

"It's not your business," Rosie shouted.

"Damn well it is," Ike answered. "Everything that happens in this town is my business." Ike moved toward Rosie threateningly, his face red and his eyes spitting fire. "This ain't gonna happen, you hear me. You are not going to embarrass me like this. I'll do what I have to do. I have friends . . ."

Rosie stepped back. "Embarrass you? What about me?" she screamed.

Jaime pitched himself between them. "Okay, son, calm down. I know how you feel, but let me handle this."

"Well, sorry, Dad, but it damn well better be handled. I'm outta here before I . . . how could she do this to the family? Marry a Jew . . ."

Jaime took Ike by the shoulders, "Please, son, let's leave this for now. I'll see you at home."

Ike stormed out of the room shouting, "No way."

Esther stopped him at the door and handed him a drink. "Here, dear. I made it for you, it will help you relax."

"Yeah," Rosie shouted from behind Jaime. "Give him some Ritalin. You need it, Ike. Asshole," she screamed after him.

Jaime whispered to her, "That ain't going to help, Rosie."

Ike obediently emptied the glass and handed it back to Esther, "Thanks, Abuelita."

"You are coming home tonight, right? We'll talk," Jaime shouted after him.

"I don't know." Ike slammed the door behind him.

Sarah cried, "He's not coming home."

Jaime shouted after him, "Watch the drinking." He sighed. "That really wasn't nice, the remark about the Ritalin, Rosie."

Rosie blew her nose and brushed away her tears. "He'll get over it."

"Your mother and I won't."

"Sorry, Daddy, I didn't want to make you look bad. I thought that if I told you and Mom, you know how the gossip goes around. Everyone would be on my case, one by one, without me being able to say my side of it. Things would go out of control. I thought it would be best if I got it all over at once, told everybody at the same time. Ray is the only one who knows, but he is no outsider. I'm sorry if I hurt your feelings."

Jaime nodded his head mournfully, "Too late now."

Sarah added, "Rosie, look at him. See what you did to your father. I am so upset I can't talk. Parents should be the first to know, it's the way we do things."

Rosie wracked her brain. What can I say to make them feel better? "Yeah, Mom, but you can still say that you knew all about it. At least I am sure you had an idea. Didn't you?"

Sarah reflected for a moment. Her voice softened. A way to save face? "Well, of course, I knew something was going on with you, but I thought you would tell me in your own time. I thought maybe someone at school."

"See," Rosie perked up. "You knew. I met Jon at school."

"This can't be happening," Jaime shook his head.

Rosie countered, "See. That's why I didn't want to tell you before, Dad."

Sarah interrupted Rosie. "Jaime, women understand such things better than men do."

Jaime shook his head from side to side slowly. "Rosie, much as I love you, the way you did this is terrible, hurtful, and disrespectful." Jaime scowled and sighed again. He met Sarah's eyes. She nodded encouragingly as he spoke, as if she were coaxing the right words out of him. "But I guess if we are asked, we can say, without too much lying, that we knew you were seeing Jon and that we discussed it at home." He thought for a moment, the words were becoming his own. "But Rosie, how you laid this on us is one thing. Maybe we can get over that. But Jon doesn't belong here."

"He is here already," Rosie said. "Isn't he doing good at the clinic? The people like him. Do you think the sick people care? Look how he helped Juan, and Poppa. Maybe it's time the town changed its attitudes."

"That ain't gonna happen," Sarah threw up her arms. "You are respected in the church. Kids look up to you. People will feel that you are rejecting them, disrespecting them, if you don't marry one of our own."

"Dad, what are you talking about? I am not rejecting anyone. To hell with what people think. This is my life. I am not a child. This has nothing to do with the church. I am not changing religions."

"Why couldn't you just find someone the same as us?" Jaime raised his voice angrily.

"Shhh, your blood pressure." Sarah cautioned.

"Don't Shhh me," Jaime snapped.

"You interrupt me all the time," Sarah growled back.

"Look at what you are doing to us, Rosie, now we are fighting," Jaime whined.

"Please. Mom and Dad, are you for me or against me?" Rosie's voice cracked. Tears cascaded down her cheeks. Sarah started weeping too. Jaime was choking back his own tears.

"That's not what it is. We are against what you are doing. Is there anything we can do to change your mind?" Sarah pleaded. Rosie did not answer.

"Never should have sent her to school," Jaime mumbled his face a deep scarlet. "I've never hit you before, Rosie, but now, so help me!" Jaime walked away. "Oh Daddy," Rosie sobbed.

"Enough," said Sarah. "I can't take any more. Come, Jaime."

Patron entered the room just as Sarah and Jaime got up to leave. "Excuse us, Poppa." Sarah wept.

"She didn't kill anybody," Patron said softly.

Sarah looked surprised. "I don't understand. Aren't you angry Poppa?

Really? Well, Rosie, don't come home too late. It's dangerous out there."

"I'll be home as soon as I can. Don't wait up for me, Mom. We'll talk more tomorrow."

Sarah pouted. "About what? You are like your father, a cement head. You won't change your mind."

Patron draped his arms around Jaime and Sarah's shoulders and steered them to the door. "I know you suspected this was happening and it was very nice that you let Rosie spring the news on the family tonight. You are good parents and she loves you very much. She is a good girl."

"Thanks, Poppa," Sarah let out a sigh of relief and kissed Patron on the cheek. He patted Jaime's back warmly several times as they walked through the doorway. "Children," he sighed, "it ain't always easy. Remember, a long time ago, before you were married, when Sarah didn't come home on time, and I went looking for her, and I caught you two behind the Cantina." Sarah and Jaime turned and looked into Patron's eyes and saw no blame or anger. It wasn't their fault. They left knowing that Patron would do all he could to make things better.

Patron returned and motioned for Rosie to follow him out to the portale. A storm of ping-pong-ball-sized hail was banging away at the flimsy latilla roof. They hurried to reach the shelter of the covered patio overlooking the plaza below. While Patron was wiping off a wooden bench for them to sit on, the electricity came on, and the fountain came to life. He gestured for Rosie to sit down next to him. For a moment they watched the raindrops fly past the bright lights of the fountain, flickering on and off like a thousand fireflies. Patron cradled Rosie's hand in his, and kissed it.

"My Rosie. Not a good night."

"Sorry, Poppa," Rosie murmured and blew her nose. Patron sighed deeply. Rosie asked if he was okay.

"No, not really. I got many different feelings, Rosie. I am trying to sort them out. The religious difference is upsetting."

Rosie nodded, and patted his hand softly. "I understand. You know I had to tell everybody like this, all together." She paused. "I am so sorry if I hurt you." She tried to smile, "but here you are, sitting holding my hand."

Patron stayed silent as Rosie began to weep harder. His heart was bursting. Why did it hurt so? Was he getting feeble in his old age? Or was he just able to feel more deeply now? He could not stand to see his Rosie so unhappy.

This was a new experience for Patron. Twenty years ago, if he had heard such an announcement from one of his own children, he would have taken to the warpath. Like he did with Paz. Twenty years ago, he would have locked up Rosie, or sent her away, and taken care of the Doc. Now, his emotions said one thing and his reason another. He reviewed his feelings; I am upset that this is happening. More than upset, angry, very angry. On the other hand, I don't want to hurt Rosie, or lose her. He squeezed her hand tightly as if she would hear his words better. "It would be so much easier if you could just be strong enough to choose someone else. If it's too hard for you I can help you get rid of the Doc."

"What?" Rosie wailed and stared up at him through her tears.

"No, no," Patron calmed her. "Not that way. Jon is a good man. I like him." He paused for a moment to switch gears. "I meant I could find him another position." He patted her hand. "Rosie, let us try to put aside how we feel for a moment and analyze the situation as if it were a business deal."

"A business deal?"

Patron continued. "Rosie, you are my precious nieta, my grand-daughter. I love you, I need you. Like your parents, your whole family, we love you and need you. Our town needs you, the young look up to you, especially the girls. You know the way people here feel about mixing with others. Most people here never met a Jew. Some have crazy ideas about them."

Rosie interrupted, "And you, Poppa?"

"I am not important right now. Rosie, it's about the others in town looking for a reason to raise hell I am worried about."

"It's not about them Poppa. It's about Jon and me. It's not about what other people think, or how the family looks at it."

Patron knew that he needed to be very careful walking the tightrope between trying to talk Rosie out of her relationship and losing her. "If you marry Jon, you will have to put up with people in town who are jealous of our family and looking to badmouth us. Then there are Ike and his friends. They do not want the likes of Jon to marry one of theirs. They won't take this lying down. Jon will be in danger. Ike and his friends will think that going along with what you want will diminish and disrespect them. It means they are not good enough for you. It sets a bad example for all the children here who look up to you. You, going to the university and all. Parents won't want their children to leave town if it means marrying outsiders."

Patron avoided Rosie's eyes and stared into the fountain. "What can I do to change your mind?"

"Poppa, you know what I am going to say."

"Yeah, but doesn't it give you second thoughts if you are making everyone unhappy?"

Rosie sighed deeply and spoke with tears streaming from her eyes. "Of course, Poppa, What do you think I am?"

Patron took her hand and felt his eyes begin to burn. Was he crying too? Such a thing would not have happened when he was a parent. He was reacting differently with Rosie. All Rosie wants is to be happy. Why am I beginning to feel like the bad guy? "Have you spoken with Fr. Raul?"

"No, I haven't had time. Anyway, what can he do?"

"He knows about suffering. He has had to face problems that require extraordinary solutions. Promise me you will talk with him. He will tell you what's wrong with marrying out of the faith, especially a Jew." Patron felt a strange feeling come over him when he said the word 'Jew.' He lingered on the feeling for a moment. Why was this, he wondered, and what was his feeling all about? He said it to himself a few more times until the word lost its meaning.

Rosie was anxious to please him. "Sure, I'll do anything you ask. But don't think Fr. Raul will talk me out of anything. And I'm not going into a convent either, Poppa." Rosie tried to force a smile and stood up. She reached out a hand to assist Patron to get up as well. "Ay!" He groaned, and rose to his feet.

"No viejo act, please." She sniffled through another feeble attempt at a smile. "Looking for sympathy, huh?"

"It's no act, Rosie." He paused, then told her, "You know that I've learned through my life that often young people your age don't know what is good for them."

"And you do, Poppa?" Rosie asked softly.

"Yes, I think I do. At least I did. Now, the older I get, the more I don't know if I am right, or if the old answers still work. This is a hard one. You, Abuelita, Paz, are all lucky you have Rosita to talk with. I don't."

This is new; do I have to reassure him? Rosie thought. "Yes you do, Poppa."

"No, that is a woman's gift. My help comes from thinking hard."

"Have you ever asked Rosita for anything?"

"No. Alcaldes don't ask saints for advice; I am supposed to come up with the answers myself." When Rosie asked him what he does when he doesn't have the answers, Patron paused for a moment and said glumly, "That hasn't happened until today."

Rosie was beginning to feel sorry for Patron, and began to question herself. Was it worth it, to make him suffer so? Then, knowing his tricks, she realized that he might be playing his guilt card. All this talk about being old and not knowing answers. I'm not going there, she thought. At the same time, Patron was searching hard for the right reasons, the right words, to change Rosie's mind. "You know that I've been down this road before with someone else." Rosie did not blink. "For the first time I am beginning to think I didn't act right back then."

When Rosie didn't answer, he continued, "I also know that if I acted now according to my old instincts, it would be terrible."

"What do you mean?" Rosie asked.

"Better I don't say. But, for example, I could fire Jon tomorrow."

"Poppa," Rosie cried. "You are scaring me!" Her next remark flew forth from the pit of her stomach. "If you did that, Poppa," the words came slow and strong, and surprised them both. "You would lose me."

The strength of her statement shook Patron and made him realize that this was not the way. He softened. "Rosie, understand, this is not easy for me."

Rosie looked directly into in his eyes. This is no weak woman, Patron thought.

Rosie cried, "Me either Poppa, please help me."

The depth of her desperation and her love were becoming clear to him. What should he do? What could he do? Should he use his power to end their relationship? Should he disown her? Could he even do anything to change things if he wanted to? He knew what most of the family wanted from him, at least he thought so. Jaime and Sarah were counting on him to get Rosie to change her mind; Ike and Jake, too. Esther and Paz would be with Rosie. One never knew with Carmela.

One more try: "Rosie, you are asking for protection from me and everybody else who opposes you. How can I agree to you marrying Jon? It goes against everything I stand for in this family, and in the town. One last time, if I asked you, begged you, to walk away from Jon for your family's sake, would you do it? For me?"

Rosie moved closer and leaned her head wearily on Patron's shoulder. He put an arm around her. "I can't, Poppa. I think I would die."

"You would die? Ay!" he said hoarsely. "Then there is no more to say." His eyes filled with tears. "Ay! My Rosie. Then I do not know how this will end. I may be too old, and too tired, to help to you avoid the consequences. There is still a part of me that feels like punishing you, but I don't have it in me."

Rosie pulled back, wiped her swollen eyes, and told Patron she must go, Jon was waiting for her at the Cantina. She would call her parents and tell them she would come back and sleep here tonight. Then she pleaded once more,

"Poppa, will you help me?"

Patron threw up his hands. "You are asking for a miracle. A miracle so we do not lose you. So you don't lose yourself. I can't make such miracles."

She said without a smile, "You always have something up your sleeve, Poppa."

"This time, preciosa, I don't even have a shirt."

They walked toward the front door in silence. Patron took his parting shot. "What about a whole year in Spain? All expenses paid?"

Rosie kissed him on the cheek and laughed.

6

La Cantina

Jon rushed into the Cantina shaking his head vigorously to shed the water that was dripping down his face. He took off his raincoat, hung it up and carefully descended the three slippery tile steps down to the bar. "Hey, Doc," Juan Torres called out.

"Pretty wet out there," Jon waved a soggy hand.

Juan grinned. "Beergarita?" This drink was one of his specialties, a mixture of beer, tequila and other secret ingredients.

Jon extended his index finger. "Just the regular."

"Okay, Doc, regular comin' up. How do you like my new hi-tech?" Juan pointed to his new CD player.

"Gloria Estefan?"

"Yeah, Gloria. Good for a rainy night, maybe pep things up. No business, so I'm gonna close early. What about this rain?" In spite of Jon's being an outsider, Juan has been friendly to him, because he owes him a lot. When Juan's 8-month-old son, Manuel, woke up vomiting and screaming with pain in the middle of the night, he and his wife, Selena, called the clinic. Fortunately, Jon was sleeping over. He told them to bring the baby right over. Jon diagnosed an acute intestinal obstruction, and said that Manuel needed emergency surgery. He immediately herded the family into his car and drove them to the hospital in Santa Fe. The operation was a success, and while the baby was still recovering, the doctors told Juan that Jon' quick actions had saved his son's life. Since then, Juan has been Jon's best P.R. person.

"Chips and salsa, Doc?"

Jon smiled. "Thanks. Damn rain. The roads are turning icy higher up. I guess I'm not going home to see my father tonight. I'd better call him." He planned to drive home to tell his father how Rosie's family meeting went.

Jon headed for the public phone at the back while Juan, working with the concentration of a pharmacist over a medicinal compound, prepared his tequila, limejuice, ice, and Triple Sec formula for Jon's margarita. After carefully pouring the mixture into a blender, Juan reached up and tugged a thick cord hanging from the large silver bell suspended over the bar. Ringing the bell is Juan's warning to anyone in hearing distance that he is turning on his blender. This is a necessity because Juan's 'signature' blender emits a very loud noise.

Patrons of the Cantina are proud that today, Juan and his noisy blender are a popular tourist attraction. Paz is so proud of his 'best in New Mexico' beergaritas and margaritas that she makes sure each customer leaves with a brochure about him. Excerpts from a North Country newspaper article describe 'Juan Torres and the Margarita Experience' at the Cantina.

◎

"Juan Torres has always liked tequila, as well as loud noises. According to his family, he was a noisy baby and a noisy kid. By the time he was a teenager, he was not only well versed in the art of growing agave and making and drinking tequila, he was most known for being a self-described motorcycle buff who had the loudest, ear-splitting motorcycle muffler in the North Country. People say that Juan or 'Cochise' as he was known then, and his motorcycle could be heard from many miles away. As one of his friends told us, 'If you want to know when Juan is coming, just watch the birds. They usually book the hell out of the area fifteen minutes before you can even hear the noise of his bike. Then you see the dust, and there comes Juan.'"

The article goes on to explain Juan's professional calling:

"When Juan was eighteen, he went out to the desert with some of his friends for a rattlesnake squashing contest. This involves roaring around the desert on a motorcycle, searching for rattlesnakes, and running them over. The contest is one hour long. The one who brings in the most dead rattlesnakes is the winner. Juan, the reigning champion at the time, was on the hunt when he spotted an especially huge rattlesnake moving all-out across the sand. When it saw Juan approaching, the snake fled up a steep rise. Juan revved his motor to follow. Just as he was about to make the kill, the snake suddenly veered to the left. Juan kept going. What the snake knew about, and Juan did not, was the twenty-foot-deep gully behind the rise. Juan sailed over the rise ('better than Evil Knievel,' one witness said) and, because all his friends saw what happened, into legend. Because Juan never let go of the handlebars, he is credited with attaining a free-flight distance record, over 150 feet. When he landed, the motorcycle shattered and so did Juan. He broke several vertebrae and assorted bones in his pelvis, left arm, and both of his lower legs. That fall ended his motorcycle career, but did not stop Juan's love affair with noise. After his rehabilitation, he turned his interest to growing agave for home brew tequila, and in making the perfect margarita. Shortly after, he recognized the potential of blenders for making a noise louder than his motorcycle. The rest is history."

@

Jon's father answered the phone after just one ring. "Hey, Jon, this weather is something. I hope you aren't driving."

"No, the roads are terrible."

"No sense taking chances," his father understood, as usual.

"Rosie is speaking with her family right about now."

"Good luck," his father sighed. "Jon, your voice is fading. Call me . . ." The phone went dead.

Jon was grateful for his father's tolerance and understanding. After all, as Jon told Rosie, "What you and I intend to do is nothing new. Many of my New Mexican ancestors, descendants of European Jewish immigrants, intermarried. My Dad is not intolerant in any way. He spends a great deal of his professional time defending the rights of poor and oppressed migrant workers and Native Americans."

Jon was also proud of his father's position on the faculty of the university law school, and of his tenure in the history department. He was an expert on the history of the Spanish and European Jews who migrated into New Mexico in past centuries. Especially those who came through Mexico. Rosie was impressed when Mr. Spielman explained his own family's history to her.

"Our ancestry dates back to 1886. We don't go as far back as you do, of course, but Jon's great-great-great-grandparents, Eastern European Jews, helped found Temple Montefiore in Las Vegas, the first synagogue in New Mexico. Along with Abraham Staab, a generous businessman from Santa Fe, Jon's great-great-grandparents contributed money toward the construction of the Saint Francis Cathedral there. In gratitude, Bishop Lamy inscribed Hebrew inscriptions and symbols over the entrance, and they can still be seen there today."

Jon and his father got on quite well, except for a running disagreement about the importance of religion. Jon was fine about following along with his father's religious beliefs until his beloved mother died of breast cancer when he was fourteen years old,

"I hate God!" was all he could articulate. "Why did he have to take Momma?"

Mr. Spielman, equally despondent, had no answer for him. He was trying to find solace by immersing himself in work and devoting his spare time to temple projects and service in the community. Jon spent his time in school and with sympathetic friends, and he took to sleeping over at their homes on weekends. He kept refusing his father's request to go to Sabbath services with him.

"God took my away my mother!" he shouted at his father. "I don't want anything to do with God."

Eventually the Rabbi became aware of the growing abyss between Mr. Spielman and his son. He tried to intervene.

"Your son needs you, David," the Rabbi counseled him. "He lost his mother and can't see past that." The elder Spielman got past his own grief and went into action. He invited his widowed sister Ethel to come out from the East to live with them. After a short while, the three of them began to function like a family again under Ethyl's care. Jon's father began spending more time with him at school and sports events. The arrangement worked well until Jon left home to attend Brown University. Eventually, Ethel died. Mr. Spielman never remarried. Jon and his father remained close. Jon's father was as taken with Rosie as his son. Although he was fully aware of the religious issues, especially as far as future grandchildren were concerned, he had gained perspective. He told his Rabbi, "I'll cross that bridge when the grandchildren come along; I'll do what I have to do. I am not going to lose my kids."

◎

Raymond noisily walked down the three steps into the bar.

Juan called out, "Ray, I'm not here for long, Doc's on the phone."

Raymond wiped off his face with a handkerchief. "What a night. Grandfather picked a heck of a time to go up on the mesa."

"I never worry about the old guy," Juan laughed, and threw Raymond a bar towel.

Raymond was wearing his usual attire: jeans, boots, and a light blue shirt. Tonight he sported a hand-painted bow tie that sat under his square-jawed, russet-colored face—it was a pale yellow butterfly resting on a field of red and green.

"Hey, Ray," Juan high-fived him, and pointed at his bowtie. "That's a beaut! What is your poison? Virgin margarita, Ginger Ale, Seven-up"

"Ginger Ale. Straight up. Jon's on the phone?"

"Yeah. Ain't Docs always on the phone?"

Jon came around the corner with a big smile. "Hey!"

Raymond grinned back. "Big night tonight."

"Don't remind me," Jon moaned. Then he spotted Raymond's bow tie. "Let me guess. A butterfly."

"Yeah," Raymond tweaked the tie. "Thought I would wear something cheerful for you guys. Made it this morning. Paint isn't completely dry."

Jon gingerly fingered the bow tie. "Feels like silk. Is it silk?"

"Yeah, it's silk."

Jon nodded. "Neckwear may be the way to go, pal. What did you say, Raymond, about walking through the doors that the Great Spirit opens . . . and being grateful? We get what we pray for, but it never comes the way we think it should!"

"Hey, you getting philosophical on me? I am the Yoda here. Yeah, yeah . . . I should be grateful . . . but making bow ties is twisted. Get it, that's a joke! Anyway, maybe I'll get some high school kids to help me, but I don't want to be anyone's boss. I am an artist . . . painting bow ties doesn't do it for me."

"Yeah, but sometimes you gotta do . . . er, what you don't want to do."

"That's a white man's neurosis."

"How's Chenoa?"

"Fine. She is visiting her sisters."

"Any baby action yet?"

"We're trying."

"Let me know if you need help."

◎

When Jon first visited Raymond in Cambridge, he was surprised to find that Raymond had taken to wearing a button down shirt with a bow tie, along with his traditional Southwest look of jeans, boots, hat and vest.

"Hey, you've gone Ivy League," Jon teased.

"Not really, just culturally sensitive. I've seen lots of professors here wearing bow ties, so I started wearing them, and making them too . . . as a hobby. It's relaxing. The shape and the colors, its good art! Look here." Raymond opened a drawer full of bow ties.

"You made these?" Jon exclaimed.

"Sure. People want to buy them, but I just give them away," Raymond grinned. "I could do a good business. Make bolo ties for wannabe Indians and bow ties for the professors who want to look like Henry Higgins—the character in *My Fair Lady*."

"My fair Lady. Jeez, Ray. You are getting educated!"

Jon had found soul mates in Raymond and his family. Early in their friendship, when Raymond and Jon were planning a camping trip along the Chama River, Raymond invited his grandfather, Elmer, to come along. After the first day, Elmer quickly recognized that Jon was bright, open-minded, and more important, eager to learn what Elmer had to teach. That same night, after dinner, Jon was complaining about his disappointment with some of the university people. Elmer interrupted in a soft voice.

"Jon, it's not about the other people. It's yourself you have to worry about. Self-inflicted misery comes from not being realistic. Having an unrealistic expectation is essentially dishonest, because we are refusing or can't see what is there. The honest person can never be disappointed or disillusioned."

Although a bit puzzled by Elmer's words, Jon admitted that he had a very strict conscience, was often much too judgmental, and excessively harsh on himself for making what he judged as minor mistakes. On the other hand, he said he had boundless compassion which confused him. He explained that often when he won at a competitive sport, he usually felt sorry for the opponent who had lost. "Is that weird? Where did that come from?" Jon asked.

Elmer smiled and nodded his head slowly, "From you. By the way, now you may call me grandfather."

The following night Elmer began to explain to Jon how the world itself is a 'living thing' and how all actions, good and bad, affect it.

"There is a layer of mind around the earth that registers everything, and there are people who are tuned in to it." Then he interrupted himself with a wide yawn. "But that is for another night. I gotta go to sleep." Elmer stretched out on the ground, covered himself with a blanket, and fell fast asleep.

Jon was so intrigued by Elmer's brief comments that he took Raymond out of Elmer's hearing range to continue the discussion. "He says so many things I've thought about, but couldn't discuss with anyone because I was afraid they would think I was nuts. Like talking to plants and understanding animals, you know, being on another level of communication. He says I could easily become a slave to material things and other people's opinions . . . and how that really isn't me. Ray, he is the first really free man I've ever met."

"Yeah," Raymond laughed. "He has what he needs, and only wants what he has. Different from Buddhists who also promote non-attachment. Grandfather is the most attached/non-attached person I ever met. He has life down to a basic truth-seeing formula—one and one make two. I knock my brains out on calculus problems, and he asks me why I go to the trouble. I am just beginning to get what he is talking about."

The following night, Jon got up the courage to ask Elmer, "What is it like to talk with everything around you . . . all the plants and animals . . . when they can't answer?"

"Who said they can't answer?" Elmer laughed in surprise.

"Well, I don't think . . ." Jon faltered, "Plants can't talk."

"That's not exactly true. They talk in their way, and when they want to. I get answers when I need them. The Great Spirit is in everything. He is around us and through us. He can be in a gecko or a cactus. He needs feedback. That's why I give him feedback about how things are going. He asks me things, and I ask him things. I get answers at the right time."

"Like what?"

"Like the sun coming up in the morning," Elmer smiled. "Now I have to go to the woods. I drank too much tea. Right now, my bladder is talking to me."

Raymond chuckled. After Elmer left, Raymond rolled his eyes. "Grandfather does not live on the earth with us fulltime. He is in touch with the air; we are in touch with the ground. He has a cosmic mind. Mine is linear. Grandfather hears the song of the universe to the fullest. We hear it only in parts. The Great Spirit makes us good for what we are good for. We all have our own work."

Jon was energized and excited about the novelty of their conversation. "Grandfather says the healing power of his medicine plants comes from the Great Spirit. The power is stored up, like a little healing bomb. He promised to show me how to collect them and make medicines."

Raymond laughed, "Just don't smoke anything he gives you."

Juan turned off the music. This made the Cantina so unusually quiet that Raymond found himself lowering his voice. "So pal, watcha' thinking?"

"What do you figure I'm thinking? I'm wondering what's happening up there." Jon pointed to up towards the hacienda. "My sweetheart is being roasted up there."

Raymond interrupted. "Like I told Rosie, save yourself some grief. Beat it out of town with her. I don't think La Tierra would follow you." Raymond paused, "I hope."

Jon threw up his hands. "Is everybody around here really so narrow-minded? Ray, what if I wanted to marry your sister? How would you, grandfather, your parents, the rest of your people feel?"

"No problem, I would love for you to marry my sister . . . if I had one. My people don't get hung up on such things. Hey, we married the Spanish, no? And whites, blacks, all the others, whatever their color. How did I get my last name of Martinez? Everybody is a mestizo, even the few who think they are not. People have been crawling under each other's tent flaps since time began."

"Please!" Jon signaled to Juan to pour another drink.

"Hungry?" Juan called.

Jon popped his right thumb up toward the ceiling. "Si."

"The regular?"

"Yeah, two beef burrito specials. Okay, Raymond?" Raymond agreed. "Extra salsa, please."

"Okay, just for you." Juan rang his bell; the blender screeched. They covered their ears and walked over to a booth in the back of the room. Jon slid into the seat along the wall. Just as Raymond sat down, four women in their early twenties appeared at the door. They were laughing and talking loud, and dressed to kill even in the rainstorm. After all, it was Friday night. They headed for a booth on the other side of the room. Juan followed them holding two bowls of chips and a large bowl of salsa. "Gotta make it quick, ladies. Closing early."

Even before they sat down, the women set to work dipping handfuls of chips into the salsa bowl, devouring them while moaning with mock sex pleasure. "Ooh, I love your chips, Juan," the tall one made her voice low and sensual. "Four margies, please." Juan went back to the bar, rang his bell four times, and set to work. About the same time, a middle-aged couple hustled down the stairs and headed for the far corner at the bar, where it was relatively dark Even though they were soaking wet, they immediately began to maul each other. "Ooh," That set another of the young women to moan so all could hear, "They are hot!"

Juan called out in the couple's direction. "We ain't gonna be open much longer."

Jon had to shout to make himself heard over the roaring blender.

"What's . . ." the blender stopped and he lowered his voice, "keeping Rosie?"

Raymond leaned back and stretched his legs under the table. "Seriously, I am very worried."

Juan rang his bell again, the blender raged. Two more for the couple at the bar. The women laughed and howled.

Jon groaned, "Man, next time I come, I am bringing earplugs. How does he get that contraption to make such a noise?"

"Extra ball bearings in the motor housing?" Raymond mused. "That would do the trick."

Juan came over with a grin, balancing two large plates in one hand and a margarita in the other.

"Something special, guys."

"Looks fancy," Jon laughed.

"Check out the decoration. They call that drizzle. Saw it in a magazine. Clever? Thought you fancy guys would like it."

"What is it?"

"Red peppers, jalapenos, squash juice . . . prickly pear . . ."

"The colors of the New Mexico flag, red, yellow—great!"

"Yeah," Juan made a bow. "My new specialty . . . yeah!"

Juan turned away with a self-satisfied grin, Raymond grimaced and whispered, "Don't say anything, but it looks like coyote scat."

He closed his eyes, mumbled thanks, and took a bite of the burrito. "I'm thinking about Ike. You know how the Great Spirit makes different kinds of people. Some, like grandfather, are selfless. Others, like Ike, are filled with too much animal self, full of drive and aggression, Right now Ike is a warrior without a war. He thinks he needs a war . . . and you need to be careful you don't become Ike's war. That's why I am worried."

"I can deal with Ike if I have to."

"But you are not a warrior."

"Says who?"

"Me. The Great Spirit did not make you that way. You are a healer. How can I explain? You know my people attribute some animal characteristics to humans, right? For example, Patron has the qualities of a bear, strong and domineering; Ike is like a wolverine, snarly and reactive; Rosie is like a cat, no, a mountain lion. I have seen her lose her temper. My grandfather, he is like an eagle. I myself have many turtle qualities.

"My people know that the Great Spirit wants us to evolve toward becoming more loving and tolerant. To this end, he has made some people move faster in this direction than others. Grandfather, Abuelita, and Paz are on the point. Rosie too, but she is young and just becoming. Guys like you and me are in the middle. Guys like Ike's friends, the criminals and druggies, are off center in their oneness with the Great Spirit. They carry negative forces and discourage others. Some carry evil within them like a virus. When something nice is happening, they turn up to ruin it. I don't want them after you!"

Jon interrupted. "I don't think Ike is like that . . . evil."

"Neither do I," Raymond agreed. "However, he does need something to get him back on center. Maybe a good bop on the head."

"That could do it, right? Ray, you are talking a lot tonight . . . for an Indian . . ."

"True." Raymond took a bite of his burrito and looked up. "Look who the wind blew in!"

Rosie walked over to them, drying her face with the bottom of her sweater. "I'm alive, believe it or not," she shrugged off rainwater.

"So, do we need the car?" Jon shouted and got up to greet her. Juan threw him a towel and he handed it to her. They brushed lips and hugged. She hugged Raymond too.

"Tell me." Jon threw up his hands.

"Ay! Pack our bags." Rosie's eyes teared up. "I told them. Total surprise. I was right. Thank God for the rain, it saved my you-know-what."

Juan yelled, "Hey Rosie, margarita. From the way you look maybe you want tequila, straight up?"

"Just white wine, Juan," she called back.

"Ay!" Juan groaned toward the women in the corner. "She's becoming a yuppie on me? I don't serve white wine to homies. Margarita for you honey."

Juan sounded the bell. The blender roared. So much for the white wine.

Rosie wiggled in the seat next to Jon, taking an angle so she was out of sight of the other customers. "So," Jon asked.

"Ike had a fit, Jake got pissed but he was too worried about the rain to make much of a fuss, Carmela was kinda quiet. I am not worried about Paz and Abuelita. But my parents . . . forget it. And Poppa, I feel like I almost killed him. Thank God, everybody had to go home early. I don't know, Jon. It's a mess."

Raymond patted her on the shoulder and pointed outside. "There's the highway!"

"Enough with ducking out, Ray. I live here. Would you duck out?" Rosie snapped.

"Only a suggestion. Take it easy," Raymond backed off.

Jon brushed away her tears with his napkin. "I would have to find a replacement . . ."

"No. We are not going anywhere. Besides, you are needed here. Who else is going to come up to work here? I want to raise our kids here. I belong here. We both belong here."

"Of course," Jon pulled her close.

"What did they actually say?" Jon asked.

"I think my parents are just as hurt because I didn't tell them first, than they are about what I said. For the moment, at least."

And Patron?" Raymond asked.

"First, he made me feel guilty, then he started to scare me, but he backed off, then he even tried a bribe. I didn't know if he was serious. Anyway, I know he is being very careful. He made mistakes in the past and he knows it."

"And Ike?"

"As expected, Ike went loco. He's probably over at Sal's getting stoned and plotting against us."

Raymond reduced his voice to a whisper. "You can joke about it, but seriously Jon, keep your car in the garage. Be careful not to walk anywhere alone. On second thought, maybe you had better sleep over at my place for a while, at least until we know where this is going."

Rosie stifled a sob and blew her nose. "It's still supposed to be a secret, family only."

"Not for long," Raymond said. "If Ike knows, the La Tierra guys will too."

Juan came over with Rosie's margarita. "You can't drink that white wine basura at my bar, especially when you are crying. And, as you notice, a diplomatic bartender doesn't ask why you are crying. Professional attitude. Read about it in the bartender's magazine."

Rosie grabbed the margarita and downed half of the glass in one swallow.

"Wow!" Juan smiled. "Now, that's my Rosie," he flashed her thumbs up and happily walked away.

Raymond reached across the table and grasped Rosie and Jon by the wrists.

"Okay, you guys. A little physics here. Let us look at this problem logically. To solve any problem we need two things, right?" He raised an index finger. "One, identify the appropriate parameters, and two," his middle finger went up, "a method to use the parameters."

"Ray . . . c'mon. What are you talking about?" Rosie groaned. "I'm going to lose it if you go on like that!"

"If you gotta lose it, lose it. Drink and listen," Raymond grinned, "Now, say we want to know the area of a rectangle. First, we need to know some parameters. We need to know the length of two of the different sides. Then we need a method to use this information to find the answer. In this case, multiplication. Then we can figure out the size of the area. Follow me?"

Jon rolled his eyes. "For God's sake, Raymond, what has this got to do with us being miserable?"

"Bear with me," Raymond laughed. "We are getting there."

"If I live that long," Jon moaned.

"What we have in your situation are lots of parameters and no method. It's like trying to figure out an area when you have the right numbers, but no way to multiply them. Can't do it!"

Jon and Rosie grimaced at one another. Rosie rolled her eyes. "Hurry up before I need to apply for social security."

"Ergo," Raymond paused for a moment to enjoy their response to his haughty word, "the necessary methods for the solution to your problem— people's love, compassion, tolerance, and acceptance, to name a few—are in question. The parameters are religious and ethnic differences, people's whacked-out attitudes and nutty personalities, primitive aggression, toxic hate and distorted thinking. You may not have a chance to work this out in Santa Rosita, so you need to consider beating it out of here, unless . . ."

"Unless what?" Rosie and Jon were in unison.

"As I said before, something unusual occurs. Find a new parameter that will give you your method. One that transcends the issues I mentioned. A unifying principle . . ."

"Are we talking physics?"

"Well, something out of the box."

"The box again." Rosie was grim: "The choices in the box are . . . I choose Jon and leave Santa Rosita, or I stay here, don't get married, and be miserable my whole life!"

"You are not getting rid of me," Jon said softly.

"Then we gotta go," Rosie started to weep.

"Maybe," said Raymond, "and maybe not."

Juan whirred his blender to get everybody's attention. "Party's over everybody! It's raining too hard, the roads are getting dangerous and I don't want to sleep here tonight."

"We are supposed to meet some guys here," shouted one of the women.

"They are probably stuck in the mud somewhere. Time to go home." Juan motioned to the couple in the corner. The group of women grabbed their coats, grumbling, but obediently headed toward the door. Raymond got up to block their view of Rosie. Jon said, "We'd better take off, too, before this roof caves in. Ray, let's drop Rosie off and then we'll go to your place."

Juan shouted again, this time more urgently, "Let's go, guys. Now, now."

The couple, still intertwined, hurried up the stairs and out the door. Jon motioned toward the people who had left. "Now the cat is out of the bag."

Rosie sighed, "Juan knows how to keep his mouth shut."

"Right," Raymond smiled, "But those women got an eyeful."

"I just don't care anymore." Rosie kissed Jon on the cheek. "I guess we can walk out arm in arm now." She pecked Raymond on the cheek, too. "All three of us."

"If that's what you want," Ray nodded. "Alright! Let's make up a bright side. New Mexico is the land of enchantment, and grandfather is on the mountain. Things happen up there."

"And Auntie Paz talks with our saint, Rosita," Rosie added.

Raymond smiled. "And there is always . . . influence from other forces."

Jon snickered, "Yeah, right. C'mon, Rosie, we'll drive you home."

Rosie offered, "Speaking of other forces, I am meeting with Fr. Raul in the morning."

"What for?" Jon asked.

"I want to see where he stands. He's a good person. Maybe he can help." Rosie reassured him.

"But he's a Catholic priest," Jon exclaimed dubiously.

"Yes, but not exactly run of the mill," Rosie smiled.

"Make sure to see him early Rosie," Raymond grinned.

Rosie smiled and rolled her eyes knowingly.

7

Fr. Raul

Saturday morning was the first time Rosie awoke with a smile since she returned home. "I did it, I really did it," she said out loud, punctuating her statement by pumping a clenched fist. "And I am still alive! Whatever happens from now on, I know I got guts."

She snuggled back under the bedcovers, closed her eyes, and remembered she had to see Fr. Raul. She reluctantly threw off the bed covers and slowly swung her feet over the side of the bed.

"Ay! I'm creaky." She mumbled as she stretched up to rid herself of the rain in her bones. Rosie slowly wrapped her bathrobe around her, and then carefully slid each foot into a sheepskin 'skating slipper.' Just as Patron taught her to do as soon as she could walk, Rosie pushed off her left foot, then her right, gliding with short steps over the slick Saltillo tiles. She sped out through the doorway and down the long hall to the kitchen, where she was greeted by the pungent smell of fresh coffee.

"God bless Abuelita," she sighed out loud. She could use a good talk with her grandmother, but not this morning. On Saturday and Sunday mornings, Esther and Patron took their breakfast in bed, snoozed at their leisure and watched TV. Do not disturb.

Rosie poured herself a cup of coffee, then stared, trance-like, out the window, enjoying the patterns the raindrops made when they struck the water puddles. Orders of the day interrupted her trance: work out, see the Padre. She washed out her coffee cup and skated back to her room, stopping to listen at her grandparents' door. No sound, except for the TV. They were probably still dozing. She yawned and told herself, "On second thought, since I am proud of myself, I'll give myself a present and pass on the workout."

Rosie showered and dressed, still in her semi-fog, threw on raingear, stepped into her boots at the front door, and scanned the terrain for the easiest way to get to the church. Rainwater rushing downhill had already littered the driveway with clumps of tree branches and muddy debris. The unpaved areas bordering the road were now soggy as quicksand.

"Stay on the blacktop, I guess," she muttered to herself as she opened her umbrella, stepped into the courtyard and slipped sideways into a flowerbed. "Shit," she yelled, and righted herself. Fortunately, it took only a minute for the rain to wash her clean.

Once she reached the plaza, it was better footing to reach the church. All was quiet except for the rain splashing on roofs and stones. When she reached the front steps of the church, she heard a faint but familiar noise. Clank, pause, clank, pause . . .

"Padre's doing his thing," she smiled to herself. Rosie followed the sound around to the back of church, careful not to step out of her boots that were being sucked down into mud.

As she walked, her mind wandered back to the time when she was a teenager and, like most of her girlfriends, she had a crush on Fr. Raul. She daydreamed about him all the time and wanted to know everything about him. An opportunity came when she and Francisca, Fr. Raul's housekeeper, were baking cookies together for a church supper. Everyone knew that he and Francisca were close, so Rosie tried to summon up the courage to ask about him.

"Of course," Francisca smiled, "He has a wonderful story, and I will be happy to tell it to you so you can tell your friends."

"Padre was born in Mexico in 1932 and raised by his grandmother until he was ten years old. When her health was failing, the family decided to sneak him across the border to the United States, where he could live with his two aunts in Las Cruces. On the day he left, his tearful grandmother asked him to take something to remember her by. He chose a centuries-old family treasure—a wood and silver crucifix once nailed to the front door frame of her house. It was a family habit to kiss the crucifix every time anyone entered or left the house. Today this hangs over his bed, the only reminder of his early days."

"I've seen that cross," Rosie interrupted.

"Yes," Francisca replied, "Sometimes he hangs it behind the altar. Now let me continue, you want to hear the entire story, right?"

"Sure," Rosie agreed, wide-eyed.

"Padre was an excellent student in school, like you Rosie, and popular with his classmates, especially the girls. He was not much interested in religion, but he respected his aunts, so he helped out in the parish church. After graduating from high school with honors, he went to the University of New Mexico, and he got a degree in psychology. He excelled at sports; he was an All-State second baseman for the baseball team. He even had a tryout with a big league team after graduation; he was thinking he could become a professional baseball player. He had met a girl at school, Elsie from California. They fell in love and wanted to get married, but they had to postpone their plans. Padre was drafted into the Army and had to go off to the Korean War. He was especially happy to do so because he loved his country and they made him a legal citizen before he left."

"That's good."

"Yes. But what came after wasn't so good. Now listen," Francisca continued.

"One night, he was at the front line when enemy soldiers attacked his position with artillery and mortars. As the artillery rounds were landing, he, and some other soldiers jumped out of their foxholes and tried to find shelter in a large bomb crater. Just as he jumped down, a mortar round hit some soldiers running behind him and everything exploded into a shower of body parts."

"Ugh!" Rosie screwed up her face.

Francisca apologized, "Sorry, dear, that's not easy to hear. I get carried away sometimes. Another shell hit the edge of the crater and the impact must have knocked him out. The poor man was lying there alone in that hole covered with blood. When he woke up, he called out to God for help."

"'I swear to you, my God,' he screamed to the sky, 'if you save me I will devote my life to you and doing your works . . . I swear.'"

"Poor Padre," Rosie started to wipe tears away.

"Don't worry, he was alright," Francisca consoled her. "His promise was the last thing he remembered before another blast came from enemy mortars. North Koreans overran the area, spotted him sprawled out in the bottom of the crater, and one must have jumped inside and stuck his bayonet deep into his right shoulder to see if he was alive. He didn't move. He poked him again in the chest and stomach to see if he moved. Again, he didn't move. So the soldier moved on. Then hours later, the Americans came back in force and drove the enemy away."

Rosie just sighed.

"Twenty-four hours later, Fr. Raul awoke in a field hospital, very confused. There was a purple heart on his pillow—that's a medal. He was told he was the only survivor of his platoon, and he would be going home as soon as he could travel. It took some time to heal from the stab wounds, but the pain in his right shoulder was still hurting terrible. The doctor told him that tendons had been damaged, and they might improve, but Fr. Raul's throwing arm would never be good. So his hopes for a baseball career were over.

"But now that didn't matter, because he had promised to devote his life to God's service. When he arrived home, there was Elsie waiting, but he was firm. He took her to a quiet place and told her about his promise to God.

"'I'm stuck. I absolutely have to do it,' he said, sobbing. 'A deal is a deal.'

"Of course, Elsie was devastated. Her depression sunk her into a pit of despair—like having a nervous breakdown. She even needed to be hospitalized."

"Poor Elsie," Rosie moaned, wiping away her tears.

"Yes, this was very sad," Francisca was moved, too. "But it's not the Padre's fault. A deal is a deal, especially with God."

Rosie was still mournful. "I guess so."

"Anyway, here's the ending. Raul went into the seminary feeling guilty and depressed, but he found some comfort when he threw himself into his studies. Again he graduated with honors, and he was posted by the Bishop to a parish in Las Cruces. Here he could get a feel for parish life before, as the Bishop said, moving on to bigger things."

"And he did when he came to us," Francisca smiled proudly.

"That's a wonderful story," Rosie hugged her.

"Isn't it," Francisca beamed.

Patron knows two more parts of Fr. Raul's story. The unhappy events relating to his first post, where he was almost defrocked, are documented and stored in the church's confidential records. These records are unknown to all the parishioners except Patron. A second, more, 'innovative' part, concerns what the parishioners have done to keep him as the priest they love.

In 1960, the Bishop, a childhood friend and distant cousin, asked Patron to consider Fr. Raul for the post at Santa Rosita. When they reviewed Raul's background, Patron was allowed to read the confidential report on why Fr. Raul was asked to resign from his position in Las Cruces.

One paragraph seemed to sum everything up: "This person is very attractive to women, in spite of himself. His natural gift for profound listening during confession, and his psychological training, offer such sincere, non-judgmental attention that some of his female parishioners are induced to pour out unusually frank and colorful confessions—powerful admissions of their deepest hopes, dreams, deeds, instincts, fantasies and desires. For women who find no place for such emotions at home, the experience of having a priest, especially someone as kind and attractive as Fr. Raul, to listen to and actually hear them, is powerful. Their husbands do not do this. Being heard so attentively and respectfully, stirs up their spirits, their minds, and their bodies. Consequently, such vulnerable women easily fall in love with their fantasy of the man inside the confessional as well as the real thing. Obviously, we have received complaints from their husbands and others."

Patron noted that the Bishop was not unsympathetic to Fr. Raul.

"He is a good priest," the Bishop said, "who should not be defrocked because he never broke his vows. It is more about judgment and boundaries."

Then he went on to explain what he felt happened when the Padre heard confessions: "He gets so interested in what the penitent is saying that he loses his boundaries; his psychological training overrides our religious teaching. He probes their experience too deeply, acting more like a psychoanalyst practicing free association, than a priest. So it is understandable that some women get, well, aroused. As a result, word of this spread around and women from other parishes came to unburden themselves to Fr. Raul. At first, we were agreeable to letting the situation rest, as we usually try to do. After all, our membership was increasing and the coffers were filling. We were able to assuage some angry husbands. However, we could not ignore what happened next. This is confidential, mind you."

Patron nodded gravely, "Of course."

"Here is what we learned about the incident, from his own hand."

The Bishop unfolded and handed over a paper, on which Patron read: "On this fateful day, I finished hearing confessions, and retired to my office. No sooner did I remove my outer garments than a female parishioner rushed into my office, shouting, 'I can't stand it anymore, take me!' She stripped off her clothes—all of her clothes—until she stood completely naked before me.

"I froze in place and stared. She was beautiful and I felt myself responding, but I crossed myself many times to summon strength. 'Put your clothes on, I beg you,' I said. But to my astonishment, she leaped up, grabbed me around the neck and kissed me. I was shocked and confused, but I gained the will power to step back, take her hands from behind my neck, push her away and flee my office.

"'Help me here,' I called to the workers outside whitewashing the walls. Help! The poor woman inside has gone crazy. Follow me!' That's when the shot rang out. She had killed herself."

Patron sighed sympathetically and handed the document back to the Bishop. He had encountered similar situations with women seeking political favors.

The Bishop continued, "The official church investigation concluded that Fr. Raul, whether intentionally or not, had been titillating and encouraging the woman when he listened to her. Therefore, some punishment was called for. He was asked to resign his post and undergo a period of rehabilitation. Of course, many of his female parishioners voiced their unhappiness with the decision. But Fr. Raul not only understood, he welcomed the decision, even suggested a more severe penalty.

"He told me that if he were forced out of the church, it would nullify his pact with God through no fault of his own. He would be free to could go back to Elsie if she wished it. He confessed that he had never stopped having her as the object of his fantasies in times of temptation. On the other hand, he tearfully spoke of the powerful, and growing, vocation he now had as a priest. He liked ministering to people; he saw an opportunity to live a tranquil life and do good at the same time. But the celibate life was proving to be a more severe challenge than he thought it would. We sent him to talk with Fr. O'Toole, an older Irish priest.

"Here are some notes on their discussion. Again, Patron, the utmost confidence."

Patron read, "Father, I get very aroused when I listen to the confessions of some women, especially the good-looking ones. When this happens, I just cannot avoid asking questions that cause us both to become more aroused."

Patron then read Fr. O'Toole's confidential and off-the-record response to Fr. Raul. "Latino priests who are straight tend to get hotter than most other priests when they listen to women. But it is better to be like that, than like our predatory brothers who take boys as prey and bring shame to the Church. Here is what I have found helpful for me. A shot or two of Jameson's Irish whiskey, or a cup of good red wine if you like it, or tequila if you prefer, and a Tic-Tac, always helps before going into the confessional. Remember that your good works count in your service to God. The rest is bullshit."

The Bishop collected the notes. "Fr. Raul has completed his period of rehabilitation and he has attended classes in behavior control. He is ready to start over. Will you take him?"

Patron agreed. "Sure, but you will owe me, Armando," he smiled.

"Of course, Ruben," the Bishop nodded. "I will tell his parishioners back in Las Cruces that he was called to do holy work again in an area that really needs it."

@

The second part of his story is well known to his Santa Rosita parishioners. When Fr. Raul arrived, he was determined not to repeat his former mistakes. He followed his spiritual advisor's advice and began to drink before and after confession. He controlled the severe temptation he must have experienced, and he was able to minister to the women in Santa Rosita in an excellent manner. He remained celibate for the first year. After that, his suffering became so apparent and noticeable, even to Patron and members of the Church Board, that some of the women who especially understood his dilemma, decided to come to his rescue. They approached Patron, who was willing to convene a private meeting about the priest's future and his needs.

Patron took the lead by acknowledging, "Our well-loved Fr. Raul is so horny that, for his own good, no parents want to leave him alone with their girls. We don't want to expose any of our vulnerable widows or unmarried women to possible . . . ."

"But he has never done anything wrong!" Carmela jumped to his defense.

"I know," Patron responded calmly, "We worry about the women, not him."

"Yes," Vincente Gomez winked at Patron and whispered, "Especially the ones who aren't gettin' any."

"I have a thought," Esther smiled and then lowered her head slightly.

"What?" Patron asked.

She brought a conspiratorial finger up to her lips, and rolled her eyes demurely. "Isn't there a precedent? Haven't we always," she paused briefly, "since the time of Fr. Miguel and Fr. Miguel, Jr., had a tradition of hiring priests who were 'real' men." She emphasized the 'real.'

"That's true, of course," they happily concurred.

"Our priests have always been real men," Paz said, "and real men need it, I mean help in their lives."

Patron caught a gleam, or half-wink, from Esther's eye. She was sending him a message.

He pondered for a while, a bit for effect, then rubbed his chin. "Fr. Raul needs . . . a housekeeper! How about . . . Francisca"

At first, the group fell quiet, and then heads started to nod. Esther smiled broadly. He got it. Esther said. "Yes Ruben. Francisca. She's a fine person. Good idea, Ruben. I'll call her and see what see says. Everyone agree." Nods all around.

At the time, Francisca was a 33-year-old widow with coppery skin, full lips, slightly slanted dark eyes and long black hair. The men admired her physical beauty and revered her body almost as much as she, herself, revered her Church. She was devoutly religious after her husband's death had left her alone, childless, and tentative about social contacts. She spent many hours confessing confusion about herself, her goals, and her future to Fr. Raul, so she listened to Esther's offer with a serious attitude. "I would be helping our parish," she concluded.

The board quickly appointed Francisca to the position on a trial basis, stipulating that if she worked out in a satisfactory manner, Fr. Raul could decide to keep her on permanently. This happened sooner than everybody expected.

Only days later, Fr. Raul thought he had finished hearing his last penitent and the church was empty, when Francisca entered the confessional. He listened to her confession in his inimitable manner. Francisca lamented her late husband, mourned the lost companionship and intimacy, and moaned that she would always miss sexual love. She poured out that she was in love with a priest who wouldn't even touch her because he was so ethical and pure of spirit. Then she started to sob uncontrollably. Fr. Raul lost all his composure, burst out of the confessional, opened the other door and took Francisca into his arms. He carried her to his quarters and found her willing to respond to the real man as they made love under his grandmother's crucifix.

After two weeks of exploring their passions, leaving the bedroom only for professional obligations, they acknowledged that they were wildly in love. Francisca was permanently hired.

Unfortunately, this arrangement caused Fr. Raul to question his legitimacy as a true Catholic priest. His guilt also came from drinking to excess, as he often chastised himself in private as a despicable fraud to the parish. He would often prostrate himself in front of the altar and plead with God for a sign, any sign, that he was fit to be a priest. He never saw or heard a sign.

The board had an additional motive for assigning Francisca to look after Fr. Raul. His drinking problem had been getting worse, frequent tequila was the only treatment that controlled his sexual frustration. The unfortunate consequence was he had become an alcoholic. Francisca agreed to the task of helping him overcome his need to drink so much alcohol. First, she managed to convince him to stop drinking tequila; he switched to wine, and with the lower alcohol content, he was able to function better. Next, she obtained his pledge to never drink before lunch, a rule he found it easy to follow. Eventually, she elicited a further promise from him to stop drinking on Wednesdays and Saturdays, the busiest confession days. Otherwise, he is allowed to carry a small flask of wine in his garments in case he needs to lubricate his 'dry throat.'

Abstinence from alcohol on Wednesdays and Saturdays has helped their romance. The priest and Francisca have fallen into a domestic routine, so that these nights are reserved for them to be together as a couple. Francisca makes her confession, and then they can enjoy the sensual ritual of candles in the bathtub and intimacy in their bed. They know that their God sees all they do and hears all they say.

"Why not have our pleasures? Who are we hurting?" asks Francisca. "If it is good for us, it is good. No?"

"I don't know," he answers. "I would feel better about our life together if I had a sign from God that what we are doing meets with his approval."

As Fr. Raul's 'dry throat treatment' became known around the parish, everybody in his flock learned when, and at what time of day, to talk him if they had something serious to discuss. Those who desire a regular confession go on Wednesdays or Saturdays. If they want a Fr. Raul 'special confession', which, the women agree, aren't as interesting now as they used to be before Francisca, they go on the other days.

Aside from the quirks known to the parish, and the private struggles he has faced, Fr. Raul is a force of good for Santa Rosita. His works of charity and compassion have brought him high respect. The men of La Tierra have good will toward him, and he and Francisca help feed the poor and hungry, comfort the aged, sick and dying—all the people in need. The priest intervenes, when asked, in family feuds that could turn deadly, preaches against drug dealers and gang violence and works well with the Church board and diocese.

The couple has encountered only one serious problem. Francisca wanted to have a child. Much as he understood, Fr. Raul could not bring himself to agree because of the scandal it would cause, even in Santa Rosita. He considered the possibility of leaving the Catholic Church for the

Episcopalian faith. That way they could get married and have a family of their own. However, he knew if he chose that way, he would have to leave town; there are no Episcopalians in Santa Rosita. They finally agreed that they might fulfill their parenting instincts by caring about other people's children as they grew up. Like Rosie, for example.

@

Rosie spotted the Padre standing under a large makeshift tent, about to dump a shovelful of dirt into a sieve. He wore his standard attire of white collar, black shirt and black pants, and, in deference to the weather, he had on a pair of knee-high rubber boots instead of his highly polished black shoes. A yellow rain hat that had seen better days was perched sideways on his head, adding a comic touch to his outfit.

"Hi, Padre, you're lookin' cool. What are you doing outside in this weather?" Rosie called to him and hurried to get under the tent. Although he was obviously working hard, she noticed there was no sweat on his brow. He doesn't sweat, no wrinkles either. She wondered about how priests manage that."

"Hola, Rosie. Digging some earth for La Noche." Rain or shine, Fr. Raul had to dig up the weekend's quota of sacred soil to be blessed by Rosita and made available to pilgrims in search of healing. Rosie quickly checked the color of the priest's nose to assess the state of his sobriety. Since his nose lights up bright red after his first drink of the day, this is easy to do. He might try to explain it away as Rosacea, but everybody knows better. Rosie noticed that Fr. Raul had changed little since she had last seen him. He was sturdily built and, except for the slight paunch, in good physical condition. The good looks of his youth were still evident in his animated face, broad smile and his large, warm brown eyes that appeared to float on a rim of tears. Such endearing eyes and expressions had never escaped notice from the parish women.

"A little soggy for La Noche, no?" Rosie smiled.

Fr. Raul flashed his grin. "Never to soggy for La Noche. So, how is it going with you?"

He asked with affection for her that went back to her being an impertinent little girl, daring him with questions in catechism class. He was explaining the importance of confession to the class when Rosie, then nine years old, jumped out of her seat waving her hand furiously.

"Padre, Padre, I don't have to go to confession."

Fr. Raul said patiently, "Yes, you must. To ask God to forgive your sins."

"Well," Rosie retorted, "You told us that Jesus died for our sins."

"Yes, he did," Fr. Raul nodded earnestly.

"Then I am free and clear! I do not have any more sins. I don't have to go to confession anymore."

"Well, it doesn't exactly work like that . . ." He repressed a chuckle and found himself at a loss for words.

"But what's the point in confessing if I am already forgiven?"

The priest had to bite his lower lip to keep a straight face. However, when he noticed some of her classmates nodding in agreement, he quickly dismissed the class.

"Watch out for this one," he cautioned himself. Now here she was, all grown up.

"Padre," Rosie said, "I have to talk with you." Not one to ignore the urgency in her expression, the priest put down his shovel. "No time like the present. First, give me a hand with the sieve. Rosita doesn't like lumpy soil."

֍

Fr. Raul leaned his shovel against a post and stuck his hands out into the rain to wash them clean. "That should be enough." He smiled.

Rosie unsnapped her raincoat. Fr. Raul helped her off with the raincoat, folded it neatly and placed it over a chair.

"Patron called me last night to say you were coming to see me. But he didn't say why. Do you wish to confess?"

"Not too much."

"Well, you don't do anything very sinful anyway, do you?" He laughed.

"That's not exactly true," she shook her head.

"Okay. Well, it is relative. Here, bow your head. Whatever you feel guilt about, I absolve you. Say a couple of Hail Mary's just to be safe."

Rosie stood up. "Padre, I need your help. To make it simple, one, I am in love with Jon. Two, we want to get married. Three, my family doesn't want me to marry him."

Now Fr. Raul was all seriousness. "Jon. Not the clinic doctor!"

Rosie nodded yes.

Oh! Oh!"

"So, Padre! What?"

"Ay! Rosie, Doc is a good person, but he is Jewish. You can't possibly marry him."

"Why not?"

"Because he's not Catholic. We don't mix."

"Why?"

"We just don't mix. That's why! Ay! This is trouble."

"That's why I'm here, Padre."

"Hold on a minute." Fr. Raul moved away towards the edge of the tent. He bent down, reached outside into the rain and stuck a finger of his right hand into the mound of soil he considered sacred. Then he walked back to Rosie and told her to close her eyes. He placed his left hand on the back of her head, made it a point not to look down her blouse, said a few words, and drew a muddy cross in the middle of her forehead.

"You will need protection."

"Thanks, can you help me? Talk to my parents?"

"I need time to think. Your family . . .?"

"They are in shock!"

Fr. Raul arranged two chairs facing each other and motioned for her to sit down.

"Okay. One thing at a time. Patron told me you were coming to talk with me. I'm supposed to talk you out of it, because we all know it would bring you great trouble to marry outside of your faith."

Tears welled up in Rosie's eyes. "I know all that, Padre."

Fr. Raul knew what he should do, but that was not the way he felt.

"Don't cry, dear. Let me just tell you what I am supposed to say, then . . . God help me . . . it would be easier for me if I did not understand. Other priests may not understand, the church may not understand, but I . . . I know about love and rules. I can tell you, you are heading for trouble. But what I think doesn't matter. We just don't want to lose you. Your family, the church, the town, we don't want to lose you."

"You're not angry with me?" Rosie cried.

"Angry with you? Never. I just don't see how this is going to work. I really don't. Jon, Santa Rosita, both ways you lose something. What I can do is pray for you to find your way. Maybe I can get answers for you, some guidance from somewhere." He was thinking, I can't get guidance for myself, how can I get any for her? How worthy am I of divine guidance?

Fr. Raul fell to his knees, clasped his hands and started to pray.

"Kneel beside me, pray."

Rosie stayed put on her chair. "I don't feel like praying right now, Padre. You go ahead."

Just as she finished her sentence, a powerful gust of wind hammered the tent so hard it began to wobble. Rosie got scared and fell to her knees.

"Don't want to get anyone mad, Padre. I'll pray with you." She kneeled down next to Fr. Raul, who opened his eyes wide and, all of a sudden, let forth a joyful whoop.

He turned and grabbed Rosie's shoulder. His face became excited, beaming.

"Rosie, I got a message." Tears filled his eyes. "Me, a message."

"A message?"

"Yes. Praise God, I got a message! Do you know what this means?"

Rosie had never seen Fr. Raul so joyful and animated before.

"What?"

"I'm alright, Rosie, I am alright."

"I'm glad you are alright, but what about me?"

"Yes, I heard about you, too. You are to wait, dear. Just wait."

"Wait? You said wait?" Rosie said skeptically.

"Yes, wait." He smiled and pointed up to the darkened sky. Then he took his head in his hands and tears welled up in his eyes.

"I got a message. Rosie, I don't have to do anything. You don't have to do anything. You know, of course, that doing nothing is not really doing nothing. It is doing something."

"What?"

"Never mind. Go be with Rosita. Maybe she will tell you more. I won't bring her outside tonight. She'll get pneumonia in the rain." He laughed aloud at his remark. He liked to laugh at his own jokes, and people often laughed at him enjoying at his own jokes.

"Thank you so much for coming here."

"Well, yes. I am glad you are happy," Rosie agreed. "So, Padre, I am supposed to wait and do nothing. How can I do that? I have decisions to make."

He was still incredulous. "Rosie, I actually got a message. Do you know what that means?"

"Not really, but I am glad for you, Padre."

"Thank you, I was concerned that . . ." He stopped short. He reminded himself, this is my concern, not Rosie's. He continued, "Rosie, go sit with Rosita inside, and then go home." Fr. Raul watched silently as Rosie made her way back into the church. He was thinking about Francisca. "I can't wait to tell her! Imagine, I got a message. God would never send me a message if he thought I had done wrong. Would he?"

Rosie went into the church and sat down in front of the statue of Rosita. After a while, Rosita eyes looked up at the sky, and Rosie saw her smile.

@

Ike woke up late Saturday afternoon with a hangover and a malevolent purpose. Although he had intended to see his friend, Sal, after leaving his grandparents' home on Friday night, he started to feel ill and headed home. There he found a bottle of cough medicine containing a sedative in the refrigerator, downed a quarter of the bottle and took two bottles of beer to bed with him. He called Sal, told him Rosie's news, and then passed out for fourteen hours.

By the time he got out of bed and showered, he felt better.

"Got to see Sal," he told himself. He said goodbye to his parents, took off on his motorcycle and drove to check on the arts and crafts center where he worked. No employees, no customers. "Damn rain is killing business," Ike grumbled to himself and headed for Sal's place. The going was tough, however. The road was slick and treacherous where water had pooled. Ike found himself sliding the motorcycle through rivulets of running water, deep puddles in potholes, and loose rocks that had fallen from higher up. He fell twice before he finally reached Sal's place in the Pinon trailer park. The mud was so deep Ike had to tug and push his bike over to Sal's trailer. He arrived sweaty and soaked, his head throbbing, sat on the front steps, opened a bottle he had brought and downed it, then pounded on the door with the empty.

"Hey, Sal, abierto! Open up."

"Okay, coming." Sal opened the door. "You look like a wet coyote."

"I feel like one." Ike brushed off as much water as he could. "God damn. I almost broke my ass on the way over. Skidded twice. Got a towel?"

"Sure! Hey, Ike, you tore your shirt."

"Shit, shit . . . So, did you call Romeo?"

"Yeah, I told him about Rosie. He's pissed. Man, a Jew . . . chinga . . . your family must be really mad."

"Yeah, but not as much as they should be. Damn doctor comes up here and nails my sister." Ike slammed his fist against the wall.

"How do you know that?"

"They were seeing each other in Albuquerque. Alone."

"Odds are yes, she's nailed."

"Chinga, he's out of here." Ike punched the wall again. "Ow!"

"What are we going to do?"

"First, we scare the shit out of him. And we call our boss, Alcalde."

"Yeah! He knows what to do with gringos . . ."

Ike sat down. "We start slow. Scare him. Spray paint 'Get out Gringo Jew' on his car. No. I got something better, let's see, gringo Jew is too long. Let's put the words together. Yeah, make up a new word: Jew plus gringo. How about Jingo? Yeah! Jingo!"

"Yeah, we spray paint 'Beat it Jingo.'"

"Then we spray paint the clinic, and then we bust his windshield and cut his tires. Then if he don't go . . ."

"The spray paint will run in this rain."

"We use oil paint. Then we bust his car."

"What about Rosie?"

"Hey. She's my sister. No, we only do the Jingo."

"I mean, what's Rosie gonna do?"

"It doesn't matter . . . when she sees him run, she'll get over it." Ike ran his hand through his hair.

Sal frowned, "Let's not spray paint the clinic."

"Why not?"

"My mother works there. She'll have to clean it up."

"Okay. We won't spray paint the clinic."

"Who else can we get to join us, what about Eduardo?"

"I don't think so," Sal said.

"Why?"

"The Doc set his broken leg, and for free. I don't think his heart would be in beating up a doctor who helped him, gringo or not. It comes down to values."

"Yeah, we have to protect our values! How about Romeo for this plan," Ike clenched his fist. "He likes to kick ass."

"Yeah, Romeo, he's for La Tierra!"

"Hey," Ike jumped up. "Call him up."

"Okay." Ike picked up the phone and dialed. Romeo answered after the first ring. Everyone was home tonight. "Hey, Romeo. Yeah, you heard?"

Romeo answered, "Heard what?" Ike took the phone and told him about the Jingo messing with his little sister. "Yeah, tonight. We'll do it tonight. You can't! Your truck got stuck. Damn, then it's me and Sal. Yeah, next time."

Ike hung up. "What an idiot, doesn't know how to handle his truck when it rains like this! We'll take my bike."

Sal looked out the window and his eyes went wide: "I don't think so. Take a look!"

"Shit!" Ike shouted. His bike was sliding away from the trailer, sinking deeper into the mud. "Shit!"

"We're stuck here for the night."

"Well, Sal, let's get drunk. Got some brews in my saddle bags."

"Never mind. Got some in the kitchen."

"Got any good stuff, tequila gold."

"Yeah."

"Are the chicks next door at home?"

"Yeah. Where is anybody gonna go in this rain?"

"Got any weed?"

"Sure."

"Then call 'em to come over and party. We'll get the Jingo tomorrow. Alcalde is coming down this way. We'll let him know what's going down here."

⊚

The hacienda roof was leaking badly, forcing Esther to move around the kitchen placing pots and pans to catch the rainwater. "Ruben," she shouted, "get more buckets, anything!"

"Okay, hold your temper!" Patron rushed into the kitchen with plastic buckets and metal pails. "Thank God, it hardly ever rains. Look at the bright side, the floor is extra clean." They laughed.

"So, Ruben, what about our Rosie?"

"Ay! What about her? Why is she doing this to us?"

"Ruben, that doesn't matter. She is doing it and she is heading for trouble. The question is, how we can prevent this trouble."

"Why are you asking me? I'm part of the trouble."

"But you're always the strategist . . ."

"I'm stumped."

"While you are stumped, I'm worried that Ike and his friends will get crazy and do some harm."

Patron nodded, "I'll talk with them."

Esther frowned. "I don't want Rosie to get hurt."

Patron lamented. "Rosie, Rosie. My heart is in one place, my head is in another. I keep thinking about what happened with Paz. But now is not twenty years ago, and Rosie isn't Paz."

Esther rolled her eyes. "Then was then, that's for sure, Ruben," she sighed. "Would it really be the end of the world, my dearest, if we let the young ones marry outsiders?"

Patron laughed. "Not the end of the big world, but the end of our world. Our culture would become diluted! God knows, there is an irony about all this."

Esther smiled. "You are so right! The bottom of the gravestones, right?" She gave a nervous laugh. "The words . . ."

Patron shook his head. "Rosie and Doc. Ay!"

"I will talk with Rosita," Esther said, "and see what she tells me."

Without thinking about it, Patron took out his lucky charm, an old, worn piece of silver in the shape of a large thumbnail, and began to rub it gently. It had an indentation in the middle that separated markings, illegible to him, arranged in two columns. "If I do what I believe I should do, it will be a disaster. So I need to do something else. Ask Rosita about that."

"We need a miracle, right?" Esther said.

"That's what Rosie said," he replied.

Patron helped Esther on with her raincoat. "Be careful and don't slip. We don't need any broken hips in this family." He stopped her: "On second thought, you shouldn't be out there alone. I will go with you. I can hold the umbrella for you."

Just as they were about to leave, Rosie came barging through the door.

"Oh, you're soaking wet," cried Esther.

"It's hailing out there and it hurts."

"Was it hard to get up the hill?"

"I just made it slipping and sliding. I hope you're not going to walk out there. You need the four-wheel drive. I had better call Jon. He's at Raymond's house."

"Sure, my dear," Abuelita answered softly. "How did it go with Padre?"

"Okay, I guess."

"What did he say to you?"

"He prayed, and then he told me to wait and do nothing. I don't understand."

"Hmmm," Patron mumbled. "Do nothing. What is that about? How can we do nothing?"

"I sat with Rosita, too."

"And?" Esther asked.

"She looked up to the sky and smiled."

"She smiled?" Esther said, wide eyed.

"Yes!"

That's good, Esther thought.

Patron peeked outside. "Four wheeler or not, Esther, there is no going down to the church tonight. We are stuck here."

"I'm going to call Jon," Rosie said. She tried to call Raymond's house, but got no answer.

"The phones are down; damn, they never work when you need them. I need to call my parents, too. "

Esther draped a comforting arm around Rosie's shoulder. "They will all be okay without you. I spoke with your mother earlier and said you are staying here again tonight. Now let's have something hot to drink."

Patron perked up. If Padre said to do nothing, he thought, then he must be waiting for something to happen. Maybe I am off the hook.

❧

Jon spent that Friday night at Raymond's home, a neat adobe building just off the central plaza of the pueblo. In the morning, Chenoa tried to go to work, but soon returned. "The mud is too deep. The car was sinking down instead of going forward. I am worried about grandfather; he's been away since Wednesday."

"Should we go get him?" Jon was concerned.

"We probably couldn't make it. Anyway, he can take care of himself until the weather clears." Raymond told him. "Our people have been using the cave up there for as far back as memory can reach. Actually, it is quite dry inside and stocked with plenty of wood for a fire. The rain can't keep up like this. Even if it's a hundred-year rain. On TV they say this storm will pass in a day or two."

"TV?" Jon laughed. "Don't you use the old Indian signs?"

"You mean watching the leaves turning upside down on the trees, and stuff like that?"

"Yeah!"

"Give me a satellite photo anytime."

"Jon, I am worried about you and Rosie," Chenoa said.

Jon threw up his hands, "Join the club."

Chenoa closed her eyes. "Something unusual is going to happen. I feel it."

Jon went to put on his coat. "I hope it's good, but I'd better go now."

Raymond jumped up, blocked the door, and looked through the small window. "No way!" He wiped away the condensation with the palm of his hand. "Take a look out there. You are not going anywhere until the rain stops."

Jon looked out and saw that his car had settled into the mud. "Damn," he grumbled. Raymond said he was sorry. "Even a horse couldn't travel out there. Call Rosie and tell her you are stuck. I'm going out back to collect some of this mud . . . good for making pots."

Chenoa shouted, "You are out of your mind!" but Raymond headed out the door.

Jon picked up the phone to call Rosie. No dial tone.

"Damn, I'll have to walk," he said.

"No way!" Chenoa was firm with him, and then Raymond bounded in, saying, "Chenoa's right! Something is strange about this rain. It's too heavy, even for a hundred-year-rain. Something unusual is going on." He smiled what Jon called his 'Indian smile.'

"Can you feel it Jon?" Chenoa asked. "Close your eyes."

"Feel what?" Jon frowned.

"Something." Raymond winked at Chenoa. "Jon, just close your eyes and don't talk."

8

The Flood

Sunday, August 12, 2000.

Elmer was the first person around Santa Rosita to see the floodwater com-ing. He was in good spirits at the time. After spending five cold and rainy days on the mesa, he had finally received a sign. It came on the fourth day of the storm, after he took a break from meditation to brew a cup of tea. He be-gan to boil some water, when he suddenly remembered that he had used the last of his tea that morning.

"Now I got to go outside . . . dig up more herbs . . . in that downpour," he grumbled.

With a sigh, he grabbed his plastic poncho, draped it over his head and made his way to the mouth of the cave. Striding as fast as he could, he made a beeline for a small flat patch of vegetation about a hundred yards away. About fifty feet away from the cave, the mud began to wash away under his feet, making him slip on the path. At the same time, water ran down his face creating tiny prisms of raindrops that dripped from his eyelids and blurred his vision. After a false step, he slid downward until he was kneeling on a flat, jet-black rock ledge covered with a veneer of running water. After he wiped his eyes to see better, he looked down and noticed a cluster of designs cut into the rock.

"Whoa!" he shouted in delight, and grabbed on to an overhanging limb to steady himself. He began to run his fingers ever so lightly over the designs. Cut deeply . . . but very old, worn by the wind . . . a spiral and a sun design, a mudhead and a sandman. He looked more closely. Ah! These are new. Now this is something. Could this be . . . ? His thoughts were interrupted by a bolt of lightning that shot out of the center of the large, black cloud directly above him. Elmer looked up, said, "Thanks," joyfully pulled himself to his feet, and made for the cave. "A piece of Osha in hot water will do me fine," he decided.

The rain ended just before dawn the next morning. By six o'clock, the sun was beginning to rise, all bright and shining. The air was crisp and clear, as if it had been 'windexed' as Raymond called it when he was a little boy. Elmer was already awake and dressed in jeans, boots, cowboy shirt painted with his own sunburst design, and leather vest.

"Time to clean up and get my stuff together," he announced to the spirits in the cave, while he tied up the sage he had collected into small bundles and placed them in his pack. "A good harvest," he smiled to himself. "Top quality stuff."

The sage would be used for the purification ritual at his pueblo's harvest celebration. Next, he carefully wrapped several small stone animals he had carved, 'cold cash' he thought to himself. He would sell these at the Arts and Crafts Center. He reached into his pack for the plastic bags he used to wrap up the Osha—a native root with curative powers—that he had harvested on his way up to the mesa. He bit off a large chew of Osha, then broke off a second piece and stuffed it into his boot to fend off any rattlesnakes he might encounter on the path down.

After cleaning the area, he removed his silver and turquoise bolo tie and medicine bag from the pockets in his vest, draped them around his neck, carefully placed his Stetson on his head, said a parting prayer of thanks, and walked out of the cave into the sunshine. Tonight he would tell his people everything that had been revealed to him, and, as soon as possible, return to the mesa with Raymond to examine much more thoroughly the new signs he had discovered.

He started down from the mesa with short, careful steps, vigilant to avoid slipping on the steep and muddy path. Considering his age, he felt proud that he could still evade the large and painful spines of the prickly pear, cholla, and other types of cactus that grew all over the hillside.

"I'm almost as frisky as the kids," he chuckled to himself. As always, he was engaged in a running conversation with every living thing around him; uttering steady, soft, often-unintelligible soft mumbles—blessings, explanations, questions and commentary—in his dialogue with the seen and unseen, and always a bit more condescending to the plants than to the animals.

"You are beautiful," he complimented a large and menacing cholla. "But keep your spines to yourself. I won't hurt you. You don't hurt me. It's a deal," he said. Just to be sure, he made a plea to the earth mother who watches over her children. "I hope your cholla is in a good mood this morning."

The path was slippery from the rain, which made the going very tough on him. Elmer tired quickly and decided to rest. "Not as frisky as I thought," he mused, and looked around to see if there was an easier way down from the mesa. The ground was too wet to sit on, so he nudged aside a juniper branch to make room for him to squat down.

"Thank you for making room for me," he said to the bush. He surveyed the landscape once more and then cocked an ear, listening for the sound of rattles. There were many rattlesnakes guarding Red Mesa. That is why this Red Mesa is often called Rattlesnake Mountain. Elmer knew the snakes would have been hiding out of the rain and wouldn't come out until the sun was high; nevertheless, he needed to be extra careful. He was obliged to practice what he preached to the children.

"Most rattlesnakes don't want to be bothered, but some of them are very ornery, so ya' gotta be careful—always." He also taught the children to talk to rattlesnakes, just in case. So he said aloud, "Rattlesnake, you are probably feeling mean, cooped up underground so long. But just wait until I leave before you come out."

Just as he was about to spit Osha juice into the four directions to seal the deal, he heard a very loud rumbling sound. Like thunder, but coming from somewhere below him.

"What is this noise? Is something or someone speaking to me?" He looked up into the sky and closed his eyes to hear better. The sound got louder. Is the Great Spirit making a move? he wondered. After all, for the past five days Elmer had tried hard to convince the Great Spirit to return the earth on center. Indians know that the earth is slightly off the center of its axis. This is why there is so much trouble in the world, why humans act so badly, and why there are wars, earthquakes and great storms. This is why too many people are not acting like human beings should. Instead, they are mean-spirited, drinking and poisoning themselves and the land, and exploiting and hurting one another.

As Elmer explained to Raymond years ago, when his grandson asked him why there was so much misery in the world, "There is nothing a human being can really do to change terrible things—it is out of our hands. Not the tribal council, not even the healers. People can change nothing. No, this is a job for the Great Spirit. He has to set the earth back in its right place, and then people will be right again. All we human beings can do is pray, dance, and ask the Great Spirit to get on with it. Until he does, nothing will change. That is just the way it is. People can knock their brains out to change things themselves, but it ain't gonna happen."

While Elmer strained to figure out where the noise was coming from, a six-inch gecko lizard sidled up to him. Elmer greeted it with a grin. "Hey! You scared of the noise too? Is the earth beginning to move back where it belongs?" Elmer moved closer until he was eyeball to eyeball with the transfixed gecko. "That would be something," Elmer murmured, "Don't you think?"

He glanced up toward the top of the mesa. All quiet. No noise from the cave, or the sky, or from anywhere up there. He turned to his left, to the east, sizing up the broad expanse of the valley below. By that time, sun and a breeze were starting to dry out a portion of the old Santa Fe Trail, but it was still hard to make it out from the surrounding sea of mud. The trail was starting to bake like a pie, crusty on top but soft underfoot. He searched for the point where the ancient trail entered his pueblo and followed its winding to the central plaza, where his people held their sacred rites and dances. His own home, two stories high, was easy to see among the low adobe buildings circling the plaza. From there, the trail veered north, passing alongside the ceremonial lodge, and through the dump with its carcasses of cars and trucks. Then it veered eastward out of the pueblo, continuing a mile to an intersection with a side road leading to the Pinon Trailer Park. This unpaved road branched off, swooped down a steep incline into the trailer park, and disappeared among the twenty or so trailers arranged in several rows. Elmer saw four abandoned cars scattered along the side of the road, stuck in mud up to their windows.

Elmer's eyes followed the trail as it left the trailer park and continued over higher ground, where it widened and became the shiny black surface of a state road. After cresting a small hill, it dove down out of sight into a canyon, then up to the hilly region where many of the townspeople lived. The old trail continued north, heading straight as an arrow into the town center, where it joined several other roads from different directions. From this junction on, the trail was a paved pathway running straight through the plaza to the fountain. Here it split into two pathways that circled the fountain, joined again and continued to the steps of the Santa Rosita church. From there, it continued, unpaved, through the arch that marked the entrance to the old cemetery and then the trail meandered through ancient tombs and headstones.

"No sound over there," Elmer said to himself, pausing for a moment to admire the multi-colored mosaic formed by the slanted gravestones reflecting the early morning sun. Those people go to a lot of trouble for their dead, he reflected. We bury our dead three or four on top of one another. They do a lot of work for nothing, he thought. Everybody's spirit is around whether they are vertical or horizontal.

Elmer peered in the direction of Black Mesa, another high plateau several miles away. He was hesitant to look there, for fear of re-experiencing a painful memory. "That's where I got it, he remembered back hundreds of years when Spanish soldiers killed him on that mesa. As he tells it, "They murdered all of us. They got me in the stomach with three of those long spears with a hook on the end. One stuck in me and I could not get it out. So very painful, and it took me a long time to die, and they just watched me. Some even spat on me. What kind of men wouldn't finish me off with some merciful blow . . . ?"

All of a sudden, Elmer heard a deafening roar. He craned his neck, looking even further east, past the plaza. "What was that?" he cried. He looked toward the Arts and Crafts Center, with its complex of shops: jewelry, pottery, rugs, paintings and carvings. No one was moving about. Still too early. People were still sleeping. No signs of movement near the coffee shop, the barbershop, not even the hotel and restaurant. Nothing at the government complex, the clinic or the town hall. "It's Sunday, of course," he muttered.

Then he turned looking to his right, to the west. "Wahee!" he shouted, and jumped up to his feet. A ten-foot-high, hundred-foot-wide wave of mud-colored water was racing toward the town.

⊚

Jon and Raymond woke to see the muddy water pouring through the pueblo's ceremonial grounds without damaging even one of the houses.

Rosie saw the flood from her grandparents' hacienda on the hillside. She had gotten out of bed early, well before her grandmother, and made herself a cup of coffee. When she went out onto the patio to watch the sunrise, now that the storm had passed, she saw floodwaters filling the plaza.

Carmela, Jake and their daughter, Lisa, slept through most of it.

Residents of the trailer park were not so lucky. Ike, Sal, and the girls who had spent the night with them, awoke with hangovers. When Ike looked out the window, he yelled, "Sal, we are floating out of the fucking trailer park!"

⊚

Fr. Raul and Francisca planned to sleep late, having cancelled Sunday morning services because of the rain. They were thrown out of their bed by the rushing waters pounding the foundation of the church. "The church is shaking," Fr. Raul cried and fell to his knees. "Can this be another sign?"

⊚

Elmer followed every twist and turn of the floodwaters as they raced through Santa Rosita. After two hours, the water began to recede, allowing Elmer to start out for home. An hour later, while everybody else was still housebound and waiting for the mud to dry out, Elmer had succeeded in working his way down to the bottom of the mesa. Since the road to town was impossible to navigate, he decided to take an alternative, more precarious route home along a rock outcropping that overlooked the road below. When he finally reached the top of the last rise before his pueblo, Elmer sat down to rest.

⊚   140   ⊚

That is when he saw it.

☉

By Sunday afternoon, word got out around the pueblo that Elmer was back. Since he had been the first person to see the flood, the tribal council called a meeting for that evening. When Elmer entered the council room, a group of excited children swarmed over him. "Tell us about the water, grandfather," they shouted in unison. Although Elmer was caught off guard, he wasn't one to pass up an opportunity to tell a good tale.

"Okay, Okay," he said, without even a smile, "breaking news first."

He mounted the podium, and slowly, with great authority, raised his hand to bring the turmoil to order. Several clusters of children ran up and sat at his feet, while scores of adults moved noisily to find places at the tables scattered around the large room. While he waited, Elmer studied the posters plastered over the walls; they warned about the perils of obesity, diabetes, alcoholism and assorted ailments. We Indians never rush, he reminded himself, savoring the thought. He spotted his family settling in at a table at the back of the room and winked playfully at them. His daughter was busy unpacking the substantial fried chicken dinner that she had made for her family. She saw Elmer's signal and winked back.

When all was quiet, Elmer gazed down at the children.

"So you want to hear about the flood; well, as you all seem to know," he nodded and pointed in the direction of the mesa, "I was on top during the rain." He paused.

"We know!" a young girl called. Elmer ignored the child's remark, but in a respectful way so that people could learn a lesson about how to relate to children. "I was getting ready to come down from the mesa, when I heard this loud noise. I looked down . . . and then I saw a huge wave of water rushing along the bottom of the canyon as quick and straight as an arrow. In front of it was a huge rock blocking the exit of the canyon. You know what the water did?"

"No, grandfather," a chorus of children answered.

"It climbed up on both sides of the canyon wall, almost as if it had legs. Then . . ." He paused, enjoying the sight of the children's eyes growing wider. "It rested for a moment, as if it was thinking where to go next."

As one, the audience tilted forward. A few wide-eyed children, sitting cross-legged and arm-in-arm in front of him, rocked in unison to his every word, like a living sculpture—a grandmother's doll, without the grandmother.

"Water thinks?" a child exclaimed.

"Shhh," the body of the sculpture responded.

He went on, "The water began to whirl around." Pause for effect. "I started to wonder, what is the water doing? Then, with a powerful heave, the water broke the rock apart, poured through it, and ran right down the wash to the old trail." Elmer locked eyes with a teenager; the girl looked away shyly. "Then I realized something . . ."

"What?" yelled a young boy.

"Glad you asked," Elmer smiled and some listeners chuckled. "The water knew exactly what it was doing and where it was going." Pause. The children leaned closer. Elmer spoke slowly and mysteriously. "As if . . . it had a mind . . . of its own."

Pause.

"Oooh," the children moaned. Elmer sped up the tempo of his words. "It turned into a raging river speeding along the old trail, and it ran right through our pueblo." A communal sigh came from the audience. "I saw it," a girl cried out.

"Yes, Ella," Elmer nodded. "From your window, but I saw it from up high on the mesa. I saw it rip through the center of the plaza. And . . ." he paused, "it didn't touch any of our homes. Ella, think about that."

Another audible sigh filled the room.

"Anybody know why?" Elmer asked, and pointed to a small group of young girls together in the far corner. No response.

"Anyone, why do you think?"

"We dunno," answered one of the girls.

"Anybody wanna guess?" Elmer grinned and looked around the room.

"Noooo," the girls mumbled, and several elder women shook their heads.

"Okay!" Elmer took back their attention in his quiet way. "Because the flood was not for our people, we have not been harmed."

A loud sigh of relief rippled through the crowd. Elmer held back a smile and winked again in the direction of Raymond's table. Raymond and Chenoa were both grinning. Raymond's mother shook her head. "For an Indian, he sure knows how to show off."

Elmer continued without taking a breath. "There is more. The floodwaters picked up speed and flew around our ceremonial lodge, raced into the dump, tossed and tumbled all the junk and trash, and dragged a bunch of cars and pick-ups behind it. Then it rushed out of the pueblo and headed toward town."

"Are you sure it really wasn't for us, grandfather?" asked a boy.

"Joe, I told you it was not. You need to listen carefully to the story. That's the way you learn." As Elmer admonished him, Joe lowered his head and let his shoulders slump. He shifted his eyes to the floor.

Elmer changed his tone, "But I see you are listening to me now." He smiled. "Good, Joe. You are a learner." Joe straightened himself up to show them all that he was paying attention now.

"The water turned toward the trailer park, rushed down the roadway, and went through the entrance with such strength that it lifted the trailers off their slabs, floating them all over the place."

"Wow," a little boy cried, and jumped up. "Wow, trailers floating all over the place." The audience snickered, some people laughed aloud. "Sounds like not only trailers floating all over," a man's voice was heard from the back. "Grandfather is in fine form tonight," a woman shouted.

Undaunted, Elmer held up his hand to quiet the people playfully heckling him, while they sipped drinks and crunched peanuts. Elmer was having a great time. Why not? Elders in his tribe have been storytellers since the people came from the center of the earth. And since a person can't be too pompous or act better than others, taking a ribbing was part of it. Everyone knew the rules of the game. Laughing at oneself was the first; don't talk too long was the second.

He continued unfazed. "The main part of the flood went along the road to town, climbed up the blacktop, and went down over the other side until it reached the fountain in the center of the plaza. It held back for a fraction of a moment, so I thought it was finished. But no!"

Silence.

"What happened, grandfather?" a little girl asked.

"The water tore around both sides of the fountain, came together at the back and raced forward toward the steps of the church. I never saw anything like that before in all my life."

The children's eyes grew wide again.

"At the steps, this river of water split in two again, and, roared, I mean roared," Elmer bellowed, "around both sides of the church. It boiled like a pot of tea water along the walls on the right side, and the Padre's residence on the left, as if it was angry about something. Then it came together again at the back of the church and spread into a broad wave that flooded over the old cemetery."

"The cemetery! Did it stop there?" another girl asked hesitantly.

"No, but that is a good question, Anna." The girl beamed. "For a moment, like Anna said, it did seem to stop. But then it dove downward into the ground and disappeared. I asked myself, 'Where is the water going?'"

"Where?" Anna called out, more confidently.

Elmer looked down. "I am not allowed to tell you that part tonight, Anna." The audience groaned.

"Why, grandfather?" the living sculpture shouted, this time in unison.

Elmer smiled. "Because I have been sworn to secrecy. But I can tell you what I did afterward."

Dead silence.

"I looked up at the sky and I said, 'You sure know how to get a guy's attention.'"

Laughter.

"What is the secret?" Anna yelled, now getting rambunctious. Elmer shook his head. "I can't say now. But it doesn't concern us too much. Someday I will be able to tell you the rest of this story, but for now, a promise is a promise. You agree, don't you?"

Respectful nodding. A promise must be kept. Elmer rested. Keep them wanting more.

As if on cue, Flora, secretary of the tribal council, yelled from the back of the room. "So what happened on the mesa that we need to know about?"

Elmer nodded his head up and down to acknowledge her question, but kept his eyes fixed on the children. "Don't be disappointed. Next week I promise another story for you."

He looked around at the audience. "Now I will answer Flora's question. I found something special on the mesa that I believe is a message for us. However, I do not want to say any more about it until I go back in clear weather with Raymond and study the signs. Then we will tell you all about it."

"Is it for us?" asked Anna, now on her feet, waving her hands and jumping up and down.

"Yes, Anna."

"From the Great Spirit?" Anna was excited.

"I am sure, Anna. The Great Spirit has been very frisky lately. That is all for now. I gotta go somewhere . . ."

"Is it about the secret?" Anna called, and the crowd roared.

"Yes, Anna," Elmer answered solemnly. "It's about the secret."

"Yeah. Grandfather has to go to a meeting at the church later," shouted a male voice from the back of the room, "with the Padre."

Elmer ignored the remark and walked off before someone read his mind.

@

Raymond drove Elmer to the church meeting after his talk at the tribal council. "So what's this about a secret?" Raymond asked

"Well," Elmer grinned slyly, "You keep a secret as good as me, right?" Raymond laughed. "I guess. So?"

Elmer nodded proudly and cleared his throat. "OK. Let's see how much I can tell you before we get to the church. Where did I leave off at the meeting? Okay, after the flood passed through the old cemetery, I saw a waterspout shoot out of the ground. I would say about thirty feet high into the air, give or take a few feet. And it carried a big, square block with it. The block tumbled down and landed near the back wall."

"Grandfather," Raymond asked incredulously, "you saw a block shot out of the ground?"

"Yes," Elmer replied. "Like a missile. So, of course, I needed a closer look. I was at the overlook, where I could see the trailer park. What a mess! All of the trailers were off their pads, scattered all over. The trailer people were trying to move around but they were stuck in the mud. Some up to their knees. That was something to see. How are those people gonna' get their trailers back on the slabs?" Elmer paused. "Am I getting off the point?"

Raymond nodded yes, but said that was all right because he wanted to hear all the details.

"OK, grandson, Tell me if I am wearing out your ears," he laughed. "I have a lot of words stored up. Well . . . I walked carefully down the hillside, crossed the road and headed for the old cemetery. The sun was very hot, so I sat down in the shade of a pinon tree to cool off. I looked up into the canopy of the tree and asked, 'What do you think shot out of the ground?' It looked like a big square box to me. Was it a coffin? The tree didn't know."

Raymond laughed softly. Grandfather at his best, he thought.

"After I cooled off, I walked over to the cemetery, and went through the arch. Another mess. The gravestones were all over the place; some leaned against the far wall where the water had left them, others were piled on top of each other. It looked like someone threw a deck of playing cards in the air, and let them fall wherever. The block was lying on its side in the far left corner of the cemetery. When I got close, I saw it was rectangular, made of wood, very hard, almost petrified. It was several feet high and wide, and in good shape. The three surfaces exposed to the air were almost dry, but caked all over with dirt and mud, and shreds of waxy cloth. I could see some designs on the surfaces. I gathered some reeds and short sticks, tied them together and made a brush to clean away some of the dirt. One side of the block had holes near each corner. On one corner, there was a round piece of wood, like a peg, sticking out of one of the holes. It looked like it was once attached to something, and broke off."

They were nearing the church. Elmer wanted to finish his story so he asked Raymond to slow down.

"I need to finish," Elmer said. "I saw an indentation, about a foot square, on the top of the block. I tried to push down on it but nothing happened. I scraped away some of the mud on the underside of the block and made out several lines, about two feet long, that criss-crossed each other. After more scraping, I saw that the lines were deeply etched into the wood. There were figures on each side of the block, and writing too. I tried to tip the block up on its end to check out the side lying in the mud, but the block was too heavy to lift. Then I remembered there was a hose at the entrance of the cemetery. I dragged it over and washed and scraped away some of the crusty dirt. The lines etched into the wood came together to make a six-pointed star with writing in the center. I wiped off the sides of the block as best I could and saw an outline of several carved figures. A woman wearing a scarf around her head and a man dressed in a long coat were on one side. There was an old, stooped man with a long beard on the other side. He was holding a staff, like people use for herding sheep. All of the figures looked up toward the top of the block. There was writing around the figures; I couldn't read it but the letters were very striking. From an old language that contained much power. I thought that they may have come from the center of the earth. Then I looked up and saw Fr. Raul and Francisca running toward me."

By this time, Raymond had arrived at the entrance to the church.

Elmer clucked his tongue in regret. "That's it for now. They are waiting for me, so I'll finish my story later." Elmer got out of the car and walked up the church steps.

@

Fr. Raul and Francisca had been sound asleep when the flood hit. The force of the water battered the outside wall of the kitchen, knocked plates off shelves, shattered bottles and scattered the pots and pans. After the initial shock, they ran into the church to inspect the damage and were stunned to find the statue of Rosita lying on her side next to the altar. Her old, rusted metal pedestal lay twisted and broken about twelve feet away.

"Rosita," wailed Francisca, who ran to her side. "She's unhurt, thank God! She could have been destroyed!"

She stood silent for a moment, then cried, "Padre, her eyes . . . they are looking right at me."

Fr. Raul ran over to her side. "I see, and now they are closing," he mumbled, then fell to his knees and crossed himself.

Francisca said, "Her eyes, Padre, did I see right? They moved. Yes? No? Yes?"

"Yes," Fr. Raul answered with a pat on her arm. "I believe it is another sign. Remember, the message."

Francisca nodded. "You mean that things are going to happen? Will we be saved?"

Fr. Raul smiled.

Francisca cried, "We must stand her up. But she is too heavy for the two of us. I will stuff a pillow under her head." She ran to get a pillow from the nearest pew. When she returned, they strained to lift the statue just high enough so that Francisca could put the pillow under her head. Rosita's eyes opened and closed for a brief moment.

Fr. Raul whispered, "Is she looking for something?"

"Could be," echoed Francisca. "But what?"

"I don't know." Fr. Raul looked up to the heavens.

"Do you think this has to do with your message?" Francisca asked adoringly. "Perhaps," he said tenderly. "Perhaps." Francisca glowed.

After making Rosita comfortable, Fr. Raul proceeded to clean up the debris around her. In so doing he glanced up at the bottom of the slab of wood attached to her feet, and noticed four holes, one near each corner. "What is this?" he wondered. He had never noticed such a thing before, but of course, he had never looked there before, either.

Francisca was at the window and uttered a loud cry. "Padre, Padre, Come quick, there is somebody in the old cemetery. Oh, the gravestones are scattered all over the place."

Fr. Raul ran over to the window. "Oh, my God!" he exclaimed and crossed himself.

"Are the dead going to rise, Padre?" Francisca cried.

"No, Francisca, they are dead. But who is that out there?"

"I don't know, I can only see his back." She was crossing herself repeatedly when Fr. Raul grabbed her by the hand and pulled her toward the door.

"We must go and see."

Francisca recognized Elmer immediately. "Grandfather, what are you doing here? Are you okay?"

Elmer smiled. "Sure, just drying out."

Fr. Raul exclaimed. "What's that?"

Elmer beckoned him over. "This block of wood shot out of the ground."

"Shot out of the ground!" Fr. Raul and Francisca cried in unison.

"Yeah, like a missile. I was up on the mesa for five days." He waved his hand in that direction. "Early this morning I saw the floodwaters coming toward the cemetery and this object came shooting up out of the ground. Something is up."

"What's up?" Francisca asked.

A slight grin appeared at the left corner of Elmer's mouth. "Something's up. That's a joke. Things don't shoot up out of the ground for nothing,"

"What could it be?" Fr. Raul asked.

Elmer shrugged his shoulders. "It's very old, with carving on it, and a place on one end that may open. The other end has a star on it. And there are carvings of people on the sides. I do not know what could be on the side it is resting on. It's too heavy for me to lift by myself."

Fr. Raul bent down and examined the odd-shaped star, the figures and the writing. Then he turned pale.

"Padre, you okay?" Francisca asked. "Do you know what this is?"

"Madre de Dios," he muttered. "Holy Mother of God! How could this be?" Fr. Raul kept repeating, "Madre de Dios," several times.

Elmer told him to grab the top end of the block. "Help me tip this over and we can see what is on this side. Then I got to get on home. I have a meeting to get to."

By lifting and pushing, the three of them managed to tip the block to a standing position. They could not see much at first, since large clumps of mud covered the side that had been in the ground. Without saying a word, they began to clean away the dirt: Fr. Raul with the makeshift brush, Elmer with the knife, and Francisca with the hose. It took about ten minutes of scrubbing to see that this side was unlike the other three sides. The carving on this side projected far out from the block. After more scrubbing and scraping, they stepped back to view the carving in its entirety. When Fr. Raul and Francisca saw it, they fell to their knees and started praying.

The priest moaned softly, "Can this be the message? That our world is to be turned upside down?"

Francisca grabbed his arm. "What do you mean?" But he was so dumbstruck that he could not answer.

Francisca tried to console him. "It doesn't matter if you know or not. Getting a message means you were chosen, you were spoken to . . . a message is a message."

Elmer backed off and watched in silence. There is going to be a hot time in the old town tonight, he thought to himself.

⊚

"Calm, Padre, calm," Francisca whispered, and gently stroked his arm.

Fr. Raul could not hear what she said for the pounding of his heart. "A minute," he motioned to both Elmer and Francisca. "Give me a minute."

He swung around, moved several paces away, and then turned around hesitantly, as if he were almost afraid to look at the block. After he ran his eyes over the wood surface, one section at a time, he walked over to Elmer until he stood face-to-face with him. He looked intently into his eyes. When Elmer returned the gaze, he took the opportunity to explore the depths of Fr. Raul's soul. Yes, he decided, the Padre is a 'human being.' That is good.

When Fr. Raul broke eye contact with Elmer, he suddenly became aware of a force coursing through his veins. A sense of purpose began to stir in his mind. "Francisca," he commanded, "We need to fetch Patron, and Esther, too."

He pressed his index finger over his lips, and looked around furtively. "Don't say a word to anyone else about this, Francisca. Do not even look like you want to tell anyone. Okay?"

Francisca nodded in agreement.

"Grandfather, I need your promise, too."

⊚ 150 ⊚

Elmer nodded to indicate he would do his best. "This is not all there is," Elmer added.

Fr. Raul looked at him intently. "What do you mean?" he asked. As preoccupied as he was, Fr. Raul always listened to others. That was part of his gift of listening.

Elmer proceeded to tell him about the figures he had discovered on the mesa ledge, and said he was going to tell his people about them tonight. But he really needed go back to study them more deeply with Raymond.

"There is a message there for us. Like this is for you," he said.

Fr. Raul raised his eyebrows when he heard the word 'message.'

"So you think this could be a message?" Fr. Raul asked, and pointed to the block.

"Why do you think it shot up out of the earth? And why now? The messages are coming like crazy." Elmer grinned. "Our job is to figure them out."

Fr. Raul's eyes widened. "How do you know?"

"I just know. That is my job."

The priest felt overjoyed that Elmer had confirmed his own feelings about the message.

"Do you know what these figures mean? What they could be telling us?"

"Sure," Elmer teased. They are going to keep you jumping for a while, he thought, but he did not say it. He spoke reverently, "This block of wood is the message. I have seen these designs elsewhere."

"I know, grandfather. Designs that go way back."

Elmer agreed. "Yes. I have seen similar marks on the bottom of those gravestones over there. Come over to the wall with me." Elmer led Fr. Raul to the far wall where the toppled gravestones lay scattered. "Look at the bottom of this one here, buried under the sand for many years."

The priest looked out of the corner of his eyes and held his breath. He did not want to look. Elmer waited until he got Padre's full attention. "See. A six-pointed star on the bottom. And the writing. Yes, look over there. That one says 1745."

"I see," replied Fr. Raul glumly.

Elmer grinned wryly, "This could upset your religious friends."

Fr. Raul tightened his lips, but being a man with a sense of irony, he could not hold back a faint smile. "Depends," he said. "Who you tell . . . or who finds out."

Elmer met his smile. "That's up to you."

Fr. Raul knew Elmer was enjoying himself, but not in a malicious way. What a strong person in that frail body, he thought.

Elmer knew it was time to leave the Padre alone. He was thinking, the Great Spirit is on the move. As the old man turned to leave, he saw Francisca and Patron coming through the cemetery archway. Francisca was holding an armful of newspapers. Esther came shuffling close behind. Elmer greeted them, and decided to stay to witness the action. He sat down on one of the large overturned gravestones, now being warmed by the sun.

"Ah! Feels good," he felt a chill and rubbed the warmth into his body.

Francisca dropped the papers, straightened her clothes, and rearranged her long hair. "Padre, Rosie was at the house when I got there. She said she wants to come over too. I didn't tell her anything."

"Ay! Now there are six of us that know," Fr. Raul moaned.

"Know what?" Patron asked. The priest answered that he would soon find out. "Francisca did not tell us anything," Patron said, "she just told us to come quick."

Francisca smiled proudly.

Fr. Raul acknowledged her, pointed to the block, and announced, "This," he paused, "came out of the ground after the flood."

Patron asked what it was. Fr. Raul motioned that he should look closer and Patron walked around the block slowly, inspecting every detail. Then he stopped cold in his tracks and motioned to Fr. Raul to come over.

"This is unbelievable," he whispered.

Esther hurried over to join them. When she saw what was on the block, she cried. "Dios mio! Oh my God, Ruben. Look at that!" She grabbed Patron's arm to steady herself.

Francisca grabbed Fr. Raul's arm, so the four of them were huddled close together.

"Kneel," said Esther. "We must kneel."

"That's why I brought the newspapers," Francisca smiled a self-satisfied smile.

She carefully spread the newspapers on the ground and Fr. Raul helped Patron and Esther to kneel in front of the three-dimensional relief. The carving was in the form of a cross, but unlike any they had ever seen before. The vertical beam of the cross protruded more than two inches from the side of the block, traversing its full length, top to bottom. The horizontal crossbeam stood out two and a half inches at both ends, and narrowed down to one inch in depth at the point where they joined the vertical beam. The changing depth of the crossbeam made it appear to be reaching out toward the viewer like a pair of embracing arms. Two delicate figures were carved into the bottom of the vertical shaft, a woman on the left, and a man on the right, both gazing up toward a six-pointed star, in one-inch relief, placed where the beams crossed. The star bore faint traces of gold paint. Bits and pieces of teardrop-shaped splotches of crimson flowed out from its center, and down to the lowest point of the star, onto the vertical beam of the cross and into the eyes of the two figures.

Fr. Raul, Francisca, Esther and Patron could only stare, transfixed by the sight. Esther broke the silence and pointed out that the expressions on the faces of the two figures appeared to be changing. Patron wanted to hear none of that. "It's the sun that's moving."

Esther interrupted him, "Well, Ruben . . ." but stopped herself short. Not here, she thought, and changed the subject. "My leg is cramping, I need to get up."

Fr. Raul responded quickly and, with Francisca's help, pulled Esther and Patron to their feet. At that moment, a beam of sunlight clearly outlined the indentation on the top of the block. "Patron, look here," Fr. Raul said, "from this angle."

Patron mentioned that it looked like a small door. "Should we open it?" he asked.

Francisca and the priest stared at one another in silence. Esther was quiet as well.

"Do we?" asked Fr. Raul. Patron stared at Esther. She nodded in the affirmative, but Patron disagreed, "Not now. Enough for one day. We need to consider this one step at a time."

Francisca looked at Esther. Answers were needed, and Esther was the expert in such matters. Grandfather, too, of course.

"Where did this, whatever it is, come from?" Francisca asked.

"From long ago," Esther answered. Was Patron thinking the same thing she was? Of course, she already knew the answer. Esther smiled. "Now, Padre, Ruben, what are you going to do with this?"

Patron's eyes started to burn. He had to make a conscious effort not to squint, but he couldn't help himself. When he did, he saw a fuzzy image of Rosie hurrying toward him through the archway. She waved to Elmer, who now was reclining peacefully on a gravestone, chewing an Osha root. Without looking, he waved back on cue.

"Why is grandfather over there all alone?" Rosie asked Francisca.

"He's tired," Francisca replied.

"Sorry it took me so long to get here. I was trying to get through to Jon. The telephones are still out. Nothing is going right today. I guess I will have to walk over to the pueblo . . ." Then she noticed the block and the newspapers around it. "What's that?" she asked.

Fr. Raul was quick to brush off her question. "Nothing Rosie, just some of the mess here." He turned toward the cemetery entrance and said it was time to go. "It's okay Rosie, everything is under control. You do not have to stay. Better we all get out of the sun now."

Rosie walked closer to the block and spotted the carving. "My God, that is beautiful," she gasped. "Look at that. A cross and a star, and the star is bleeding, and the people below are looking up at it and, and, they seem sad. They are sad. They are so sad! Oh, it makes me cry." She began to sniffle and Francisca joined her.

Fr. Raul moved in front of Rosie, but too late. She was about to let loose her usual barrage of questions. "What is this thing? Where does it come from? Who are these people? What is this writing? Why is there a six-pointed star on the crucifix? Why are these people so sad?"

"Very sad," Francisca agreed, and blew her nose loudly.

"Yes, very, very sad," Esther added, also teary-eyed.

Rosie cried, "Look at those faces, where did this come from, Padre? "

"Shot right up out of the ground," Elmer shouted.

Fr. Raul knew he had no hope now of discouraging Rosie's questions. "We can call the university; I've got a friend there . . ." she was eager to find answers.

He motioned for Rosie to slow down. "Please, Rosie, this turned up a only couple of hours ago. No university, no outsiders," he urged.

"All right," Rosie answered. "You know I have more important things on my mind anyway."

Fr. Raul nodded knowingly. "Of course. You need not bother about this. We will call a meeting of the church executive board tonight to discuss what it is and what to do with it. Maybe we should just bury it and let in rest in peace."

"Or not!" Rosie added, "I'm a member of the board. I'll come to the meeting. This may be something historic."

"Whatever," Fr. Raul mumbled. His face was beet red. "Let's all go home and leave everything be. There is a lot of cleaning up to do. I will arrange an emergency meeting of the church board for tonight to talk this over. You can all come."

"But I am not on the board," Esther said.

He reflected for a moment. "Technically you are right. Okay, Abuelita will not come tonight. I will ask the board members if you can come to the next meeting. Patron will tell you what happens tonight. But no word to anyone. Promise?"

Esther nodded. "Sure."

Fr. Raul added that he wanted grandfather to come as well because it was he who had discovered the wooden block. When Francisca mentioned that Elmer was not on the church board, the priest merely told her that since Elmer wasn't Catholic, the rules do not apply to him. "Okay with you, grandfather?" he called. "Francisca will let you know what time."

Elmer got up, signaled his agreement, waved goodbye and walked off without a word. Fr. Raul and the others began to file out, when Rosie announced, "I'll be along soon. I want to look at the gravestones. My relatives are piled up all over the place. I'll fetch Jon to help me clean up." Fr. Raul bellowed. "Not Jon. The boys will clean up," he said firmly. "Leave it to my workers. Pablo will be here any minute with his crew. Rosie, whatever you do, don't say anything to Jon. I beg you. I am going to cover up the block as soon as you all leave."

"I understand," Rosie said. "But I don't agree. Jon should see this."

"He is not one of us," Fr. Raul was surprised at what he had blurted out and apologized when he saw he had hurt Rosie. "Sorry," he mumbled. "I didn't mean it that way. I mean, this is a lot to handle; I want to keep it just between us. Please."

"Jon is us . . . to me," Rosie said softly.

Fr. Raul scolded her. "Rosie, remember, when I said to do nothing? Maybe this is part of it. Bringing Jon here is not doing nothing."

His frustration touched Rosie's heart. She tried again. "Jon knows how to keep his mouth shut. He is a doctor . . ." She interrupted herself and reflected for a moment, "I am going to walk over to the pueblo to meet Jon, Padre. But tell me first, do you really believe that what is happening here has something to do with what you told me . . . about doing nothing?"

Fr. Raul sighed and half-closed his eyes. "We need time to see. Now please do as I say." As he spoke, images of his message, and the memory of Rosita opening her eyes, rushed into his mind. He did not know why, but he suddenly called out Francisca's name. She was walking ahead with Esther and Patron. She turned. During a long, quiet moment, they drank from each other's eyes until they were filled, then he followed her out.

Patron stopped under the archway and stretched his arms skyward. He shuffled his feet back and forth slightly, as if he wanted to grow roots. One by one, he tensed and relaxed his arm, leg and back muscles. When he finished, he stretched up straight, then stood still, like a warrior about to don his armor. The figure of his hero, Don Quixote de la Mancha, flashed before his mind.

Esther came up behind him and locked arms. She felt her skin tingle. No question at all, the spirit was moving. Patron was more filled with it now than when he woke up this morning.

9

The Name of God

Rosie took the path to the pueblo. Her mind was racing; when Fr. Raul said she should "wait," did he already know that mysterious forces were at work? Was Rosita involved? After all, I asked her for help. Why was she always looking up at the sky? The path was deeply rutted so she had to keep her eyes on the ground. Fifteen minutes later, she heard Jon call. She looked up; there he was, weaving his way towards her. She aimed herself at his open arms and hurried to him as fast as she could.

"Our first public hug," Jon kissed her.

"And more," she kissed back.

Jon pulled back and looked her square in the eyes. "What's this? You are all smiles. What's going on?"

"A lot," she smiled coquettishly. "Don't know exactly what, but something is happening."

Jon nuzzled her face with his open palm. "Mysteries, mysteries."

Rosie nuzzled him back.

Jon hugged her again. "The pueblo grounds are a mess. The water turned up a jumble of pots, tools, arrowheads and whatever. Everyone is out there picking up stuff."

"Tell me about that later, Right now you got to come with me to the cemetery," she bubbled.

Jon looked confused. "What's going on? I just ran into grandfather, he seemed well, 'up,' for him I mean. He said something about talking with his people tonight, and a meeting after at the church, and going to Red Mesa with Raymond tomorrow to check out some drawings on a rock."

Rosie tugged at his sleeve. "Later, later. Come with me now. I have something to show you. I promised not to tell anyone but . . ."

Jon interrupted, "Then don't tell me."

"See for yourself first, then tell me if I did right," she glowed.

They climbed over the cemetery wall, and Jon stopped short. "Maybe we should not go in," he said, "some people might not want me here."

"You are going to be surprised at what, and who, is here," she laughed. Rosie pointed to the block on the far wall, now was covered with a blue tarpaulin. Padre worked fast, she thought, "Over there, that's what you need to see." Rosie steered him toward the block and removed the covering.

Jon circled the block slowly, inspecting each figure carefully.

"My God," he shouted, "isn't that something? A cross with a six-pointed star at its center."

Rosie smirked, "Look at the people at the bottom of the cross."

Jon kneeled down for a closer look. "They are looking up at the cross and the star," he stopped. "They seem to be crying." His words caught in his throat and he swallowed hard. "Who, where did this come from?"

Rosie had never seen Jon so moved before. She sidled closer, circled her two arms around his waist, and laid her head on his shoulder. She felt him tremble slightly and enjoyed it. That's his soul. She whispered, "Maybe someone from long ago wants to help us."

Jon started rubbing his forehead to clear his mind. "What do you mean?"

She placed her finger over his lips. "Come, there is more I have to show you. Get the hose."

Jon's incredulity had rendered him more compliant than usual, so he dragged the hose over to a pile of gravestones and rinsed them while Rosie wiped away the mud. This quiet respite allowed him to regain his composure.

"Rosie sweetheart, I am fighting a mad urge to spray you." he said playfully, swinging the stream of water close to Rosie, "and I am losing . . ."

"Don't you dare. I'll get mad," she said, feigning anger. He capitulated, but reluctantly.

"You owe me one."

"Be serious," Rosie pointed to a six-foot tall tombstone lying face up in the mud. "Come and look," she enthused, "this one dates back to the 1600's. And this one, I have never seen this one before. It must have been completely buried." She crouched down and ran a finger over a blurred name and date. "Can you make this out? This is very old, great- great- great, who knows how many greats. I can just about make out the name, Alonzo. That's Poppa's name! The date looks like, looks like, 16 . . . something. Look here at the part of the stone that was buried. The writing is clear."

Jon dropped down next to her. 'There is a six-pointed star here too, and this writing. I recognize it."

Rosie laughed, "Padre is right. Something is happening."

Jon was at a loss for words.

She laughed. "I guess you can do anything you want in this cemetery after all." Rosie nestled in his arms and became so soft she could feel her bones melt. "This is fantastic!"

Jon wet his finger and traced the words on the stone. "This is Hebrew. It says Yahweh, the Jewish name for God. These are the same as the letters carved over the front door of the cathedral in Santa Fe. But I don't know the other words."

Rosie peeked out from the nest of his embrace. She raised herself up slowly and languorously and walked over to a wall of small headstones that were still standing upright. The soil underneath had been almost completely washed away so they seemed to be suspended in air. "Look here, Jon, the same six-pointed stars, all on the Alonzo's, and these other names, they have stars on them too. See here, on the very bottom of the stones. They were buried so no one could see them."

My father told me about buried gravestone," Jon said. "He showed me pictures of others, all around the state."

Suddenly they heard, "Hey, hey, leave those stones be." Fr. Raul was running toward them waving his arms frantically. "Rosie, for God's sake, what is Doc doing here? I told you . . ."

He scowled angrily, whirled around, and beckoned to Pablo who was behind him riding astride a small tractor, to come ahead. Then, with a hammering motion of one fist in his other palm, he signaled for Pablo to nail the "Quarantine" sign he had just prepared to the top of the entrance arch to the cemetery.

"Pablo," he shouted over the noise of the tractor, "when you finish, get your crew in here and put these stones back where they belong, and quickly. Make sure to sink them deep." Pablo flipped him a thumbs up, and waved to Rosie and Jon.

Fr. Raul turned to them. "For God's sake Rosie, Doc, keep what you have seen here to yourselves, please. I don't know what we've got on our hands. I will try to keep things quiet by warning people away from here. I am saying it's for sanitary reason. Doc, I want you to agree."

Rosie interrupted with a grimace, "Sanitary reasons?"

"I know, I know. It is not exactly true. Well, it could be true, the ground being turned over and all that. I want to keep this as quiet as possible until the meeting tonight."

"Sanitary reasons," Jon smiled. "Sure, I'll back you up."

Fr. Raul thanked Jon with a sigh of relief. What is Doc thinking? He wondered. Is he gloating over my predicament? No, he decided. He is not that kind of man.

"Padre," Rosie asked Fr. Raul sweetly, "Look at the gravestones. These names and these stars. Doesn't this say that our ancestors were Jews? Can this be the miracle I asked Rosita for? Do you know what this discovery could mean for Jon and me?"

Fr. Raul moaned. "Ay, Rosie, first things first."

"Well, it's true. Right?" Rosie persevered. "You need to say so."

Fr. Raul's face reddened. "Don't jump to conclusions. Not all of our ancestors . . . I am Catholic from way back, from Mexico."

Rosie was not going to let him off the hook. She was forming her plan and needed to know where he stood. "That doesn't mean anything. These ancestors buried here, some of them came from Mexico too. I studied the history of Mexico." Fr. Raul reached down and felt for his flask. Thank God, he had it. But he thought twice about imbibing. Things were different now, hasn't he been directly called to serve? No drinking, he ordered himself with an unusually strong, and new, inner voice. He would need all his faculties to assert his clerical authority in this matter.

"Rosie," he said, in his newfound voice, "We will talk everything over at the meeting tonight. Doc, my son, can I call you my son?"

Jon smiled. "If you wish," he shrugged his shoulders.

Fr. Raul looked him in the eyes imploringly. "I need you to keep this to yourself"

Jon acquiesced respectfully. "Privileged information, I understand and agree. Can I tell Raymond? He'll have something to say."

Rosie interrupted. "Padre, I am sure grandfather already told him."

Fr. Raul slumped in frustration. "True. Those people have no secrets between them."

Jon laughed. He just had to say it, in spite of what Fr. Raul was feeling. "Imagine, Jews, sleeping all around us."

"And maybe above ground too." Rosie laughed loudly. "Imagine that." She grabbed Jon's arm. "A lot of people here are going to need a shrink when they find this out. Especially Ike." She laughed again.

Fr. Raul moaned again. "Not funny, Rosie. That's not the attitude we need."

"Maybe not for you, Padre," Rosie could not stop laughing even though she felt sympathetic for the Fr. Raul's quandary. He wasn't the enemy, she decided. Better to let him figure it out. "So what now?"

"Pray and praise God," Fr. Raul understood the irony of the situation. "It will be what it will be," he said forlornly. Then, to Rosie and Jon's surprise, he tossed his head back and addressed the sky. "You called me to do a special assignment." Then he added, "Ay! Let it be what it will be. Rosie, Jon, you two go home and Rosie, please, for now, for God's and my sake, keep this under your hat until tonight." He smiled at them, "You know, I am not who I was yesterday."

Rosie bounced toward Fr. Raul and kissed his cheek, then happily grabbed Jon by the arm and swaggered off. "Whatever you say, Padre. See you tonight. Make sure to get a good nap."

❦

After Elmer left the cemetery and sauntered into the pueblo, he found hordes of excited people bustling around the central plaza. They were foraging for artifacts unearthed by the flood. One six-year-old ran up to his mother brandishing an old turquoise neckpiece that he had pulled out of a large chunk of mud.

"Very good," his mother smiled. "This is very old. Keep it for your grandchildren." When she saw Elmer coming, she dangled it for him to see, and alerted the others.

"So?" An older woman asked Elmer, "How did you make out up there?" She pointed to the mesa.

"Tell you tonight" Elmer answered, "Wanna hint?" She nodded. "Something is up. We will see what the Great Spirit is trying to tell us."

"What happened over at the old cemetery?" shouted a young mother sitting in a lawn chair, nursing her infant.

"A lot, but secret for now," Elmer grinned. "I'll tell you what I can at the meeting tonight. Bring the kids. Right now I need some food and a nap."

Raymond and Chenoa hurried over to him. "Grandfather, are you well?" Chenoa, a worrier by nature, peered at him with compassion and concern as if she was waiting for bad news. Elmer was very fond of her. Such a good human being, he thought, always thinks of everyone else before herself. "Very, very well, Chenoa," he answered.

Raymond laughed. "That means very well!"

"But the rain, grandfather . . ." Chenoa persisted. Was it possible that grandfather had not even one complaint that needed tending?

"Don't need a bath for a week," Elmer laughed. He turned to Raymond. "I found two rock drawings on the mesa I've never seen before. We need to go to see them tomorrow early, and figure them out, O.K?" Elmer's remark filled Raymond with pride; he grinned and glanced at Chenoa. She smiled. His look said, "See what a great guy you married, grandfather wants me on the mesa with him."

"Don't get too puffed up," Elmer kidded, and mumbled a brief prayer. "The Great Spirit is awake and on the move."

Raymond's expression turned grave, "About the casino issue . . .?"

Elmer pointed up to the mesa. "Answers are up there, we will see if your college education helps us to figure them out."

Chenoa lovingly locked her arms with theirs and guided them across the plaza to Raymond's parents. They were happily lounging in front of their house. His father was scanning the plaza with a pair of binoculars and spotted them. When Elmer came within hearing distance, Raymond's father laughed loudly and called to him,

"Grandfather, you look like a hungry coyote. Oh, oh, sorry, I am looking through the wrong side of the glasses."

Raymond's mother laughed loudly. "Ho, back in one piece. I was worried. Are you tired, hungry?"

"Both, but in reverse." Elmer embraced her. "One thing at a time. For right now, first the beef, then the bed."

◎

After Jon and Rosie left the cemetery, Fr. Raul hastily re-wrapped the block and directed Pablo and his crew to winch it up onto the flatbed attached to the tractor. This done, Pablo drove the tractor around to the front of the church, where they hauled the block up the church stairs on to the landing, loaded it on a dolly, and wheeled it into the church. "Behind the altar," Fr. Raul ordered breathlessly, "Keep it covered, don't let Rosita see it."

Pablo nodded in approval; he was thinking, this is big stuff, and winked assuringly to his workers, all relatives of one sort or the other. They were scrutinizing the recent events carefully. "So far, Padre is doing it right," they silently agreed.

In the meantime, Francisca was nervously calling the church executive board members requesting their urgent attendance at a 'top secret' meeting.

Be firm and not too pushy, she cautioned herself, knowing they would rather speak to Padre directly about such important things. She paused in her thoughts to smile, but I will have to do.

Fr. Raul and Patron have selected each member of the church board executive committee to represent different constituencies of the congregation. Patron, for example, speaks for the senior, old guard, and the political and business members of the community.

Paz represents the most devout churchwomen, the bible study group and charismatic members of the church. She oversees a group called Saints Alive offering intercessory prayer for those in need.

Rosie was the official representative of the younger generation before she went away to school, and, as time allows, remains involved in youth activities.

Carmela stands for, in her words, "the modern women in the church, and feminist causes that sometimes put me at odds with Fr. Raul and the Pope." In spite of her feminist bent, she and Fr. Raul work very well together, especially when it comes to raising funds for charitable causes.

Esther also participates. She originally declined an invitation to join the executive committee because she felt that "people would say that too many of my family have their nose in everybody's business." However, she is often invited to attend meetings dealing with community health and spiritual issues, as a non-voting, highly respected consultant. In other words, she is 'there' but not 'there.' A common way of getting around administrative corners in Santa Rosita.

Vincente and Vickie Lopez represent the interests of low income and rural parishioners living on 'the edge,' economically struggling folks who live on small farms, in trailers and the like. The Lopez's are descended from a long line of traditional Catholics. They are related to Pablo Montoya, (the keeper of the church) who is descended from an especially zealous branch of the Montoya family. In addition to his church duties, Pablo also serves as the church liaison to those in the 'non-conforming' part of the community who congregate in Diego's bar on the outskirts of town. This fringe element includes the chronically unemployed, drug dealers, and criminals going to, or having just left, prison.

@

Francisca was greatly enjoying her newfound authority. "Informal dress," she told everyone, "meeting starts at nine o'clock sharp. And tell no one. I can't answer any questions because I am sworn to secrecy." Francisca's enjoyment was cut short after she interrupted Carmela's afternoon beauty nap.

"Who is this," Carmela asked sleepily. "Francisca? What is going on, Francisca? Why are you calling me during siesta?"

When Francisca started to explain to her about the meeting, Carmela interrupted her to ask why Padre didn't call her personally.

"Padre is very busy," Francisca answered, and explained that the meeting was being held later than usual because there will be fewer people on the streets, thus better for secrecy. "Padre said not to tell anyone about the meeting, except for Jake," she added with some hint of authority. "Grandfather is going to be there too."

"Grandfather?" Carmela repeated.

"Yes, grandfather," Francisca said his name slowly and secretively, "After he finishes up at the pueblo. I can't say any more. You will understand later. Now I have to go. I must call others. See you later." It felt good when she hung up.

After finishing her calls, Francisca realized that she had an unexpected opportunity to get directly involved in Fr. Raul's affairs. After all, she thought, wasn't I one of the first to see the block? Didn't I stand next to it with Patron, Esther, Grandfather, Rosie and Padre? Even if I am technically only a housekeeper, aren't I more than that? Don't I have the right to see that the meeting goes well for Fr. Raul, perhaps even participate?

"Yes," she told herself. "I won't ask others what to do this time, I will go ahead and do what I think is necessary. Padre is under such pressure that some cheering up will do him good, and I will do it." With this self-accorded mandate to 'up' her status, she set to work preparing the field of action. First, she draped the altar with a blue silk, gold-trimmed cloth. Rosita's favorite colors. This done, she rushed out to purchase coffee and refreshments, and special ingredients for a 'surprise' she planned for the meeting. It's like inviting people to my home, she thought, smiling proudly. Maybe a blessing time is upon us. She had heard about such times.

At eight-forty-five that evening, Fr. Raul walked out to the landing at the top of the church steps to await the arrival of the board members. The night was oddly quiet. Even the cicadas were silent. Unusual for this time of year. Must be the flood, he thought. He looked up at the clear night sky, breathed in the cool clear air, and began to count the stars, one way he often prayed. A wave of questions rolled through his mind. How will the church board feel about the block? Would they be willing to face up to what it means, if it means what I think it does? Will they want to stifle its meaning and bury it again? And what about Rosita herself? Obviously, this block is related to her. What is she feeling? Certainly, she wants to be complete again. What are the carvings about, the figures and the writing on the block? What is inside the block, and why did it show up now, at this specific time?

"Oh God!" he cried, "Give me strength. You have placed a great responsibility upon me. What will happen if La Tierra finds out? What if, God forbid, the story gets out to the press, or the university, or worse if the church authorities hear of it? Reporters and researchers, and monsignors and bishops will swarm all over us. Our lives will never be the same."

He paused from his entreaties when he spotted Patron, Paz and Rosie hurrying down the hill towards the church. Then he continued his entreaty, but quickly, "And Rosie. What does this have to do with her? God, what are you telling me?" He rubbed his forehead hard. "Maybe I should call the Bishop . . ."

Carmela pulled up in her new SUV just as Patron, Paz, and Rosie began to climb the stairs to the landing in front of the church. Vincente and Vickie, who were tailing Carmela in their pick-up truck, rattled and bumped to a halt behind her.

"Okay to park here, Padre?" Vincente called to Fr. Raul who flashed thumbs up. Raymond pulled up into the cloud of black smoke pouring out of Vincente's exhaust pipe, then backed up quickly, and proceeded forward swerving around Vincente's truck. He parked in front of Carmela. Elmer threw open the right front door of the car and emerged coughing.

"What are you cooking in there?" he shouted to Vincente. Everyone laughed.

Raymond waved to Fr. Raul. "Pretty prompt for Indians, eh?"

Fr. Raul bantered back. "Indian time disappeared with television."

Raymond laughed. "Naw, college did it to me. Hey, take good care of my grandfather. He talked more today than in the past three years."

Elmer grumbled. "I talk when there is something to say."

"We will watch out for him," agreed Fr. Raul with a grin.

Raymond got back into his car. "I'll be at the Cantina. Call when the meeting is finished."

Carmela shouted, "I'll drive grandfather back, no problem."

Raymond answered. "Okay, thanks. Appreciate it, Carmela. Okay, grandfather?"

"Sure, she is prettier than you," Elmer grinned.

Raymond smiled to himself. Grandfather is certainly frisky tonight.

Carmela fluttered her eyelids, placed her hands on her hips, and assumed a model's pose. Raymond flipped a thumb up to Rosie and rolled his eyes. "See you later," he shouted, winked, and drove off.

Vincente pulled Fr. Raul aside. "Is this meeting about Rosie and the doctor? We just heard . . . they kissed on the old pueblo trail . . ."

"You heard! No, the meeting isn't about them. Well," he hesitated, and then murmured, "not exactly."

Just as Fr. Raul herded the last member of the group into the church, Ike and Alcalde, the fifty-five year old regional boss of la Tierra, roared up to the church on Ike's motorcycle. Earlier, Alcalde had arrived in town for his monthly visit and headed over to Diego's bar to 'dry his thirst,' and take a siesta in a back room 'office' he uses when he is in town. Ike joined him there soon after his arrival and told him about Rosie's announcement. Alcalde already knew via the La Tierra grapevine that something unusual was 'going down at the church' that night. By the time Alcalde downed his fifth shot of tequila, he was ready to have a talk with Rosie and the Doc, and, of course, check out the action in the church. A full agenda.

"These new events," he proclaimed to his drinking companions with authority, "about the gringo, outsider, Jew with Rosie, and the secret meeting at the church tonight, need my attention." He paused to empty his glass, then added angrily. "This secret meeting, well, it better not be about the chinga casino." His informant let him know that Rosie was attending the church meeting. Therefore, he could deal with both issues at the same time. Before he left Diego's, Alcalde called Sal and issued him an executive order to 'waste' Jon's car while he and Ike checked out the church meeting.

Fr. Raul groaned under his breath when he saw Ike and Alcalde disembarking from the motorcycle. "Shit. Shit, shit."

"What's that racket out there?" Paz called from the church. Fr. Raul shouted back that it was nothing, and that he would be right in. Rosie was halfway down the aisle when she heard the noise and rushed outside.

"I know that sound. It's Ike's bike. You didn't invite him, did you? He is not a member."

"Of course not." Fr. Raul sighed. "He's got company too."

Rosie stood in front of the church door. "Oh, no. That loser, Alcalde. Want me to get rid of them, Padre?"

Fr. Raul stepped in front of her. "No, that's my job. Remember you were told to do nothing. Nothing! Please go back inside, get some refreshments. I will take care of them. Now do what I say."

Seeing his desperation, Rosie frowned, nodded her head and found it surprisingly easy to obey. "Do nothing," she repeated dutifully. "Do nothing. Why not? The less I do, the better it gets."

Fr. Raul motioned to Ike and Alcalde to remain at the bottom of the stairs; he would walk down and join them. The two were dressed in almost similar outfits of jeans, black leather jackets and boots. Each wore a black T-shirt and the La Tierra headband. The only difference was that Alcalde was wearing snakeskin boots, and Ike was wearing plain brown leather ones. When Fr. Raul reached the bottom step, he noted that Alcalde's pockmarked face seemed unusually red. He reflected on the time when he first met Alcalde, before he joined La Tierra and his name was Angel Garcia. The priest knew Alcalde well enough to be extra careful in dealing with him when he reeked of alcohol. Why were they here? He wondered. He patted the handlebars on Ike's motorcycle. "Great bike."

"Thanks, Padre. Want to go for a ride?" Ike glowed. He liked to show off that Fr. Raul was a pal.

"Definitely." Fr. Raul smiled.

"Okay, Padre, Let's do it," Ike slurred with well-oiled enthusiasm.

Fr. Raul patted him on the shoulder. "Can't right now."

"Just name the time," Ike beamed.

Alcalde had little interest in religion aside from political motives and was trying hard to relate to Fr. Raul. Ike, on the other hand, took religion seriously, in spite of his radical attitude and anti-social antics. Since some of La Tierra's militant manifesto conflicted with what Fr. Raul preached, Ike often found himself caught in the middle of their differing philosophies.

"You can't be a great Santero with hate in your heart," Fr. Raul had often reminded him. Once, there was talk of Ike becoming a priest. However, this ended when Ike and his fellow altar boys began to sample Fr. Raul's stash of wine. Their crimes became apparent one Sunday morning after Ike and a couple of other boys began to stagger around the altar during mass. There was also the time when a couple of Ike's friends pilfered the poor box in the Fr. Miguel sanctuary, and Ike didn't tell who they were because he 'wasn't a rat.' As Fr. Raul explained to his disappointed parents, "Ike is sensitive and spiritual; however, he is more of an artist than a priest. Maybe someday, something will knock some sense into him. I'm praying for that to happen."

Fr. Raul managed a smile. "So, what are you guys doing here? Confessions are over."

"It's not that." Alcalde answered with some irritation. After all, Fr. Raul was not a supportive priest when it came to La Tierra. "I haven't been to confession for years," he laughed.

"Don't think I don't know that, Angel, I mean, Alcalde." Fr. Raul smiled and playfully waved a finger at him. "If you did I would probably have to be in the confessional for a week."

Alcalde froze for a moment. Was that a put down? He had been getting a lot of those lately. "Okay, Padre," he said, sensing that Fr. Raul was covering up something.

Ike tried to lighten the mood. "What's happenin' tonight, Padre? We heard that something was going down."

Fr. Raul responded matter-of-factly. "Not much, the flood did a lot of damage. We are going to discuss how to make repairs, you know, get things back to normal."

"Sure," Alcalde's eyes narrowed. He decided to try again. "We heard you found something."

"Where did you hear that?"

"You know we got our sources," Alcalde smiled slyly.

Fr. Raul smiled back. "Some of the gravestones got messed up by the flood."

"Well, our intelligence says that something's up that may interest La Tierra, and maybe we should just check it out."

Fr. Raul's eyes narrowed. How did they get wind of the block? Then it hit him. Pablo's helpers hung out at Diego's bar, damn!

Alcalde relaxed his stare and asked as courteously as he could, "Padre, we would like to attend the meeting."

Fr. Raul replied in his most earnest and agreeable voice. "You are always welcome here, however, tonight the meeting is closed. Church board executive committee members only. You understand," he smiled, and patted Alcalde reassuringly on the shoulder.

Still saccharine, Alcalde continued. "Father, you know I respect you, we all respect you, but there is nothing that happens here that I can't know about. If something is going down, it is better that we know about it before it happens, not after. You know what I mean?" Then he backed off. "This way we can work together . . ."

Ike found himself resenting the tone of voice Alcalde was using with Fr. Raul.

Fr. Raul replied in a measured and even firmer voice. "I don't believe we have a problem that concerns you. If we do, and it is something you need to know about, I will tell Ike to let you know all about it. Now I must go."

Alcalde clenched his teeth so hard they began to hurt. It was time for an executive decision. Not a good idea to fight with a priest. Need another strategy, he thought, and another drink. The image of the tequila bottle he had tucked away in the motorcycle's saddlebag appeared in his mind.

"Okay, Father, if that's the way you want it, I understand. C'mon, Ike," he said abruptly and turned to go.

"Wait a minute, Alcalde," Ike shouted. The meeting was one thing, his sister another. "Rosie, you got to talk to Rosie. Padre, could you ask Rosie to come out for a minute?"

"Rosie?" Fr. Raul turned away and began to climb the steps.

"You know, to talk about this stuff with the Jingo."

"Jingo, what's a Jingo, Ike?"

Well, the gringo Jew . . . never mind . . . I want to see Rosie. Alcalde wants to talk to her."

Fr. Raul put up his hand and blocked Ike as he started to climb the stairs. "Another time. People are waiting for me . . ."

Alcalde narrowed his eyes. Find another way. He shouted, "Ike, let's just go. We don't want to interrupt the Padre's meeting."

"You sure?" Ike asked.

"Yeah." Alcalde pointed toward the motorcycle.

"Well, okay," Ike agreed quizzically.

Father Raul smiled appreciatively, "Thanks guys. We've got a lot to do . . . the flood, you know."

Alcalde whispered to Ike. "Something is up. We need to check out what's happening."

"But you told him we were going." Ike said.

"La Tierra, bro, La Tierra." Alcalde noticed that Ike was not very enthusiastic. "What's the matter, Ike?" he said.

Ike replied with a forlorn expression. "Don't feel right. Lying to Padre and spyin' on my family," he grumbled.

Alcalde quickly recognized that he needed to switch gears. Use the soft approach, he told himself. It works better with softies like Ike who like the fun part of La Tierra business, but can't handle the dirty work. "We are family too, Ike. My gang was more my family growing up than my own blood. Think for a minute. Who knows what they are doin' in there? Maybe they're planning to allow more gringos in, or a hotel chain, or a casino."

However, Ike was having a hard time paying attention and he was becoming agitated. The alcohol was wearing off. He began to rub his throbbing forehead. "What do you mean? We all know the Indians don't want a casino. Also, they feel the same as us about keeping outsiders away."

Alcalde did not want any further discussion. "La Tierra, Ike, I am pulling rank here. We are goin' in the side door. Something's up, and we have to find out what it is. Then we will take care of your sister and the Jingo."

❦

Fr. Raul walked back into the church to find everybody enjoying Francisca's flan surprise. Carmela popped out of her seat when she saw him. "Here, Padre," she thrust a plate in his direction. "A big slice of flan, a spoon, and a napkin. Sit and enjoy."

"Yes, Padre, you need strength." Francisca jumped in, winking at him in her special way. "Anyone need anything else?"

Fr. Raul acknowledged her wink with his patronizing, reserved-for-Francisca-in-public smile. "You have done a lot on such short notice," he praised her and she raised her head high and beamed. She was important to the church and pleased when it was publicly acknowledged. However, Carmela was not going to let the moment pass.

"Francisca," she began, "How do you make your flan so firm, and so quickly? It takes me such a long time." Carmela could not resist keeping Francisca in her place. Some of her attitude comes from never forgetting the crush she had on Fr. Raul when she was a teenager, well before Francisca came along. Carmela was so obsessed about going to confession her parents became concerned about her. When they asked Fr. Raul what he thought about her devotion he naively responded that Carmela was exceptionally spiritual. "What? Carmela, spiritual?" her astonished mother chuckled and decided on the spot that Padre knew nothing about women. She mentioned to Carmela, who was quite a favorite with the young men in town, what the Padre had said about her being spiritual.

"Have you thought about becoming a nun?" her mother proposed with a straight face. Carmela did not answer but she got the message. Her religious fervor decreased rapidly in the weeks that followed. Another reason for Carmela's attitude had to do with her feelings about social standing. She had even aired her concerns about Francisca rising above her place with Jake one morning. "Francisca is acting a bit high and mighty, don't you think, Jake? After all, it's not that she is Fr. Raul's real wife."

Jake groaned and replied that he had another half hour to sleep before he had to get up, and why did she have to bring up something negative the first thing in the morning. "Husbands need to listen to their wives," she shouted. "Go make your own breakfast."

Carmela's question about the flan hit Francisca like a stomach punch. "I stick it in the refrigerator to help it set quickly," she muttered and lowered her eyes.

"But doesn't that affect the flavor?" Carmela broadcast for all to hear. She tasted the flan again, this time like a wine connoisseur, being careful to scoop up just a bit on the tip of the spoon, admiring it, smelling it and finally tasting. "Mine takes a whole day to get there. But this is . . . good. Of course it would taste better with a regular spoon instead of this plastic . . ."

Fr. Raul had had enough of watching Francisca deflate like a leaky balloon. Vincente and Vickie, allies of the underdogs, also began to be irritated by Carmela's sniping. They gave the high sign to Fr. Raul.

"Enough about food," Padre said firmly, turning away from Carmela. "Time to get to work." He smiled at Francisca, motioned for her to get the tape recorder and notebook ready, and cleared his throat. "I open this private meeting for urgent business. First, I make a motion to skip all of the old business, and anything else, and get to this matter. Anyone second the motion?"

"Me." Carmela, as vice president of the church board, responded in her best administrative voice. Enough of Francisca, back to business. She sat up ramrod straight, and raised her right hand.

Fr. Raul continued. "Okay, anyone against the motion? No one. That is good. Okay. Now we vote on the motion. Yes, raise your hands." Everyone raised hands. "Okay, just new business. Francisca will record the proceedings." He eyeballed Carmela to see her reaction, but there was no response, the point was made. Francisca sat down as close to Fr. Raul as propriety would allow under the circumstances, and began to arrange her writing materials neatly on the table. Fr. Raul shifted a bit to increase the distance between them, but not too far away. Before he moved however, he reached under the table and patted her thigh.

"So, Padre, what's so hush-hush?" asked Vickie Lopez, a short and squarely built woman with an open, pleasant face and big brown eyes. Her thick lips and broad nose were set among the rivulets of wrinkles running over her well-bronzed skin.

Fr. Raul smiled and answered her gently, respectfully. "Vickie. This is a very sensitive issue. You need to get the whole picture so we will start at the beginning. Grandfather will begin. Grandfather . . ."

Elmer cleared his throat and began his story. At the same time, Ike and Alcalde had parked the motorcycle out of sight, retrieved the bottle of tequila from the saddlebag and served themselves. After a brief strategy session, they decided to sneak back into the church via the gravel-covered courtyard leading into the Fr. Miguel Sanctuary. From there they could ease into a pew and hear what was going on. They proceeded through the entry arch and tiptoed through the cactus garden, weaving their way between the statues of the saints until they arrived at the open sanctuary door.

"Like a detective movie, no?" Alcalde snickered. Stifling their amusement, they tiptoed into the sanctuary, easing along the 'wall of miracles'—a collection of retablos, religious objects and colorful carved wood figures of saints, some in glass cases. Ike was careful not to disturb the piles of assorted crutches, statues, medals and artificial limbs hanging from the walls and ceiling, as well as discarded leg casts and melted candles littering the floor. That would be a sin. He was especially careful not to step into the hole in the floor containing the sacred soil. Alcalde followed, much less carefully.

When they arrived at the passageway leading from the sanctuary to the church, Ike crouched down and peeked around the doorway.

"Everyone is in front of the altar eating," he whispered. A loud stomach rumble punctuated his words.

"Shhh," Alcalde nudged him.

Ike looked up with a sorrowful expression. "I forgot to eat dinner. I am starving! Sneaking around in my church is not helping my stomach, either."

Alcalde scoffed. "Forget your stomach. I can't hear a word from here. Gotta get closer. C'mon." Alcalde peeked in around the corner. The main entrance was on his left, the altar on the right. "We need to get over to the other side of the church," Alcalde whispered, and pointed to the confessional on the opposite wall. They could hear from there without being seen. He signaled Ike to follow. They crawled along the left wall of the church, passed quickly across the church entrance, and proceeded down along the right wall until they reached the confessional. "You go in there; I'll go in on the priest's side." Alcalde slurred his words.

Ike grabbed Alcalde's sleeve. "The priest's side on the confessional? Could be blasphemy. God may not like it."

Alcalde giggled, "Confessional or not, this is the only place we can hear from. C'mon."

Ike hesitated again. "I dunno."

Alcalde grabbed Ike's arm. "That's an order."

"I don't want to cross Padre." Ike was adamant. "I don't want to go into the confessional."

"You have to. Now do it. I said, that's an order."

Ike thought. "This is not good. What's the matter with him? This is not the guy I knew." He was thinking of the time he first met Alcalde and how he was impressed that Alcalde came from a long line of farmers and cattle ranchers who were known for their long-standing feuds and separatist revolts against both the United States and the state of New Mexico. Alcalde was devoted to the separatist tradition Ike respected—keeping the outsiders out, and the insiders in—everyone and everything in their place. Ike was also aware that Alcalde was unhappy about his demotion to the job of regional director of the far North Country, a place no one else wanted to work. This happened after Alcalde's efforts to defeat the Indian gaming movement failed, and casinos started to sprout up like cacti along the north-south corridor in New Mexico.

After hearing Alcalde's order, Ike began to have second thoughts. Should I have told him that what is happening here is an opportunity for him to get back into some old-fashioned action, and redeem himself with La Tierra? This is about my church and my sister, my Padre and my grandfather.

Alcalde peered through the confessional partition and whispered. "Excuse me, Father, for I have sinned."

"Fuck off," whispered Ike and crossed himself.

"That's not nice." Alcalde whipped his hand over his mouth to contain his laughter.

Ike tried to listen hard but he couldn't make out what Elmer was saying.

"When I was going down from the mesa, I heard a noise . . ."

Fr. Raul interrupted. "Could you jump ahead and tell us what you saw come out of the ground?"

"Okay. Well, I was looking at the old cemetery that the water knocked the hell out of, and I saw a waterspout, and this block shoots up into the air."

Vickie's eyelids stretched wide open. Paz's mouth dropped open.

Vincente blurted, "You're kidding me, right? You say something came out of the ground."

"Right out." Elmer shot his hand up toward the ceiling. "Like a missile."

"Holy Mother of God!" Paz crossed herself.

"How high?" asked Patron.

"Very, very high," Elmer laughed to himself, aware that he could really gild the lily. "Then it fell to the ground, into the mud, but it didn't get busted because the ground was so soft, and then it rolled over a couple of times . . ."

"Thanks, grandfather," Fr. Raul cut him short. "We thank you for taking your time to tell us what happened. This afternoon Patron, Esther, Rosie and I inspected the block and now I want to show it to you all. "

Elmer's face fell. "Is that all?"

Fr. Raul nodded yes.

Elmer mumbled. "Pretty short . . ."

Ike whispered to Alcalde, "grandfather said something about a block."

"What block? I don't see any block." Alcalde slurred almost intelligibly. The tequila was working fast.

Ike said, "Shhh. For God's sake. It's that blue covered thing behind the altar. We need to move closer to see it."

Alcalde slowly opened the door of the confessional, crawled out on his hands and knees, headed back along the wall toward the church entrance, crossed over to the other side of the room, and stood up behind a statue. This gave him an excellent view of the block. He beckoned to Ike to follow him. When Ike arrived, Alcalde was reeling, and choking back laughter.

"Here," Alcalde said, reaching into his pocket for the tequila bottle. "Drink."

Ike smiled. "Give it here," and guzzled it.

Alcalde held up the bottle. "This is my agave home brew, numero uno tequila. La Tierra, bro'."

Fr. Raul walked over to the side of the altar and peeled the cover from the block. "Take a look. One by one. And take your time to examine every side. When you finish, we will talk."

Everyone got up and reverently approached the block. What was this strange thing?

"Alcalde," Ike complained. "I can't see a thing from here. They are standing between us and the block."

"Yeah," said Alcalde. "Let's go back to where we were. At least we can hear better."

The group circled the block as one. When they saw the side with the cross, Paz fell to her knees as if she were thunderstruck. Her eyes glazed over and she threw both hands over her head and started muttering unintelligibly. Vickie raised her right hand.

"Shhh, everybody, Paz is speaking to the spirits."

Fr. Raul walked over to Paz and gently tapped her on the shoulder. "Come back, Paz."

She lowered her arms and brushed the tears from her eyes.

Vincente rubbed his chin. "What is that star thing doing in the middle of the cross? And where is Jesus?" he asked.

Fr. Raul ignored his question. "Please, everyone, take your eyes off the cross because it is too . . . well, it's going to take us away from the business at hand." He pointed to the holes on top of the block. "Please look carefully at the top here, see the markings, the six-pointed star, and the outline of some type of compartment. Now look at these four holes. Remember how they are positioned. Now follow me."

He walked the group over to Rosita. "Now Pablo and I are going to slide Rosita out of her nicho and tip her backwards. I want you all to look down at the bottom of her feet."

Everyone else stared intently at the bottom of the statue.

"Well, I'll be damned," Vincente said. "It is the same. She's got matching holes."

"Shhh," said Vickie.

Rosie caught her breath, and then blurted, "Oh my God."

Ike was having a hard time hearing. "I heard something about matching holes," he mumbled. "Did you say matching holes?" Ike held his hand over his mouth to hold back a snort and heard Alcalde chortling. "Chinga, I am going to lose it, Ike . . . what kind of holes?"

Fr. Raul and Pablo righted the statue and asked everyone to be seated.

"Discussion open. Anyone have anything to say?" Rosie kept her eyes fixed on him, but he avoided her gaze.

Carmela stood up, and cleared her throat in her most elegant manner. "Well, it's obvious that since the holes in this block match the holes in Rosita, this block belongs to Rosita." Carmela was pleased when she saw everyone's heads bobbing up and down in agreement.

Francisca added. "It's a pedestal. Not a block. Rosita has her original pedestal back."

"Pedestal. Yes. Everyone agree?" Fr. Raul nodded solemnly.

"Sure," said Rosie, a bit sarcastically. "Someone must have buried the pedestal on purpose. Why would someone do that? "

Fr. Raul admonished her with a glare. "One thing at a time, Rosie. I told you . . ."

Vickie said, "Yes, Rosie. Why would anybody would bury her pedestal?"

Grandfather said, "The block is hollow, perhaps the answer is inside."

Rosie shouted, "Why are you all beating around the bush? You don't have to look inside the block to see anything. Just look at the figures and the writing on the outside. And the cross, the crying cross. The block or pedestal is Jewish. Jon said the writing is God's name in Hebrew characters."

Silence. Fr. Raul swallowed audibly.

Francisca jumped to her feet. "I'll get you some water."

Fr. Raul regained his voice. "Thank you, Rosie. Okay everybody, let us not jump to conclusions. Do we want to look inside? Let's take a vote. "

Rosie and Paz shot up their hands. The others looked back and forth at each other then tentatively raised their hands. "I guess," Carmela said.

"And are we ready to deal with what we find?" Patron interjected.

Rosie added. "Poppa, you mean what we have already found out. That Rosita is . . . Jewish." She paused. "Say it. Our beloved saint is Jewish. What's the matter with you guys?"

"Rosie!" Vickie shot up out of her chair and shouted angrily. "You should be ashamed of yourself for saying such a thing. Rosita is not Jewish; I do not want to hear this, Padre. Vincente, I want to go."

Fr. Raul moved to calm her. He eyed Francisca, who went into action. "Vickie, I understand how you feel, but please don't leave. We must face this together. All of us." With such personal attention, Vickie was not only reassured; she was overwhelmed that she was being singled out. This meant she mattered. She basked in this good feeling while Fr. Raul also consoled her.

"Whatever we find, we can deal with."

Francisca handed Fr. Raul a glass of water, and hurried to Vickie's side.

"We need you," she crooned softly. Vickie relaxed even more. If Francisca can take this, so can I, she thought, Francisca is only a housekeeper, after all.

"Maybe Vickie is right," Vincente bellowed. "What if we find out something that we don't want to know?"

"You already did," Rosie shouted back. "Don't you see?"

"I know what you want," Vincente barked. "And why."

Patron glowered at Vincente and signaled for Rosie to be quiet. "Let's see what there is to see, Padre."

"Okay," Fr. Raul agreed. "We open up the block. Okay?" Everyone nodded in agreement. "What we find here stays here. Agreed?" All hands went up.

"Like Las Vegas," smiled Carmela. "Nevada, that is."

Paz winked at Rosie and popped up her thumb. "My guys are working," she mouthed. Rosie smiled and conspiratorially wiggled her eyebrows.

Elmer signaled to Fr. Raul that he had something to say. The priest raised his hands to silence everyone, and then nodded to Elmer, who proceeded to clear his throat until all eyes were upon him.

"Still got the taste of your exhaust in my mouth," he teased Vincente, who had learned long ago not to take Elmer's humor personally. Elmer spoke slowly and with authority. "Now that we all have decided to go ahead, we can't just chop it open, we need to figure a way to get in. See, these markings here at the top. Looks like a door, right? But it's not. These markings are a trick."

"A trick!" Vickie exclaimed.

"A very old trick." Elmer smiled. "See. The markings take your attention away from where the lock is located. My people have used this type of trick for a long time and I would not be surprised if whoever made this one learned it from us." Elmer put both hands on the block and lightly ran his fingers from left to right across the top edge. "Here," he felt something on the top right corner. He took out his pocketknife, and using its butt end, tapped horizontally, from left to right, along the top outside edge of the block. After several taps, a one-inch wide lath of wood edged out of the top right corner of the block.

"Grandfather," Vickie exclaimed in admiration. "How did you know that?" Elmer nodded knowingly. "This piece of wood covers the ends of two horizontal dowels that hold up a panel on the top side of the block. Once I remove this piece of wood, I can pull out the dowels, and the hidden door on top will fall in. This kind of setup is airtight when the inside of the block is waxed and oiled. Bug proof and waterproof too. We will see."

"What if there is a curse about opening it?" Paz mumbled.

"A curse!" Vickie chewed her lower lip. Carmela pondered the idea for a brief moment and quietly stepped back.

"There are no curses," Vincente scolded. "Why scare . . ."

"You are wrong, Vincente, there are curses," Paz interrupted him and looked imploringly at Fr. Raul. "Remember . . ."

"Not now, please. Let's pray; that will neutralize any curses," Fr. Raul interrupted them both.

"No jinx here," Elmer stated with a sure tone.

Vickie asked. "You sure? How do you know?"

"Because the Great Spirit is on the move. This is a good thing. That is, if we do not screw it up like we do to everything else the Great Spirit does for us."

Ike was becoming increasingly irritated because he was hearing only bits and pieces of the conversation. He turned to Alcalde, who was dozing against the wall.

Ike nudged him. "Wake up. You can't sleep now. Listen, can you make sense of what they are saying?" Ike recoiled from the strong smell of alcohol on his breath.

"I hear tapping," Alcalde snickered. He was thinking; imagine me hiding in the confessional. This is one to tell the boys.

Ike was also thinking: Alcalde has nothing to lose here. This is not his family. He signaled to Alcalde to listen and lay off the tequila.

"No problema," Alcalde mouthed back. He had drained the bottle anyway.

Ike was beginning to think some unpleasant thoughts about Alcalde, and didn't like it.

Elmer glanced at Patron for the go-ahead to open the door on the top of the pedestal. When Rosie, who was by now greatly enjoying the proceedings, light-heartedly asked if it could be booby-trapped, Elmer smiled and shook his head, "No."

Patron bestowed his permission with an almost imperceptible nod and Elmer set to work. He removed the lath from the side of the pedestal, and slowly extracted the two long wooden dowels.

Admiring "Ooohs" and "Aaahs" filled the room. Next, he tapped gently on the center of top of the block. Slowly the outlined area began to give way until the panel fell inward.

Paz cried out, "Bravo, grandfather!"

Elmer was pleased, but did not change his expression. He was somewhere else, thanking his long dead ancestor who had just shown him how to do what he did.

"Now we will see," Fr. Raul said quietly and respectfully. He reminded himself of the message he had received and crossed himself.

"Yes, friends, we will see," echoed Patron.

"The moment of truth," Rosie grinned.

Elmer slowly and reverently lifted the panel away from the pedestal. "Before I look in I will say something," he said and reached for the medicine bag around his neck.

"So will I," said Fr. Raul. "Let us all pray."

Everyone bowed their heads.

"In case there is a curse." Vickie added.

Vincente barked, "Vickie, you gotta stop watching those horror films."

"Shhh," Fr. Raul whispered. "Pray in silence." After a moment, Elmer announced. "I cannot see down inside too well. Anyone got a flashlight?"

"I do," Vincente said, happy to be of use. "Here, a small one, on my key chain."

Elmer thanked him and peered inside carefully. "I just see . . . a bunch of packages. No bugs. And no curses." He laughed. "Doesn't smell too good . . ."

Alcalde was feeling giddy and dizzy, and sick to his stomach. He had to urinate badly. "Ike, what's happenin', man? You got a better view than me."

Ike whispered. "I dunno. Grandfather said he was sticking his hand in the block or something . . . maybe Vickie."

"Damn, don't make me laugh. I'm gonna pee my pants."

"Yeah," Ike decided to rub it in; Alcalde was getting on his nerves. Either Ike was growing up or Alcalde was going down. "Yeah, right, grandfather is sticking his hand in Vickie."

"Damn, Ike, That's lame, stupid. You know once I get laughin' I can't stop."

"Okay. Yes, grandfather is sticking his hand in . . . Vickie . . . whoops, sorry. I mean the block." Ike heard a series of gagging and choking sounds from the other side of the confessional. The door creaked open, followed by a series of scraping sounds, then the sound of footsteps shuffling toward the church entrance. Seconds later, the church door slammed shut, and he heard an unearthly howl.

Everyone at the front of the church whipped around. "Did you hear that?" yelled Vickie. "The curse."

"Don't be silly, it's the wind," said Patron.

"There is no wind tonight," Vincente grunted impatiently.

"Oh, oh," Paz murmured. Elmer gestured for calm. "I told you. This is a good thing, good spirits."

Fr. Raul said he would investigate the noise and hurried up the center aisle and through the doorway to the landing. Once outside, he made out the silhouette of a man, bent over and laughing loudly, staggering along at the far end of the plaza. A Kokopelli image came to mind. Was this a sign? "No," Fr. Raul chuckled in relief, "Only a drunk." He walked back into the church and exclaimed. "It's nothing, just some borracho walking down the road, drunk and laughing."

"Are you sure!" Vickie exclaimed in a shrill voice. "Evil spirits can shapeshift, change their form, make believe they are something they are not."

Elmer interrupted. "Vickie, I am the expert on shapeshifting here. This is not evil. Would I say this if it were not true?"

"Of course not," Fr. Raul said, not to be outdone in spiritual matters. "We are in church, right? Our Lord is right up there . . ."

"And Rosita too," Paz added.

Vickie turned away from the group. For insurance, she crossed herself, put the thumb of her right hand between her index and middle finger, pointed them straight ahead, and spit three times—something her grandmother had taught her to do to ward off evil spirits.

Alcalde was outside, relieving himself mightily and laughing at the same time. When he finished, he headed for the Cantina. When he arrived, he slipped into the restroom off the vestibule, and cleaned up as best he could. After a period of rest on a stool, he carefully guided himself down the stairs to the bar, and under Juan's inquisitive gaze made it to a corner barstool out of sight of most of the other customers. His head was pounding. "Two aspirin and double tequila," he mumbled.

"You O.K?" Juan knew him well from his younger days.

"No," Alcalde muttered, trying to contain his nausea. "Just want sit here in the corner by myself. Need something strong and straight."

"Sure," Juan said and poured him a drink from the watered down bottle of tequila. Alcalde downed it quickly, paused for a moment, peered into the glass curiously and set it down. He was too drunk to taste the difference. He checked out the room and spied Raymond in the back. He was talking to the gringo Doc. When Raymond caught his eye, he managed a feeble wave. Raymond returned a cursory greeting and turned away.

"Don't look now, Jon," Raymond said. "Alcalde just walked in."

"Who?"

"Alcalde, the guy from La Tierra. Over, there, he looks like he needs somebody's help." Raymond laughed. "I wonder what he is doing here. He is a Diego's guy. Gotta watch out for him."

"Do I need a gun?"

Raymond did not laugh. "I'll let you know after tomorrow."

"What is going to be different tomorrow?"

"Maybe a lot. I am going to the mesa with grandfather at first light. You people here got your message. Now it is our turn."

Jon wrinkled his brow. "What are you talking about?

"Our money problems. Our people are just about making ends meet with our art business. The other pueblos along the north-south highway have faced the same problem and they chose to build casinos. Now they are doing great, financially at least, but grandfather thinks they are selling out, and paying a great spiritual price. We need to find something else besides building a casino to solve our problems."

Jon sat up straight and, with a hint of uncertainty, said, "So you are going to study the rock drawings, petroglyphs, for an answer?"

Raymond nodded. "Grandfather just discovered two new ones we need to figure out."

Jon's interest perked up, but he was now culturally sensitive enough to know this was not his business. "I would love to come with you, but I guess I can't," he assumed, with a touch of disappointment.

"I'm sorry."

"Sure. Why do you have to be there by first light?"

"Good question, grasshopper," Raymond teased. "Gotta give you one of these keep-it-between-us-Indian answers. Since everything is alive, the drawings change with the light. Like a movie. We have to see the message from first light to last light. Like life, gotta be there from beginning to end to get it all."

Jon searched for a way to get into the action. "How about if I drive you?" Raymond agreed heartily. "That works."

Jon laughed. "Deliver you before the sun comes up. Pick-up at sunset."

Raymond flashed a thumbs-up. "You got it."

Jon smiled. "Ray, if you don't get your answer from the rock drawings I've got an idea for you."

Raymond laughed. "You know what we think about white man's ideas for us Indians . . ."

Raymond peeked over at Alcalde who was now dead asleep on the bar. His head was cradled in one arm, the other arm hung down to the bar rail. Juan caught Raymond's eye and placed both hands up to the side of his face, palms together, tilted his head to the side, and put his thumb in his mouth to complete his impression of a sleeping baby.

Raymond flipped him a thumbs-up. Jon was safe, at least for the moment. It was time to leave.

10

La Palabra de Dios

"Here goes," Elmer slid his hand gently into the block. While he felt around very gingerly, he caught each person's eyes for a brief moment, inviting them to explore along with him. Patron stood at his side, consciously restraining himself from taking charge. It would be bad form to interfere with Elmer's deliberate way of doing things or attempt to usurp Fr. Raul's authority in matters of the church. Nevertheless, he was weighing the consequences of what he suspected the block contained. Maybe I should call an end to this right now, bury the block, and tell everyone to forget this ever happened, he told himself.

Carmela put her hands over her eyes and squealed a warning, "Watch out for bugs and spiders."

Vincente shot an index finger up to his lips. "Shhh, Carmela. God knows how long that block has been shut tight. How can there be something alive in there?"

Carmela moaned turned away and uncovered her eyes. "I don't care. Grandfather, don't stick your hand where you can't see."

Elmer grinned, "See, I am still alive and kicking. Listen up all of you, the inside of this block is lined with oilskin, and wax. That's to keep the water out. There are parcels covered with a waxy coating. They seem solid, not brittle. There are three of them, standing on end. One feels like two rolls of paper towels, pointy at the top. One is hard, feels like wood. This other one is also flat, but heavy, hard, like stone. Everything feels solid. Nothing rattles. Should I take them out, Padre, Patron?"

Carmela pouted. "What about germs? You cannot see germs. There may be an old disease in there."

"You are vaccinated, no? Besides this isn't a U.F.O," scolded Vincente.

Rosie was having second thoughts about proceeding. "Maybe we shouldn't touch these things, maybe wait and get someone here who knows about this . . . from the university, an archeo . . ."

Patron barked, "No, Rosie. We do not want any strangers, reporters or university people here to spread this around. What if we find something . . . that shouldn't be found? No, everything stays here, private. You hear?"

"Yes," Rosie obeyed. Fr. Raul added. "We promised, remember? Private."

"Yes. Poppa, I said yes." Rosie acquiesced with an obedient, even graceful expression implying that Patron owed her one. After all, he was the one who taught her that a chip is a chip. If anyone needed chips, it was Rosie.

"That's right! No outsiders," Vincente said between clenched teeth, with the emphasis on "outsider."

Rosie wanted to challenge Vincente about "outsiders," but decided to leave well enough alone. "Okay, Vincente, if you say so. No outsiders." Now he would owe her too. Agree with someone in public in Santa Rosita and you have made a friend.

Fr. Raul motioned to Elmer not to remove anything from the block until he prepared the table. "Whatever is in there is old and can fall apart."

Rosie snapped. "We don't need to call it the block anymore. It's Rosita's pedestal. Right?"

Fr. Raul barked back. "No, Rosie, for now it's a block. Remember, one thing at a time. Hold your horses. We do not change anything until we change it. Rosie, remember the message . . . wait, wait, wait. For God's sake, wait."

Patron agreed, "Enough Rosie,"

She backed off. Are they going to close their eyes to what this means, she wondered; better not.

"More light, please." Fr. Raul signaled to Pablo who was standing as close as he could to seem invisible. While Pablo was lighting new candles, Fr. Raul closed his eyes reverently and signaled everyone to follow.

When Pablo finished, Elmer broke the silence. "Ready everyone, here comes the first package. It is wedged pretty good. Ugh! Here, Carmela, take it from me." He thrust the package at Carmela who pushed it away.

"Not me, it's dirty."

Vincente elbowed Carmela aside. "Give it to me," he cried, "and give Vickie the next one."

Francisca arrived with a roll of paper towels and some newspaper, which she handed to Pablo who quickly spread them over the table.

Vickie moved forward hesitantly, "I am not touching whatever that is with my bare hands. I need a paper towel or something, maybe rubber gloves, to hold it with."

Francisca agreed, and went off to get some more supplies.

Elmer, so intent on fishing for packages, ignored the confusion. He tugged. "Here comes another one. Careful, its heavy."

"Give it here." Paz commanded. "Oh, you are right. It is very heavy," she groaned, and let it slide down onto the table with a thump.

Elmer grunted, and hauled out the next package. "This is the biggest," he groaned.

"That's not my package," said Vickie.

"I'll take it," said Patron, then rolled his eyes in mild disgust when Vickie moaned, "Paz has my package."

Paz heard what Vickie said, and motioned for her to come closer.

"It will be our package, Vickie, dear," she said sweetly.

Elmer strained to reach in as deeply as he could.

Rosie laughed and playfully warned him to be careful not to fall in. No one thought her remark funny, except Elmer. Then he feigned surprise. "Wait. Something else. There is a little package here in the corner. Got it!" Elmer took it out and examined it. "Well, look at this. Rosie, I believe it is for you."

Rosie smiled, "For me. Why for me?"

Elmer grinned again; he was having a good time. "I do not give away trade secrets."

"It's so tiny," Rosie grinned gleefully.

At the same moment, Patron saw a smile cross Esther's face and was overcome by a strange feeling.

In the meantime, Ike was wondering why Alcalde had not returned. Some leader, leaving me here alone, he whispered to himself. I'll get the goods myself. Have to get closer so I can see what they are doing. Ike crawled out of his hiding place, keeping as low a profile as he could, and headed for the pews. When he reached the end of the pew at the center aisle, he got a clear view of the table and the people crowded around it. He saw Elmer pick up a flat package, but he did not hear him ask if he could open it. All eyes were fixed on Patron for the go-ahead. When he nodded yes, and Fr. Raul nodded in agreement, they began to cut away the coating on the packages. Vincente drew out a large utility knife from its leather holder on his belt.

"Start on the heavy package with Vickie," Elmer suggested. "I'll start on this one."

Patron unfolded his own pocketknife and started to scrape away the coating on the large package.

"I'll open this little one," Rosie said.

"Here's a kitchen knife," Francisca offered.

"I'll help you," Carmela said, and asked Francisca if she had any latex disposable gloves.

"No. I don't use them, too expensive," Francisca said with a tinge of authority, and then politely suggested that everyone try to keep the scrapings off the floor.

The wax coatings were finally scraped off the packages, but not without occasional grunts, complaints, and stifled curses. Fr. Raul took command. "Now we carefully remove the wrappings. The little one first."

With all eyes upon her, Rosie gently scratched at the wrapping with her fingernail until she found an edge. She lifted it up and peeled off several layers of oilskin that came off more easily than she anticipated. A perfectly preserved silver artifact fell into her open palm. "Look, a charm," she bubbled.

"Let me see," Patron reached over and gently removed the charm from Rosie's hand. Conscious that he needed to stretch his eyes open to avoid a series of unwanted nervous blinks, he reached into his vest, took out his own lucky charm and held both pieces side-by-side. It was as he had feared.

Rosie hugged him, "Look, Poppa, peas in a pod."

Patron stood wide-mouthed, transfixed.

Seeing his distress, Fr. Raul jumped into action. He placed the charm in Rosie's hand, wrapped her fingers around it, and placed his hand over hers. "Remember, do nothing," he said softly. Then he turned to the others and motioned to Vincente to proceed.

Vincente peeled away the oilskin covering his flat parcel and raised the object up for all to see. Carmela cried, "Look. It is a tablet, with writing on it. Five lines on each side, I don't understand the writing." She crossed herself.

"Give it here," Fr. Raul said and took it from her. "La Palabra de Dios," he choked. Tears welled up in his eyes. "La Palabra de Dios."

Elmer broke the silence. "That's a good carving," he said, "that white stone is not from here. Never seen stone like that before."

Fr. Raul gingerly laid the stone on the table. "It could be from Spain," he said weakly. Francisca brushed Fr. Raul's hand tenderly as she reached out to touch the tablet with a finger. She kissed it and blew the kiss to the heavens.

Elmer lightly touched the deeply etched letters. "Very powerful, very, very powerful. Strong medicine, as Indians say in the movies."

"Enough for one night," Vickie groaned. "I don't feel so good. The candle smell is making me sick. I need air, open a door."

Paz cut her short "And have the whole town in here? Sorry, cannot open a door. It's not the candles, honey, it's the emotion. Let's just get it over with, see everything and then talk it over." She did not want to hurt Vickie's feelings so she added, warmly, "Dear, it's La Palabra de Dios, the Word of God. The Ten Commandments, right Padre?"

Fr. Raul nodded in agreement. "Looks like it."

Paz dove into herself, closed her eyes and saw the beautiful face of her long dead great-grandmother smiling at her. So what are you up to? Paz asked her.

The moment had come for Patron to intervene.

"One moment, please. Like my daughter Paz said, we need to check everything out. Then we can decide what to do. Hold the comments for now." He picked up the tall package, turned his back to the group and carefully unwrapped it. What could this be? He wondered. When the wrapping was off, he held the object behind him and turned around to face the group. "Everyone sit down before I show this to you," he said quietly.

When everyone was seated, he slowly brought the object out from behind his back and removed the worn and tattered cloth covering. There were two gold covered rollers, connected by a scroll of parchment. "Know what this is?" he asked.

Fr. Raul jumped to his feet, leaned over the table and touched the scroll with two fingers. "My God, it's the holy book of the Jews. The Torah. Look, how the parchment is so delicate. How could it have survived? It surely must be blessed."

Francisca and Vickie nodded in agreement.

Rosie felt as if her head would burst. Her thoughts fled her mind. Her body became void of feelings.

Elmer muttered, "Very powerful."

Patron unrolled a small portion of the scroll exposing a segment of the parchment.

"The writing is the same as the writing on the side of the pedestal," Vickie announced.

"The colors, so beautiful, so alive, vibrant," added Paz.

"Very powerful," Elmer mumbled repeatedly. Then he smiled, "No question. The Great Spirit is on the move."

Now mindless, and drawn by an unseen force, Rosie felt herself drifting silently towards Rosita, as if her feet were not touching the floor. She looked up and saw that Rosita was smiling, a soft, barely perceptible smile." When Rosie's consciousness returned, she whispered, "So, you brought the rain . . ?"

Paz glanced up and saw Rosie at Rosita's feet. A shiver started in her lower back and rippled all through her body. "Oh boy!" she said aloud.

In the meantime, Vincente was becoming increasingly agitated. "Okay, I do not know anything about this . . . er, Torah here or whatever it is. The Ten Commandments I know. Let's keep going. Get it all out on the table. What is in the other package? Here, pass it to me. I'll open it." Vincente proceeded to tear off the wrapping. "It's a bunch of wood panels, five of them. Oh, look, retablos . . . pictures on one side, look, very beautiful. And look at this one, on the other side..."

"Writing . . . lists . . . dates," added Vickie.

Suddenly, Rosie broke away from her reverie and rushed back to the table.

"Let me see," she cried and grabbed the panel with the writing out of Vincente's hands.

"Hey," Vincente grunted.

Rosie ignored him and began to speak quickly and shrilly. "The writing is Spanish. I can make this out. The letters are burned into the wood. Let's see, this one has names of people and their families. Like a family tree, there are dates too. Many names are illegible but I can make out some of them. Here, this one lists those who left to go north in 1570. Oh, my gosh. Mendez, Laguna, Tamuz, Abale, Jaramillo, Gomez, Lopez, and Alonzo—here us, Alonzo—and . . . Carrillo, Garcia . . ."

"Abale, Gomez," Vincente shouted.

"Wait," Rosie urged, "there are lots more." The dates are 1500, here is one with three generations 1570, and here is another panel . . . auto-da-fe (burned at the stake), killed by the Inquisition, Campos, Butos, and Espinosa. Lots more name and dates.

Rosie picked up another panel and studied it carefully. "This panel tells about the person who made all this . . . I can translate it. Listen."

"Let me," Fr. Raul interrupted. Patron held up his hand and said with pride, "It's okay Padre, Rosie speaks perfect Spanish. Now read, Rosie."

Rosie began to read.

> I, Luis Alonzo, born in Spain in the year of our lord 1510, having escaped to New Spain in the year of our lord 1540, to avoid persecution by the Inquisition, and, having settled in Nuevo Leon since that time, and, having again been judged and sentenced to be burned at the stake unless I renounce my religious beliefs, which I cannot do in good conscience, hereby state that I am therefore prepared to die.
>
> I leave behind a saintly woman whom God placed into my mind, and had me carve her out of my heart. She is my last holy work. God has told me he will give her a name in the future. She is to embody the spirit of the women of my people. Her destiny is to illuminate a different land, at a different time. My son, Abraham Alonzo, will take her to where she must go. I have placed the holy words the Lord God gave my people inside of her, so no matter what happens to us, they will always be safe. I have placed the names of the many wronged people inside her as well.

She represents both love and hope. When her spirit moves, it will testify to the cruel and unwarranted suffering inflicted on us by stupid and frightened people. If we are able to receive her within, she gives the power to see what is right, and to transform thoughts and acts born of ignorance and suffering into love, compassion, understanding, learning, forgiveness and tolerance.

She will warm the heart of the receivers, and help them to be far seeing, to heal, to banish cruelty, to be one with all, as God's people, to teach unity, not separateness and to help us overcome our own faults. She is to teach that we are all related and what we do to one, we do to all. She is to teach women to educate their sons, from their first days, not to murder innocents.

Respectfully signed, in the presence of the Lord, our God, Yahweh.

Luis Alonzo, Nuevo Leon, New Spain, August 5, 1570.

Patron fell back in his chair. Luis Alonzo. Could this be my ancestor? I wish Esther were here.

"Did I hear right? Did the writer say that Rosita will . . . manifest, come to life?" Fr. Raul exclaimed. "It says when her spirit moves . . ."

"Same thing," Paz clicked her tongue in surprise that Padre said such a thing.

Carmela shook her head in disbelief. "This is getting too creepy." She looked over to the block: "Those faces . . ." Tears filled her eyes.

Vickie looked over. She paled. "They are crying."

Vincente feared the women were going off the deep end. "No, it's just the shadows from the candles," he explained tentatively, "candlelight flickers and makes shadows. Wood don't cry."

Paz jumped in decisively. "They are crying. And everyone here who isn't stupid knows why they are crying, right?"

"What are you talking about?" "Vincente snapped, "Nothing is crying. I told you, wood does not cry. I work with wood all the time."

Patron chimed in impatiently. "Stop, Vincente is right. The candlelight is playing on the faces. It's condensation."

Vickie answered. "No, Patron. They are crying, look. Madre de Dios . . ."

Patron picked up the plastic cover and threw it over the block. "That's enough," he said firmly. "You are all going loco."

Vickie grabbed Fr. Raul by the arm. "Do you think so, Padre? Is this block cursed?"

Fr. Raul rubbed his chin hard and muttered, "Maybe it is condensation, maybe it is the shadows, and maybe not. Who knows anymore? For now, let us all be quiet and thankful and do nothing. Let us just . . . pray."

While everyone sat in quiet prayer, Rosie stood up, tucked the retablo panels under her arm and slowly walked over to the bank of half-spent candles in front of the altar.

When Fr. Raul ended the prayer with an "Amen" everyone opened their eyes and looked to the altar to see Rosie silhouetted against the soft red-orange glow of the candles that bathed her in an aura.

"What," Rosie turned and snapped, "is everybody looking at?"

Silence. Even Paz remained speechless.

Elmer mumbled, "Whoa!"

Pablo crossed himself.

Ike saw the packages being examined and heard the words 'Ten Commandments,' 'Torah,' and 'charm,' and some of the names and dates that Rosie read out loud. Headache and all, his curiosity went into overdrive. What's that roll of paper? And what's this about a historic something or other, he said to himself. Then, he saw Rosie silhouetted against the candlelight. He felt the blood drain from his face and he became light-headed. His mind filled with the image of Rosie as a young girl. He was back to a time in their lives when he was the big brother she adored. "She is my little sister, and she looks like an angel," he said softly. "An angel." Then his eyes moved to Rosita. He saw her smile at him.

"Holy shit," he muttered, "Holy shit! What the hell was in that booze?"

Rosie was not frightened, even though she felt herself drifting out of herself. Time seemed to stop. I don't like this, she told herself and forced a deep breath to bring herself back as Esther had taught her to do. Everyone was staring at her.

Fr. Raul broke the silence. "Too much, too much," he mumbled.

Patron thought. Do I need new glasses? Am I getting senile? Esther, come here. He tried to contact her mind. No answer.

Carmela was at a loss for words, so she rubbed her eyes and adjusted her contact lenses.

Vickie stiffened her body to gain strength and grabbed Vincente's arm. He sat as still as a fencepost.

Francisca was trembling and got up to leave the room to compose herself.

Fr. Raul broke the spell. "Okay, what does the executive committee think?"

"Rosie . . ." Vickie started.

Fr. Raul cut her short. "No, not Rosie. Not now. About the block."

Vincente was more than happy to ignore what happened. The night was getting more and more weird, and he wanted to go home. "Maybe we should just put the block . . ."

"Rosita's pedestal, please," Rosie interrupted, but weakly. She felt sapped of all energy. The phrase, "right future wrongs," she had read aloud from Luis's document raced through her mind. Francisca nodded in agreement.

"Okay, Rosita's pedestal, whatever," Vincente responded, almost obsequiously.

Rosie smiled back weakly. She did not understand why all of a sudden, Vincente addressed her so respectfully.

Vincente continued. "There is no question about what we have to do. We need to put it back in the ground. That will save us a lot of trouble."

"I am leaning the same way," Patron said. "Or we could put Rosita back on this block, er, her pedestal, where she belongs, and remove, or cover the figures on the side so no one can see them. It would make her happy to be complete again. And no one would know . . ."

"And her insides?" Paz asked, "Back in the pedestal?"

Patron said, "What else?"

"But, Poppa," Paz argued, "how can you bury what we have learned here tonight? This knowledge upsets everything that some of us believe about ourselves, and our attitudes . . . it affirms that some of us are descended from Jews, in fact most of the people in this room, except for grandfather and perhaps Fr. Raul."

Elmer interrupted, "Well, it's not that simple. I just want to say that the Jews are probably descended from my people. After all, we have been around longer than anyone else." He smiled to himself, I just I had to get that one in.

Vincente thought for a moment. "I am not descended from any Jews, not me."

"Don't be too sure," Patron shook his head and said glumly, "You heard the names."

Ike strained hard to hear what they were saying. What he heard sounded like "some of us are descended from Jews." The ecstatic feeling he experienced seeing Rosie in the candlelight disappeared in a flash. What is all this shit about Jews, he said to himself. He was trying hard to stifle a strong urge to make his appearance known. No, he told himself, keep hidden; it would upset Fr. Raul if he knew I was spying on him. I will stick around until they leave and check everything out. He ducked down behind the pew just before Pablo, who was beginning to sense an additional presence in the room, turned around to investigate.

It was getting past midnight and everyone was tired. Elmer's eyelids were beginning to droop. Why are some human beings so strange about respecting their origins? Doesn't the branch die if it abandons the tree? Enough philosophy for one night, he said to himself, yawned loudly and announced. "I need to go home and get some sleep. I am going back up to the mesa early tomorrow morning. Whatever you are going to do with what we learned today is not for me to decide anyway."

Fr. Raul disagreed, but respectfully. "I don't feel that way grandfather. God, and our Great Spirit, have brought us into this together."

Elmer smiled. Fr. Raul had said "our Great Spirit." 'Our' is a good word. However, I still have to go home. Elmer became aware that he had never used the word 'however' in his conversations with himself before. Is my vocabulary changing because I am hanging out with these people?

Carmela dragged herself to her feet. "I have had enough for one night. C'mon, grandfather, I'll drive you home." Elmer beamed, more delighted than he wanted to show.

Fr. Raul shouted, "Just a minute, everyone. Excuse me, grandfather, but I need everyone to swear that we will not utter a word of what happened here tonight, or what we have seen, to anyone. That means not Jake, Jon, or anyone. Patron can tell Esther because she saw the block, that is, pedestal, and I want her to come to the next meeting. Is that O.K?"

No objections.

"Now please, everyone, before we leave, let us pray for strength and guidance about how to proceed. Then we will meet back here tomorrow night. Same time. Now promise." Everyone promised. "Anyone who so desires can remain for communion. Short version."

Patron and Elmer headed for the door.

Carmela motioned to Elmer to wait for her and followed Rosie, Vincente, Vickie, Pablo and Paz to the front pew. When they kneeled down Fr. Raul began the abbreviated mass.

"Dear Lord," he said, "we have been given a terrible responsibility to figure out why you have dumped this problem in our laps. What are we supposed to do with this knowledge? Help us to do our best. Amen."

Then, to everyone's surprise, he turned to address Rosita. "I have a feeling you are involved. At least we have found your missing pedestal. I hope you are happy about that. One way or the other you will get it back. That I promise."

Fr. Raul invited everyone to light a candle at Rosita's feet. Rosie asked him.

"What about, you know . . .?"

Fr. Raul responded solemnly. "Later. Give me a hand to bring the things we found to my office. I will lock them in the safe. Then I will pray on these events. Maybe I will have some answers for you." He turned to the group. "Please, for God's sake, and mine, tell no one. Good night and God bless you."

After everyone had left the church, Fr. Raul and Francisca retired to their quarters. When Ike heard their door slam, he left his hiding place, moved up to the altar and removed the cover from the pedestal. He noticed the carving with the 'reaching out cross,' as Elmer called it, shimmering in the fading candlelight. He squatted down in front of it to get a closer look.

"What is all this?" he asked himself. "The names they mentioned, on the list, and this beautiful work?" Ike became transfixed until he noticed some drops of blood on the star in the center of the crucifix begin to pulsate.

"La Palabra de Dios," he whispered.

Then the room began to spin. He tried to stand up, but his feet abruptly slid out from under him. He fell backwards and the back of his head bounced off the Saltillo tile floor. Lights out. From that moment on, and for the rest of his days, Ike would never know if the reason he passed out that night was due to Alcalde's tequila or whether, indeed, the Holy Spirit had touched him.

11

The Word According to Petroglyphs

Elmer and Raymond were waiting in the small guardhouse at the entrance to the pueblo when Jon sped into the parking lot at five-thirty Monday morning. His SUV was covered with graffiti, and the back window was cracked in two.

"What happened?" Raymond shouted and opened the door. "What's that written here, 'Jingo go home, or else.' You okay?"

Jon nodded and waved Elmer into the front seat. Raymond got in the back and stretched out. "Unbelievable, those jerks," Raymond yelled.

Jon groaned. "I tried to rinse off the Jingo crap but it's oil paint, won't come off. Anyway, it's not the end of the world. Here, I brought a thermos of hot tea for you guys."

Raymond filled two plastic cups and handed one to Elmer.

"Thanks," he smiled, "Hey, what's a Jingo?"

"Beats me," Jon yawned. Raymond yawned in return, "La Tierra for sure."

"Screw 'em," Jon snapped, and stepped hard on the accelerator.

"Good attitude," Elmer chuckled.

"Think I should get that gun?" Jon scoffed.

"So now you are a warrior?" Elmer laughed, "No gun, Jon."

"Why not?" Jon asked, suddenly aware that his foot was pressing too hard on the accelerator.

"Don't let crazies make you veer off center and act crazy too. Fix your car and forget about La Tierra. If you do not react, they do not exist. Get it? Now please, slow down."

"What if they go after Rosie?" Jon asked.

"Then you get a gun." Elmer laughed. "Don't worry. Ike wouldn't let anyone hurt Rosie."

"Voila." Jon brought the car to a halt at the foot of the Mesa.

"On the other hand, Jon," Elmer teased; "if you need a bow and arrow . . ." He stopped in mid-sentence, distracted by a tinge of brilliant orange color beginning to edge up over the eastern hills. He absorbed it for a moment, and then said urgently, "First light, gotta hurry." Elmer was now all business.

"Jon. Remember, you do nothing."

"Yes, grandfather, I'll see you this evening."

"Not if we see you first," Elmer smiled, flipped Jon a thumbs up, and pointed Raymond in the direction of the stone trail. "No cactus there. I don't want to get spiked in the dark."

The stone trail, a three-foot deep, two-foot wide passageway carved into the soft white rock, was made by a million footsteps. It winds up the side of the mesa to about one hundred feet short of the top, and then flattens out and becomes a rocky path. When it rains, the trail is as slippery as a water slide. Consequently, experienced climbers take a longer, but safer, trail in bad weather. Numerous stone caves yawn over the trail. The caves were shaped eons ago by volcanic forces that spewed a mixture of dust, ash, silica and minerals—tuff—through the layers of sandstone. Over time, the tuff eroded away more quickly than the sandstone, leaving a variety of talc-white caves that have served animals and people as a source of shelter.

As soon as Elmer began to climb, he retreated into a contemplative state of mind. Raymond learned early in life to respect his grandfather's ability to 'leave' the present on a moment's notice. The higher they climbed, and with Elmer quiet, Raymond became increasingly curious about the interior of the caves. He stopped to peek into one of the larger caves, but Elmer barked wordlessly, and pointed a finger skyward indicating that it was getting lighter. There was no time for exploration, so Raymond picked up the pace. Moments later, they reached the end of the stone trail, and an easy trek to the top of the mesa. After they crested the edge of the mesa, Elmer motioned to Raymond that he wanted to enter the sacred cave alone.

Once inside, Elmer lit a bundle of sage, blew the smoke to the four directions, and performed his blessing ceremony. Raymond stood quietly outside until Elmer beckoned him to come in. After Raymond entered, they stood silently together in the footprints of the countless others who stood here since ancient times. Raymond looked around him.

The cave is irregular in circumference, averaging about eighteen feet in diameter and is ten feet high. It is surprisingly well lit, both by daylight and firelight, because its brilliant white color reflects the light so well. A firepit sits opposite the entrance and has a small, black-rimmed smoke hole in the ceiling above it. The walls are covered with colorful paintings of animals and people, some very old, as well as etchings of spirals, wavy lines, hourglasses, crosses, sacred figures, fish, snakes and more. Academic experts say that their purpose is to tell stories, share information, depict relationships, portray beliefs, describe history and cosmology, communicate messages and infinitely more. Only people like Elmer possess the ancestral spiritual decoder necessary to actually know what mysteries they hold.

Elmer eased down cross-legged on the soft, sandy floor and grunted with satisfaction. "The trail gets longer every year. Okay, grandson, let us drink now, and then we need to light sage again. Watch how I do it. Someday you will sit here with your own grandson. Then we go outside and sit until sunset and observe the two new figures I found. We must not miss anything because messages can go by as fast as a shooting star. And no talking. First, we must watch until the sun is at its highest. Then we can take a break, eat and rest for an hour. When the sun starts down, we go back to work. Savvy?"

"Yes, grandfather." Raymond felt a warm surge of pride pass through his chest.

"And then," Elmer continued, "when we have finished, we go home and tell the people what has been revealed, and what we are supposed to do with what we learned. Above all, grandson, keep an open mind. Sometimes the Great Spirit comes at you from left field."

Raymond laughed. "That's a mixed metaphor."

"That's the Great Spirit for you. He's a mindbender." Elmer smiled.

Elmer removed a bundle of sage from his bag, lit it, and began to chant melodiously to the powers that live in each of the four directions. He motioned to Raymond to join in, and they repeated the ceremony together. When they finished, they repeated, "All, my relatives," three times in unison. Then Elmer grinned mischievously.

"Grandson, we only need to do that ceremony once, but I did it when I first came into the cave in case we screwed it up when we did it together."

Raymond laughed and Elmer placed both hands on his shoulders. "Okay, grandson. We woke them up and they know we are coming. Let us get on with it. I will show you the figures. I take one, and you take the other. When we are as one with them, the vision will follow." Elmer chuckled, "At least that's the way it goes with us old guys. Maybe it's different for college guys."

Raymond sassed back. "No peyote? No mushrooms, grandfather? Like the old guys?"

"Nah. This is a drug-free cave. Those guys that go on vision quests or whatever and take drugs only fool themselves. What they think are revelations, are their own daydreams, movies on the back of their eyelids. The spirits don't waste their time talking to druggies." Elmer sighed. "Believe me, I know. I tried the other way. Damn mescaline, almost killed me. Made me think I could fly by myself. I started speeding down the runway trying to take off, but I never got off the ground. I tripped over a rock and got knocked cold for two days. But that's a story for another day."

Raymond laughed, loudly this time. "I gotta make a pit stop, grandfather."

"Okay, aim downwind."

Raymond laughed again. "You are frisky for sure . . ."

Elmer was smiling when he met Raymond outside. "I want to tell you, grandson, that this is a fine moment for me. Being here with you. Together, trying to help our people."

"Me, too," Raymond was deeply moved.

Elmer patted Raymond's cheek firmly, but gently. "Isn't this just like the movies?"

❧

Jon and Rosie had agreed to get together that morning after Jon delivered Raymond and Elmer to the mesa. When Rosie heard Jon's car approaching she picked up her picnic basket bursting with coffee, rolls, butter, bacon, jam and honey, and walked out into the courtyard. Then she spotted the graffiti on Jon's car.

"Oh my God!" she shouted, "Goddamn, sons of bitches, what did they do? Are you okay?"

"I'm fine."

"What happened?" she yelled, her eyes spitting fire.

"I found the car like this in the morning."

"What's this 'Jingo'?"

"I haven't the slightest . . . got any turpentine."

"Yeah, in the garage."

"Good, I'll clean this off. It's oil paint."

"Okay, but first," Rosie smiled.

"What, Rosie?"

"This." Rosie jumped into his arms and wrapped her legs tightly around him.

"Mmmm! I love you," Jon whispered as they kissed. "Now let's clean off the car."

Rosie hurried into the garage and emerged with a can of turpentine and a handful of rags. "My grandparents have everything," she smiled. Jon poured the turpentine over the cloths and began to wipe off the graffiti. "Great, it works, there goes Jingo. So are you going to tell me what happened last night at the church?"

"A lot. But I cannot say because I am sworn to secrecy about you-know-what for the moment," she said coyly.

"You told me about the cemetery," Jon teased.

"That was different, but I'll give you a hint. Do you remember when I asked Fr. Raul for advice, he told me to wait, and I thought that was ridiculous? And remember when Raymond said that the answer to our dilemma had to come from outside."

"Sort of . . ."

Rosie smiled, "Well, something is happening that is no one's doing."

Jon sighed, "Honey, I haven't the slightest idea what you are talking about."

"Bear with me. Look, isn't it weird that I haven't gotten any aggravation from my family since my announcement? Mostly grim faces and head scratching. That is already unusual. Normally they would be in an uproar. Everybody would be mad at me and the crazies would be after your scalp. Do they have other things on their minds? Maybe the flood is the reason. But with all that happened at the cemetery, that block being discovered . . . Wouldn't you think, the way the word spreads so fast around here . . . that, I don't know. Last night, the people at the church meeting looked at me funny, like I was weird."

"What do you mean weird?"

"I don't have another word to describe what happened. All of a sudden, everyone got quiet and looked at me. Differently than ever before. Like it wasn't me. I felt funny too."

Jon shook his head, wiped off the last of the graffiti and gathered the rags together. He smiled, "Nothing unusual about you being weird. "

Rosie punched him in the arm and pointed to the trashcan. "Rags in there," she frowned. "I'll put the turpentine back where it belongs. You go wash your hands in the sink. Clean them good."

Jon obeyed. "Seriously. What do you mean, something is going on?" he asked.

Rosie came over to the sink and intertwined her hands with Jon's. "You have to live up here a long time to understand such things. How about washing my hands too?"

"Oh," Jon smiled warmly, "anytime."

Rosie snuggled closer. "I think we should just lie low for the time being. And wait and see what happens."

"Lying low sounds good to me," Jon dried off their hands and embraced her. "How low do you want to lie?"

Rosie smiled coquettishly. "Got a blanket in the car?"

"Better believe it, New Mexico standard equipment."

Rosie whispered in his ear, "Well, how about we spread the blanket next to the river; eat some breakfast and . . ."

Jon nuzzled her neck. "Something good is happening. We've never, er, in Santa Rosita . . ." Jon laughed.

"I mean a picnic by the river." Rosie punched him in the shoulder again, but not too hard.

◎

Night fell very fast on the mesa. It was time to leave as soon as Elmer began to feel the air beginning to cool down. The sun was setting fast. He opened his eyes and stretched up from his sitting position. Raymond sat upright at his side. He was sound asleep. Elmer nudged him gently and Raymond awoke with a start. "I was awake, grandfather."

"Of course," Elmer smiled. "Before we go, I need to thank the Great Spirit. Would you like to do this with me?"

Raymond grinned, "Of course." A great honor.

Elmer grinned back. "You did good today. This will only take five minutes, and then the spirits go off duty."

After the brief ceremony, they gathered up their gear and started down the mesa. Elmer led the way. Suddenly he stopped, turned around, and looked into Raymond's eyes as deeply as only he could, "So . . ."

"You mean what happened?"

Elmer nodded.

"Well, grandfather, my figure resembled, I guess . . . a butterfly. At first, I could not make it out, until it took shape, narrow at the center, wide at the sides. I did not see it move until late afternoon. First, it wiggled a bit, and then it started to beat its wings, very slowly at first. Like the butterfly in that Microsoft logo."

"What's that?"

"You know, computer . . ."

"Oh, never mind that. Go on."

"Well, then it started moving faster and faster. Then I guess I fell asleep and started to dream. The figure became many butterflies. Millions of them. They flew toward a house with a lot of lights and a big parking lot, and beat their wings together and made a powerful wind that tumbled the house.

When the wreckage settled, a lot of small flat round pebbles tumbled out of the wreckage followed by lots of small people who ran all over like ants. Next, the butterflies flew into a crowd of very tall people and landed on their heads and their shoulders."

"Very good," Elmer exclaimed. "Very good."

"And then, crazy as it sounds, I saw the butterflies smile, and the people, too."

Elmer drew Raymond close and placed his hands on Raymond's shoulders. "That's very good for a college boy. Now tell me what that was that all about?"

Raymond scratched his head, "I haven't the slightest idea."

"Be an Indian and not a physicist."

"I need time to think it over. What about you, grandfather?"

"Let's walk first."

They walked until they reached the stone trail. Elmer asked Raymond to go first so he could lean on Raymond's shoulder. "My figure looked like a bunch of stick people holding hands in a circle, as seen from above. Their heads were inside of the circle, and their bodies and legs outside.

"Like people doing a water ballet in the old Esther Williams movies."

"Who?" Elmer asked.

"Never mind, grandfather, go on."

"Well, the figure started to turn, slowly at first, then faster, and then it got a hundred times bigger. I had to jump back so it did not hit me when it took off."

"It took off?" Raymond echoed.

"Sure, it flew up from the ground, picked up speed, flew down into the valley, crossed over the reservation, touched every building, every home and the Santa Rosita church and the Arts and Crafts Center. Then it flew way up into the heavens and came back. Like one of those flying saucers. Then it became smaller, whirled slower and slower, and settled back into the ground. And that was it."

"That's something," Raymond said.

"Yes. We got what we asked for."

"What, grandfather?"

"A reminder that we have an opportunity to hold hands with others. That we can do something good for all of us if we do it together. "

"Is that it?"

"That's part of it, my grandson." Elmer knew that since there were two figures, the message had two parts. The first part was his; everyone was supposed to do something together. Raymond's part was about what everybody was supposed to do.

"And you, grandson. What did you get?"

"Butterflies on the brain."

"And . . ."

Raymond drew a deep breath. "Well, the butterflies blew over a building built of pebbles and landed on the shoulders of people and made them happy."

Elmer stopped; they had almost reached the bottom of the trail. "And . . .?"

"That's all I can do for now . . ."

"Okay, ask Jon when we get in his car. He knows."

"What? C'mon, grandfather. How would Jon know?"

"He knows. Wanna bet?"

Raymond laughed. "Okay. What do we bet for?"

"If I win, we do a week on the mesa together. You need a post-graduate course in vision interpretation."

"Okay, and if I win? Raymond grinned.

"We do the same."

@

Jon was waiting at the bottom of the mesa with a spotless SUV and a new rear window. Elmer was going to remark about it, but chose to remain silent. The less said about bad things, the less power they have. Raymond checked out the car and flipped Jon a thumbs up, but he was mostly thinking about why grandfather said that Jon knew something he did not. When they got in the car, he tapped Jon on the shoulder.

"Hey, Jon. My grandfather said that you could explain my vision today."

Jon pressed his foot on the accelerator. Was he being put on? "I don't know about your stuff," he said, "I'm a white man from Santa Fe."

"Grandfather says you know. But since you are a white man, you don't know that you know," Raymond laughed.

Elmer joined in lightheartedly. "My knucklehead grandson genius knows what E=Mc2—whatever—means, but can't make sense of a basic vision any Indian kid can figure out in a heartbeat."

Raymond said, "Thanks, grandfather," greatly enjoying the banter. After all, Indian or not, he was a physicist, and a quantum physicist to boot. Mystery was his specialty, scientific mystery, that is.

"Hmm. So I know what it is, eh?" Jon smiled. "Ray, my friend I'd love nothing more than to one-up you in front of grandfather but I haven't the slightest idea what I am supposed to know."

Raymond feigned annoyance and settled back in his seat.

"Indians don't one-up one another. But then you are not an Indian." Raymond looked at Elmer for permission to go on. After all this was sacred material. Elmer nodded, yes.

"Okay, Jon. I saw a butterfly, then a lot of butterflies, and they knocked over a house and small round flat pebbles rolled out, and the butterflies landed on the heads and shoulders of all shapes and colors of smiling people."

Elmer started chuckling louder than Raymond ever heard him laugh before.

"What, you guys?" Raymond threw up his hands.

"Butterflies, c'mon . . ." Jon roared. "You didn't have to go to all that trouble. I told you the same thing the other night."

"What are you talking about?" Raymond asked. Elmer was chortling so hard he was having a hard time catching his breath.

"Butterflies," Jon howled, "Sure. You are being told that you don't need to build a casino to go into business."

"Business, what kind of business?"

"Butterflies. C'mon, Ray, butterflies. What looks like butterflies? Bow ties. And what goes with that? Bolo ties, and hatbands and headbands as well . . . no?"

"Not bad, my boy," Elmer patted Jon on the back. "Not bad at all."

"Oh!" Raymond sighed, "Hmmm. Butterflies. Right. Even if we were to consider such a thing, we will need a lot of capital. Butterflies ain't free," he grinned, very pleased with his pun. "Get it?"

"Ughhh," Jon groaned.

Elmer interrupted. "Let's get serious. We have been told that we need to go into business with others. Considering what has happened lately, the others means the Alonzos."

Elmer locked his hands together. "See, all the people holding hands together. Simple."

"Simple. Not for me." Raymond asked, "How do you make a vision come true?"

"You don't," Elmer answered. "Visions are likes leaves in the wind. They float by, and you grab them. Opportunity is in the air. We need to grab it."

❧

The first thing Ike remembered when he regained consciousness on the floor of the darkened church was the image of Rosie framed in candlelight.

"She looked so . . ." Ike searched for words, but none came. He edged up slowly, not to agitate his throbbing headache. "Ow!" Any movement made it worse. What the hell. Am I getting weird, am I losing it? He got to his feet and wobbled over to Rosita. It was too dark to see very much, so he picked up a few half-spent candles, lit them, and placed them at Rosita's feet. He kneeled down in front of her and stared up into her eyes. Did I see her eyes move? He asked himself, and felt his feet turn ice cold. Am I going loco? He shouted aloud and noticed a cold chill at the back of his neck that crawled slowly down his body. He opened and shut his eyes several times. No, I ain't loco. He choked and felt his eyes filled with tears.

She is staring at me. She is. "You are," he cried, and Rosita's eyes moved slightly sideways, very slowly, demurely. Oh God, I am losing it.

Alcalde, you son-of-a-bitch, you poisoned me. My mind is gone. I am loco. He began to sob, hiding his face in his hands. When he gathered his courage to look again, he peered out through the corner of his eyes. I don't fuc...er, believe it! I hear you talking in my head. What, are you saying? What, you are telling me . . . that I am . . . more than I am right now. That I have things to do. That I am a good man. You are saying this to me! To me, Ike, the loser?

Ike's heart was pumping blood so fast it flushed the cobwebs from his mind. This can't be true. Statues can't talk. What is going on? Am I dead? Did I break my skull? Did Alcalde poison me? He listened again. What? I should look at the pedestal. Ike staggered over to the pedestal, and came face to face with the relief. He squatted down, fixing his eyes on the bleeding six-pointed star at the heart of the cross. He began to feel great warmth in his chest, as if his heart was becoming one with the star. The dripping blood became his own. He started to weep, softly at first, then with deep wrenching sobs. He stared at the figures at the foot of the cross, and allowed their sadness to penetrate every cell of his being. He felt he was dissolving, all boundaries disappeared, curiously however, he became unafraid.

Then he heard Rosita's voice. "Do you know who those people are?"

Ike turned quickly to face her. "No," Ike answered.

"Mary and Joseph and Abraham, crying over what people have done with their gifts. They are crying because we have corrupted God's sacred words, and divided the people that God wants connected."

"But I didn't do anything . . ."

"Really?"

"What do you mean?"

"Never mind. What is important is what you are going to do now that you know."

"Know what?"

Rosita's voice became stronger, more urgent. "Think about it. What do you know?"

"Oh!"

"Do something about it, Ike," she spoke in a voice as gentle as a soft breeze.

Ike felt like a small child. "Who me? Do what?"

"You know."

"Got a hint?"

"Close your eyes."

Ike closed his eyes. A whirlwind of lines and circles rushed into his mind. The lines and circles came together to form a circle of many people together holding hands. He felt a rush of compassion. "We are one," Rosita said. "Now do something about it."

Then there was silence.

It took some time for Ike to gather himself together. After he did, he left the church, slogged his way up the hill to his parents' house, ran to his room and passed out on his bed. When he awoke at 10 A.M., the back of his head was still throbbing.

What the hell happened to me last night, he asked himself. Was I dreaming? Then he fell back asleep. At 2 P.M., he got up, showered, dressed and went to work. Surprisingly, when he sat down at his loom, his headache improved, although his mind was still spinning with memories of the night before. She said to do something about it, he muttered to himself. Do something about it. He removed the shuttle from the loom and detached the rug he was weaving. Ike had a new project in mind.

❀

Earlier that morning, Patron was eating his breakfast at their oversized, well-worn kitchen table, updating Esther about the meeting the night before.

"Want some more bacon?" Esther called from the stove.

"No thanks, dear, more coffee would be nice."

Esther poured the coffee and sat down at the table. "Oh Ruben," she groaned, "It used to be harder to get up than to sit down. Now it is all the same."

"You should have been there last night. Fr. Raul wants you to come tonight."

"I was there, I can see through your eyes, you know." she smiled.

Patron waved her off. "Don't say such things; you know it gives me the willies."

Esther laughed. "You only need to worry if you are naughty."

That was something he had thought about in the past, so he didn't laugh and hastened to change the subject.

"Esther, I thought I'd seen it all at my age. But this . . ." he sighed with deep apprehension.

Esther was enjoying herself. "At last the cat is out of the bag—something we always knew, somewhere deep inside, but never said." Esther remembered taking heat about her candle lighting. Now it was payback time.

"Ruben, we knew that many of our ancestors were forced to become Catholic centuries ago, but we ignore it like it never happened. We change the subject when we are asked why we continue to circumcise our boys, or else we fabricate a medical excuse. Why we say our family is 'allergic' to pork and shellfish, even though some of us have never tried it. And the bonfires for seven nights at Christmas. Why was I chosen to carry on the Friday night ceremony? Why do I want Rosie to continue my ways?"

"Rosie?" Patron asked, "So Rosie is chosen?"

"What else?" Esther smiled. "Ruben," Esther continued. "We never asked why, because we don't even want to think why. Why not speak the truth? Are we afraid the Inquisition will get us? I am not saying that we have to change anything. I am what I am: Catholic, Hispanic, and proud of it. I am staying that way. But what if we came out and addressed this issue in public? After all, isn't it about honoring and respecting our true history? And it might shut up some haters. Wouldn't that be a good thing?"

"Shutting up the haters is a good thing. But the people would go loco."

"But Ruben, truth must be always be acknowledged. Even if it takes 500 years."

"Esther, mi amor, how is this truth going to better our lives? Sometimes the truth is better buried."

"Maybe and maybe not. But what if somebody like you acknowledges that we are all part of everything, and everyone that came before. Maybe people can learn to be more tolerant, less critical of others, especially when they know we are all in the same boat. That no one is any better than anyone else, that no one has all the right answers, certainly not more than anyone else. That hate is just ignorance. And, of course, there is . . ."

Patron groaned, "I know."

Esther smiled, "Rosie and Jon . . ."

Patron grunted, "Ay! Don't remind me."

Esther began to speak but Patron raised his hand to shush her. "Please dear. One thing at a time. We don't want to make a problem when there isn't a problem. Who is ready for such a message? Anyway, we are not Jews because our ancestors were Jews. We are Catholics. This discovery has no relevance to our lives."

Esther answered in measured tones. "True, if we look at our lives like a snapshot in time, and that our personal experience is all there is. There is a larger context, Ruben. A beginning and an end. The snapshot is one picture in a book; the album contains what came before us, and what will come after."

Patron grimaced, "Snapshots, albums, what are you talking about?"

"Rosie and Jon. How can we object to her marrying a Jew when we would be Jewish if the Inquisition hadn't happened?"

"We are what we are, not what we could be." Patron tried to steer her into the realm of logical practicality, but that is not where Esther lived.

"It has relevance to our ancestors' spirits. Aren't they always with us? Aren't they watching us now? Don't you feel them here? They ask us if we going to rise above prejudice and stupidity in our old age, or continue on the same divisive path. They ask if we will allow them back in our lives. Why should we accept the Spanish part and not the Jewish part?" Esther stopped. "Ruben, why are you blinking your eyes so much?"

"I am not blinking my eyes."

"Yes, you are, Ruben. You blink when you are nervous."

"So I'm nervous. Esther, no wonder I am nervous. This isn't easy for me. When I was younger, I only related to my own kind, wanted no part of outsiders and gringos. I disliked some of the grabby Jews I met in the big cities who owned the big stores, controlled rug distribution, who were tough in business. I felt the same way Ike feels now."

Esther leaned forward. "All the Jews you met were bad? Now come on . . ."

"Well, of course I met some good regular people, storekeepers, artists, lawyers, and some university people." He reflected for a moment. "It's true that I always looked for the bad."

Esther interrupted. "See!"

Patron held up a hand. "Wait now. Let me finish. I'll give you one thing. I must confess, as I get older, I feel bad that I encouraged Ike to have the same attitudes."

Esther decided to be quiet and hear him out, so she nodded her approval. Ruben has to get where he is going in his own way.

Patron spoke quickly and fearfully. "This is not just about me. Esther, can you imagine what will happen if our neighbors find out they are descended from Jews? What will this do to this town? Our religion is the core of our life. People could start comparing—for good or bad —who is descended from Jews and who is not. Why open a Pandora's Box? You know how loco people can get. There are not only people among us who don't like Jews; others hate them, even if they never met a Jew in their life. What are they going to do if they find out they are exactly what they hate? We have enough to deal with the idiots who spend their time measuring whose skin is whiter. Are they going to start comparing how Jewish they are, or are not?"

"Probably," Esther threw up her hands and shrugged her shoulders.

Patron continued his litany with more confidence. "What do you think will happen to our church if this comes out? Won't people start to wonder if they have the right to go to church at all if they are descended from Jews? Then what do they do? Where would we all belong? Abandon our church that we love? No Esther, if we go public our lives as we know it would be over. Not to say the town would become a media zoo. Is that good?"

Esther chuckled, "You are speaking about things you never wanted to discuss before, isn't that good? And won't it be harder for any one of us who knows the secret to give Rosie and Jon a hard time? Isn't this already a blessing? A miracle? Wouldn't you like to be a fly on the wall when someone who badmouths Jon for being a Jew finds out that their ancestors were too?" Esther laughed heartily.

"That's not funny!" Patron waved a finger at her.

"Yes, it is," she roared.

Patron could not stop himself from cracking a smile. "Jon is still an outsider." Patron reached for his lucky charm and held it up. His voice softened.

"Can you believe it, Esther, all these years I've been reciting the Rosary with my beads and this—the Ten Commandments?"

She smiled slyly. "C'mon, Ruben, you knew, somewhere deep inside, you knew."

He frowned. "Well, I'm not that stupid. When we do not want to know, we do not know. There is something else, Esther."

"What's that?" Patron blinked hard to clear his eyes. "Well, this may sound strange, but Rosita, whom we love and adore, is—I don't know how to say this—well, we have been worshipping a Jewish . . . statue . . . all these years."

Esther chuckled. "Ruben, you are losing it. Jesus Christ was Jewish, the disciples were Jewish, but a statue cannot be Jewish. Anyway, what is the difference? Christian, Jewish. What does she care? It is only stupidos that make such distinctions."

"Ay! So now I am a stupido?"

Esther giggled. "At least you are a cute one. Like Paz said, you men have to struggle to learn things that women naturally know. But it is very cute to watch you struggle. Whoever heard of a Jewish statue? Enough dear, have some more bacon and stop blinking your eyes."

Patron relaxed and told Esther that he was not blinking and that he had something in his eye. He picked up a piece of bacon and bit hard. "See. Jews don't eat bacon, do they?"

◎

Fr. Raul slipped out of bed before sunrise, opened the safe in his bedroom, removed the Ten Commandments, the panels, and the Torah, and placed them on his bed. Francisca was awake, but still snuggled deep under the covers.

"What do you think, Francisca? Do we put these back in Rosita's pedestal and forget about them? Should we bring them out on Sunday morning for everyone to see and discuss? Do I call the Bishop? What does this holy message mean for us? And why now? What does Rosie have to do with this? You saw her last night. I don't even dare to say what I think about that."

Francisca smiled. "Rosie shone like a saint."

"All this is beyond me. I am a simple parish priest."

"No dear." Francisca beamed warmly and stroked Fr. Raul's face. "Not beyond you at all. Remember when you played baseball, you told me about what a good clutch hitter you were."

Raul had learned to pay attention to Francisca's often-unrecognized wisdom. "Yes," he laughed. "Yes. But now I'm a priest and tonight we must decide what to do. Thank God Esther is coming. I will pray all day."

"All day! What about your lunch?"

"At noon."

"What do you want?"

"A big burrito, Colorado filling, and a Pepsi."

"Diet Pepsi."

Fr. Raul grinned. "Regular today. I need the sugar."

"Should I bring lunch into the church?"

"No, call me when you are ready. I'll eat in the kitchen, with you."

"Okay," she smiled happily. "Chips and salsa?"

"I guess so."

"Yes, you do need to eat."

"Pico de Gallo too. You know, I haven't had a drink for a while."

"Yes, I am very proud."

"I have made a decision," he said with great conviction. Strength oozed from his pores.

Francisca's heart beat faster. "I am sure it's right, whatever it is."

"Whatever the committee decides to do about the contents of the pedestal and the names on the retablos, I have decided, and I hope they agree with me, that Rosita should stand outside on her new pedestal at sunset. I will cover it so no one will see the carvings."

"Brilliant," Francisca blushed.

"Make sure everyone knows Rosita will be out tonight," he said. He suddenly felt warm all over.

"Of course," She responded with great enthusiasm. Another direct assignment. "I'll get the word out, mi amor. You are so smart, and so good. And you are doing such a great job with this difficult task." She was getting hot too.

"Francisca," Fr. Raul blushed, "we have a little time . . ."

Francisca smiled. "Always. We always have time." Francisca lifted the bed covers and Fr. Raul slipped in.

"God is good," he smiled.

"You too," she sighed.

◎

Paz dusted off her saints and fetishes and re-arranged them neatly. "Darlings, you all get first class treatment today because you have answered my prayers. Fancy you being in cahoots with Rosita." Paz placed a pinch of corn meal laced with turquoise dust in front of the stone animals. "This is for you guys, and some extra for you, turtle, for giving Rosie extra patience, which, God knows, she needs." Then she reached behind the row of saints and plucked out St. Anthony, who was leaning upside down against the wall, still in exile. "Okay, sentence over. Back to work with the others. All is forgiven." She kissed him with a big, loud, smack, "Mmm-aaaah," and lined him up next to his fellows.

"But don't forget you-know-what."

◎

Hand-in-hand, Vincente and Vickie took their usual walk after breakfast. Vincente lifted Vickie's hand to his face and kissed it tenderly. "Vickie, remember when Rosie read out the names of the people that came here long ago?"

"Yes, dear."

"The Abales are on that list."

"I know, dear."

"So are we."

"So what do we do?"

"The best we can."

"Which means?" Vickie looked straight into Vincente's eyes.

"Forget about it."

"But aren't you curious?"

"Forget about it."

"But . . ." Vickie murmured.

❁

Alcalde called Ike at work.

"Ike, I am really sick. My head is killing me and I got the runs."

"I got sick, too." Ike wanted to brush him off.

Alcalde continued in a hoarse voice. "Must have mixed a bad batch. Chinga, the two of us stuck in the confessional, hardly hearing a thing that was going on, and when you said that about Elmer's hand in Vickie. I lost it. I went over to the Cantina to cool down, but I got too sick and couldn't make it back to see you. Anyway, tell me what happened that I need to know about. What is with that block? I need to set your sister straight about the Jingo, but I am too sick to do anything today, so I am going home to recuperate. I'll take care of things on my next visit. Sal wasted the Jingo's car last night. Hear anything about it?"

Ike made an effort to disguise his disappointment and annoyance. "Er, no, heard nothing, so far." Alcalde was the last person he wanted to deal with now. Since Alcalde had abandoned him, he lost all respect for him. Didn't he make me hide in the confessional, a blasphemous act, and then poison me to boot? Didn't he run out of the church and abandon me? Ike was thinking hard. That wasn't loyal and respectful. What kind of a leader is that? Yeah, I got to face the truth, Alcalde isn't a bad guy, personally, but if he represents La Tierra nowadays, spying from the confessional, that has nothing to do with saving our heritage. One thing for sure, I can't let him loose on Rosie.

He spoke quickly. "Not much happened after you left. They got some stuff out of the block but it didn't seem important. They are going to have another meeting tonight. I think it is about whether they should use the block for Rosita's pedestal. That's about it. Hey. About my sister. Tell everyone to back off. I will handle her. Tell Sal not to do anything more with the Doc right now."

"The Doc," Alcalde laughed hoarsely. "You mean the Jingo."

"Yeah, right, the Jingo."

"You alright, Ike? You sound different."

"Just wore out."

Alcalde was glad to get off the hook. He needed to assert his authority but he felt too sick to do so.

"Ike, I hope you are not going soft." He could not afford to lose another member, especially a member of the Alonzo family.

"Waddya' mean, soft?" Ike shot back. "I said I'll take care of it."

"Okay, don't get sensitive. Just doing my job." Alcalde was pleased to delegate responsibility for the matter to Ike. He had what he needed to file a report and show his superiors that he was on the ball. "Okay amigo, whatever you want, I've got lots of things to do as soon as I feel better. Let me know if you need me. La Tierra is always here for you."

"Right! I'll be in touch."

"Ike, I almost peed my pants laughing last night."

"A night to remember . . ."

"Yeah. Adios. La Tierra, bro', I gotta go to the head."

"Yeah," Ike hung up the phone, walked into the bathroom, took off his headband and threw it into the garbage pail. Immediately, his headache disappeared. He stared at the garbage pail for some time, wondering.

He was at his loom setting up his new design when Sal walked in and moaned, "Man, I am going nuts."

"What happened?" Ike asked, not too enthusiastically.

"My chinga trailer, it's stuck fast in chinga dried mud five hundred feet from where it belongs."

Ike tried to muster up some sympathy, but his mind was elsewhere. "It wasn't that far when I left."

"It kept sliding around until the ground dried hard. Why did this happen to me, Ike? I'm a good guy."

"Yeah." Ike stared expressionless.

Sal stepped closer and looked into his eyes. "You Okay?"

"I drank some bad shit last night. Listen; I just talked with Alcalde, about the Rosie thing."

Sal interrupted. "Hey. I did the deed last night. Sprayed shit all over the Doc's car, 'Jingo go home' in oil paint. He will have a hell of a job getting that off. Busted his 'shield too."

Ike did not react. "I gotta talk to you, Sal."

Sal looked puzzled. "Hey, I thought you would be pleased." Ike's respect and approval meant the world to him.

"Sal, I gotta talk to you."

"Sure, Ike, but first I gotta say that you and me, we're like this, y'know." Sal crossed the index and middle fingers on his right hand. "And I don't want you to think that I'm not with you on the Rosie thing but I gotta pass for a while. The flood, y'know. I gotta find a place to live until I get my trailer back to where it belongs. I don't want to let you down, bro. I know this is important to you."

Ike hid a sigh of relief, and smiled. "That's okay. Bad timing, the flood and all."

Sal was surprised. "You are not mad?"

"Change of plans," Ike said.

Sal smiled back. Then he noticed Ike's bare forehead. "Where's your headband. You always wear your headband. Even in the shower."

"Took it off"

"Took it off. Why did you take it off?" Sal asked curiously. What was going on with Ike? He was different.

"Headache."

"You Okay?"

"Yeah." Ike smiled weakly.

"Ike, you seem different."

"How?"

"Well, kind of out of it, your eyes are different."

"How different?"

Sal squinted and looked closely at Ike's eyes. "Your eyes are ... shinier."

"What's shinier?"

"I dunno, shinier."

Ike sniffled. "Maybe I'm getting a cold. Gotta get back to work. A new design."

Sal turned to leave. "Gotta go, need to figure out what to do with the chinga trailer. I feel cursed lately."

"Could be," Ike nodded solemnly, "could be. Maybe somebody is telling us something."

⊚

Jake got back in bed after his regular 6 A.M. bathroom sortie. Carmela snuggled up and whispered, "Honey, are you Okay?" Jake yawned and said he had a bad night because of Rosie. "Why can't things be easy?" he moaned. He rolled over to face Carmela, and put his arms around her. Her soft and delicious body made him feels amorous, so his power rose. "My little plumpy," he said as he kissed her cheek, and moved his hand over her chest. "In the mood?"

"Not right now, dear, maybe later. I have something on my mind, too."

"Okay, what is it?" Jake feigned annoyance. "Hurry before the mood goes."

"What if you found out we were Jewish?"

Jake moved back, but not so far as to break contact. "Geez, Carmela, what are you talking about now?' He withdrew an arm and she put it back.

"I mean from your people, way back, long ago."

"Carmela, Jewish? What Jewish? I am not Jewish. I'm Catholic."

"But what if you found out you were."

"What if I found out I was a walrus?"

"C'mon, Jake."

"Don't be silly," he scoffed, profoundly disappointed that his power was fading fast.

Carmela continued. "Well, darling, the Jews have done many good things in this world. They have always been persecuted and were nearly wiped out in Germany. Of course, our religion is against them, but they are people like anyone else. One of our wool suppliers is Jewish and he is a good man, with a nice family. Some Jews are very charitable, professional. Look at Jon. Of course some are cheap and bossy too, especially those smelly ones I see in New York with beards and long hair, who break into lines."

"There's a reason people are down on the Jews. That thing about killing Christ."

"Do you know any Jews?"

"Well, in the army, a couple, but they weren't like regular Jews."

"How?"

"They were just regular guys, okay?"

Carmela withdrew his hand and rolled away. "I mean I wouldn't want not to be Catholic, but it would be special to say that we have Jewish blood running through our veins, the culture not the religion. We could accept that part."

He reached over. "Carmela, your uppity thing about white skin is one thing, now you want to be a Jew. C'mon."

Carmela pouted. "I don't want to be a Jew, Jake. I was just thinking what that would mean for Lisa to say that we have Jewish ancestors . . . the culture part."

"We have enough trouble with racist gringos and blacks who hate us for being Hispanics and get us mixed up with illegal immigrants; you want to add the Jew thing to it? It is just asking for more trouble," Jake groaned, "lots and lots of trouble. Carmela, you are a trip." Jake started chuckling.

"Thanks honey." Carmela said. "You really think I am special?"

"One of a kind."

Carmela rolled back toward Jake and wiggled around until Jake's hand landed in the right place. "You adore me, don't you?"

Jake grinned, "And how, baby. He sighed a happy sigh. "It's going to be a good day."

@

Elmer was having dinner with Raymond and Chenoa at the pueblo, Chenoa handed Elmer a plate filled with two toasted tuna fish salad with tomato sandwiches, his favorite meal.

"Grandfather," she asked, "what's with these messages, the block, and the drawings on the mesa?"

"First, Chenoa, need some more mayo, please." Elmer took a swig of tea from the super-sized, adobe-colored ceramic cup with 'Big Chief' written on the side Raymond had made for him. "Chenoa, we are getting messages, helpful ones. The Great Spirit has suggested a way to keep going without building a casino. As Jon figured out, and your smart husband did not." He teased Raymond, who feigned disappointment.

Chenoa laughed too, and hugged Raymond. "Not to worry dear, I love you. Gotta hear more tonight. Off to work for me." She kissed them both and left.

Elmer continued with his mouth full, "Grandson, the butterfly means you need to expand your bow tie business. That is the solution you have been offered. My circle of figures means that if we take this opportunity, your ties and headbands will become world famous and the pueblo will prosper."

"What?" Raymond retorted. "Bow ties, bolo ties and headbands? World famous? Very funny. It's a hobby, not a profession."

"Don't use your thinker. The way has been prepared. You have been chosen. That is why you were sent to Massachusetts to learn about the market."

"But bow ties are out of fashion, except in university towns."

"That is true if you say it. But when you get serious, the Great Spirit will change the layer of mind around the world to make bow ties fashionable."

"How do you know that?"

"The figures said so. But we have to do our part."

Raymond asked, "What's that?"

"Marketing," answered Elmer. "Marketing. The Great Spirit will help us with marketing. How do you think ideas get around?"

Raymond chuckled. "Grandfather, what do you know about marketing?"

"Why do people come from all over the world to buy our art? Marketing. Rosie knows about marketing. The way has been prepared for her to help. Why do you think she is our little sister? It is because we are destined to work together for the good of all. Her people picked her. The Great Spirit has picked you. Remember how the image in my vision flew all over the land. That means that your creations will go all over. It also means that it can only happen if our people and Rosie's people do it together. You make them, she creates the market, and we distribute them. All together, Rosie, Patron, his family, our people and us. All in a circle holding hands."

"Then you think the world will want to buy bowties?" Raymond asked.

Elmer answered with a satisfied grin. "Not all, but enough. Then we invest the profits."

Raymond grinned, "Invest the profits. I have to discuss this with Chenoa."

Elmer nodded, "If you like. She knows all about it anyway. Bear clan women know everything." He rolled his eyes, "Sometimes I wish they didn't."

Raymond asked, "And the big pow-wow at the church?"

Elmer whispered, even though there was no one there to hear, "Hush-hush. They received an old letter. I have no idea what they will do with it. It may be too powerful for them to use right now. Whatever, there is some heavy stuff going on. That's for sure."

12

More Than Meets the Eye

Pablo awoke feeling happy and enthusiastic about placing Rosita back on her pedestal. After a quick breakfast, he meticulously cleaned the peg holes on the top and bottom of the statue and the block to prepare them for new pegs. He found a sturdy oak leg from a discarded table and carved out four new, very solid pegs. After sanding them to the proper dimensions, he glued them deeply into the holes on the block. That's when Pablo got the idea to make Rosita easy to move around and save on some backbreaking work. To this purpose, he salvaged the undercarriage from a discarded baby stroller and carefully attached it to the bottom of the pedestal.

When this was done, it was time to test out his work.

He called Fr. Raul to help him. "Padre, I will rig a pulley above Rosita and wrap a strong rope around her waist so we can to raise her up and slip her pedestal under her." He then tugged on the rope and slowly raised Rosita into the air. Fr. Raul moved the pedestal under her and lined up the pegs correctly, and Pablo lowered her down.

"Perfecto," beamed Francisca. "Wonderful Pablo. You are so clever."

Pablo grinned uncharacteristically, and bowed low in appreciation of her compliment. Fr. Raul motioned to them that a prayer was in order. He took Francisca's hand in his and squeezed it gently.

"See how happy she is," Francisca smiled.

Pablo began to weep. "At last," he choked. "She is one. This is a great day."

Fr. Raul and Francisca looked at him curiously, but did not ask him to explain his words. After all, he was a Montoya, and had the right to mysteries. Francisca commented to Fr. Raul that although Pablo seemed very 'dense' at times, especially after drinking at Diego's with his cronies, at other times, he seemed very 'haughty' like a spirit watching.

When they finished their prayer, Pablo asked Fr. Raul if he should glue the pegs into the statue. "We could lift her up and do it right now," he said eagerly.

Fr. Raul shook his head. "No, Rosita has her pedestal back, but this may not be permanent. We need to see what the committee decides."

Francisca and Pablo protested, gently at first. "She does not want to lose her pedestal again, Padre." Francisca was emphatic. "She is whole."

"Yes," echoed Pablo at full volume, as if he had suddenly accumulated more substance. "There must be no question that she needs to keep her pedestal, Padre."

Some part of Fr. Raul bristled about taking an order from Pablo. However, he held his tongue. He knew that, as a Montoya—a direct descendant of the church founders, Fr. Miguel and Fr. Miguel Jr.—Pablo was a repository of little known church history. For example, one story he was privy to concerned the true origins of the church's and diocese's eternal indebtedness to the financial acumen of Fr. Miguel Jr.

As Pablo tells it, after Rosita's initial 'illumination' long ago, Fr. Miguel Jr., the presiding priest at the time, at his mother Felice's urging, created the weekly ritual they called the Noche ceremony. He wheeled Rosita out of the church and placed her on the landing at the top of the church steps to 'bathe' in the sunset. Eventually, Rosita and the Noche ritual began to be associated with many miracles and cures. Some people actually have referred to Santa Rosita as the Lourdes of America. Sensing the possibilities, Fr. Miguel Jr. invented an additional 'tradition'—consecrating 'sacred soil'—to satisfy those who desired to take a piece of the sacred experience home with them, spread the word, and leave a donation behind. This donation has supported the church in fine style ever since then.

This tradition is currently explained in the church brochure entitled 'Sacred Soil' which reads: "On Saturday morning, before the Noche ceremony, the priest spreads special soil in front the place where Rosita will stand. After the evening 'illumination' of Rosita, the priest takes the now-consecrated soil into the Fr. Miguel Sanctuary of Healing. He then places the soil into a large hole in the center of the floor. Here, pilgrims and worshippers who come to the sanctuary to pray for healing are free to reach down and take a pinch of soil home with them to use as they may."

After Pablo and Fr. Raul placed Rosita on her pedestal, Pablo suggested to Fr. Raul that they hold a special Noche ceremony that night. Fr. Raul agreed and asked Pablo and Francisca to spread the word.

Francisca beamed her words into the wind and they spread to everyone in the area. Her message carried through the Arts and Crafts Complex, the supermarket, the barbershop, the schools, the government complex and the pueblo. Parents dispatched their children to alert those who were not present to come quickly. By late afternoon, the crowd began to gather at the church steps. About a half hour before sunset, when members of the church committee were straggling up to the church, and Fr. Raul and Pablo had finished piling up the sacred soil, it was time to roll Rosita onto the landing at the top of the church steps. After they brought her out, Fr. Raul slowly uncovered her. A hush came over the crowd. Something was different, they noticed. No doubt about it. She was standing much taller and on a new silk-covered pedestal.

What happened next remains indelibly embedded in the souls of those who witnessed the spectacle. As the sun began its slow descent behind the mountains, Raymond saw five golden-red rays of brilliant light fly up toward the sky, recoil off the fast-moving, wispy clouds winging over the town, rebound to earth, and illuminate the plaza. Time froze the sunset in place for a long time.

Jon saw four separate rainbows materialize from each corner of the horizon. They arched upward toward the apex of the sky and filled the heavens with plumes of red, gold and orange that slowly blended, forming a colorful skydome. A rainbow slowly appeared at its center and bolted straight down from the apex of the dome to touch Rosita's golden crown.

Jake was pulling up to the church steps with Carmela when it happened. At first, he was speechless and frightened, but soon felt a calm come over him. He turned off the ignition, reached out for the trembling Carmela and squeezed her close. He described it to his friends the next day: "Rosita flashed her eyes: red, blue, and orange. Then she looked up and around, slowly. Her gaze went through everybody's hearts. The crowd stopped cold, people cried, 'Ahhh.' Then her smile shone, red and gold colors, and her crown glittered so bright I could not look at it. All at once, something, I think it was her soul, flashed out of her and flew into the air. It, she, touched everyone in the plaza; actually, it went through us. Then it shot up to the center of the sky and came back into her again, and then her chest lit up with the color of blood.

"'Sangre de Cristo,' one woman screamed.

"Then, a light came forth from her breast and everyone was surrounded by it and everyone started to dissolve so that there were no individual people anymore, only light. That's when I had to close my eyes. Then it was over. Carmela and I were shaking and crying and laughing. But we weren't afraid. We weren't afraid."

When all the rainbow light had disappeared, and the sun went down behind the hills, the people knew that Rosita had come into their world for a brief moment. Flesh and blood, in person, for real. And she was not alone.

Elmer saw everyone who ever was, now briefly liberated from their earthly forms, soaring all around him. Others with a similar gift sensed their ancestors' presence in the red, gold, and emerald green colors that floated over the plaza. Great-great-great-great grandmothers materialized over their loved ones, covering them with tears of joy so strong that droplets of water fell from the sky.

"A summer squall?" one woman asked. However, there were no rain clouds to be seen.

At the moment it happened, Esther was standing on the church steps, next to Patron, Paz, Ike and Rosie. She squeezed Patron's hand tightly, and he squeezed back. No words were necessary. Esther knew, in the part of herself that is much older than words, that the spirit of Luis Alonzo had materialized out of the universe to be with them, and to see if his messages had arrived. Then the words, 'goodness is never unrewarded' came into Patron's mind. From where he did not know, but Esther did.

The people stayed on and lit candles when darkness fell. When Pablo motioned that it was time to take Rosita inside, the crowd yelled, "Not yet!" They proceeded to encircle her with candles and lit the plaza with luminarias. Fr. Raul announced that he had a meeting with the church committee, but would leave Rosita out on the steps under the care of Pablo Montoya, who was standing taller, stronger, and in charge.

The members of the committee, with their official invited guests, Elmer and Esther, solemnly filed into the church. As they were about to close the door, Ike came running up the church steps and asked Fr. Raul if he could attend the meeting. Fr. Raul sensed that Ike's request belied something important, especially tonight, of all nights.

"He is not himself," he spoke to himself. "Seems out of it, depersonalized," reverting to his psychological terminology. "Like he has PTSD."

Rosie noticed the change in Ike as well. So did Esther. Rosie moved closer to him and whispered in his ear. "Are you okay?" "You seem different." She noticed that Ike was not wearing his headband; perhaps out of respect. She asked, a bit sarcastically, "No headband tonight?"

"No. Don't need it anymore," he said, and gently grabbed Rosie's shoulders and stared into her eyes. "Sis, I need to say that I love you and am proud that you are my little sister."

Rosie gasped. Her eyes filled. "Are you putting me on?" She caught her breath and swallowed hard. "I don't know what to say. I guess I should say, I love you too."

Patron, Esther, and Paz watched them, dazzled. Great things were happening.

Ike pleaded, "Please, Padre, I need to attend the meeting. I need to know more." Fr. Raul jumped at the opportunity to sway Ike for the good.

"But no spying for La Tierra, Ike; this meeting is confidential. If you want to come as our Ike, you can. "

"I will come as your Ike," he said, as contritely as a chastised child.

"Our Ike. Not La Tierra's."

"Okay."

Fr. Raul asked the others if they would agree to allow Ike to attend the meeting and they readily agreed. Vincente fought a sudden urge to ask Fr. Raul for permission for his own son to attend. After all, what was good for the

Alonzos was good for his family as well. Realistically though, it was probably too late.

After what had just happened, Rosie tried to suppress her annoyance with Ike, but could not help asking the group, "Do you all know what happened to Jon's car?"

"It wasn't me," Ike jumped in, "but it was my fault indirectly. I'm sorry and promise it will not happen again. I am quitting La Tierra, Sis."

Fr. Raul interrupted. "Then come in, Ike."

Rosie puzzled. "He called me Sis," she mumbled. "He used to call me Sis when I was little." She inched her arm around Ike's waist. It felt good and he returned the gesture, but more weakly. Rosie noted that his body was almost limp. She hugged him closer. "Did you get hit in the head or something?"

❧

Fr. Raul cleared his throat, called the meeting to order and welcomed Ike and Esther. "Ike is not here to spy for La Tierra," he added, "and he promises to keep our secrets." Everyone agreed Ike could stay. Vincente, still recovering from shock, noted with concern that Ike didn't look right.

"What's up, Ike?" he asked.

Ike murmured, "A lot," slowly flipped him thumbs up, and motioned that he would continue the discussion after the meeting. Paz inquired if he was okay, and Ike reassured her with a nod and a smile. Esther took hold of his arm and glanced knowingly at Paz. They both saw the signs, no doubt about it; at long last, Ike had been touched.

Fr. Raul announced a prayer. "Okay. After what we seen tonight, Lord, give us strength and wisdom."

"Amen," echoed Vickie loudly. Fr. Raul rapped the table three times. "We need to set some rules, O.K? Everyone will have an opinion tonight, so we need to be orderly. First off, stay put in your seats. If someone has something to say, raise your hand. When I recognize you, stand up. Except for Patron, grandfather, and Esther, if they do not want to stand up, they do not have to. And no interrupting. If you want to say something, but someone else is talking, do not interrupt; instead, raise a hand to be recognized. If you are recognized, the speaker has to sit down and you get up. Okay?"

Everyone nodded yes, except Vickie, who was still trying to make sense of the instructions.

"I guess so," she answered.

Rosie stayed quiet. "Button the lips and watch," she urged herself.

Fr. Raul waited for absolute silence to begin. "You all saw what happened out there. We have a great responsibility before us. We have important questions to deal with. Here are some. What exactly have we found? Why is it here in Santa Rosita? What is it for? Why now? Why us? And what do we do about it? So let us address these questions one at a time. Who wants to start?"

Rosie and Paz shot their hands up in the air.

"Paz has the floor," Fr. Raul exclaimed in his most official voice, and, with an almost imperceptible nod of his head, signaled Rosie to cool it. So far, so good.

Paz stretched up to her full height. "God has spoken to us, and I think I know why."

Everyone leaned forward to hear what she had to say, aware that Paz, like her mother, had a direct connection to the saints. Paz waited a moment to bask in the glow of respect flowing from her audience's eyes, and then began to speak in slow and measured tones.

"We have received a message, especially for my family, because my family and probably everyone else in town, and especially Ike there, were about to give Rosie a hard time about marrying the Doc. We were forcing her to choose between the man she loves and her family. Having to make such a choice would make her sick, or make her leave town."

Patron shifted in his chair and strained to keep still.

"Also," Paz continued, "putting the Doc, who is a nice guy, in peril from the likes of our local terrorists, like La Tierra." She looked up toward the heavens and crossed herself. "The Lord has reminded us to get rid of our stupid attitudes and to remember that we are more alike than not, and that we need to get with it and stop acting and thinking like jerks."

Elmer muttered a blessing in her direction, thinking, she flies straight for a slightly bent arrow. One of my people must be running through her blood.

Vincente raised his hand, and was duly recognized. He rose to his feet. Paz sat down.

"I have the greatest respect for your contact with the saints, Paz, but do you actually think that God sent the Alonzo family a message? What about my family. Don't we get a message too? Why only your family?"

Vickie flipped Vincente a big smile and a thumbs up.

"Yes," she shouted, riding on his coattails. "What about us? Wasn't what happened out there for everyone?"

Paz stood up again so that she and Vincente were both standing.

"Well, yes, for my family, but sure, of course, yours too. Of course, for everyone. God is fed up with the way everyone is acting."

Elmer silently agreed with Paz. That's for sure. The earth is off center. Don't these people get it? Why do they think the weather has been so terrible lately?

"That's going a little too far, Paz dear," Patron interrupted.

"No, Poppa," Paz persevered. "Not far enough. You know what we need to do."

"Will we be punished if we don't?" Vickie interrupted. Paz ignored her and went on: "What other reason can there be why this block, pedestal or whatever Rosita stands on tonight, has appeared to us?"

Rosie could not restrain herself any longer so she raised her hand. Fr. Raul reluctantly acknowledged her, and was pleased to see that when Rosie stood up, Paz and Vincente dutifully sat down.

"Whoever believes that God raised the pedestal to send us a message, show your hands."

Everyone raised their hands.

"I will too," Vincente said, "but only if we agree that the message is for everybody, not just your family."

"Well, then," Rosie continued. "Okay, a message for all. Who are we to ignore a message that God has sent us, all of us? Grandfather, anything to say?"

Elmer broke out of his reverie. "I say, why not?" He smiled. "I'm gonna talk and sit. I only got a few ups and downs in me this late at night. The Great Spirit, what you call God, sends us messages every day. It does not have to be with a flood, either. Yours came in a block. Mine came in a figure carved in stone. Sometimes they come by Federal Express," he teased.

Esther interrupted. "What do you think is the message?"

"You asking me?" Elmer looked surprised because he figured that she knew the answer.

"Yes, grandfather," she said with a smile indicating that she did know the answer. She just wanted him to say it out loud.

"Well, the message is, and I say this with respect, and don't want to criticize all of you and the way you live your lives, but the message of the Great Spirit is . . . all, my relatives. We are all the same. We think we are different, and we are not. We should not divide ourselves into categories, as people always seem to want to do. No one is better than anyone else, or more right than anyone else. All that humans do to convince themselves that someone is better than someone else is a lie, whatever form it comes in. We need to work together and not against one another. I just got a fresh reminder about this when I was on the mesa. And that applies to Rosie and Jon's situation as well. Love is being together—united—one. Why divide it, or measure it, or interfere with it, or mess it up?"

Esther winked at him, "Good job."

He winked back.

Carmela raised her hand and was duly recognized. She uncoiled herself upward very, very slowly. When she attained her full height, she pulled back her shoulders just enough so the sparkling turquoise necklace resting on her ivory bodice could catch the candlelight and illuminate her face in a soft, bluish glow, her most flattering color.

"Well, what I have learned here is that some of you are descended from the Jewish people who came here from New Spain—Mexico—hundreds of years ago, to escape being killed by the Inquisition. Your Jewish ancestors had to change their religion or be wiped out. That, of course, is them, and not you here. You are not religious Jews anymore, although you may have Jewish genes in your blood. You can't get rid of that." She stopped for a moment, as if she ran out of words, but then resumed. "Rosita has reminded us that some of you are the great-great-, way back, great grandchildren of Jews. So that's where we must start our discussion and then see where we go."

Elmer was thinking, the same crazy people that killed the Jews tried to wipe us out too. The Jews could change their religion if they wanted to survive, but we couldn't change anything.

Carmela continued. "Now since I am married to Jake, in a manner of speaking, I too am Jewish, because I have, well, Jewish . . . you know, in me too." She blushed, and then continued, "and our Lisa has half Jewish blood." Fr. Raul motioned that she was finished.

"Thanks, Carmela. First things first. Does everyone agree about the message?"

"What?" Vincente asked Vickie, who was equally puzzled.

Fr. Raul motioned for Carmela to sit down. "That some of you have Jewish ancestors. Everyone who agrees raise your hands."

"Some of us," Vincente added.

"Sure," said Fr. Raul, "some of us here, unless we go back 2000 years. Then we all have Jewish ancestors."

Elmer chuckled to himself. "Why not say that if you go back before the Jews, you all have Indian ancestors."

Patron interrupted. "What's the difference, 400 years or 2000 years? We are what we are today."

"Right," Vickie enthusiastically agreed. "Now that makes sense."

Vincente grabbed her arm. "Shhh," he whispered, "you are talking too much. Leave it to me. How many glasses of wine did you have at dinner?"

Vickie pulled his hand off her arm, turned away and pouted. "Only two . . . and if I want to say something, I will."

Patron ignored the spat and continued. "All this talk about blood doesn't mean anything."

Esther interrupted with a soft smile. "Dear, it's not only OF the blood, it is IN the blood. What do you do with that?"

"With what?" Vickie asked. Then, without saying a word, she let Vincente know that Esther had just contradicted Patron, and in public too. And what was good for Esther . . .

Rosie jumped in, "So when we say that we don't like Jews, or say bad things about them, or want to hurt them, or protest if one of us wants to marry one of them . . ." Rosie stopped to emphasize the word marry and glared at Ike who was almost inert, "we are talking about ourselves. In case you don't remember, our family name was on Luis Alonzo's list of people who escaped from New Spain—Mexico." Ike stayed quiet after she baited him. Instead of reacting as usual, he put his hand up to his forehead and rubbed it gently.

"Are you okay, Ike?" Rosie asked worriedly.

"I guess," Ike sighed. He was beginning to enjoy the attention.

Paz raised her hand and was acknowledged. "Did you see the carving on Rosie's pedestal? The star in the middle of the cross. And the people looking up and crying? You know what that means? It means that they are crying for us. We are being told not to forget that some of our blood ancestors had to run for their lives from the crazy people of our church. Rosita is saying that we should not repeat that wrong. She is testing us to see how we react to Rosie and Doc's situation now that she revealed these secrets to us. And she is watching."

Ike jumped up out of his trance. "Yeah! That's true! I gotta lay off Jon and Rosie. Padre, I need to confess . . ."

Fr. Raul smiled, "Later."

Esther said tenderly, "Paz is right. The figures on the pedestal are telling us that our love for God was split up. We are killing each other, ignoring the message. Like grandfather says, 'All, my relatives.' We are all one, and yet we blow it off."

Elmer murmured to himself, "Hmm! She got it for sure."

Vickie could not contain herself any longer and leaped to her feet. "Now, hold on. I did not do anything bad. Why should I be responsible for what the church did hundreds of years ago? I was not even born then. I go to church, pray, and try to be as good a person as I can. What is wrong with that? I am only responsible for what I do. I'm a good daughter, wife, mother, grandmother. I help people."

Esther gently motioned for her to sit down. "Dear, I don't mean for you to feel responsible, none of us had anything to do with the Inquisition. You did not do anything wrong. None of us did."

Vincente interrupted, "Damn sure I didn't."

"So why is Rosita mad at us?" Vickie asked tearfully.

Paz lifted her arms in the air as if she were to confer a blessing. "Vickie, Rosita isn't mad at us. We are just being reminded that our people would have rejected Rosie, even exiled her or worse, when the word got out that she had fallen for Doc. The Inquisition did the same thing to some of our ancestors hundreds of years ago. Have we changed in four hundred years?" Paz threw up her hands. "Don't you see? We have an opportunity to do something different."

Ike, who was back in a trance, softly mumbled, "Yeah. To do something about it," but no one paid attention.

Vickie struggled to stand up but only made it halfway. "Rosie, I was angry when I heard about you and Doc. A lot of bad things went through my mind."

Rosie stiffened. "How did you find out about us?"

"Someone saw you kissing on the road near the cemetery. Everybody knows."

Fr. Raul clucked his tongue in disapproval. "Yeah! Pablo's helpers."

Vincente mused aloud, "We have a lot to think about." He patted Vickie's arm, and she grasped his hand tight.

Ike raised his hand to be recognized. Fr. Raul gave him the nod. "I've got something to confess to everyone."

"Confess?" Fr. Raul asked. "I said later."

"This is different, Padre. Forgive me. I was here late last night."

Fr. Raul broke the stunned silence. "What, you were here? You weren't supposed to be in here."

"Please," Ike pleaded. "I am sorry, but hear me out. Something has happened to me."

"Something has happened," cried Esther. "I hope not anything you smoked or drank. I am so worried about that basura you smoke and drink with your friends."

"What? Tell us, Ike." Rosie touched his arm gently.

"Yes, dear, tell us," Paz urged.

Patron wondered if Ike was stoned, and signaled to Esther to check him out. .

Esther walked over to Ike and felt his forehead. "No fever." She ran her other hand over the back of his head. "Wow. You have a big bump back here. What happened?"

Ike shook his head from side to side. "Don't exactly know."

Esther whispered in his ear, "Dear, you come home with me after the meeting. I'll fix something . . ."

"Sure, Abuelita, sure," he said, in a childish voice.

"Tell us what happened," Francisca said.

"Yes, tell us, your family and your friends," Carmela added.

Ike leaned his elbows on the table and let his head sink into his hands. "Rosita spoke to me last night, I think."

"So?" Paz and Esther replied in unison. "She talks all the time."

Ike looked up. "Not to me, she doesn't. I thought that maybe I was losing it."

Esther looked at Patron reassuringly. "If that's all, he'll be okay," she sighed with relief and thought, "It's hard to grow up in one night. Rosita probably laid it on him."

Fr. Raul reminded Ike that he would be hearing confessions next morning.

Patron felt satisfied that he knew why Ike was acting so weirdly, so he decided to say his piece. He cleared his throat to get everyone's attention. "Now, what we need to do . . . what we have to do here is . . . now listen, everybody. We agree that the message says that some of us are descended from Jews. Right? We hear that Rosita is sad because people act cruelly to one another, because they worship the same God in different ways, and this is a bad way to do things because it causes trouble."

"You got it, Poppa," Paz interrupted. "Now what else?"

"Yes," Rosie added. "What else?"

"What else?"

Rosie cleared her throat. "About me and Jon."

"Yes," Paz added, "about being kinder to one another, more understanding."

"Yeah," Vincente interrupted, "That sounds great, but I can't do it. I am only human and it is human nature for people to see the same thing differently, and to fight, compete, and argue."

"What is this about human nature?" Carmela cut in.

Vickie jumped to Vincente's aid as quickly as a mother rescuing her child. "Well, Carmela. Human nature means people are naturally critical of one another, measure other people, try to be better, try to beat out each other, richer or poorer, white or dark, choose the best religion, to think their way is the best and only way."

Carmela recoiled. "Whoa! That's some opinion. So you are saying that we are all that dumb?"

Fr. Raul interrupted. "Stop right there. Let us look at the positive part of the message. Rosita is telling us that we can do better. If we do what she says, we can begin at home, for example, start with Rosie and Jon. What do you think, grandfather?"

Elmer was listening attentively and thinking that the meeting would be more orderly if they had a talking stick. "Why not? Sounds good to me." Elmer nodded sagely.

Fr. Raul continued, "Glad you agree. If we, as the executive committee, come out and support Rosie and Jon openly, it will be easier for the Doc to be accepted, and, if we do this right, it will not be so bad for Rosie to marry him. This way we can avoid her being the subject of gossip and criticism, or bringing disrespect to the Alonzo family or her being run out of town."

"That would be a good thing," Elmer mumbled under his breath.

Carmela said, "And we could have a doctor in the family."

To his surprise, Patron found himself on the bandwagon. Was this his opportunity to seal the deal of Rosie staying home? "Yes," he added, "and bring a lot of health care money into the community. Could this be a win-win?"

"Sounds okay to me," Vincente agreed. Several of his relatives worked at the clinic.

Patron saw his opening. "One question before us is if we tell about Rosita's origins or do we keep it a secret? According to what we read on the panel, Rosita is not Christian, a Jew made her, so she's Jewish. You all know what this means, and you also know we cannot let this be known, because the sacred soil, the pilgrimages, the healing, are all related to Rosita. We need to figure something out." Everyone nodded in agreement.

Vincente became quiet. Many of his family members made the

religious articles the vendors sold to the visitors. If it came out that Rosita was Jewish . . . he became even more attentive.

Patron continued, "Now, follow my logic here. Since some of us are descended from these Jews then . . . Rosita is still, technically, ours. Right? Even if she is Jewish, and we are Christians." More murmurs of agreement from his audience.

"Since she is ours, we can continue as before. Nothing has changed. If she came along with our ancestors, she is converted, like they were."

Everyone agreed enthusiastically. "Absolutely, she is ours," Paz added. "Bless her; she is like us, and our saint."

"Yes, absolutely," Vincente added with authority.

"Definitely," Vickie echoed. "Now you are talking."

Esther sparkled, and then flashed Patron a 'you did it again, dear' smile. Patron sat up straight and tall. He knew what it felt like to make lemonade out of lemons. "That settles it. Her Jewish origins are the same as some of us. We are not Jewish anymore, so neither is Rosita. But, and this is important, because of our origins, it's okay to carry on some of the old practices because we would be respectful Christians carrying on the practices of our ancestors. It does not have to be related to anything religious-Jewish, just cultural-Jewish. That makes sense, Padre, no?"

"Okay," said Fr. Raul. "If you say so."

Vickie, however, expressed some doubts. "Are you sure Padre? Are you sure, we don't have to give her back to the Jews? Is it all right for Catholics, to have a Jewish saint? Is she still good for us even though we are not Jews anymore? Maybe she wants to go back to her people. Maybe they want her back. Are you sure we are not stealing her from the Jews, Padre?"

Everyone turned to Fr. Raul.

Francisca sighed, bathing him with adoration. He felt the rush, and turned off his conscious mind. Time stopped. He imagined himself back in school playing baseball. Funny, he thought, why he would think of this now? He had not played baseball for many years, except for having an occasional catch with the children. Back in time, he recalled several occasions when he played in college and the outcome of the game was in his hands. He relived the time he batted in the game-winning run in a clutch situation, and felt the exhilaration of his teammates joyously piling on as he crossed home plate. Here he was in another clutch situation. He took a deep breath and drew himself up to his full height. In his mind, he swung his bat a couple of times, and looked the pitcher square in the eye. Then he spoke.

"Okay, of course, Rosita is ours. There is no question of it. Here is why. She is a saint. Jews don't have saints," he announced.

"Jews don't have saints," Vickie parroted. "Really? Is that true?"

"From my mouth to God's ear," Fr. Raul dropped his voice to its deepest tone.

Vincente and Vickie grinned with relief. "Jews don't have saints," Vincente echoed the words. Certainly, he thought, one for their side and one less problem. Fr. Raul was certainly smart. How lucky they were to have such a man as their priest.

"That's true. Brilliant, Padre!" Vincente exulted. Patron nodded in admiration.

Vickie wiped the tears from her eyes. Paz, too. Ike screwed up his face as if it would help his concentration, then he nodded, yes! Patron and Esther glanced at each other, rolled their eyes, and smiled. Rosie watched and waited.

Fr. Raul had slugged the ball out of the park. Now he was running around the bases.

"Okay, there is something else. Although we are all to benefit from this revelation, I feel there is a special connection between Rosie and Rosita. You saw what happened last night. Rosie, for some reason, has been chosen. Maybe she's the first in Santa Rosita to show us a new way, by marrying an outsider and a Jew."

"Also a gringo," Vincente interrupted.

Fr. Raul ignored him and locked eyes with Patron.

"I believe Rosita wants," he paused, searching his mind for the right words. "No, let me say it this way, Rosita needs Rosie to stay in this town and help to bring love and peace and prosperity. That is her destiny. We have to help her do that."

"Not bad," murmured Patron, and he thought, "Thank you, God. I am off the hook."

Elmer said to him, "And Rosie will do marketing for our businesses."

"And that is why," Fr. Raul smiled widely, "I got the message from above to tell her to wait."

After a short silence, he placed his palms together in a prayerful gesture. "Listen, everyone. Another idea has come to me. Praise God."

Francisca took a deep breath. "Praise God. Another brilliance."

"Next week," he smiled. "When all this commotion dies down, maybe . . ."

Everyone leaned forward.

"I can baptize Rosita. Just to be sure."

Francisca felt her heart soar. "Wow!" she cried to herself.

"Great idea," Patron shouted and slammed the table. What a genius! Patron thought. He should go into politics.

"What a priest!" Vickie whispered to Vincente, who asked, "Padre, is it okay to baptize a statue?"

Fr. Raul was riding the undaunted express. He thought for a moment, and then delivered with confidence, "It is, now!"

Everyone laughed in a satisfied way. Padre had answered like a real Santa Rositan, with attitude. They high-fived one another as if to say, yeah, we make our own rules in Santa Rosita.

"That will do it," laughed Paz.

Rosie rolled her eyes in disbelief. If it helps me, she thought, who cares?

"That will do it," repeated Vincente.

Ike stood up and cleared his throat. "I wanna say something about what happened to me last night."

Fr Raul placed an arm on Ike's shoulder. "You were drinking, no?"

"Not that much, more that I was poisoned . . ."

"Stoned, maybe?"

"Not that I remember."

"Okay, Ike. Let's talk about this later if it is alright."

"Sure, Padre. For now, I want to say to everyone that since I talked with Rosita last night I am quitting La Tierra and I am trying to be okay about Rosie and Jon being married, and I am going to devote my life to being a Santero."

Elmer thought, he did get hit on the head.

Patron smiled. "So you spoke with Rosita?"

"Yes, Poppa. Rosie is not the only one." He tried to squelch the rising tide of rivalrous thoughts.

Patron sidestepped nicely. "I am very happy, nieto, very happy, very proud. Of course. Rosita didn't say anything about you moving away, I hope. You can be a Santero here, right?"

"Yes, Poppa."

"That's very good."

"So, she showed you . . ." Esther had prayed long and hard for Ike.

Ike leaned back in his chair. "Myself and my place, Abuelita."

"That's good, Ike. I want to know more about that." Fr. Raul smiled. "But right now we need to decide what we are to do with all we have learned."

Patron responded with certainty. "If we tell the people outside what we know, they will go loco, the word will get around, and then the whole state and maybe the whole country will go crazy too. So we have only one option."

"Yeah," Vincente added, "people got enough worries without opening a can of worms about Jews."

"My parents told me Jews had horns," Vickie interrupted.

"That's ridiculous," Carmela jumped in, "But it's not ridiculous that a lot of the families in Santa Rosita are on the list of the Jews who came. But what about the families that are not mentioned on the list? Do you think they might feel, well, superior, or inferior, or like outsiders? That's only more trouble."

"Excuse me, Carmela," Patron gently interrupted, "All things considered, the town doesn't need, nor can it handle this kind of news. I want to keep this just between us. I propose we put a permanent cover over the pedestal, and leave Rosita's secrets inside of her where they belong. That will be the end of it, and nothing ever leaves this room. Nothing."

"So," Fr. Raul said respectfully, "if I understand you correctly, you believe that the people shouldn't hear the truth?"

Ike interrupted, "Are people ever ready to hear the truth, Padre? I wasn't until it hit me in the head."

Elmer stood up quietly, and waited until he had everyone's attention.

"That is true. Most of us are not ready to hear the truth. That is because, sad as it is and I do not know why, the Great Spirit has not made all of us in the same way. Some can hear his sound, and make the music. Others can hear the sound, but they cannot make the music. Others do not hear the sound at all. I think that we here in this room have heard the sound in our own ways. And we will make different music. I agree with Patron that most people may not be ready to hear this message. That is why we have special people in our tribe to guard the Great Spirit's messages. Now we have become the guardians of this message as well. Especially Rosie and Ike, who will carry this message for a long time because they are young. We can play the music for everyone else, in our own way, so they do not know it is being played. Get it? That is what we have been told to do. We must market the message of the Great Spirit."

Rosie was surprised that she understood everything Elmer had said. Not only understood it, she agreed with him.

"What in the world is he talking about?" Carmela asked herself. Then she stood up. "Excuse me, grandfather, please, I want to say something. Now although I didn't notice any of my ancestors on the list, I do not entirely agree that keeping this information quiet is the right thing to do. I think that acknowledging any Jewish blood could be a good thing because of some good things that Jews have done, and how they are respected in some places. For example, there are Jewish people who often come into the store to buy rugs. Some of them are good customers. Now I could tell them about having a common background and . . ."

Vickie interrupted her. "I don't want to know, or anyone else to know I have Jewish blood if I had it. I want to stay the way I am, and I don't want to hear about anything else. I have enough troubles. I don't want people to look at me cross-eyed if they think I am a Jew."

"Hold it, Vickie," Carmela interrupted. "One has nothing to do with the other. Why can't I be Catholic with Jewish blood? That's what it seems most of us are anyway? Padre made the point that Jesus was Jewish. That does it for me. Jews were pre-Catholics anyway. No? We can tell the truth to everyone, and stay the way we are."

Vincente's face reddened. "What about the fact that the Jews killed Jesus? Think about that. People have a right to hate you if you killed Jesus. The Jews did, that's the truth."

"That's hogwash," Rosie raised her voice. "The Jews didn't kill Jesus. How can you believe that?"

"Well, a lot of people say that. I learned that in Sunday school."

Rosie was right back at him. "Right, so even if it were true and a distant relative of yours killed Jesus? What does that have to do with you?"

"I would have a problem," Vincente stuttered.

"Well," Rosie forged ahead, "the Jews didn't kill Jesus, that's propaganda. Pontius Pilate, a Roman, had Jesus killed."

Patron thought, politics killed Jesus.

Vickie smiled, "That's good to hear. Nevertheless, Vincente has a point. If some of us come out and say we are descended from Jews, the Jew-haters would hate us. Even if we go to church. Then we would be different. I don't want to be different."

"Yeah," Vincente added. "I like being the same."

"I get where you are coming from," Rosie nodded; the less said the better.

"My head is killing me," Vincente groaned.

"Being different is good," Paz mumbled.

"For you, maybe. But not for me. Me and Vincente want to be the same," Vickie sulked.

"Enough please." Patron bellowed loudly. "I don't think that the blood discussion is relevant, if we decide to forget the whole thing. Carmela, I respect how you feel, but you will have to keep this secret."

Carmela waited a moment to answer. All eyes were on her. "Of course, Poppa. I promise, but it does make me feel, you know, how to put it, more interesting, if you know what I mean." She turned to Esther. "Can I come over early next Friday night and light the candles with you?"

"Now it's candles," Patron moaned.

Esther smiled, "Of course, dear."

"Me, too," added Rosie defiantly.

Vickie whispered in her husband's ear, "Vincente, my mother lit candles on Friday night, too."

"Ay!" Patron moaned in frustration, but quickly regained his composure. He gestured toward Fr. Raul. "We need to vote on what we should do with the pedestal. We have three choices. Bury it, keep it out and cover it, or tell everyone about it, and deal with the people, the press and the university, and create a madhouse."

Esther and Paz sprang into action. "Bury it? No way! Rosita keeps her pedestal! Who is against Rosita keeping her pedestal?" They glared around the table.

No one raised their hands. "Who wants to bury the pedestal?" Everyone glanced around tentatively; however, no one completely raised their hand.

Patron was on his game. "It would be the easiest to bury the pedestal, and forget all about it, but it seems that no one wants to do that." He was about to draw in his net when Fr. Raul interrupted.

"Who is in favor of showing the pedestal to the people, including what was inside it?"

"Me. Full disclosure to all," Paz shouted. "It's the people's right."

"That depends," said Rosie. "I have a stake here. If everybody knew that some of us have Jewish ancestors, it would create a lot of confusion for sure. But then who could object to me and Jon?"

Vincente added, "Right now, when everybody in town who doesn't already know, finds out about you and Jon, it will hit the fan. But if people knew they had Jewish ancestors, what could they say? Jon would not be that different, except for being an outsider and a gringo. But he's also bringing good medical care and money and jobs to the clinic."

"Very good, dear," Vickie smiled, "you make a lot of sense, too."

"Good thinking, Vincente," Esther added. "The fact that he is a good doctor could prevent the outsider criticism. We need a good doctor here."

Patron sensed that Vincente needed just a bit more convincing; he had a lot of influence with the parish constituency.

"Did you know, Vincente, that Jon is from Santa Fe, and speaks better

Spanish than most of us?" Good point, he thought, but not good enough. Was he losing his touch?

Esther sent a message to his mind: you can do better.

Patron rubbed his lucky charm and said to himself, I'll work on it.

Carmela was lost in a pleasing thought. Wouldn't it be good for business if she wore a six-pointed star around her neck? Actually, she could have one made out of silver, with a turquoise cross in the middle. And manufacture and sell them.

Paz was self-absorbed, wondering why Rosita's pedestal had not surfaced when *she* needed help.

Rosie announced, with some firmness. "I will agree to go along with whatever the committee decides, with one point. I don't want any more trouble for Jon or myself, especially from Ike and his buddies. You know that Jon's car was wasted, and Alcalde was here yesterday."

"Yeah," Ike responded. "I told Sal and Alcalde to lay off. Anyway, now I am a fraud as far as La Tierra is concerned. This Jewish thing is sure to get around."

"Alcalde. Alcalde from the north. He was here?" Vincente cried.

"Yeah. He was with me in the church, but he left. He didn't hear anything."

"Are you sure?" Fr. Raul groaned.

"Yes. I brushed him off earlier today. He's too hung-over to be any trouble."

Fr. Raul doubted Ike's assurances, but he was eager to conclude the evening. "Okay, I propose that we wrap Rosita's belongings in new protective, waterproof cases and put them back in her pedestal. Then we seal her pedestal in metal—copper would be nice. Then we permanently attach Rosita and her pedestal together."

He smiled warmly and pointed at Rosie, "If no one objects, Rosie can keep the little charm as a wedding gift."

"Ohhh," the group sighed.

"How thoughtful," murmured Paz. "Padre is such a nice guy."

Francisca beamed. It is going be a hot night tonight.

"And we forget this ever happened," said Patron.

"No, we won't," exclaimed Paz, Esther and Rosie in unison. "No, we won't."

Fr. Raul backed off quickly. "We won't forget about it, but we won't talk about it in public."

"What about among ourselves?" Vickie asked.

"Let's try not to," Fr. Raul replied wearily. And then thought to himself: fat chance.

Esther raised her hand to speak. "We can try to forget about the rising of the pedestal, but we will never forget about the message. Spreading this message, and living it is now our work. Remember, we have been chosen to receive the message. Now let us hold hands and make a promise to devote our lives to spreading the word. You, too, grandfather. Pablo, come too."

Elmer added, "If you can't talk about the message, it doesn't mean you can't use it," and winked at Rosie, who returned the smile.

Elmer grinned. She gets it. Marketing, he was thinking, marketing.

Fr. Raul rapped the table. "All in favor of keeping Rosita on her pedestal, covering up this whole deal, and keeping all this to ourselves to our dying days raise your hands."

"And," Esther added.

Fr. Raul smiled, "Spreading Rosita's message. Okay."

He continued. "Okay. Everyone is raising their hands except Paz."

Paz said earnestly. "I am for the message, but I am against the secrecy." Then she smiled. "I'll promise secrecy only if I have to."

Fr. Raul sighed. "You have to. Motion passed. Meeting over. Now, let's go outside."

The group walked out of the church, into a throng of people kneeling at Rosita's feet. Carmela spotted Jake, together with Sarah and Jaime, and waved to them. Patron, Esther, Ike, Paz and Rosie hurried over to join them. Jon was standing with Raymond and his family. When he spotted Rosie, he started to edge his way through the crowd to her.

Vickie was thinking, my God, could it be that most of the people out there praying to Rosita are Jewish?

Elmer walked behind her and heard her thoughts. There are no Jews, or Christians, or Moslems or anything else, silly girl, only Indians. He was surprised at the number of his own people he saw among those outlined by the bright lights of the fountain. When he saw his own family, he felt a pleasant tingle all over his body. "Things ain't that bad," he chuckled to himself.

Fr. Raul walked to the edge of the landing, raised both hands over his head, and shouted to attract the crowd's attention, but no one paid him any notice. Pablo walked in front of Fr. Raul, raised his hand to signal Fr. Raul to step back, reached back under his shirt and into his belt, took out a forty-five revolver and fired two shots into the air.

"Attention, attention please," Pablo called and got the crowd's attention. "Padre needs to tell you something." Then he smiled and deferred to Fr. Raul.

Fr. Raul moved to the edge of the landing. "I want to tell you all that a wonderful thing has happened. A blessing. The flood brought Rosita back her pedestal. Rosita is whole once again. The Lord has sent us a message. That message is to do our best to love one another, to overlook our differences, and to be good and to be kind. The message is, as our respected friend grandfather says, that we are all relatives. Now we must live our lives in a manner to respect this holy message. No more hate, let us live with our similarities and not our differences. So if you hear of any events in which you can put Rosita's message to work, for example, anything to do with new and different people wanting to settle here, or marry one of ours, and live here and raise a family, or anything like that, remember that it is the right thing to do."

Fr. Raul reached up and made the sign of the cross.

"Rosita will be here to watch over us and to see that we fulfill her message. Now she needs to go to bed, and so do we."

Elmer winked up at the night sky. "And start marketing."

13

What Really Matters

The following Friday, Esther was setting the table for dinner when the phone rang. It was Rosie.

"Hi, Abuelita, I hear you and Poppa had a busy week."

Esther laughed. "Lots to do."

Rosie's voice wavered a bit. "You talk to Mom and Dad, and Jake . . .?"

"Yes, everybody. Not too bad, considering. Ike sure did a 360." She knew what Rosie was going to ask next.

"Think I can bring Jon with me tonight?"

"Well, why not?" Esther laughed, "We got to start somewhere. How about coming over a little earlier to give me a hand and talk?"

Rosie sighed, a mixture of relief and joy. "I would love to Abuelita, but I've got a lot of work to catch up on at the clinic. You know the outages from the flood, no electricity, no computer."

"Okay, dear." Rosie heard the disappointment in Esther's voice, so she offered to make the flan for dessert. She could pick up the ingredients on the way to work and cook it in the clinic kitchen during the afternoon. Esther was pleased. "Sure. But when you make it, be sure to . . ." Rosie knew the directions by heart and teased, "Let the eggs sit for a while before I mix them with . . ."

Esther laughed, "Would you like to light candles with me tonight?"

Around dinnertime, Rosie called Abuelita to say that she had indeed made the flan, but that she and Jon would be late for dinner because Jon had an emergency.

"Not a problem," Esther said. "Everyone is inside talking about you and Jon."

"Really. Is that bad?" Rosie asked anxiously. "I talked with them so much this week. Jon did too. Is there something I don't know about?"

"Not really. You know Poppa, he doesn't want any surprises," Esther answered. "And, of course, he has to fill in Jake and your Mom and Dad about the secret."

A half hour later, Jon and Rosie arrived at her grandparent's door. She took three deep meditative breaths, and gave Jon a quick kiss for good luck. Then, with their best smiles, they bounced through the vestibule into the dining room, and into the middle of a sober discussion.

Esther greeted them enthusiastically.

"Welcome, Jon. Poppa is just finishing telling everyone about Rosita."

Rosie wondered about the pledge of secrecy for a brief moment, then quickly put it out of her mind.

"I know what you are thinking, Rosie," Esther laughed. "But there are no secrets from family." Patron nodded in their direction, and signaled for them to wait until he finished speaking.

Patron had been very busy since the last meeting at the church. Once he knew that he had to accept the 'Rosie and Doc' deal, as he called it, he set to work and spread the word about Rosie and Jon. He announced that although he was not pleased, he intended to bless the union because it was the Christian thing to do. In short, people had better like it, or else. It helped that the Doc would stay at the Clinic and that no one disliked him. Those of Patron's 'muchacho' friends who knew what great influence he had jumped to his support.

"You are right, after all, how long can we keep the outside world from our door?" one old friend agreed. Feeble arguments, Patron thought, but the best he could do under the circumstances.

Before Rosie and Jon arrived, Patron shared the new information about the family's ancestry with those who hadn't known. He tried to make the point that Jon was not so different after all. "So that's it," he wrapped up. "Now you all figure out how this affects how you feel about you-know-what." Then, one at a time, he locked eyes with Jake, Jaime, and Sarah, making it clear where he stood. He already had Paz, Esther, Ike, and Carmela on his side. Having said his piece, Patron leaned back to signal that his part of the conversation was over.

After Rosie walked in, she tried to break the somber mood.

"Everyone looks too serious," she joked, but nervously. Jake waved them over to the table and said blandly, "We just got an earful. Come sit down. I'm starving."

Paz winked enthusiastically at Rosie and nodded a reassuring signal. Ike was still foggy-minded and could only manage a weak smile.

Sarah and Jaime got up and embraced Jon tentatively, but when he hugged them back, they responded in kind, especially Sarah. For her, a good hug was a good hug no matter where it came from. It was evident that Jaime was having a particularly hard time with the situation. But after he finished embracing Rosie, he shouted "What the hell!" and laughed. Jaime's display of humorous acceptance melted the tension. After all was said and done, he thought, he was a lucky man. His daughter wanted to live near the family. That is what she said when he and Sarah got together with Rosie and Jon to hash over the situation. Jaime was proud that he was able to keep his emotions in check and be civil. Patron and Abuelita didn't seem disturbed so why should he? He always trusted their judgment. And, after all, it wasn't about his pride; it was about Rosie's happiness. He emphasized that point to Jake and Ike, too. Easier said than done, of course, but he was going to try hard to set a good example and forget about the religious difference. At least for now. After all, that is what good fathers do.

Carmela smiled warmly at Jon, but it was evident that Jake was having a problem. His pride was involved. He told her, "I'm gonna take a lot of crap from some of the boys." Carmela, as usual, knew how to lift up her man and assure him that someone as wonderful as he could easily handle such a situation. He smiled and took a deep breath, "What the hell," he said. "You are right. I can handle it."

Jake knew that he was being scrutinized for a sign of acceptance. With all eyes on him, he took a deep breath and signaled to Jon to come over, and said matter-of-factly. "Doc, you are going to make the family bigger, so we added an extra leaf to the table. You sit down on Momma's right."

Rosie lit up. She winked at Jake, who winked back and tried to hold back a smile.

So Rosie's happy, Jake said to himself. Things are better when Rosie is happy. Carmela will be happy. Things are better when the women are happy.

What the hell. I ain't gonna bother about all this Jew stuff. I got enough troubles.

Jake's acceptance made Jon feel more at ease and he took the opportunity to apologize for being late because of his last minute emergency. To his surprise, everyone nodded gravely, even respectfully. After all, they never had a doctor in the family before. Jake started thinking.

"Carmela thinks it's good he is a doctor. I wonder if he thinks that makes him special," He was not going to call him doctor, or Doc. "Hey, Jon," he asked emphasizing the 'Jon.' "So what was the emergency about?"

Was this a sincere question or a challenge? Rosie wondered.

Jon asked Jake if he was sure he wanted to hear the details, and that it might be boring.

"No, Jon," Jake relaxed and told him to go ahead. He was satisfied that Jon passed the test.

Jon smiled and continued, "A car hit a biker near the plaza, threw him into a parked car, beat him up pretty bad. They brought him into the clinic and I x-rayed him. Found a broken clavicle, two broken ribs, and a broken wrist. Concussion, too. I called in a helicopter from Albuquerque to Medevac him to the trauma center."

"Will he live, Doctor?" Carmela asked, wide-eyed.

Rosie interrupted. "Call him Jon. Of course he will live; Jon does the right things."

"Who was it?" Ike asked.

Jon smiled, "Can't say Ike; confidentiality."

"Doctors can't say the names of patients or talk about them," Carmela chimed in.

Jon continued, "He'll be okay His vital signs were stable when he left. The fractures will heal, and hopefully the concussion will too."

"Vital signs, fractures?" Jaime squinted hard.

"Yeah," Jon said. "You know: respiration, temperature, blood pressure, oxygen level, pulse. All systems working."

Jaime nodded. Vital signs, good to know. He was listening and learning. So was Jake.

Carmela beamed. "That's interesting, Jon." Interesting was a word rarely said around that table. Jake started to think that maybe Carmela was right when she was busting his chops about having a doctor in the family, especially when it could save them a lot of money with free medical care. Besides, how many of his cronies know what vital signs are?

Esther smiled mysteriously. "Now for my surprise." She walked into the kitchen and beckoned Paz to join her. After a moment, they returned with shawls over their heads. Esther carried two candlesticks, which she placed on the table.

Then she announced, "After what I learned this week, actually what we all learned about where we came from, I am coming out of the closet."

Everyone looked puzzled. Ike perked up. He thought that was a funny thing for Abuelita to say, because he was sure she did not know what 'coming out of the closet' meant.

"Now what?" Sarah whispered to Jaime.

Patron knew what was coming. He felt his eyes burning and swallowed hard, and then he took out his lucky charm.

"Anyone want to join me?" Esther asked.

"Me!" Rosie and Carmela said in unison and stood up. Jake grabbed Carmela's arm. "What are you doing? You ain't Jewish."

Carmela pushed his hand away. "I can do this, even if I don't know if I am legal or not. Why can't I have two religions like people who have two citizenships? Besides, I know you are. And I am your wife. Aren't I Jewish by injection?"

Everyone laughed.

"Well, I guess." Jake liked that remark and started laughing, too.

Carmela continued. "Anyway, if Catholics were Jews two thousand years ago, that gives me some kind of personal privilege, don't you think?"

"If you put it that way," Jake grinned and patted her rear gently for all to see. Everyone laughed again. Carmela rolled her eyes in seductive way so everyone could see she liked it and that her Jake was a stud.

Esther looked around the table, stopping for a brief second to catch each person's eye. Ike knew what she wanted, so he got to his feet. So did Jon. Jake, Jaime and Patron did not move. Esther noticed that Patron raised his left eyebrow, a subtle signal to show his annoyance. She stared him down until he lowered it. Her message was, if you are not going to join us, do not get in the way. Now satisfied that everyone was in accord, Esther lit the candles, waved her arms back and forth over them, and whispered some words. Then she and Paz, said "Amen" together. Another "Amen" echoed through the room, this time from Ike, Rosie and Carmela.

"Is that it, Abuelita?" Jake asked.

Esther smiled, "That's it. Now our ancestors are happy." Esther removed her shawl, stretched herself up as tall as she could, and, with her chin as high as she could raise it, announced, "Let's eat."

"Finally," Patron said to himself enthusiastically, while making sure that he maintained a blasé outward expression.

After a relatively uneventful dinner, and to the delight of all, Rosie ceremoniously served the first piece of her flan, and a huge one at that, to Ike, who moaned with pleasure after the first bite.

"I made it," Rosie beamed proudly.

"I know," Ike winked at Esther. "Abuelita told me. She said I'd better like it. Actually, I do like it."

"Really," Rosie almost blushed. "I don't know what to say, Ike."

"Yeah, I am acting weird, ain't I?" Rosie grinned with delight at her parents. "Mom, Dad, Ike actually said he likes my flan."

Jaime laughed, "Now that's a miracle." Jon was laughing as well.

When Jon passed Jake a slice of flan, Jake asked him if he would mind looking at a black spot on his hand after they finished dinner. "Sure," Jon smiled.

Sarah hastened to join the queue. "My joints have been aching lately, Jon. My cures are not working too well. Any ideas?"

"This is good," Carmela thought. She could see herself saying, "So, you have something wrong with you, eh! What are the symptoms? I'll see what my brother-in-law the doctor says about it, and let you know."

After coffee, Patron was ready to do what needed to be done. He wiped his mouth with his napkin, folded it neatly, three folds this way and three folds that way, inserted it carefully into his napkin holder, and placed it to the left of his plate. "Okay, everybody, showtime! I heard that on TV." He laughed. "Now let's get things straight. You know about Rosita and her pedestal. From now on, whatever we discuss stays here, in this room, in the family. As family, we have no secrets between us. Everything out on the table. We have just learned that Rosie and Jon want to get married. According to our family tradition, we try to stay with our own kind, because time has shown it keeps the family close. In Rosie's case, Jon is not only an outsider; he has a different religion."

"But a good person," Paz interrupted. "And the religion . . ."

Patron glared at Paz. "I am going one step at a time."

Paz backed off.

Patron continued. "Normally, their union goes against everything we believe in. Jon has to understand this is hard for us. Especially Ike, last week he was very upset about Rosie wanting to marry Jon."

Ike rubbed the back of his head. Did Poppa approve, or not? "Yeah, But I've changed," he declared.

"We know why," Rosie sassed. Rosie asked Patron if he had told them about Rosita. Patron answered that he thought he had covered everything.

"You told them that Rosita was Jewish?" Rosie questioned.

Jake moaned. "Jeez. Rosita is the reason this town has so many Christian tourists. We can't make a living off Jews. There aren't enough."

Ike smiled and exclaimed. "No problemo, bro.' That will be taken care of."

Patron interrupted, "Maybe we should stop here."

"Let's go all the way, Poppa." Ike spoke gently and respectfully.

"Yes," said Esther. "There's more. My candle lighting is a Jewish thing. I do it like my mother and grandmother did, although I do not know exactly the reason for it. I just do it because I need to do it. Like some unnamed force is controlling me. Like making the bread for Friday night."

"The bread," Jaime and Jake echoed.

Esther continued. "Yes, it is Jewish bread. The recipe has been handed down in my family from way, way back."

"Wow," Jake exclaimed. "Wow. Imagine that, my favorite bread is Jewish."

Rosie chimed in as if she were addressing her students at the university. "There are many things we do that are linked to our ancestors, but we do not know why. Did you ever ask yourselves why we play games after Friday night dinner?"

"Sure," Sarah said. "Because Momma did that with her own parents. That is something that we just do." Sarah threw up her hands.

"That's my point," Rosie smiled. "The real reason we do it is because during the Inquisition, Jews were not allowed to assemble for prayer on Friday nights. Therefore, when the soldiers came around to check on them, the Jews hid their prayer books and pretended to play games. It became a tradition that outlived its original reason for coming into being. Like observant Jews not mixing meat and dairy today."

Jaime screwed up his face in puzzlement. "Jews don't mix meat and dairy?"

Sarah said, "Whoever heard of such a thing?" Rosie asked her why some of the other families in town only eat fish on Friday. Sarah could not answer. To counter, she asked Rosie where she got her information.

Rosie answered respectfully. "Mom, this week I went on the Internet and spoke with a friend at the university who specializes in the history of New Mexico. Of course, I didn't tell her our secret. I just asked her about the Jews in New Mexico, said I was doing some research. I learned that we are called 'crypto-Jews' or secret Jews. Like us, most crypto-Jews don't even know that they are descended from Jews. The proof is on the bottom of the gravestones in the cemetery. When I was there, I came across a gravestone I never saw before. It belonged to Abraham Alonzo, our ancestor. Right, Jon?"

Jon nodded. "I saw it, too."

Rosie continued. "On the bottom of his gravestone was a Jewish star. And there were stars on the bottoms of a lot of the other old ones, too. My friend told me that when the Jews came to New Mexico they had to practice their religion on the sly."

"Why did they come here?" Jake asked.

"We," Rosie paused to emphasize the word. "We came here from Spain via Mexico. The Jews lived peacefully among the Moors in Spain until the army of King Ferdinand and Queen Isabella drove the Moors out. The Jews were told to either convert to Christianity or be killed. Some fled; those who converted were called conversos. After a while, many of the conversos were killed, too. There was no escape. So when Columbus sailed to this, the new world, in the 1500's, many Jews came here with him to escape the Inquisition. Unfortunately, the Inquisition followed them here, so the Jews moved on. Our ancestors fled from Mexico north to this place. But the priests and soldiers eventually caught up with them. The Jews had literally to go underground. When a Jew died, the family etched a six-pointed star into the bottom of the gravestone, so it would be out of sight. They feared that any passerby who saw the star would denounce the family. The Jews who stayed on assimilated. Eventually, the few remaining rituals and practices became entwined with parts of Catholic culture. These rituals and practices were handed down though the generations, like lighting candles on Friday night, Abuelita's bread and more."

Jon added, "Some of the Jews in New Mexico today are not from Spain. They came from Europe over the past two centuries. My ancestors came here in the mid-1800's and although they worked and lived here, we still faced the same rejection and anti-Semitism that Jews who don't live in Israel have to deal with every day."

Jake was listening intensively to Jon's words.

"Ay!" he moaned. "What you say is true. I am prejudiced against Jews. I have said awful things about them."

"Join the club," Jon sighed.

"So now people can call me a dirty Jew," Jake laughed, and so did everyone else.

Jon smiled. "If you wish."

Paz put the discussion back on track. "Just remember that no one in this family can say that Jon is an outsider as far as religion is concerned. Our blood ancestry is as Jewish as his."

"But our religion is different." Carmela said.

Jake looked perplexed. "What's with this 'our' thing?" he wondered.

"Blood is blood," Ike mumbled and rubbed his head again. No change in the size of his bump. "Blood is blood."

"So what now?" Sarah asked.

Patron straightened up in his chair. "We do nothing, we change nothing. Maybe we are Jews in blood, but we are Catholics in religion. I love the church. I love my religion. I love our community."

The family nodded in assent.

"What we need to do is to keep everything the same, no changes, and keep this news to ourselves. We can do what we want to do personally. Whoever wants to explore the past, fine. I am more interested in the present and our future. I have learned a great lesson from Rosita, a lesson in tolerance and acceptance. We have been given a divine message that we need to get over our prejudices so we can accept Jon into the family. Otherwise, it is blasphemy. That is that. Case closed."

Esther smiled. "So I can light my candles out here on Friday nights?"

"Of course, dear," Patron smiled. "Everyone okay with that?"

"No problem," said Jake. "As long as we keep it in our family. It is no one's business what we do at home. My Abuelita's happy, I'm happy!" He threw Esther a kiss.

With all eyes on him, Patron got up slowly, walked over to Jon and embraced him. "You don't by any chance want to convert?" Then he paused a while and grinned. Everyone got the joke.

Jon laughed. "Thanks for the offer. We are what we are."

Patron laughed. "That's what I used to think. Now look at us. I am sure we can work it all out. You are one of us now." One by one, everyone got up and embraced Rosie and Jon.

Esther smiled. "This is what really matters."

@

At exactly the same moment Patron was embracing Jon, Fr. Raul and Francisca were on the church floor, prostrating themselves at Rosita's feet. They were in the middle of praying hard for strength and understanding, when a blast of wind whistled through the open front door of the church. A beam of bright, white moonlight followed and flashed over Rosita's face. She was smiling.

Esther, Paz and Rosie all felt that smile, too.

14

All, My Relatives

Saturday August 4, 2001

> All, my relatives.
> We are all the same stuff formed differently.
> It makes trouble when we forget that.
> All, my relatives.
>
> —Elmer Ceoptewa. Santa Rosita Pueblo

One year later, Rosie finished her studies at the University of New Mexico and married Jon in a dual religious ceremony in the newly built Rosita wing of the Santa Rosita church. Paz sat on Patron's right during the ceremony.

Ike and Raymond had designed and built the new wing of the church with the help of local artisans. They took special care to construct Rosita's new window in a way to express her message. With the help of Fr. Raul, it took three months to shape and fit hundreds of pieces of dark bentonite, black obsidian, red quartz and blue turquoise stones, with stained glass of many colors, into a geometric pattern of six-pointed stars, circles, crosses, butterflies, rainbows and designs found on the rocks of the mesa.

They designed the room so the visitor entering through the arched doorway at the side of the main church views Rosita dramatically silhouetted against her window. The visitor who looks up sees four rainbows, rendered in glossy multicolored tile, streaming into each corner of the room from the apex of the ceiling and ending at each corner of the floor. Twenty rows of candles, all in amber-colored glasses, continually flicker at Rosita's feet.

The wedding ceremony was presided over by Fr. Raul and a reform Rabbi from Santa Fe. Raymond was best man. Elmer occupied a place of honor on Jon's family's side of the aisle. During the ceremony, both Elmer and the photographer who posed the wedding party in front of Rosita, noticed something very strange. But that is for the end of the story.

After the ceremony, and the picture taking, Patron called out. "A mi casa"—everyone to my place. Rosie and Jon hurried out of the church into a cloud of grains and seeds and bread crumbs (so the birds could feast too) sprinkled over them by the wedding party. They hopped into the back seat of Ike's new convertible (he had sold his motorcycle) and drove slowly, leading the procession of guests up the hill to Rosie's grandparents' hacienda.

The moment the wedding party entered the courtyard, the waiting and colorfully attired mariachi band struck up a brassy version of 'Cielito Lindo.' Under Paz's watchful eye, smiling servers greeted the crowd with trays of margaritas and sangria that Juan had mass-produced in the kitchen. Esther and Sarah had the dinner tables arranged in a horseshoe shape around the fountain. The head table, extending along the front of the house, was reserved for the newlyweds and their immediate families. Rosie's family sat on her left, Jon's father and a few other relatives on his right.

Fr. Raul and Francisca's place was at the first table that branched off to the right of the head table. A place of honor. Fr. Raul sported his new burgundy cap and frock, his new formal attire since he had been promoted to Monsignor. Francisca had taken to wearing matching burgundy colored blouses and skirts, too. Fr. Raul was enjoying the festivities with a pleased grin across his face. Good luck comes in threes, he thought. He was recently made Monsignor, the wedding came off without a hitch, and he was pleased about the letter he had received the day before.

"Dear Monsignor," it read. "We are pleased to inform you that the Bishop has approved your request to stay at your current posting until you desire to retire, or reasons beyond your control impede you from continuing your duties. Our thanks for your contributions to the Church. Our best wishes for your continued success."

His dream had come true. He could stay in Santa Rosita forever. He had not told Francisca yet, and fantasized about her response when she learned the news. How happy she will be when I read this letter to her tonight, he mused.

Francisca, who by this time had learned to read his mind, walked over to him with two margaritas, and winked. "All you want, always, mi amor."

For the past year, Fr. Raul had worked hard to apply what he learned from his experience. He recently completed the first of what he hoped would be an annual fiesta called 'We Are All One.' This first event coincided with the annual pilgrimage to Santa Rosita, filling the hearts of the faithful, as well as the coffers of the church.

"The purpose of this event," he wrote in his fundraising brochure, "is to commemorate and celebrate the history of all Santa Rositans, both Indians and townspeople, to welcome newcomers, and to promote the 'We are all one' philosophy."

Fr. Raul declared the opening day of the fiesta as the day for 'Rosita's message.' He started a tradition of re-reading the speech he made on the steps of the church the year before. Fortunately, Francisca was so taken by his speech at the time that she remembered it verbatim, and wrote it down. Last Christmas, she presented him with a framed version of the speech, written in her beautiful handwriting. He hung it on the wall over his bed, next to his crucifix. On Saturday nights, Francisca liked to ask Fr. Raul, "read it to me again, dear."

The first 'We Are All One' fiesta was a great success. Fr. Raul, Patron, Ike and Raymond presided over the festivities, which included mariachi bands, Indian dances, and drumming. The tourists loved it. Juan ran the Cantina concession, and made enough money to purchase a very expensive amplifier for his blender. Rosita was on display every day so she could share in the fun. There was only one glitch. The considerable volumes of people placed a serious strain on the supply of sacred soil. When they heard of the shortage, a group of crooks conceived a plot to peddle bogus sacred soil to gullible tourists. Fr. Raul asked Ike and Sal to stop what he considered a sacrilege. After a phone call to Alcalde, the problem, as well as two people involved in causing the problem, disappeared within two days. Alcalde reported his success to an answering machine in the state office of La Tierra. No one returned his call.

Patron sat in an old, ornate and oversized ceremonial chair to Rosie's left. He wore a black suit with silver buttons, and a dashing white lace shirt with an open collar, partially covered by a black leather vest. The shirt and vest provided a striking background for a massive silver bolo tie studded with turquoise jewels—a gift from Raymond. Patron acknowledged each guest individually with a bow of his noble head.

Esther, on his left, whispered, "Stop acting like the Pope," but he ignored her. With utmost dignity, of course. Patron had kept busy in the past year attempting to apply Rosita's theme of unity and cooperation to some serious wheeling and dealing. After conferring with Jon, Rosie and Raymond, Patron decided to call in his political chips. He 'scrounged,' in his words, substantial grants, 'to the tune of several million dollars' from state, federal and private sources. The funds had been designated to "support a model community, demonstrate tolerance for ethnic and religious diversity, and support mutual economic cooperation." Right up his new-found alley.

Patron used the money to fund several new companies, which he placed under the banner of a new entity—Alonzo Enterprises. Jaime Flores became President, and Rosie Flores the CFO. The company was already in the black.

Alonzo Enterprises includes the Red Mesa Company (with offices planned in New York, London, Boston and Paris), with Raymond Martinez as President. The Red Mesa Company manufactures bow ties, bolo ties, and headbands. They are expanding into southwestern footwear, jewelry and women's clothing. 'The Sacred Rug Company' is a spin-off from Alonzo's Arts and Crafts Enterprises. Ike Flores is President. This division specializes in rugs for all religions (one big seller for Muslim clientele is a prayer rug with an embedded, almost invisible, design of the call to prayer).

Patron also helped Jake expand his platform as Director of the Recycling Center, by creating the Santa Rosita Waste Management Company, in partnership with Chenoa Martinez, cultural coordinator. This business has already received national recognition for recycling scrap metal from discarded automobiles, trailers and old pickup trucks. They have contracts with over twenty small towns and twelve Indian pueblos.

Patron also obtained a ten-year federal development grant to establish a rural health care demonstration program in Santa Rosita. Jon Spielman, Director of the Clinic, now the hub of a regional health care system, helped obtain the grant. The grant supports twenty new jobs. Jon and Esther are training locals as 'barefoot doctors' who go into the countryside to meet patients on their own turf. Their motto is, "If they can't come to us, we go to them." Patron made it clear to everyone in town that Jon had to sign on for ten years in order to keep the grant. That done, and because Jon still had not made any enemies, it was an easy matter to formally announce his marriage to Rosie. Things went as smooth as silk.

"Two birds with one stone," Esther said. She is very proud and thankful for the way Patron eased the path for Rosie and Jon. That is why, at the wedding feast, she whispered in his ear, "Ruben, you could have made it miserable for all of us, but man that you are, you saved the day." He grinned, but without taking his eyes off the crowd. Esther continued. "Amor, you are something. "

"I know," he grinned and whispered without turning his head. "It's amazing, isn't it? And so are you."

Jon came to understand the Santa Rositans' attitude about insularity and applied the concept to advantage by developing the 'barefoot doctor' practice. Locals were much more trusted and effective than highly trained health workers from the outside. Consequently, he decided to make his clinic a showplace for culturally sensitive rural medicine. Jon gathered and trained the local curanderas, medicine men and women, shamans and more, in the practice of modern medicine.

In a short time, Jon's efforts have already improved the devastation caused by illnesses and conditions such as depression, alcoholism, obesity, diabetes, and high blood pressure, as well as spousal violence and teenage pregnancy. He is currently planning to create programs for the schools to benefit children. As expected, some people from the pueblo are resistant to his efforts because of their belief that nothing positive can happen until the Great Spirit puts the earth back on center. Nevertheless, he has sworn to persevere until the Great Spirit does so.

Patron met Elmer's eyes, smiled, and raised his glass. Raymond raised his glass of non-alcoholic beer, toasted "Back to you," and tugged playfully at his bow tie. They had had a busy year as well. Elmer and Raymond had called a meeting after they returned from the mesa last year to shared what they learned with their people.

After a lengthy discussion, it was accepted that the signs they received about cooperation, and togetherness—'All, my relatives'— meant that everyone needed to work together—Indians and non-Indians as well. A mutually profitable business would make it possible for them to create jobs, increase the cash flow and keep their world as stable as possible.

Their action plan called for Raymond and Rosie to start the Red Mesa Company. With the start-up money that Patron obtained, the businesses prospered quickly. Rosie's marketing campaign, using catalogs, telemarketing and the Internet, quickly increased sales. Good P.R. helped, too.

They were so successful that the tribe could finally put away the idea of building a casino. Because of their efforts, many of the pueblo's youth are now making a living as artists, creating innovative designs for neckwear, headbands and hatbands. Others are working in computer marketing and sales via their very popular website. Bolo ties are selling like hotcakes overseas. The Red Mesa Company has a large sign on the wall of the front office with the Indian word, and newly created symbol for 'Marketing.' It is a butterfly in the middle of a circle of stick figures of people holding hands. Their little heads are on the inside, and their bodies and feet are on the outside.

Paz was swimming in the sea of good feelings around her. She was especially pleased when Rosie asked her to be maid of honor. When Rosie popped the question, she replied,

"Rosie, dear, shouldn't you ask a girlfriend?" Of course, Rosie knew what she wanted to hear and said it.

"Auntie Paz, you are my best girlfriend."

Paz hugged her and laughed. "You know that you are already in my will but today, today, my dear, your percentage goes up."

After the turmoil around Rosie's announcement died down and the issues around the rising of Rosita's pedestal were settled, Paz expressed her deep gratitude to her saints. She thanked them profusely for intervening and informing God that it was necessary to raise Rosita's pedestal out of the ground to wake people up with a divine message—love, peace, and as little aggravation as possible. However, her saints were not finished with her.

After word got out about Paz's 'direct pipeline' to the saints, she was approached to write a book. Her recently published, 'The Saint Whisperer' is climbing on the bestseller list, leading to an offer to do a radio talk show. She has also mentioned that she might enter a theological seminary "when I get really old."

With bartender Juan's help, she has expanded the restaurant business to include a mail order center featuring Paz's Chili, and Juan's unique blenders (three sizes: loud, louder and loudest), Margarita and Beergarita Mix, baseball caps, T-shirts, and, of course, Margarita-themed headbands (specially designed by Ike).

Vincente and Vickie were in a jovial mood, having already downed a pitcher and a half of very strong sangria. They, too, worked hard to apply what they learned from what they called the 'Rosita Experience' to their daily lives. To his credit, Vincente approached the Abales, and attempted to settle their differences. Unfortunately, the head of the Abale clan, not being privy to what happened with Rosita, said, "I don't know what the hell you are talking about. You must be sucking agave. We have always fought each other and we always will. After all, if we do not keep to tradition, what else do we have? So get the hell out of here."

So, that was that. At least he had tried. Vincente cleared himself of any guilt. Rosita will not blame me, he said to himself. Rosita knows that Abale is a son of a bitch. Vincente also notched back a bit on his 'warrior' talk with the grandkids, two of whom are now working with Ike. He often ponders the notion that anyone in Santa Rosita who hates the Jews, hates their own ancestors, because their ancestors were Jews. That is something he never thought about before. He often talks about it with Vickie on their morning walks. She is on salary at the health clinic, and doing good work in the outreach program. They spend a lot of time together helping each other keep Rosita's secret.

Ike was chatting and laughing loudly with his girlfriend Consuela, Sal, his cousin Lisa, and her boyfriend, Pedro. Continuingly inspired by the special mission Rosita had given him, Ike applied what he learned about 'spiritual illumination and transformation' in his art. He started a new organization with Raymond called 'Todos, Nuestra Tierra' (All, Our land). Their new headband logo has been adopted by many environmental organizations. It is a picture of Rosita, dressed as a Kachina, with her arms reaching out toward the viewer. She rests on a background of the map of New Mexico, painted a beautiful soft Santa Fe blue. A golden arc of figures, stars, symbols and crosses, representing most of the known religious belief systems, range over her head like a tiara.

Next year, Ike plans to marry Consuela, who is twenty-two years old. She is a childhood acquaintance who returned to Santa Rosita from military service six months earlier. He used to think she was a 'goodie-goodie' until, as he told many of his cronies, "We made out in my car" after a night on the town.

Consuela says she fell madly in love with Ike after, in her words, "Ike got rid of that goddamn headband and motorcycle, changed the way he dressed, and grew up."

Ike continues his friendship with Sal. Being the loyal friend that he is, Ike gave him a job as his executive assistant. Sal is calming down, although he has to curtail the vulgar language that angers Consuela. The passage of time helped Ike get over his disappointment with Alcalde. After all, he was grateful that Alcalde did not press the issue about Rosie. As a reward, Ike hired him to manage a company outlet store near the four corners area (New Mexico, Arizona, Colorado, and Utah) after La Tierra, as Alcalde described it, "went belly up because all the chinga bosses went into politics." The store just about breaks even financially, but the office parties are the best in the organization. Consuela does not mind going up to party occasionally.

In the future, Ike would become a celebrated santero, especially known for weaving beautifully colored, subtle, configurations of crosses and six-pointed stars into his rugs and tapestries. The media would portray Ike as embodying the 'Spirit of the Mystical West.'

Carmela was working the crowd wearing her new pendant, a tiny six-pointed star placed at the center of a large turquoise cross. She has taken to lighting candles on Friday night with Esther, Paz and Rosie. The girls, as they call themselves, have also taken to drinking a second glass of sacramental wine and upping its quality. On the Friday preceding, the wedding, Carmela, the most adamant about upgrading the wine portion of the ritual, brought over a bottle of Chateau Gloria from France. Everyone loved it.

Carmela has also added something new to her mystique. During her marketing trips to New York City, selling 'Alonzo's Rugs' to design stores and galleries, she has learned to capitalize on the New York glitterati's fascination with her as a self-proclaimed 'Crypto-Jew.' It has gotten to the point where she lectures to groups about the meaning of the symbols woven into the rugs, and shows people how and where to look for them. Consequently, she has become popular with the American Jewish community as well as other cultural, historical and environmental groups; they come to Santa Rosita at her invitation. There is a special rate for them at the Inn and a discount for the 'Crypto-Jew' tour.

Carmela has appeared on several morning talk shows, and been approached by several publishers to write a book about her discovery of her Jewish descent. Jake is happy that she is happy, and crows that their sex is better than ever. As he says, "She is really horny when she comes back from New York City."

Esther was feeling very contented watching her loved ones, Jon and Rosie, and their parents, joyfully mingle with the wedding guests.

"Something done right," she said to herself.

Esther works one day a week at the Health Center teaching young people about herbal medicine. She is paid as a consultant under one of the grants Patron received from a national foundation interested in alternative medicine. Elmer also works at the clinic, teaching what he knows about medicinal herbs and teas. He is paid under the Native American Healer section of the grant. He spends a lot of time with his new baby granddaughter, and visits Red Mesa once a month to enjoy the company of the spirits. Jon wants Elmer and Esther to write a book with him about their healing methods, but Elmer is not interested in doing so.

He told Jon, "We just do it. The more we talk about it, the more it does not work. Do not worry. One day you will understand." Elmer is still waiting for the earth to get back on center.

As the night wore on, the music played, and it was time for Rosie and Jon to dance their wedding dance. They held each other close. "Whoever thought," Jon whispered, "that the future is going to be wonderful, and so very interesting." Rosie kissed him hard, and the crowd whooped.

After her honeymoon, Rosie plans to start a center for tolerance and understanding in Northern New Mexico called the 'Rosita Center' where she will teach the power of sometimes doing nothing, and unconditional acceptance of diversity. She plans to spend the next year collecting research for a book she will call 'Rosita's Miracle.'

"After all," Rosie says, "I asked Rosita and she delivered. I want to spend the next year researching who she is, where she came from and what is her story. I will ask grandfather, Fr. Raul, Pablo, and Jon's father to help, as well as some people at the university."

Rosie intends to unveil Rosita's pedestal in the future, but only after those who have promised to keep it secret pass on. And, of course, if Rosita wants her to.

Now for the curiosity.

When the photographer developed the wedding pictures, he was surprised that Rosita's face displayed a variety of expressions. When asked by his assistant to explain how such a thing could happen, he answered, "This is unusual, of course. However it is probably due to the effect of the shadows generated by the changing light coming through the stained glass window, as well as the candles at the foot of the statue."

When the assistant asked why the expressions on Rosita's face exactly matched the expressions on Rosie's face, and vice versa, the photographer answered impatiently. "It's obvious. Similar expressions result from similar lighting effects."

"I guess," the assistant agreed. "After all, a wooden statue cannot smile."

However, when Rosie, Elmer, Ike and the members of the executive committee saw the pictures, they knew better.

Jon said, "Why not?"

Many years later, Jon learned to take Rosie's word for such things. Actually, on their fiftieth wedding anniversary, they were able to read each other's minds, although Rosie would be much better at it.

Epilogue: Rosita's Story

True to her word, on a Sunday afternoon about a year after her wedding, Rosie was ready to meet Jon and Raymond at the Cantina to discuss the material that would be the basis of her new book. Many months earlier, she had given each one an assignment to help her gather information from their own sources. Today, she intended to review and discuss what they all had learned, and assemble their knowledge.

Rosie had devoted many hours at the university to researching the history of 'Crypto-Jews' by reviewing old documents and talking with the faculty. She also worked with Pablo, who allowed her access to private family files, and Fr. Raul, who helped her access some relevant church files. Together with Jon, who often accompanied her on field research, she learned a great deal from her new father-in-law, David Spielman. He had access to well-guarded information pertaining to the experiences of Jews who had come to New Mexico. Their visits together to sites of interest became a favorite pastime.

Raymond was tasked to learn what he could from the tribal records, and to ask Grandfather to travel back through the boundless dream world to learn about Rosita's origins. Elmer was happy to do so, and they spent days on the mesa so he could teach Raymond to access the dream world as well and do 'Indian Research' as he called it.

◎

Rosie arrived at the Cantina carrying her briefcase under one arm, and a tape recorder under the other. Since it was Sunday afternoon, the Cantina's patio was overflowing with exuberant locals, gesturing and talking loudly as they crowded around the old wooden tables. The town's weavers gathered at one table, Santeros and wood carvers, at their own. The people were still enthusiastic about last year's events that had made the local economy boom. Armando, the town's most esteemed retablo artist, climbed up on a bench, glass of tequila in hand, and, as his friends held him straight, praised Fr. Raul's pronouncement of the previous year's events as a bonafide miracle.

"Didn't he call it right?" Armando shouted, "Prosperity is here. Didn't our blessed Padre assure us that when word got out about the miracle, new business would come to the town? Isn't this a golden age for us and our neighbors?" He threw out his arms in a gesture of embrace and pointed in the direction of the pueblo.

Jose, an apprentice rug weaver, grabbed Armando's arm and pulled himself up next to him. "Let's drink to the Padre," he shouted, and the crowd raised their glasses.

"And Patron, too," another artisan joined him.

Everyone waved to Rosie as she passed. Some even tipped their hats.

She waved and smiled back.

Jon had arrived before Rosie. By the time he got there, most of the customers were outside, so he had no trouble slipping into the family's 'reserved' booth. Earlier that afternoon, he had let the bartender, Juan, know that he was meeting Raymond and Rosie.

With a smile of anticipation, Jon settled himself at the back of the booth, turned over the well-worn 'Reserved' sign, and threw off the protective cloth towel Juan had spread over a bowl of tortilla chips, cup of salsa, two margaritas on ice, a plate of guacamole, and a large unopened ginger ale for Raymond. Jon reached for the margarita and took a long, slow sip.

Since he was the only outsider to have witnessed the event, Jon had spent the last year trying to make sense of what he had seen. He often talked his ideas over with Rosie, and now he was looking forward to discussing them with Raymond before she arrived. By this time, he had already admitted to himself that any attempt to use scientific principles—time, space, causality and logic—to make sense of what had happened, was useless. Like it or not, his rational mind was the wrong tool for this particular job.

Think outside the box, forget common sense and logic, he told himself. Jump over the rational boundaries, come up with alternative ways to understand what Grandfather talks about.

He was silently reviewing his ideas when he felt a tap on his shoulder. Raymond was standing over him and eyeing the feast on the table. Jon handed up the bottle of ginger ale.

"You got a dent between your eyes deep as a canyon." Raymond picked up a handful of chips and dipped one in the guacamole. "Been thinking too hard again?"

"Better believe it!" Jon searched for the crevice and rubbed his forehead.

"Don't bust your head. Like I said, your way of thinking can go only so far, you know, like driving a car to the edge of the mesa, and then you can't go any farther. Because there is no more road. Get what I mean?" Raymond opened the bottle of ginger ale and scooped up another chip with salsa. "So, where is Rosie?"

"She'll be along," Jon said. "You're right; I can't explain what I saw. But I saw it. So, I ask myself, how could such a thing happen?"

Raymond snapped another chip in two. "You can't drive in a nail with a screwdriver! So did you find the words?"

"Well, I tried to do like you and grandfather say; don't use my thinker, use imagination."

Raymond nodded in approval. Jon continued, "So how about this? I'm imagining if—how to put it—what I saw could be explained; if it was possible, for example, to say that life on earth was restricted to a finite dimension of physical existence?"

He hesitated for a moment, straining, ". . . which is stratified among layers of other dimensions, all floating within an endless universe—follow me?"

Raymond grinned, enjoying his friend's mental gymnastics. Poor Jon, he thought affectionately, there he is struggling to discover and understand, or re-invent, a cosmology that every Indian has in his bones. Curious how intellectual smarts and spiritual smarts do not necessarily go hand in hand. It's not Jon's fault, he said to himself, nobody ever taught him this stuff. When ya' don't know, ya' don't know.

Jon nodded his head vigorously as he spoke, as if he hoped to agree with his own words, "Let's consider the relationship between our human physical body and this narrow dimension of ours. Our body is born into it, like when a waiter in an Italian restaurant pours balsamic vinegar into a bowl of olive oil and a form appears. What about that?"

Raymond licked his lips. "Italian restaurants, dipping bread in olive oil—sounds good to me!"

"Okay, now, it's a given that our personal consciousness lives in the physical body, right?"

"Why not?" Raymond agreed, sort of.

Jon continued, "Maybe it is possible that since our consciousness—thinking, feeling—is non-material, it is able to simultaneously inhabit the physical body, as well as other places, dimensions, at the same time?"

"That's why we have vision quests and can time and space travel in our sleep."

Jon leaned forward, aware that he was getting a little closer to what Raymond had said. "Well, I can't do that. However, if you or Grandfather can do it, it is because your consciousness, or whatever, has to be connected to the infinite at the time. If that's so, then it follows that everything that is, or was, or will be, is also connected. "

Raymond tapped Jon's head with a chip. "You get a sparrow feather for that," he laughed. "Grandfather would be proud."

"So you don't think I'm loco?" Jon sighed. "I'm thinking that I might be talking loco."

Raymond grinned. "No, not loco! You just got promoted to Indian first grade."

Jon breathed out, more with exhaustion than relief. "If everything I said was possible, it could explain what happened out there last year, don't you think?"

"Why not? But you don't need to knock yourself out. No one needs to explain what happened. It just happened. It is not about who, what, when or why. It just is! Imagine you drive your car to the edge of the mesa, pal. Now read the signpost. What does it say?" Raymond grabbed his bottle of ginger ale, sipped it slowly, and looked deep into Jon's eyes. He tapped his temple several times with a finger, and then tapped his heart. "Open up whatever is in there . . ."

"It's open, it's open."

"The sign says, why not?"

"Why not?" Jon noticed that his headache was gone.

"Sure," Raymond continued. "You say 'seamless,' we say 'all is one.' This is not an Indian pipe dream. Science supports the idea that the universe is seamless and connected—that all is one. Therefore, we can be here and everywhere at the same time. Imagine, amigo, you are focusing a super- power electron microscope on a room where eight people are having dinner. Using life-sized resolution, the people appear to be clearly defined, separate entities. Right?"

Jon agreed.

"Now increase the power of magnification and what do you see? The physical boundaries defining each individual fade away. More magnification and they completely dissolve. Even more magnification and everything you thought was separate starts to merge. Nothing is there except an ocean of pulsating atoms—the cosmic soup. This is like what we see when we look up at the sky with a powerful telescope. Infinity inward, infinity outward. All separation disappears. The universe is a state of undifferentiated continuity and unity. Matter, time and space become one. And listen to this: since no space-time exists, and all is intertwined, events can even occur simultaneously."

Jon grimaced. "Theoretically, it makes sense that what happens 'earth-years apart' could occur simultaneously if the universe were boundless." He felt his headache coming back.

Raymond leaned forward. "Exactly. With no space-time, it's possible that anything outside our dimension could manifest itself here in ways we can't understand: energy, material things in different forms, thoughts, emotions, perceptions, actions. Phenomena may become 'real' here as pure energy, arriving and vanishing in an eye-blink, like the flash of ecstasy in my sister's eyes when she saw her new baby. Some people are more tuned in to this than others. Medicine men and women, and some others among us, can dip into the cosmic soup and feel it as emotions, or thoughts, or physically. The cosmic soup can pour over us."

"So you are saying that's what happened?" Jon asked.

"Could be, poured all over us. And it doesn't have to make sense." Raymond hit the table with his fist to punctuate his comment. "That's because your normal sense has run out of road. But, if you could ignore your physical sense, and know with something else, well, why not? Well?"

"Why not? Okay, why not? Let's forget how it happened, but then, why did it happen?"

"That's a very good question!" Raymond smiled because he had spotted Rosie. "Look who's here—maybe she has some answers."

@

Rosie walked up to their booth. They got up, Jon kissed her and Raymond hugged her. So guys," she said, "Ready for . . ."

"The big story." Jon settled them down in the booth.

Raymond smiled. "Did Grandfather's research help?"

"Indispensable," Rosie agreed.

". . . in his sleep, right?" Jon asked.

Rosie smiled. "That's the way he does it."

"So let's hear it." Raymond was eager to hear what she had pieced together.

"Here we go." Rosie reached into her briefcase and removed her manuscript. Then she turned on her tape recorder. "Technology," she smiled. "Okay. Thanks to Grandfather, we go back to August 5, 1570, to an artist's studio in the village of Nuevo Leon, capital of the colony of New Spain. Grandfather saw Maestro Luis Alonzo, the most celebrated wood carver of saints and angels at that time, dozing in his studio. He was awakened by a gentle, but resolute voice. 'Luis, it is time,' the voice said. 'Luis, it is time.' That's what Grandfather said, and now, here's my story version of what grandfather reported."

"Today?" Luis mumbled, as he awoke with the now familiar sense of dread rising in his stomach. Sleep, fitful or not, had been his best escape.

"Yes," the voice answered, almost forlornly. Luis listened, momentarily distracted by how his warm breath condensed into a cloud of vapor as it hit the cold air in the room—as if it materialized his fear. No time for such reflections, he told himself, and shuffled over to the center of the room to admire his latest creation. There stood a six-foot-tall wooden statue of a woman, so delicately balanced on her three-foot high, elaborately carved pedestal that she appeared to float above it. Luis gazed critically at the position of her hands. Did he get them right? Her right hand reached out toward him with upturned palm, her left hand extended out from her side, as if she were expecting someone to take her hand. She was perfect!

Luis spoke to her tenderly, ". . . a few more touches, my lady." He snatched up a thin paintbrush from his worktable and dipped it in a pot of gold paint. With brush in hand, he carefully climbed up the scaffold beside the statue, and set to work touching up her intricate tiara. When he finished, he let the paintbrush fall from his hands and gingerly placed them over her face. Closing his eyes for a moment to focus on his sense of touch, Luis ran his fingertips ever so gently over her sculpted cheekbones, her thin nose, tiny ears and gently rounded chin, stopping at the point where her neck met the edge of the crimson, flared collar embellishing the top of her robe.

"Not a splinter," he marveled to himself, and ran his hands lightly over the gilt trim around her collar.

"Good," he whispered. Moving quickly, he floated his hands downward, rising and falling over and under the folds of the gold-trimmed, blue and crimson robe cascading away from her neck and down to her feet.

"Like silk." Luis was as satisfied with his work as any perfectionist could ever be.

Did his muse agree? He put a hand up to his ear to listen. There was no sound. He asked in his mind, satisfactory? He listened again. Still no response. So be it. He could proceed. He smiled at the statue.

Now Senorita, for your eyes. Luis's most challenging task was to create her eyes and set them in place.

Helped by a burst of unexpected energy, he collected several logs and heaved them onto the fire, picked up an iron candelabrum, inserted a fresh candle into each of its eight receptacles, and lit them carefully. This done, he walked over to the cabinet set against the north wall of his studio, where he kept his supplies. It was especially cold in that part of his studio, farthest away from the fireplace, so he tied his heavy robe tight around him, and draped his colorful woven serape around his neck. While he gathered up paints, brushes and a palette, an icy sting on the back of his neck startled him.

What's this? Luis reached back quickly. The back of his neck was wet and cold. He looked up to see a thread of water droplets—iridescent jewels—running along the underside of the latillas supporting the roof, reflecting the candlelight in a rainbow of colors. Always the artist, he forgot his discomfort. But no time for that, he thought, and spoke aloud to reassure his muse. "I will finish my statue tonight." No answer, but not unexpected. Luis knew the way of the muse, and loved trying to explain her to his students during the years he had been allowed to teach.

"The muse communicates God's instructions to the artist. You, the artist, are the instrument, the technician, the way into this earthly realm of existence. You must listen with respect and humility." He added a disclaimer that always amused his students, "Even if you may have to do what the muse says, it does not mean you have to like it."

Luis's muses instructed him to carve, shape, and paint the statue's eyes in a new and unique way.

"Her eyes must seem alive," the muse insisted, "the color, Luis, especially the color . . . must be like no other."

He set to work mixing powders, searching for the right shade of blue. It was frustrating work. He muttered the same words over and over again: "No good. Must reflect the light better." Samples littered the floor.

"Try again," he urged himself. Twice he cleaned off his palette and started over. On the third round, he threw up his hands in frustration. "No good, no good," he cried, then he fell quiet. The muse's presence filled the room.

"Luis, I instructed you that you must close your eyes to see," the voice sounded impatient.

He closed his eyes and saw with his imagination. "Yes! The blue of the sky, with a touch of orange and amber, too. Like her skin." He opened his eyes and stirred the colors together. "Sky blue and brilliant. A bit more gold, a flash of sunlight. Silver too, yes, silver for the ring of light around her turquoise pupils. Yes, this will do," he smiled to himself. "This will do nicely. Do you agree?"

He listened. No comment. He took that as approval.

His next task was unprecedented: her eyes had to move. He had never done such a thing before; the eyes of his statues had always been unchanging, immovable. He had already spent months struggling with experiments that failed and pleading with his muse for help. No answer. Just silence.

Help had come one torrid afternoon, when Luis was stretched out on a couch dozing. He was pondering his problem, and listening to the snoring of his assistant, Primero, leaning back against the fireplace wall.

Luis heard the words in his head, "Willow pegs!"

"Willow pegs." He stirred from his reverie and repeated the words slowly.

"Yes, of course!" He jumped up and shouted, "Willow pegs, Primero! Wake up. Willow pegs contract and expand with changes in temperature and humidity. Right?"

Primero yawned loudly and nodded his head. He had no idea what the Maestro was taking about.

"Tell me, Primero, what will happen if we attach her eyeballs to the sockets with willow pegs?" Luis asked him enthusiastically.

Primero's eyes widened with excitement. "Oh!"

"Right! The eyes will move when the pegs expand and contract. Yes?"

"Yes, Maestro," Primero nodded his head with a sure sense of understanding. "Of course, Maestro. They will roll upward when it is hot and dry, because the willow contracts, and downward when the humidity is high and the willow expands."

Primero beamed with pride. "What a privilege to work with such a genius," he thought, but then he realized, sadly, "Ay! How can the priests call such a man 'the devil Jew,' the 'Christ Killer,' the heretic?" He lamented to himself.

Primero was taught to believe that the priests' words were infallible, because God inspired them. Personal experience, however, had taught him that Luis was nothing like a devil. No, he was a fair man, a good father, and a great artist. "Such a pity," he regularly complained to his wife. "Such a pity."

Luis felt the sadness reflected in the eyes of his short, dark-skinned, powerfully built protégé, and his heart warmed. Ah, Primero, he reflected— Primero of the perpetual smile, and the bright brown eyes. Primero, who knew so much more than he could say. Primero, the orphan boy Luis had rescued from the streets decades earlier. Now he was thankful that Primero returned the favor by remaining devoted to him, loyal and diligent. He was unique among the assistants; the others had abandoned Luis as soon as they heard that the artist had been targeted by agents of the Inquisition. No, thought Primero, who wept inconsolably when he heard the news and vowed to stay with Luis. He was clever enough to offer his help in conspiring with Luis to dupe the authorities.

They plotted that Primero would inform the Church investigators that he would 'spy' on Luis and steal his artistic secrets for the Crown. These authorities agreed, knowing that Primero was the only assistant left with access to Luis's unique wood carving techniques, special colors and dyes and technical inventions. This scheme helped Primero buy time for Luis. The officials agreed that they would not take Luis away until Primero had captured his most important secret— making wood like iron—the process of fossilizing wood quickly. Luis had worked out the technique with a renowned holy man and potter from the area named Miguel. They had met soon after Luis arrived in a ship from Spain, bewildered at the prospect of making art in a new world.

This was an unusual arrangement for the time; colonials like Luis were forbidden to fraternize with natives. Natives were slaves. But incorporating Miguel's teachings into his own work enabled Luis to create wonderful carvings, retablos, statues like this one that would be almost impervious to the effects of time. The products of their collaboration were so exceptional that the Crown initially welcomed it—until the Inquisition gained force.

Then there was a formal prohibition against fraternizing in any way between the native people and colonials, especially those who had been religious and political exiles from Spain. When fraternization actually became a capital offense, Miguel had to flee Nuevo Leon to survive.

As Luis saw their work together coming to an end, he confided many secrets to Primero to assure him future prosperity as a Santero. But Primero was more concerned about his master's safety than exploiting his gifts. Lately, the Inquisition agents had become increasingly impatient and belligerent about allowing Luis to continue without converting to Catholicism, and Luis scornfully disregarded the idea. Primero, however, continued to plead with him, even after Luis's frustrated family abandoned their own attempts to sway him.

"Maestro, just do what the authorities want!" he would tearfully beseech Luis, who always returned the same answer, "Never." Primero would cry out, "Do you want to die?"

Luis would answer calmly. "What has to be, has to be." Primero would cry even louder, "For God's sake, Maestro, tell them you will convert, but just pretend. A lie will protect you! Who cares? God himself knows what you do, and why."

"I can't," Luis would say firmly, shaking his head from side to side, then gazing upward, and raising his right arm toward the heavens as if responding to someone's invisible scrutiny.

This would predictably cause Primero to bellow, "Ay!" throw up his hands, and stomp out of the room.

Luis was beginning to install the statue's eyes when he noticed that the willow pegs were somewhat swollen, due to the rainy weather of the past few days. After a few calculations, he decided to position the eyes with a slight downward gaze.

Primero approved. "Yes. When the wood dries, she will look straight ahead. Now she looks down, like a sweet angel, Maestro." Primero nodded his head. "And she will last forever."

Once the eyes were in place, Luis climbed up on the scaffold, faced the statue squarely and placed his hands on her shoulders. Then, as Santeros do, he began to breathe life into her. He stared through her turquoise pupils so that his gaze penetrated straight through to the back of her eyes. All the while, he smiled with a fond expression, like a mother face-to-face with her newborn infant. "My work is done," he whispered, Primero watched from below. A female voice entered Luis's mind. It sounded soft, sweet, and perplexed, so young and vulnerable, but not frightened.

"Who are you? Who am I? What am I to do?" Luis did not perceive the voice as a physical sound. He experienced it as a bodily sensation, goose bumps rising all over his skin, a common occurrence when people deal with a presence they don't know or understand. Primero was aware that Luis was 'connecting;' he had learned to watch and listen at such times.

Luis spoke: "Child, you came through me to do something wonderful. Where or when, or how, I do not know, but you will at the right time." A soft turquoise light emanated from her eyes and began to fill the room. It became so intense that Primero threw his hands to his face to shield his eyes from the glare. The light grew even brighter, then, in a flash, disappeared.

"Nashamah," Luis said softly.

Primero choked. "Holy Mary, Mother of God," the words caught in his throat. He fell to his knees and, starting at his forehead, began a frenzy of crossing his eyes, mouth and his heart with a trembling hand. "The Holy Ghost."

Luis nodded reaching down to pat Primero's shoulder. "All the same."

"God, here in this room. A great privilege," Primero exulted, and crossed himself again.

"Yes," Luis repeated softly. A great sadness enveloped Primero again as he thought, "Ay! How can they want to punish this man in the name of God, when God comes to him?"

Luis looked deeply into Primero's eyes. "No need to worry . . ."

Seeing no fear in Luis's eyes, his assistant turned away, tears streaming down his face. "I don't understand why . . ."

"Because, Primero," Luis spoke slowly, "I have learned there are different humans on the earth; primitive beings and, as the natives say, human beings."

Primero knit his brow hard and listened intently. Sometimes the Maestro's words strained the boundaries of his understanding. Luis continued, "The primitives are full of self and little spirit, they take everything for themselves." Primero nodded in agreement, "You and I, Maestro, we are not primitive. We are 'human beings.'"

Luis agreed.

Primero continued, "But why does God allow the primitives in the church, Maestro?"

Luis answered that he did not know why, but that man made the church, not God.

"Yes, Maestro," Primero agreed. "The primitives go where there is power to be had. We go where there is art and love . . . that is why we are so easy to kill."

Luis reflected. "Remember Primero, I am counting on you to carry on." He turned to the statue. "You will leave with Abraham tonight. Get ready for a long sleep."

The artist motioned to Primero and together, in silence, they draped the statue with a gold-trimmed, blue silk shawl that Luis's wife, Sarah, had made especially for her. Primero's tears were spattering it.

Luis turned away and announced solemnly, "Leave me, my dear friend, I must write my declaration."

Without a word, Primero shuffled out of the room. Luis reached over to his worktable and picked up a retablo—a flat rectangular panel of wood with a colorful image of Adam and Eve in the Garden of Eden. But the back side of the retablo was stark white; Primero had coated it with gesso the previous day to make it ready for Luis's declaration. He tucked the retablo under his arm, moved closer to the fireplace, and sat down on a small wooden bench. After a moment of thought, he reached into the fireplace and gingerly extracted a thin, metal etching instrument from the coals. Placing it carefully in its wooden holder, he set the retablo on his lap, and began to write, "I, Luis Alonzo, born in Spain . . .

So," Jon interrupted. "You are telling me that Grandfather saw all this happening?"

Raymond nodded, "Yes!" Rosie concurred.

Jon shook his head, "How could he possibly know what Luis thought and felt?"

Raymond grinned. "The dream world is boundless. No boundaries, no time limits no inside or outside. . ."

"No boundaries." Rosie echoed.

"A boundless dream world," Jon responded, "no time or space; all is seamless, you say, no boundaries—Ray, that's what I was talking about before!"

Ray smiled and Rosie interrupted, "Tell me later, but now, where was I?"

"Luis's declaration . . ." Jon prompted her.

"Glad you were listening," Raymond chuckled quietly.

"Here we go," Rosie said.

◎

Luis put down his etching tool just as the morning sun began to light up the steamy east window of his studio. He sighed deeply, stretched slowly as if loosening one stiffened joint at a time, and shuffled over to the plush brocade bench nestled under the window. After settling into its soft, welcoming cushions, he reworked his declaration with care, scribing over a few letters to make them stand out more clearly against the white background of the retablo. When it satisfied him, he walked over to a concealed door at the back of the studio. He opened it and entered another, smaller workspace, where he created artwork forbidden by the authorities. Once inside, he collected several other retablos and brought them out into the main studio.

Working quickly, Luis wrapped the retablos in oilskin, dipped them in the vat of hot wax that Primero kept near the fire, and set them to dry. While the wax set, he re-entered the small room, collected three other packages that were already sealed and waterproofed and placed them next to the pedestal.

"That's everything," he said to himself. He knelt down beside the pedestal and proceeded to slide the fingers of his right hand under the trim overhanging the top of the pedestal. He searched for the edge of a thin lath of wood. When he found it, he pulled hard to remove it, exposing the edges of the two dowels supporting a hidden panel at the top of the pedestal. When he removed the dowels, the panel fell in. Primero shouted through the closed door.

"Maestro, I could only get two natives to help. The townspeople are too afraid to come."

Luis called back, "They will do. Bring them in when I tell you."

"Of course, Maestro," Primero was wondering what his master intended. Although he knew about the secret workroom, and that Luis was going to place his declaration in the pedestal, he was unaware of the other objects Luis was including.

Satisfied that everything was packed securely, Luis set the waterproof covering in place, fixed the panel over it, reset the dowels, and replaced the lath of wood.

"Come ahead, Primero," he shouted. "Time to attach our lady to her pedestal, and prepare her for the journey."

Primero and his helpers were in the room before Luis finished the sentence. Under Luis's direction, they lifted the statue and turned her upside down, revealing the four holes Luis had drilled on the bottom. After Luis filled the holes with glue and placed wooden pegs in them, he instructed the workers to lift the statue, and place her on the pedestal, fitting each peg into the corresponding holes on the pedestal. This done, they wrapped the final assembly in oilskin and coated it heavily with wax. Luis inspected his creation to assure that everything was sealed and watertight. Satisfied, he wrapped the statue in burlap, applied another coat of oilskin, layered it with wax, and had the workers set her in a creosote and oilskin-lined wooden crate filled with straw.

Just as Primero raised his hammer to drive in the last nail, Luis's 35-year-old son Abraham burst into the room. "The cart is outside, the rain is awful. We must hurry," he yelled. Luis held out his arms to embrace him, and then pulled back, as if the closeness was too much to bear at this moment.

"They say it's a hundred-year rain," Primero said. Abraham ignored him; he was thinking hard. How could he convince his stubborn father to come away with him? He had failed to do so many times before. "Father, there is no time left. We must go immediately," he urged.

Luis ignored him. His main desire was to get Abraham and his family to safety as soon as possible. "De Sosa. What about De Sosa?" Luis inquired about Abraham's partner in the exodus.

"Packed and ready to leave, and without the Crown's permission . . . he is fed up with their stalling. Yesterday was the end of it. They sang the same song: unless we bring along soldiers and priests, we cannot leave."

"So?"

"I thought they were going to arrest me on the spot. Instead, they sent someone to follow me to see where I went and who I talked with. Fortunately, he drinks too much; I can leave a wine flask here and there and lose him when I want." Abraham grinned.

Luis only pointed to the crate. "Let's get her on the cart. Then you must go."

"We go! We . . ." Abraham's eyes pleaded.

"Abraham, no." Luis stiffened.

"Please, Father?" Abraham grabbed Luis' shoulder so hard that Primero instinctively moved forward to protect Luis, but then pulled back. Abraham would never hurt his father. "Don't waste your breath, Abraham." Primero sighed and placed his hand on Abraham's shoulder.

Luis grabbed Abraham's other shoulder. "Think clearly, for God's sake. The authorities think you will not leave without me, right? So as long as they believe I am here, they believe you are here, too." Abraham stood mute. "They will come for me after the morning muster. If I am not here, they will go right to our home and take the rest of the family. If you leave right now, and I am here when they come, you will have a good head start. The rain will cover your tracks. It will be a week before it stops and they can organize a search."

Abraham tightened his jaw in exasperation. "I understand. But you can always buy us more time if you convert, like they want. You know how important it would be to them if someone like you . . ."

"Never a Marrano!" Luis barked. "Never!"

Abraham responded sharply, "But you made me do it, and mother and Rebecca."

"Look how much time it bought us." For what seemed an endless moment, the two men stared deeply and lovingly, into each other's eyes. Luis felt a sob rising up inside him, dissolving his heart. Abraham stepped back. "You will be burned at the stake, Father. Auto-da-fe . . . like the others."

Luis turned away. "Abraham, I need you to listen carefully, to believe and obey, what I am about to say." Primero sensed the intimate moment and began to disengage in the way he had learned from his Indian friends—the way to be absent while the body stays. Luis spoke warmly, reassuringly, "From time to time, God curses our people. I do not know why. It is now my turn. As hard as it may be for you to understand, please believe me when I say I will be comforted. Why? Because, my son, I have been told not to be afraid. I will not be here when they come for me. " Abraham stared dumbfounded for a moment, but recovered quickly. He had learned to accept his father's mysterious ways. "Doesn't that mean you should escape with us?"

"No, that's not it. The voice was clear. I need to stay here, but I will not be here when they come for me. Your mother understands." Luis pulled Abraham close and whispered secretively, "I have a message for you. Listen most carefully. This lady is very important; take her with you to the north. Your task is to guard her. You will have many trials along the way but you will succeed. When you arrive at the right place, you will know it. Then bury her. That is what you have to do."

Abraham fell limp in his arms.

Luis squeezed him close once again, then nudged Abraham toward the door. "Go." Primero and his two helpers picked up the crate and followed them outside into the downpour.

"Hurry," Luis implored. "The guards will come for me after their morning meal." Luis pushed his reluctant son up into the driver's seat. Abraham grabbed the reins and steadied the horse while Primero and his helpers slid the crate into the cart, piled many bales of hay on top, and covered the cargo with a heavy tarpaulin.

"Good," shivered Luis, "She is dry and safe." Luis nodded his thanks to the helpers and gestured for Primero to dismiss them. Then he embraced Primero. "Thank you. Profit from what I have taught you. Everything here is now yours. I have written it all down in a letter for you. Look in the drawer in my work table." Primero, wide-eyed with terror, stood frozen to the spot. His bright eyes dimmed, as if his soul had taken flight. "Now, go inside," Luis ordered sternly. "You must not be out here when they come." Primero's tears mixed with the rain dripping down his face. "Yes, Maestro." His sadness blended with the morning's dreariness.

Luis squeezed his son's hand, then slapped the horse's rear. "Go," he cried. The cart jerked forward and was away. Luis turned away from Abraham's parting look and saw a contingent of soldiers appearing out of the storm at a distance. The captain leading the guard was squinting hard to see through the rain when he spotted the hazy outline of the cart moving away. "Stop!" he shouted and signaled two soldiers to run after the cart. Fortunately for Abraham, they began to slip and slide on the wet cobblestones and had to slow down to a walk. Seconds later, the cart turned a corner and disappeared. No sooner did Luis threw up his arms to block the two soldiers from going any further, he felt a burning pain slash through his chest that knocked him to the ground.

When he opened his eyes, he was lying in a puddle of water. He saw Primero framed in the studio doorway, beginning to move toward him. Luis lifted his left arm to signal to Primero to come no further. Then he heard the voice, "Come along, Luis, we are leaving."

By the time the first soldier's sword sliced through Luis's side, he and his muse had already dissolved into the universe. The soldiers who skewered the fallen Luis with their swords and spears expressed puzzlement that he had been able to maintain a faint smile at the corners of his mouth during the slaughter. They also were incredulous that he continued to babble unintelligibly while they struck him, and that he did not seem to feel any pain.

"These Jew devils, they don't die like Christians," one soldier said, "They talk even after they are dead."

"Yes, it's like he didn't care that we were killing him," another added, "as if he wasn't there. Surely the devil's work!"

"Yes," the Captain affirmed, "Jews are the devil's work," shaking his head from side to side disdainfully. "Very unsatisfying. This old Jew should have suffered more—like a normal person."

"Horrible," Jon sighed, surprised to find that he had finished his second margarita. He raised his hand to signal Juan for another, but Raymond stopped him.

"How about hearing this sober?"

Jon ignored him. "Is the next part what Pablo and my father talked about?"

"Yes," Rosie said.

"Then shoot," Jon smiled.

"Remember, my white brother, good stories ain't quick stories," Raymond admonished him. Rosie leafed through her papers. "Where were we? Oh! After Luis died."

Abraham pulled the cart up to the veranda of their home. His mother was waiting with her shawl wrapped tightly around her, making her seem smaller than usual.

"Thank God!" she called to him.

Abraham shouted, "But Father didn't come!" and watched tears well up in her eyes. "We need to leave now, before the roads become impassable." He stepped down from the cart.

"Yes," she choked up and began to turn away.

Abraham embraced her. "He will find us, Mother," he whispered. As mothers do, she strained to offer words to comfort his pain before her own, but she found it impossible. She knew that she would never see her beloved husband again, at least not on earth, and now she needed to tend to the children.

"Fetch Rebecca, she's with the horses," she ordered, and went inside to gather their belongings.

Abraham left to find his sister, briefly stopping to alert several other families to be ready to leave within the hour. When he found his fifteen-year-old sister, she was sitting alone in the barn. Her eyes were reddened, her cheeks flushed and wet with tears because she had seen him drive up without her father. He drew her close for a moment, and then, gently, pointed her toward the house, where their mother was putting bundles on the veranda. Abraham went to find help in moving the crated statue from the cart into the larger prairie wagon they would use for their journey. Then, possessions loaded, Abraham settled his distraught mother and sister inside, and, numbing himself to the sound of their weeping, took leave of Nuevo Leon forever.

The plan was for Abraham to rendezvous with his business partner and friend, Gaspar Castano De Sosa and a band of at least a hundred and fifty artisans, merchants, and traders. All of them were fleeing Nuevo Leon for religious or political reasons. Abraham trusted De Sosa's intelligence and courage to rebel against what he considered oppressive authorities. He was caught up in enthusiasm about De Sosa's dream to start a different kind of community in a new place—where artists could create freely and express themselves. They would no longer submit to restrictions like producing only church-approved religious art, as it had been in Nuevo Leon.

When they met up three days later, De Sosa was profoundly disappointed that Luis had not come. He had been counting on Luis to oversee the founding of the art settlement. After a brief strategy meeting, they decided to travel northeast, cross the big river, the Rio Grande, and into unmapped territory. This route would take them inland, away from the military and priestly traffic on the north-south trail linking the missions of the Pacific coast.

On the fifteenth day of their journey, eluding all Spaniards and seeing only a few nomadic groups of Indians, they arrived at the southern bank of the big river. It was a beautiful, sunny day, where they could see in the distance the green of shrubs filled with game birds. De Sosa was pleased, eager to settle down in what he called his 'new New World.'

"Abraham, you said you would know when we arrive at the right place, and I agreed. Certainly, dear friend, this must be it." Abraham wanted to please his friend and agree, but a voice inside told him otherwise, so he pointed off to the north.

"This is too close to where we have come from. Native people saw us, and they will tell others." Although disappointed, De Sosa was in good spirits about finding such a suitable place, that he agreed, with a touch of magnanimity.

"It's so fine here, a little farther north may be even better. So you want us to get wet, friend? Agreed. We cross the river. But . . ." he laughed, "we will go just so far on the other side, and then we stay until you find the promised land for us."

Abraham eagerly agreed. After they had crossed the Rio Grande and traveled for three more days, De Sosa became impatient. "We will camp here Abraham, and now it is up to you." Without objecting, Abraham organized a scouting party and pressed on to the north. Six days later, he returned with the conviction that their promised land was only a three days' ride to the north. He had discovered a place along the river where the canyon walls were so steep that they formed a natural dam, with a waterfall on the lower side. This would make irrigation of farmland much easier. Abraham could find no sign that anyone had lived there before. So the migrating group moved northward and made homes on their new land.

The joy of these settlers was relatively short-lived. After some years of relative peace and seclusion, a party of Spanish hunters discovered them and lost no time in sending back word to the authorities in New Spain. They, in turn, dispatched an expedition of soldiers, priests, and five hundred additional settlers to the colony.

De Sosa was furious and drunk when Abraham conferred with him. "Are we doomed to a nomadic life, Abraham, wandering endlessly in the desert?" De Sosa slurred his words and dashed his wine glass against the wall. "I know how you feel, Gaspar," Abraham consoled him. "But we must go on, go further north, to the snow country, and we must leave quickly." De Sosa answered mournfully, "My friend," he sighed and pointed to himself, "this Gaspar is fading away, like the dusk outside."

Abraham said, "You know what we have to do." But De Sosa refused. He intended to stay.

What neither of them knew was that the Inquisition officials had become obsessed about finding and returning them to New Spain—especially De Sosa. It was based on his defiance when he publicly denounced soldiers and priests, unwilling to have them join his expedition; he had set a precedent for rebellion.

Abraham packed up all his family's belongings once more. Accompanied by half of the colony, mostly Jews, they traveled northward. In the winter of 1588, Abraham was scouting ahead of the group when he came upon a narrow canyon, rode through it, and mounted a steep slope. Cresting the hill, he viewed a valley covered with grasslands, bordered on both sides by steep wooded hills. The valley extended northwards for a distance until it blended into the green foothills of a snow-peaked mountain range. Seen from above, it resembled an enormous bird's nest, bordered by mountains and the tallest trees he had seen. A closer look revealed an abundance of deer, elk and other game grazing. Fresh water flowed down from a high mesa and fish were abundant in the mountain streams joined to create a small lake surrounded by rich bottomland, a promising place for farms. No people had made marks of occupying this area. He slept by the lake that night and set off eagerly the next morning to lead his group back, thinking the whole time, "I have found our place. Thanks to God. I will call it Santuario." Sanctuary."

⊚

Jon smiled. "Took a long time."

"Don't be irreverent," Raymond chastised him. "Abraham was well loved by my people."

"How do you know?" Jon asked.

"All of us know about Abraham and Great Owl. That's in first grade. He was part of our pueblo's beginnings. Abraham's dream came true." Raymond smiled.

Rosie added, "At least for a while. Here's more. This is where your Jon's father and the university historians helped me a lot."

⊚

As the years passed, Santuario prospered under Abraham's stewardship. The group elected him their first Alcalde—Mayor of the town.

His first project was to lay out the footprint of the town, and this time they would be able to construct permanent homes. The excellent clay from the river worked well for baking adobe bricks, so the people used them to build homes and stables around a large, square plaza that Abraham chose for the community and commercial heart of the village. Farmers like Abraham preferred to build their homes and outbuildings on expansive homesteads in the hills or along the riverbed. He skillfully guided his people and, as time passed, native clans passing through the region took note of the way these artisans and farmers lived in harmony. Eventually many nomadic natives settled adjacent to the village and built structures to make their own pueblo a short distance away.

One of Abraham's greatest achievements was becoming friends with Great Owl, the leader of the pueblo people. Together they established a precedent for inter-cultural cooperation that was radically different from the exploitative, oppressive Spanish colonists. Their enlightened leadership allowed settlers and natives to enjoy the advantages of their mutual efforts without fear of violence. Over time, the people in the region came to work together, celebrate and intermarry, nurture a new culture and a new breed of American. Abraham was so highly esteemed by the natives that his mother's death in 1596 brought the offer of an honor—an Indian burial ceremony. Abraham politely refused.

Santuario's peace and tranquility was threatened only once. In the second decade after Abraham founded the village, an expedition led by Juan de Onate left New Spain and eventually headed in their direction. De Onate's expedition consisted of a large contingent of heavily armed soldiers and many priests. They were searching for the reputed 'Seven Cities of Cibola.' De Onate's mandate was to gather riches, exploit savage labor, and spread the Holy Catholic faith.

When the people of Santuario heard the news about de Onate, they agreed that this time they would not flee, but would stay and fight. The native people offered to join them and dispatched scouts to track the Spanish expedition. Abraham and the strongest men were committed to fortifying a perimeter around the town and training fighters. One evening, as he made his rounds of the fortifications, he remembered the statue his father had entrusted to him. When he first arrived in Santuario, he had buried the statue for its safety and built his barn on the site. A safe place, he thought at the time, but now he reconsidered. When de Onate's men decided to attack, they would try to torch everything. The statue would never survive the heat of such a conflagration, so Abraham decided to hide it elsewhere.

That night when moonlight lit up the plaza, he surveyed the landscape around him. Where would it be safe? He searched the surrounding hills for barren spots. "Not good," he said aloud. "Floods have come down those ways." He inspected the string of adobe houses along the periphery of the plaza as well as his own home on a hill overlooking the plaza. "No, danger of mudslides and fires." As he turned to examine the north border of the plaza, he stepped into a ground squirrel hole and sank into it, down to his knee. Struggling to stand again, he noticed that his foot and leg had created a deep impression in the soft sand. I had the shape of a woman.

"A sign," he smiled in appreciation, "to bury her right here in the marketplace, under everybody's nose. Yes, right here, deep in this sand!"

At three in the morning, all quiet, Abraham summoned the help of his two sons, David and Adam, who were also standing guard duty that night. They dug up the crate, loaded it into a cart, and brought it down the hill to the spot on the plaza where he had tripped. Abraham kept watch while the boys dug a deep hole and buried the crate. He was sure no one had seen them.

Several days later, the Indian scouts returned to the village and reported the welcome news that de Onate's party had turned eastward to avoid the worst winter snows. Santuario was saved. When David asked his father what would become of the statue, Abraham said, "My son, if we dig her up, we will only have to bury her again. Let her sleep there, in the middle of our community."

"Here, under the marketplace?"

"Yes. My father told me I would know the right place. This is it. My father said she will do what she has to do, when it is time to do it. And it will be something wonderful."

"When will that be?"

Abraham threw up his hands, "I don't know."

"Can we tell anyone?" Adam asked.

"Only our family; you will tell your children when the time comes. No one else must know. The authorities must never get their hands on the statue."

"The authorities, Father?" David's eyes widened. "Surely we are out of their reach now!"

"For now, yes. However, someday, they will come. They always do. That is why my son, we need to pass on our traditions."

"I will try to do that, father," David said earnestly. "I will try."

@

De Onate never reached Santuario. The village was left in peace, and prosperity brought an increase in population. People thought of themselves as a town with a neighboring pueblo, alike in their pursuits and outlook. Abraham's descendants were spared the carnage of the bloody Indian uprising of 1680, when the native clans from all over the region went on the warpath. It was common for them to slaughter settlers, soldiers and priests indiscriminately, and the only survivors were the people who fled from their land. During this revolt, marauding war parties—Navajos and Apaches among them—passed through Santuario. However, when they found no enslaved Indians, no soldiers or priests, and heard reports from the pueblo about the settlers' good will, they moved on. Some Indians became so enticed by the beauty of the region and the peaceful nature of the local people that they stayed to join the pueblo community. But the war parties made sure that local artisans and Santeros surrendered their religious works, which they promptly hacked to pieces and burned.

Knowledge about the statue disappeared after about a century—many generations for these people. David died of pneumonia before he could marry. Adam had six children, and related the secret of the statue's location to them. But after three generations, some family members might have heard stories about a statue, but the truth was known only to a few.

@

"My father mentioned some of that," Jon interrupted.

"Yes, things spread down the generations by word of mouth. But no one knew exactly. That's why the rising of the statue was such a complete surprise."

"Rising of the statue?" Jon's eyes opened wide. "What was that about?"

"You'll see. There are a couple of versions."

"Go on, Rosie," Raymond encouraged her. "I'm enjoying this."

@

On a summer morning in 1740, Fr. Miguel Montoya, a young priest, wandered into Santuario. He was on a pilgrimage, he announced with fervor, to go away alone, as he put it, "as far north as I can, to get away from the damnable church authorities."

Santuario had changed considerably from Abraham's time. The central plaza and marketplace, formerly an expanse of sandy dirt, was now a profusion of bushes and flowers surrounding an ornate central fountain. The showy floral display had been created by the Alcalde, Samuel, one of Abraham's descendants. He devised an intricate system of tile aqueducts carrying water from the mountains to irrigation channels under the stand of cottonwood trees surrounding the plaza. This arrangement supplied water even in dry weather to sustain the gardens and fountain, besides cisterns for the community's needs. The original row of adobe houses lining the west side of the plaza had expanded back into the foothills. The east side of the plaza housed a Cantina and a large general store. The north side of the plaza led up a hill to where pens were used as animal corrals. Beyond was the burial ground. Some of the original homesteads had grown to become large farms and even larger ranches. They sold their produce of meat, vegetables and grain on the south side of the plaza, a bustling commercial complex of livery stables, livestock barns, stores, and a trading post.

The town's Catholics enthusiastically welcomed Fr. Miguel. They were the most recent arrivals, anxious to have a priest to offer mass for them, bless their marriages and baptize their babies. Fr. Miguel concluded that he had been 'called' to this town, but wondered why the people had not already built a church, or even brought a priest with them. He soon learned that the townspeople were content to keep their religious beliefs to themselves and worship at home. Upon further inquiry, he learned from members of his new flock that many families descended from the original settlers had unfamiliar practices, like Friday night celebrations. They observed the Sabbath on Saturday instead of Sunday, practiced ritual circumcision of male babies and had bizarre burial rites.

This brought about his conviction that the town needed a true church. There was an obstacle, however. Members of his potential new parish saw themselves as Santuarians first, and Catholics second. Since they enjoyed their situation as it was, they made it clear to him that they would do nothing new without the approval of Samuel, the Alcalde. Fr. Miguel was eager to talk with him.

"Make sure to do it on a Saturday," counseled the farmer who was lodging him. "He is in a better mood."

Fr. Miguel woke early on a Saturday morning, feeling both enthusiastic and apprehensive. After a breakfast of tea and rolls at the farmer's adobe, he headed up into the hills to Samuel's farm. The sun on his back quickly banished the morning chill from his bones.

"A beautiful day. Life here is good," he sighed. Soon after, he spotted Samuel moving about on the rise above him. Samuel was dressed in a dark jacket and pants, a fresh white shirt and hip boots. He was pouring feed into a line of cattle troughs.

Fr. Miguel waved and called, "Good morning!" Samuel looked up, squinting his eyes to see better. The good-looking, pale-skinned priest seemed to materialize out of the bright sun. Samuel motioned for him to come closer.

"Watch where you walk, Padre," he warned. "The gophers had a party last night."

"Senor Alcalde," Fr. Miguel smiled politely. "You seem too well dressed for this work."

Samuel laughed, "It's Saturday . . ."

"Oh! Yes," Fr. Miguel nodded.

Samuel observed him carefully, without hostility or a superior attitude. He found the priest to have a pleasant way about him—open, relaxed and friendly. The Indians had already informed Samuel that he was well meaning—so far, at least. But since he was a priest, well, Samuel needed to be on guard.

"I have a question for you, Alcalde," Fr. Miguel smiled his broadest smile.

"Of course," Samuel answered earnestly.

Fr. Miguel cleared his throat loudly. He had to say this just right: "Alcalde," he began.

Samuel interrupted, "Call me Samuel."

"Yes. Thank you, Samuel, I am curious why there is no church in Santuario, and why you have no worship on Sunday. All of the other villages . . ."

Samuel put down the feed sack and turned away from Fr. Miguel for a moment to stem the tide of emotion and the angry thoughts rising within him. "So it begins," he said to himself, and turned back to face the priest.

"Padre," Samuel answered without expression. "That is our way, the way we learned from those who settled here many generations ago. People do what they want here. Our parents and grandparents did not need a church. We don't either." He spoke in a slow, measured way, carefully observing Fr. Miguel's reactions to his words. How much of a zealot was he?

"So, how and where do people worship our Holy Family?" Fr. Miguel asked tentatively.

He is asking, not demanding, Samuel thought, good. He said calmly, "You have seen for yourself. Believers worship whatever they believe, in whatever way, and wherever they want to. Our Indian friends have their own special ways. As you know, our Catholic friends worship in their homes on Sunday. Others worship on Friday night and Saturday. And some of us don't worship at all." Samuel noticed that Fr. Miguel took his comments well. He seemed calm, respectful, interested in listening. His body language was not confrontational. So far, so good.

Fr. Miguel offered, "Do you agree that Sunday is the prescribed day of worship? It is the Lord's Day, is it not?"

Samuel smiled softly, "For you and others who believe like you. But for others the Lord's Day is Saturday, the day our parents rested. A lot of us follow our parents' ways. No one really asks why. It's tradition."

"So you are not a non-practicing Catholic?" Fr. Miguel was puzzled.

Samuel smiled again, "I guess not."

Fr. Miguel pressed on. "Do you believe in God?" he asked softly.

Samuel hesitated for a moment. Did he really want to answer this question? This priest seemed only curious, not suspicious of him, not one of those he had been warned about as a child. "When I think about it," Samuel hesitated. "I do. When I need help . . ."

"Do you believe that Jesus Christ is the Son of God?" Fr. Miguel asked more doggedly.

Samuel waited a moment before he decided to answer. "As much I believe that you and I are both sons of God." Samuel felt something stir within him, something people know without having consciously learned it.

"Oh." Fr. Miguel considered Samuel's response and found it hard to put into words what he felt. "Oh, yes. I think I understand," he said softly. "Your people came here long ago, didn't they?"

His eyed brimmed with tears and Samuel saw that he was moved and saddened. He relaxed. "This Padre is not an enemy," he thought to himself.

"What is it you understand?" he asked, and the priest replied, "That a terrible sin occurred a long time ago; that was the reason your people came here."

"That is true, Padre," Samuel nodded. Fr. Miguel locked eyes with him. "Samuel, there are sick and evil people in the world. They use anything to gain their ends; they are everywhere—in the church, too."

Samuel nodded again and Fr. Miguel cried out to him, "I am a refugee, too. I have not suffered like your people, of course. But we have common enemies. Because of the people in power in the Church, Samuel, I couldn't be the kind of priest I want to be. Like your ancestors, I also left everything behind to find a Santuario for myself, to be true to myself. And here I am, and I need a home here, and a church to do things the right way."

"Your right way, Padre," Samuel reminded him. "Not mine."

"That is true, Samuel. Nevertheless, I beg your permission."

Samuel shook his head. "No, Padre. With all due respect, for you seem well intentioned, we do not need a church. We need better homes for the poor and help for sick people who can't work in the fields. For a very long time we have been fine without a church."

Then he added, "If you are a refugee as you say you are, you know what the church has done, what it always does, what it always brings. Why not do your good work, but leave things be?"

Fr. Miguel moved closer to Samuel. When the Alcalde backed away, the priest moved closer once again, so that the distance between them remained the same. "Yes. Yes. You mean the poison, the politics, the killings, but Samuel, that is not the true church. That is the doing of the evil people who hide in the church. Samuel, I understand how you feel, and why you feel the way you do. I have prayed for the courage to come before you and humbly ask your permission, and your blessing, to build a peaceful church. Will you help me?"

Samuel listened—tried to listen—with an open mind, but his emotions were turmoil of fear, concern, hurt, and anger. His feelings were so intense they numbed his mind. "So it starts," he repeated to himself.

When he regained his composure, he blurted out, "Padre, do you know what you are asking? Don't you understand that if there is a church here, in a public place, religion will no longer be a private matter? People will begin to align themselves with one religious practice or another. Right now, we live peacefully together, whether our beliefs are similar or not. Most of us believe in God. Padre, if we have learned one thing from the Indians, it is respect for spirituality, no matter how the people express it. Here in Santuario we live with tolerance of others' ways. That is the freedom our ancestors wanted. Now you want to change this place."

Fr. Miguel remained composed, speaking softly but firmly. "I do understand how you feel. However, we Catholics need a church to stand at the center of our lives. That is our way. But my church will be only for those who want it."

"That may be true at the beginning, Padre, perhaps for as long as you are here. But, after we are gone, what then? Over time your church will change everything."

"For the better, I hope."

"That is not the lesson of history, is it? Why not just build your church somewhere else? Why stay where you are not needed or wanted? Why can't you leave us be?" Samuel sighed.

Fr. Miguel replied with earnest certainty, "Because, Samuel, this is where I am called to be. This is where I will live the rest of my life. I know that."

"You know that?" Samuels's eyes narrowed. "God told you to come here?"

The priest smiled. "In a manner of speaking, yes."

Samuel raised his eyebrows; it entered his mind that he could crush this man with one blow and that would be the end of it. "Padre, I mean no disrespect, but this is all about you, what you want, what your church wants. Why do you and your church want to go where you are not wanted?

"There are souls to save," Fr. Miguel answered. "The truth needs to be taught. And the faithful need a place with a priest to say masses for their souls."

"And after that, what always happens?" Samuel interrupted. "Although you seem well-intentioned, you carry a plague with you—the plague of divisiveness— that has slaughtered my ancestors throughout the ages. They came here to escape your plague. To find peace, that's why we call this Santuario . . ."

Fr. Miguel spoke rapidly, gesturing wildly with his hands, "I am aware of why your ancestors came here. There is evil in the church. There is always evil where good resides. The Catholic Church today, with a few exceptions, has been usurped by evil men who use it for their own gain and are fierce against heretics."

He stopped to catch his breath. "Please understand, Samuel," he pleaded, "I am not one of them. I want to build a true church and teach what is right, one that cares for people and unites them, not divides them."

Samuel frowned. "Why should it matter to me after all the evil your church has done?" However, the priest's sincerity touched him.

"I'll tell you why it matters to you, Samuel. Others will come here, and they will not rest until they make everybody fit their own image." He tapped his head several times. "Consider this, Samuel. What if I have been called here first, before the others come, to spare you their presence? Once I am installed here, I can keep them away, because there will be no reason for them to come. I can promise you that."

Samuel laughed, sarcastically, "You say you have been sent here to protect us from your own church?"

Fr. Miguel nodded his head. "Yes, in a manner of speaking, from the evil in my own church . . ."

Samuel turned his back and stared off into the distance. "So I have to choose between you or others I don't know. You are giving me an ultimatum, Padre." Fr. Miguel stood silent.

The realization that the priest was right fell on Samuel like a shroud. Of course, others would come. They always had done so.

"Do I trust him?" Samuel asked himself, while he searched Fr. Miguel's face for signs of duplicity: a sidelong glance, a sneer, hollow eyes or a sweaty brow. He said, "I need to think, Padre, and discuss your proposal with my family. I will give you my answer tonight at the fiesta."

Fr. Miguel literally jumped for joy, and seized his hand. "God is with you!"

"Whose God, Padre?" Samuel uttered the words with such an anguished tone that it suppressed the priest's joy.

"We will show what can be done," Fr. Miguel managed to say.

"Show who?" Samuel scowled, "show them what? To live in peace and tolerance is no problem. We have co-existed with each other and the Indians for a many generations."

Fr. Miguel agreed enthusiastically. "Yes, but there are others coming to this region who need to learn from such an example."

"I don't care about people outside our community. Others with the authority of the crown and church have slaughtered my people throughout history." Samuel turned away in frustration. "Padre, you want to sell me something I don't need."

Fr. Miguel held his words until Samuel turned back to him. "You can't stop people from coming here, Samuel. But when they come we will show them a better way, you and I will accept one another and be friends, Samuel— good friends."

In spite of himself, Samuel laughed, realizing that he liked the priest.

"Padre, I am just a simple farmer. As long as you are here, give me a helping hand and pick up a feed sack."

Saturday night was fiesta night in Santuario. The market closed early so people could make their way home to put on fresh clothes and share a festive meal. Families would stroll through the plaza and saunter among the vendors hawking a trinkets and sweets. By sunset, local musicians would have formed a band and filled themselves with drink, so they could blare their special brand of lively music. When darkness fell, the children lit a hundred candles arranged around the fountain. Their flickering light shone through ornate holes on the sides of their silver containers, creating a play of lights and shadows. After the dancing began, when the time was right, the young men and women formed two facing rings and began a promenade around the paved stones of the plaza; men on the outer circle and young women on the inner one. As was the custom, they paraded in opposite directions. The eyes of the women and girls signaled suggestions of passion, dreams and fantasies to the young men of their choice. As the men circled, they also winked their eyes in secret, conveying covert signs to a chosen lady about a rendezvous later. Whispers and giggles accompanied the music. A ring of sentinels, older women perched around the plaza and gossiping, kept watch on the proceedings carefully in case a couple attempted to melt away into the darkness.

Fr. Miguel spotted Samuel in the crowd and began to weave his way in his direction. Samuel saw him and motioned for the priest to meet him at the edge of the plaza, away from the crowd. Samuel greeted him soberly, "Padre, what you said about others from your church coming here has disturbed me. But you spoke your truth, and my truth is that I have been negligent—in thinking that time could stand still. There have been more strangers coming to the area lately . . ."

The priest nodded in agreement: "Yes. They are building roads and missions south of the mesa lands. So you understand that if I build a church, other priests will have no need to come, nor try to establish their authority here."

Samuel knew that without a force of armed men to drive any strangers away, he was helpless to keep Santuario isolated as time went on. "You must promise never to divide us! Not to turn us against each other!"

Fr. Miguel smiled and crossed himself. He clasped Samuel's hands tightly. "Yes, I promise."

Samuel turned his head and looked up in the direction of the cemetery on the north side of the plaza. "What choice do I have?" he cried out loud to his ancestors. There was no answer.

Fr. Miguel gently laid a hand on Samuel's shoulder. "What is troubling you?" he asked.

Samuel answered softly, "The end, Padre."

"Of a time . . ." Fr. Miguel said. "But maybe the beginning of something new."

"If only that were true," Samuel sighed. "Go ahead, build your church."

The priest pointed back towards the cemetery. "We will build it there, on the north side of the plaza downward from the cemetery, so those who rest there will be protected. Samuel, our church will be open to everybody. You will see, Alcalde, you will see that I will be true to my word and what you fear will not happen here. We will make a new way for ourselves. I swear it."

❀

Samuel did not live long enough to learn whether Fr. Miguel kept his part of the bargain. Two years after they struck their deal, the church was completed. Not long after that, Samuel died of pneumonia. Fr. Miguel said a funeral mass for his soul at the church, and proclaimed Samuel 'a great man, a Moses of our time, who now sits at the side of God.' Samuel was buried in the newly consecrated ground of the cemetery. The priest even saw to it that Samuel's dying request was honored, regarding the special words and symbols he wanted carved into his gravestone. The priest personally tended Samuel's grave until the day he himself died.

During the years of his stewardship of the Catholics, Fr. Miguel kept his word to Samuel and consequently was well loved by the townspeople and the Indians living in the pueblo. He was the only priest in New Mexico territory who built his church without the labor of Indian slaves.

His church stands on the north side of the plaza, a rectangular adobe-walled building, two stories high, with a double-layered red tile roof. A coat of stark white tuff covers the outside walls, gives them a clean and bright appearance. The roof is rimmed with weathered hand-carved wooden corbels, spaced six feet apart. They reach out, like protecting arms, over the latilla-covered portal—a walkway surrounding the church. The ceiling inside is unique: an ornate array of dark brown varnished poles of aspen and pine, arranged in Fr. Miguel's design of interlocking crosses. A stained glass window placed under a projecting arch adorns the wall behind the altar, and the church cemetery looks over mountains beyond.

Fr. Miguel's sensitivity led to his inclusion of Kachina figures depicting the Stations of the Cross, painted along the interior walls. Once the walls were prepared, Fr. Miguel invited several Indian artisans to depict the Stations of the Cross with their native figures. They felt so honored that they worked to produce beautiful images. Fr. Miguel's ecumenical attitude toward all the people of the pueblo made them feel welcome and eager to come to the church for some rituals and holy days. They would crowd in for a funeral or join in a procession on a Saint's day.

The priest became respected as 'a man of the people' by the Indians, or 'the man who paints spirits on the walls.' When he made the remark after mass one Sunday that a bell tower would be a worthy addition to the church, people who had never been inside wanted to join everybody else in the work.

True to his word, Fr. Miguel opened the church on Friday and Saturday nights for those who worshipped 'in a different way.' He also allowed anyone from the town to be buried in the consecrated ground of the churchyard. Relatives of non-Catholics still engraved the tombstones of their deceased with their own sacred symbols, as the priest had ordered to be done with Samuel's monument. He himself carved a Star of David into a beam in the ceiling above the altar to honor Samuel's contributions. "In God's eyes, we are all one. There are no differences between us," he preached.

Fr. Miguel's had steadfast dedication to preserving Santuario as Samuel had wanted. Some years after the church was completed, three priests arrived from the south bringing a message from the Bishop that Fr. Miguel needed to tighten his loose clerical practices, and they would stay to help him. That night the priest invited them to a lavish feast, where they were treated to abundant wine and sweet meal cakes from his Indian friends. The next morning the priests felt very ill, suffered close to death for several days, or so they thought. As soon as they recovered, they were anxious to leave Santuario. That was the last time Fr. Miguel heard from them. The night after the priests left, he visited Samuel's grave and knelt to whisper, "A promise is a promise, my friend. A promise is a promise."

When the priests returned to report to the church authorities of New Spain, they gave a harsh assessment: "The area was rife with illness and people there were not worthy of our efforts." That was that. The Catholic Church left the people of Santuario in peace.

◎

Rosie reached into her briefcase and removed a handful of papers. "Just in case I needed it," she smiled. "I brought along a little hard evidence."

"Hard evidence," Raymond laughed, "from hundreds of years ago?"

"Sure," Rosie answered. "Don't you remember when I was writing a paper on the history of the town for an anthropology course? I heard of an official document in the church archives relating to Fr. Miguel. It concerned Fr. Jose Francisco, a priest in Santa Rosita during the early 1800's. As part of his petition to obtain a dispensation allowing him to marry a parishioner (common law, of course), without being defrocked, this priest cited Fr. Miguel's life and ministry as a precedent. Although his original petition can't be found in the records, Fr. Jose Francisco's request was rejected. But the archives had a record of his petition, through the Montoya family, who had a copy entrusted to them."

She unfolded one of the papers. "Jon, you haven't seen some of this material. I saved it for a surprise."

"Let's hear about it. Surprises are welcome after a year of marriage." He squeezed her hand lovingly.

The document read: "In his time Fr. Miguel Montoya set a realistic standard for priests serving in remote areas. He was a beloved, even legendary, priest who ministered equally to believers and non-believers. However, in spite of himself, he fell in love with a village girl named Rosita. Since priests were viewed as being more 'natural' in those days, as local people regarded them, he took her into his household with her, and together they did good works. When she died, Fr. Miguel became so deeply depressed that he took to drinking, but he devoted his sober moments to a crusade to keep Rosita's memory alive. First, he renamed the church Santa Rosita in her honor, and soon after proposed changing the town's name to Santa Rosita. Since he had significantly expanded his parish, the townspeople agreed. As the years passed, his many children prospered and founded strong family lines. Fr. Miguel remained a priest of the people, adored by his flock for being a kind and tolerant man. His goodness was not only lavished on his congregation, but on the native people as well. That is why so many of them helped him build the church and painted the walls with the Kachina figures. Fr. Miguel is an example of how a devoted priest can live and work among people in remote areas. Such folk priests become so much a part of the community that some, if they are inclined, feel free to enter relationships, live in common-law marriage and raise children. I, Fr. Jose Francisco, want to follow in this great priest's footsteps."

"Regretfully," Rosie continued to Jon and Raymond, "When the Bishop refused his request, Fr. Jose Francisco became distraught. He had to make a choice, resign as a priest, or rebel against the church dictates like many other rural priests who lived as they desired. They could do this only because they were beyond the disciplinary reach of the church hierarchy. Such license by rural priests was so frequent, it was the reason Archbishop Jean-Baptiste Lamy regularly rode his burro on an inspection tour through northern New Mexico. He was urging his priests to clean up their practices; Willa Cather memorialized him in her account 'Death Comes for the Archbishop' and I gained insight from that book."

"Required reading in New Mexico," Jon said.

Rosie went on, "Since Fr. Jose Francisco could not find it in himself to live a double life, he left the church and married his parishioner, then became a farmer.

"Interesting," Raymond nodded.

"There's more," Rosie added. "Fr. Miguel was the first person who saw what is called the 'rising' of the old statue. There are two versions; there is an 'approved' description in the Santa Rosita church brochure. Here," Rosie handed Jon the brochure.

Jon began to read aloud: "The morning of the miracle, Fr. Miguel, the celebrated priest of Santa Rosita, who was now old and sick, sat on the front steps of his church, ready to greet the day. It had been raining unusually hard for five days, and the plaza in front of the church had flooded. While saying his prayers for God's grace and guidance, this holy man heard a loud sound. When he looked up, he saw the muddy ground in the center of the plaza crack apart and a beautiful carved figure rise out of the ground. Fr. Miguel ran over to the statue, fell to his knees, looked up at heaven and said, 'Thank you, dear God. Now I can go to you.' He smiled, and sank down dead over the statue. When word reached the Bishop about this event, he initiated an investigation to proclaim a miracle. Although that never came to pass, the Alcalde named the statue Santa Rosita, and she is with us to this day."

"That's one version," Rosie said, and she paused for dramatic effect. "However, members of Pablo's family are privy to what they say is the true version of this story. They call it 'The Legend' but the full title is 'The Legend of Fr. Miguel and the Rising of Santa Rosita.'"

She reached into her briefcase once more, removed a packet of folded papers, and smoothed them out on the table. She began to read a translated account:

"August 6, 1780, was the morning when our beloved Fr. Miguel met his maker and Rosita 'rose' from her sleep. It was the time of the monsoon rains from the south. Rain had pounded Santa Rosita for many days. Muddy rivers were turning over the ground. No one could travel. Since the rain confined Fr. Miguel to the church, he took the opportunity to drink more heavily than usual and spend time with Felice, the mother of his children and his dutiful housekeeper. She was a faithful woman who had thoroughly devoted herself to his service as soon as an appropriate time had elapsed after Rosita's death. The rain ended that night, and the morning of August 6 dawned sunny. Felice awoke happy, leaped out of bed and tugged the Padre awake. Once she got him up, she pointed him to the door. 'Go out and breathe the fresh morning air,' she urged, and left to climb up into the bell tower and ring the bell for morning prayers.

"Fr. Miguel slipped his frock over his head, and stumbled toward the church entrance. He opened the broad wooden church doors, and stepped out on the landing, all the while rubbing his eyes. As he squinted to see better in the bright sunlight, he could not believe what was slowly coming into focus.

"'Madre de Dios,' he mumbled, 'What can this be?'

"A large object covered with shreds of cloth, was emerging from the ground. Large pieces of brown colored lumps of wax and rotten wood were falling away from it, revealing a form.

"'Is that the top of a . . . statue?' he asked himself aloud.

"Did it have a face? Indeed, it was under a golden crown as well. Miracle of miracles, the face was very beautiful. "Es Nuestra Senora de Guadeloupe!' Fr. Miguel screamed, 'Milagro!' while the statue continued to rise. He staggered down the church stairs, arms outstretched. 'No, not Guadeloupe. No, Dios mio, mi Rosita, mi Rosita!'

"Meanwhile, Felice had just stepped out onto the platform of the bell tower. As she reached up for the bell rope, she looked down into the plaza to see Fr. Miguel running to the statue. Then she howled as Fr. Miguel tripped over a rock, flew through the air for a short distance and hit, head first, the statue's stone-hard breast. She heard him cry, 'Rosita. Your eyes, they see me!'

"Felice screamed directly into the dome of the church bell. The noise resonated within the metal for over a minute, then flew all over the countryside scattering every bird within miles and bringing people running. Felice shouted from the bell tower. 'I saw it. I saw it. Padre flew in the air. He touched the statue and fell dead on top of her.'"

Jon rolled his eyes. "After all those years, a statue coming up out of the ground? That's how we have . . ." He motioned in the direction of the church.

Rosie shuffled some papers. "Wait dear, there's more." She read on.

"The people of the parish proclaimed the rising of the statue as a miracle, and the death of Fr. Miguel as a holy ascension. In the days that followed, Felice became celebrated in two ways. First, as the second person to witness the rising of the statue, and as the only eyewitness to the increasingly romanticized death of Fr. Miguel, arms around the statue as he died. There was never a person who didn't weep when Felice related the story. She sounded awestruck when she described how she saw Fr. Miguel actually 'fly' toward the statue and to his death. The distance of the flight exponentially increased with the size of her audience. Songs were written in Rosita's honor. Artists carved, and painters painted many beautiful works to memorialize the occasion."

Rosie had her audience mesmerized: "Felice soon began to be called 'Mother Felice' and was successful collecting money to add the 'Fr. Miguel Memorial Sanctuary' with meditation courtyard on the east side of the church. Her son, Miguel Jr., became a priest also—Fr. Miguel Jr. He followed the Padre's example in serving the church and the community faithfully for over fifty years, most of them under the watchful eye of his mother.

"As the centuries passed, there were skeptics who attempted to dismiss the miracle of Rosita and her heavenly origin. Some church experts held that likely the statue had made by a Santero and buried during the Indian revolt by savages rioting in the area. Others thought that it 'was most likely brought by de Onate's priests or soldiers from New Spain.'"

Rosie interrupted herself. "I read that modern experts from the university, applying the latest carbon dating technology, have proved that the statue was carved and decorated before 1600. That's why no more 'experts' are allowed to get near the statue," Rosie said. "Pablo is convinced of her divine nature. He and his buddies at La Tierra will threaten or run out anyone who says different."

Jon shook his head. "I don't doubt that."

Raymond told them, "Fr. Miguel Montoya's descendants select one person from each generation, like Pablo today, to care for Rosita. That is why he calls the statue 'Abuelita' when no one else is around. And that's why, as keeper of the statue, he makes a living telling tourists about her other mysteries."

"There's even more," Rosie smiled proudly. "First, there is the curious disappearance of the pedestal of the statue described by Felice to her son, Fr.

Miguel Jr., when she was on her deathbed. He, in turn, passed the story down, and so on, until it eventually was told to Pablo by his grandmother. Here is what Pablo quotes Felice as saying." She read from another paper.

"'I could not believe what my eyes were seeing. Rosita had a large golden crown on her head. Reaching skyward from the crown were six golden spheres. She looked downward, as if she were scared, confused. Although it was muddy, I saw that her robe was a sky-blue color, like the color of heaven, and it was bordered with gold. Her robe flowed down her body, spreading out until it reached her ankles and bare feet. She was tilting sideways; it looked like she had almost broken off from a part of her that was still stuck in the ground. When I took a closer look, I saw she had two sections. The top section was Rosita herself. The other section was a pedestal. It looked like there were wooden pegs in each of the four corners that connected her to the pedestal, but three of the pegs were broken.'

"'The pedestal disappeared soon after the rising of the statue. After they removed Fr. Miguel's body from the statue, the Alcalde and his boys broke the remaining peg that had joined the statue to its pedestal, and brought the statue into the church. They had a very hard time separating the statue from the pedestal, even though only one peg connected them. I remembered thinking that the statue didn't want to leave her pedestal. When the Alcalde came back, he told me, and not politely at all, to walk away. Then he ordered boys to dig up the pedestal. I saw him examine it closely, and after a lot of arguing, he covered it with a cloth. Then he told two of his boys to guard the pedestal all night and not let anyone near it. I heard that one of Alcalde's boys got drunk that night and spread around talk of several figures carved into it and some strange writing that did not seem to fit with the statue. The next morning the pedestal was gone. When I brought this up to the Alcalde, I was told to forget about it. So I did. He is not a person to cross.'"

"The pedestal!" Jon's face lit up.

"Right," Raymond smiled.

"I'll be damned!" Jon slapped the table.

Rosie handed Jon a small brochure in English. "Take a look at the rest of the story, as Fr. Raul has written it for our visitors."

Jon read: "There are mysteries and wonder about our Rosita. Hundreds of years ago, Rosita was a real person who worked at this church as a housekeeper. Sunset was her favorite time of day. Every evening she would sit on the steps of the church at sunset to say her rosary and pray. People would remark on how beautiful and holy she looked in the colors of the sunset. Eventually other people joined with her, to be reverent, quiet and pray. Then, Rosita died. After the rising of the statue and Fr. Miguel's death, Felice, the new housekeeper, placed the statue behind the altar at the back of the church. It never saw light until decades later, when Fr. Miguel Jr. became the resident priest. One day when the church was undergoing the annual top-to-bottom cleaning, Mother Felice and two workers moved the statue outside and set it on the landing at the top of the church steps overlooking the plaza. It had rained most of the day, but the afternoon sun was bright and began to dry out the ground. As the sun began to set that evening, people passing by the front of the church on their way home noticed that Rosita's face was glowing. They gathered around and, to their surprise, her eyes flashed a bright turquoise light, and rolled upward toward the heavens. Then a warm and gentle smile crossed her mouth. People came running from everywhere as word spread. Two Indians in the crowd named her 'Golden Spirit' and 'The Woman Who Never Dies.' Since that time, artists have captured what they call 'Rosita's Moment' in many forms. Not only did Rosita bring a personal miracle into our lives, she assured the prosperity of our town for all time because of the number of people who make a pilgrimage here to see her and experience her blessing."

"That's good for business," Jon said.

"You'd better believe it; Fr. Raul does not say it publicly, but he and the diocese, are eternally grateful for Fr. Miguel Jr.'s financial savvy. After Rosita's 'illumination,' the story goes, Felice urged Fr. Miguel Jr. to begin a weekly ritual he called the Noche ceremony. You know, when they place Rosita on the landing at the top of the church steps to 'bathe' her in the setting sun's light. After the Noche ritual began to be associated with cures, Santa Rosita got the reputation of being another Lourdes. So Fr. Miguel Jr. added another way to satisfy those who wanted to keep a reminder of the sacred experience—a sort of relic to take and show others. He called it the tradition of the 'sacred soil.'"

Raymond chuckled, "Smart marketing, right? So now, we're up to date. Good job, Rosie."

"So that's what happened to the people here before us," Jon mused.

"Yes, my dearest, and thanks to them, here we are today."

Jon's eyed filled. Raymond reached out and took their hands. "You asked for a miracle and . . ."

Jon smiled. "It's wonderful to really know there is more to life than meets the eye . . ."

"Just look at us." Rosie's heart overflowed with an emotion that was impossible to express. They all fell quiet, sharing this moment beyond words.

The Rosie smiled and kissed them both on the cheeks.

* 9 7 8 0 8 6 5 3 4 8 0 6 6 *